What Love Tastes Like

ZURI DAY

Dafina
Books

Kensington Publishing Corp.

http://www.kensingtonbooks.com

DAFINA BOOKS are published by

Kensington Publishing Corp.
119 West 40th Street
New York, NY 10018

All Kensington Titles, Imprints, and Distributed Lines are
available at special quantity discounts for bulk purchases for
sales promotions, premiums, fund-raising, and educational or
institutional use. Special book excerpts or customized print-
ings can also be created to fit specific needs. For details, write
or phone the office of the Kensington special sales manager:
Kensington Publishing Corp., 119 West 40th Street, New
York, NY 10018, attn: Special Sales Department, Phone:
1-800-221-2647.

Dafina and the Dafina logo Reg. U.S. Pat. & TM Off.

ISBN-13: 978-0-7582-3872-6
ISBN-10: 0-7582-3872-X

First mass market printing: September 2010

10 9 8 7 6 5 4 3 2 1

Printed in the United States of America

For all of those who love to cook,
and who love to eat.

Acknowledgments

As always, special thanks to the A Team. You're the best! To Eden Chuislekuda, for her restaurant and food-industry expertise. To my mother, one of the finest cooks I ever met, who helped inspire my love for the kitchen, and my sister, Dee, who made it look so easy. Finally, to the Food Network, my in-home school for all things culinary! Especially my favorite chefs, the Neelys, Paula Deen, Alton Brown, Rachael Ray, and the irresistible Bobby Flay. Bon appétit!

1

Could anybody possibly be that fine? That's what Tiffany Matthews asked herself as she fastened her seat belt, took a deep breath, and clutched a teddy bear that looked as frazzled as she felt. The bear had an excuse—it was twenty-three years old. And so did Tiffany—she was exhausted. Graduating from culinary school and preparing for a month-long overseas internship had taken its toll.

There was yet another draining aspect to consider: Tiffany was terrified of flying. So much so that even after taking the anxiety pill her best friend had given her, she brazenly endured the curious stares of fellow passengers as they watched the naturally attractive, obviously adult woman sit in the airport, enter the jetway, and then board a plane with a raggedy stuffed animal clasped to her chest.

Tiffany didn't care. During a childhood where her mother worked long hours and her grandmother loved but didn't entertain, Tuffy, the teddy bear, had been her constant and sometimes only friend. No matter what happened, Tuffy was there to lend a cushy ear, an eternal smile, and wide, button-eyed support. This stuffed animal was also the first present she remembered her father giving her, when she was five years old. Unfortunately, his gift stayed around longer than Daddy did, a fact that after years of not seeing him still brought Tiffany pain. They were estranged, and while Tiffany would never admit it, having her father's first gift close by always felt like having him near. Tuffy brought comfort—during her childhood of loneliness, her teenaged years of puppy love and superficial heartbreak, her college years of first love and true pain, and now, while pursuing a dream her parents felt was beneath her. As the plane began its ascent into the magnificently blue May sky, and Tiffany squeezed her eyes shut, praying the pill would stave off an attack, she knew she'd take any help she could get to make it through this flight, even that of a furry friend.

It wasn't until the plane leveled off and her heartbeat slowed that she thought of him again—the stranger in first class. Their eyes had met when she passed by him on the way to her seat in coach. Tiffany had assessed him in an instant: fine, classy, rich. *And probably married,* she concluded, as she finally loosened the death grip she had on Tuffy and laid him on the middle seat next to her. *Clearly out of my league. . . .* Still, she couldn't help but remember how her breath caught when she entered the plane and saw him sitting there, looking like a *GQ* ad, in the second row, aisle seat. His close-cropped black hair looked soft and touchable, his cushiony lips framed nicely by just the hint of a mustache. But it was his eyes that had caused Tiffany's breath to catch: the deepest brown she'd ever seen, especially set against flawless skin that not only looked the color of maple syrup, but she imagined tasted as sweet. This information was absorbed and processed in the seconds it took the man two people in front of her to put his carry-on in the overhead bin and step aside so the people behind him could continue. The stranger had glanced up at her. Their eyes had held for a moment. Had she imagined his giving her a quick once-over before he resumed reading his magazine?

Tiffany tilted back her seat and placed Tuffy on her lap. Perhaps it was the medication or the lack of sleep the prior night, but Tiffany welcomed what she hoped would be a long slumber that would take her over the Atlantic, all the way up to the landing in Rome. If she was lucky, she thought, she'd wake up with just enough time to pull her seat forward and place her tray table back in its upright and locked position. And if she was sleeping, she wouldn't be thinking about how much she hated flying, and she especially would not be thinking about Mr. First Class. She knew she was kidding herself to think she made any kind of impression as she passed by the sexy stranger. How could she, dressed in jeans, a Baby Phat T-shirt, and clutching a tattered teddy bear? *No need to sit here fantasizing. If I'm going to dream . . . might as well do it in my sleep!*

Dominique Rollins, or Nick as he was known to friends, put down the magazine and picked up his drink. After staring at the same page for over five minutes, he realized he wasn't reading it anyway. For some inexplicable reason, his mind kept wandering to the woman back in coach, the sexy siren who'd passed him clutching a teddy bear as if she were five instead of the twentysomething she looked. His guess was that she was afraid of flying and the toy was some type of childhood relic, like a security blanket. But to carry it openly, in public, holding it as if it were a lifeline? *Too bad, because that chick is fine as chilled wine in the summertime.* Nick appreciated the stranger's natural beauty, but he liked his women successful and secure. Not that he was looking for women on this trip, he reminded himself. He wanted a carefree few days without any complications. Nick knew all too well that when it came to the words "woman" and "complication," one rarely appeared without the other.

Her eyes . . . Nick tilted his seat back and sipped his Manhattan. That was what intrigued him about her. In them was a curious blend of trepidation and intelligence, of anxiety mixed with steely resolve. The combination brought out his chivalrous side. A part of him wanted to walk back to where she was, sit her on his lap, and tell her that everything was going to be all right. His rational side quickly shot down that idea. One, she was a stranger; two, she'd hardly appreciate being treated like a child, clutched teddy bear notwithstanding; and three, Nick wasn't in the market for a woman—friend or otherwise—he reminded himself for the second time in as many minutes. He was grateful for his work and the newest acquisition that had helped to take his mind off Angelica, the woman who'd dashed his dream of their getting married and having a family together . . . and broken his heart.

Nick signaled the flight attendant for another

drink and reached for his iPod. He didn't want to think about Angelica on this trip. He wanted to enjoy this mini-vacation in Rome, one of his favorite cities, and dine at AnticaPesa, one of his favorite restaurants and the inspiration behind the upscale eatery in his newly acquired boutique hotel.

Thinking about the quaint, thirty-four-room property he and his partners had purchased in Malibu, California, and were transforming into a twenty-first-century masterpiece brought a smile to Nick's face. Following the global economic collapse, the men had outwitted their corporate competition and had gotten an incredible deal on the 1930s Spanish-style building. The group, four successful men with diverse and various corporate and entrepreneurial backgrounds, all agreed that it was the good looks and sexy swagger of Nick and another partner, Bastion Price, that sealed the deal with the sixty-something, hard-as-nails Realtor who'd handled negotiations. This trip was the calm before the storm of Le Sol's grand opening, less than one month away.

Nick pressed the button that reclined his seat to an almost fully horizontal position. He tried to relax. But every time his eyes closed, he saw the short-haired, chocolate brown, doe-eyed beauty who'd passed him hours before, with those hip-hugging jeans and bountiful breasts pressed up against a tight, pale yellow T-shirt. *You're flying to Rome for pasta, not pussy,* he mentally chastised himself. Even so, his appetite had been awakened, and the dish he wanted to taste wasn't from anybody's kitchen.

2

Tiffany took a deep breath and tried not to panic. Her purse had been here just a minute ago, in the basket of her luggage cart, right next to her laptop. She mentally retraced her footsteps in her mind, remembering specific moments when she knew she'd had the Coach bag her mother had given her for Christmas. She'd definitely had it as she exited the plane, had fiddled with the strap as she and the handsome stranger shared casual pleasantries when finding themselves separated only by a rope as they snaked through the customs line. She'd looked in her purse, prepared to boldly give the man her phone number, but his turn had come up before she could find paper and pen. She remembered carefully putting her passport back in her purse after they'd stamped it, her mother's words echoing in her head: *Treat that passport as if it's the key out of that country, because it is.*

"Yes, I had it then," she said to herself as she remembered her purse being the last thing she placed on the luggage cart, after loading on two heavy suitcases, a carry-on, her laptop, and Tuffy. Then she'd rolled out of the baggage claim area in search of ground transportation. That's when a young woman who looked American but spoke with an accent had approached her and asked for the best way to get to the tourist sites in the city center. When Tiffany said she didn't know, the woman had excitedly gone on about it being her first time in Rome and admitting how nervous she was to be there by herself. Tiffany could relate. She was nervous as well. She'd felt a kinship with the foreigner, and at the time had thought the woman's shifting eyes were due to nervousness. Now she knew it was due to something else. *That bitch was watching out for an accomplice.*

"She took my purse!" Tiffany yelled, before even realizing she was speaking out loud. Several pairs of eyes turned to stare at her, but she was too panicked to feel embarrassment. "Help, those people stole my purse!"

Belatedly, Tiffany decided to give chase, her heavily laden luggage cart careening wildly through Rome's Fiumicino Airport. She steered the clumsy vehicle as if she were back on the streets of LA, doing a drive-by.

"Excuse me," she said to a woman whom she accidentally bumped in the butt, almost knocking her over. "Coming through!" she yelled as an older gentleman decided to stop and tie his shoe. She managed to bring the cart to a halt just before she broadsided him, stopping so quickly that her carry-on toppled off the cart and Tuffy flew forward and hit the man in the head. "My bad," she said to the bewildered man, who began berating her in rapid-fire Italian. "No-a speakie, no-a speakie," she replied as she gathered up her bag and her bear and began again in the direction she thought the woman had gone.

Five minutes later, she gave up the chase. The woman was nowhere in sight and now Tiffany doubted she could even recognize her in a line-up. Was her hair dark blond or brown? Was she wearing a blue top . . . or was it purple? The woman was Tiffany's height, five foot three, but Tiffany didn't remember whether she wore jeans or slacks, or a skirt, for that matter. She'd had colosseums, not criminals, on her mind as they'd talked.

"Damn." Tiffany plopped down on her luggage and put her head in her hands. She could feel the beginnings of an anxiety attack coming on and tried to focus on breathing deeply. But the gravity of the situation began to grow in her mind. She was in a foreign country, alone, with no passport, no money, and no idea how she'd gone from triumph to tragedy so quickly. She'd been so proud of herself as she'd stepped off the plane, having made it through her first trans-Atlantic flight without throwing up or peeing on herself—both unfortunate events that had accompanied past panic attacks. Now she was precariously close to achieving a trifecta, because in addition to these two scene-stealers, she felt ready to throw a two-year-old tantrum and assure herself a place in one of Rome's asylums for the insane. Tiffany began to shake with the effort it took to hold herself together. Trying not to hyperventilate—on top of not vomiting, peeing, or sobbing like a fool—was taking its toll.

"Are you all right?"

Tiffany froze at the sound of the voice flowing down to her ears, smooth and sweet . . . like maple syrup. Without opening her eyes or raising her head, she knew who it was. *Just great. I probably look like a blubbering idiot, and here comes Mr. First Class to see me in all my crazed glory.* Tiffany hadn't imagined the handsome stranger as her knight in shining armor, but she had imagined doing things to him at night—before she'd forced herself to stop fantasizing and fallen asleep.

He placed a firm hand on Tiffany's shoulder. "What is the problem here? Can I help?"

Tiffany wiped her eyes, prayed there was no snot coming out of her nose, and stood. She took another deep breath and forced herself to look into the eyes that had melted her meow-meow on the plane. "My purse was stolen." Her voice was soft, barely a whisper. But it was all she could do. The energy that fueled her initial outburst was spent; now if she opened her mouth much wider she'd break out into an ugly cry.

He angrily clenched and unclenched his jaw. "Come with me." His tone was decisive, as were his movements. He placed his single carry-on bag on top of her luggage, took Tiffany's much smaller hand into his large one, and began navigating them through the terminal. Tiffany walked beside him silently, feeling as if the events taking place were surreal. She'd been in Rome less than an hour and already her life was upside down. When they reached the elevator, he quietly reached for the teddy bear in the luggage cart basket and handed it to Tiffany.

"Here, your friend will make you feel a little better."

His gesture was almost her undoing, yet Tiffany took Tuffy and clutched him to her chest. "Thank you," she stuttered. She knew it must seem silly to other people, but once she clasped her dear furry friend, she began to calm down.

The elevator doors opened and the stranger guided the cart and Tiffany inside it. Tiffany snuck a glance at him, and then not being able to resist it, took another, longer look. "Where are we going?"

"To the administrative offices," he replied. "I know someone there who can get us to a higher-up in airport security. We'll be able to get this straightened out without all the hassle. You'll have to fill out a report with the airport, and another with the police if you want this crime reported, which I suggest that you do. I won't ask you what happened. You'll have to repeat the despicable details at least twice as it is." He gave Tiffany's hand a reassuring squeeze. "By the way, I'm Nick Rollins."

His personable manners in the midst of madness brought a smile to Tiffany's heart, if not her face. "Tiffany Matthews."

"Even though I truly wish the circumstances were different, Tiffany Matthews, it is a pleasure to formally meet you."

Just over an hour later, Nick was once again leading Tiffany, this time out of the administrative offices and down to ground transportation. As assuring as it was to have this six-foot-tall mass of obvious authority walking beside her, looking nice and smelling good, something about his take-charge manner made her uncomfortable. For the moment, she was too grateful to complain. If Nick hadn't been there, Tiffany felt she'd still be sitting on her luggage, crying and waiting for God knew who to do Lord knew what.

"Thanks for everything you did back there," Tiffany said as they once again neared the elevator.

"No worries," Nick said comfortably. "I'm just glad I was here to help you. Trans-Atlantic flying can be exhausting. To have your purse stolen after having just landed is plain bad luck."

"I knew better than to turn my back on my cart, even for a second. But that woman, excuse me, that *thief,* distracted me on purpose, showing me a brochure of some famous fountain . . ."

"Trevi, it's the Trevi Fountain."

"It's the *trouble* fountain in my book, because that's what finding out about it cost me—nothing but trouble."

"On the good side, nothing was taken that can't be replaced, and what's more, your trip is bound to get better from here!"

The next thing Tiffany knew she was in Nick's chauffeured town car, getting whisked to the American embassy for an emergency replacement passport. On the way, Nick provided his satellite phone so that she could make calls to replace her traveler's checks, cancel her credit cards, and turn off her cell phone— all the while thanking her mother for bugging her until Tiffany had promised to write all of her credit card, passport, and related telephone numbers on a separate piece of paper and place it in her carry-on luggage. While she placed all of these calls, Nick was a calming presence beside her, handling his own items of business on the car phone. When she ended her call, he was still on his, a business call of some sort, she deduced. She busied herself looking out the window, taking in this place that looked so different from the streets of LA. They passed several stately-looking buildings adorned with statues and accented with fountains.

As she gazed out her window, Tiffany thought back over the past couple hours. How Nick Rollins had swooped in to save a modern-day damsel in distress. She remembered the deference those in the airline office had paid him, how the manager of the airport had referred to him as "Mr. Rollins." How the police had appeared out of nowhere and taken her report right there in the airline office, precluding her from having to actually travel to the station to fill out the report. Nick was obviously well known in Rome, or at least well connected.

It took just under an hour for Tiffany to fill out the paperwork regarding her stolen passport and the application to have a new one expedited to her. Throughout the process, Nick continued to be a re-assuring presence beside her. His chivalry continued once they left the embassy and got back in the car.

"Please accept my gift of a hotel room where I'm staying," he said.

Tiffany started, so engrossed in present complexities that she hadn't begun to think of future challenges—such as eating, sleeping and navigating a foreign city with no money. "Oh, I couldn't," she muttered, her mind whirling with plan-B possibilities, of which there were none.

"I insist," Nick countered easily. "It's in a very nice and convenient location, and has a great restaurant with shops nearby. It will be the perfect backdrop for your introduction to Rome, and will prevent you from having to scramble around for a room on credit." There was humor in Nick's voice as he spoke this last sentence, but Tiffany failed to find anything funny. She seriously doubted that there was a hotel on the continent that would extend credit to a traveling guest.

"I can't accept that kind of generosity," Tiffany said again, this time with less conviction. When Nick remained quiet, gently stroking his wisp of a mustache, she continued, "Only if I can pay you back, every cent."

Nick smiled, and a blessed showing of even, white teeth sent her heart flip-flopping with a different kind of anxiety. She was quickly, quietly, falling in lust.

Who is this man who's rescued me? Tiffany pondered the question as she and Nick continued casual conversation. *And what is he expecting in exchange for his kindness?*

3

The hotel was quaint, and plush at the same time—about ten minutes away from what Tiffany would later learn was the hub of Rome's city center. Tiffany's second thought, after the first one of how beautiful the building was, was the fact that it would probably take a third of this trip's budget to pay for one night's stay. She'd reserved a room in a modest bed-and-breakfast, but an inquiring phone call to the establishment had confirmed her fears and Nick's assumption that she couldn't check in without a major credit card. The thought to throw herself on the mercy of the restaurant where she'd be interning was quickly extinguished. She knew those people even less than she knew Nick, which was hardly at all. Except for one phone call, the communication regarding the internship had been by e-mail. Not only that, but Chef Riatoli was her mentor, at the top of his game. She wanted to impress him. Begging him for money before she'd even entered his kitchen was not the type of impression she had in mind. *Just one*

*night. Then my traveler's checks will be here and I can be
on my way.*

A doorman in top hat and tails stepped up to the
town car and made an exaggerated sweep of his
hands as he opened the door. "Welcome back, Mr.
Rollins, sir." His accent was lyrical and his eyes twin-
kled. "Always a pleasure to have you."

"*Grazie,* Alberto," Nick replied. He continued chatting but Tiffany couldn't understand a word he said.
What was perfectly clear, however, was how sexy
Nick sounded speaking Italian. She tried not to be
impressed, and failed, especially once they stepped
inside the extravagantly appointed hotel lobby.

Okay, maybe half my budget, Tiffany thought as they
entered. The deep mahogany wood along the walls
and the front desk gleamed under the sparkling light
from pure gold chandeliers. Tiffany's feet sank into
plush, dark carpeting before the pile gave way to a
bronzed, polished marble. All words escaped her as
she tried to appear casual and nonchalant in what
was rapidly becoming a fairy tale. But reality came
crashing down around her when she heard the manager's response to Nick's request for a second room.

"I'm sorry, sir, but there are no other rooms available."

"Excuse me?" Nick responded in English, obviously not used to being told no, no matter what the
question.

"All of the rooms are taken, sir. We are sold out,"
the manager said, a look pleading for understanding
in his eyes. "I can recommend another fine hotel
that's just down the way—"

"Never mind that," Nick interrupted, silencing the
man with a wave of his authoritative hand. And

then, seeing the fear in the eyes of an employee not wanting to piss off one of his richest customers, Nick softened. "It's okay," he continued in Italian. "I will work it out." And then he turned to Tiffany. "You'll stay in my suite."

"No," Tiffany said, without hesitation. And once again, the vague feeling of discomfort that had plagued her at various times since their meeting surfaced. "I couldn't do that," she slowly continued. Not that bedding down with this fine specimen of human flesh wasn't tempting—it was. It just wasn't prudent. Tiffany was here to launch her career into the culinary world, a competitive, all-consuming endeavor. She needed to be ready to meet Chef on Monday morning, and didn't need to be distracted by fleeting fancies of delusional love.

Nick nodded curtly to the manager before grasping Tiffany's arm and directing them both away from the desk. "This suite," he began by way of explanation, "has two bedrooms, two baths, a nice-sized living/dining area, and fully furnished kitchen. You'll be safe and secure in your own room, which is on the other side of the living room . . . if that's what you want."

"I need my own room, not one in your suite." Tiffany knew she was hardly in a position to make demands, but the feeling of losing control was increasing, along with her anxiety. She glanced over at Tuffy peeking out of her oversized travel bag, but squelched the urge to reach for teddy bear backup.

Nick followed Tiffany's gaze and released a long breath. He eyed her critically before walking back over to the desk and speaking to the manager. "He's checking on the other hotel," he announced when he rejoined her in the lobby's sitting area.

They didn't have long to wait. The hotel manager came over to where they sat, and Tiffany didn't have to speak Italian to know his search had not been successful.

"There's a cardiologist conference going on in the area," Nick translated after he and the manager had spoken. "All of the five-star hotels are booked solid."

"I don't have to stay in a five-star hotel," Tiffany said to the manager. "I'll take anything."

Instead of talking to Tiffany, the manager looked at Nick.

Why are you looking at him? Didn't you just hear me say I'd take anything? Tiffany thought this but did not voice it. No money, no ID, and no place to go were standing in between her and her much-loved independence.

Nick checked his watch. "That's fine, but we don't have time for that tonight. You're welcome to stay in my suite, and if you still want to move to another hotel tomorrow, I'll be more than happy to help you get settled in one that is more to your liking."

Tiffany hid a frown, stifled a sigh, and silently followed Nick as he walked over to the front desk to pick up the room keys. *What choice do I have?* She didn't like the feeling of helplessness that had accompanied her unspoken decision to share Nick's suite. This feeling warred with the thought that said she should be grateful that Nick was here to offer her a room. *I can't deny that,* she thoughtfully concluded, trying to shake off the angst she felt and replace it with gratitude. *After all, it's just one night.* Even so, she lifted Tuffy from the cart just as the bellhop pushed the container bearing their luggage toward the elevator, and snuck another look at the handsome man who'd become her savior. A squiggly feeling slid from her navel to her nana as she eyed the strong, capable hands, one clutching a briefcase, the other, an iPhone. Tiffany clutched the bear, hoping that more than protecting her from Nick, her furry friend could protect her from herself.

4

Later, Tiffany would congratulate herself on not gasping. Nick's penthouse suite was the most beautiful place she'd ever seen. Unlike the small, almost claustrophobic European rooms she'd seen online and for which she'd prepared herself, this suite was spacious, with towering ceilings and silk-covered walls. A large living-room window offered views of a well-landscaped park and beyond that the sparkling city lights of Rome. A large marble fireplace anchored one wall, while a formal dining room occupied the other end of the rectangular space. The velvet couch and love seat, upholstered in a rich sienna, was soft and inviting—the perfect contrast to the ivory-colored carpeting that anchored the living and dining room area. Beyond that, a deep cherry wood adorned the cabinetry as well as the appliances. Tiffany could only imagine what the bedrooms and bathrooms looked like. She began to feel as if spending twenty-four hours in the lap of luxury might not be such a bad experience after all.

"Do you like it?" Nick asked, basking in the joyful

wonder that shone on Tiffany's face. It pleased him that she was as appreciative of beauty as he was.

"It's beautiful."

"I fell in love with it the first time I stayed here. Especially this." Nick stood at the large picture window and swept his hand to indicate the view of Rome, with the ancient ruins of the Colosseum outlined against a near-dark sky.

"You come here often?" Tiffany walked over and stood by the window.

"Not as often as I'd like. But when I do, I stay here."

They were silent a moment, taking in the greenery of the landscape, the water spouting from a fountain, a full moon overhead, and the city center's beckoning lights.

"What brought you here in the first place, to Italy?"

Nick hesitated before answering. The memory of his first visit to Rome, ten years ago, brought with it subtle heartache. That trip was a thirtieth birthday present to himself, one that Angelica had encouraged. They'd been just friends then when she, along with eight of Nick's good friends, had swept into the Eternal City like a cyclone, partied like it was 1999, took the tours, ate the food, and promptly fell in love with all things Italy.

But as he stared out the window, watching the moon rise higher in the sky, Nick was all too aware that the woman beside him now was not Angelica. She was an exquisite woman-child, vulnerable yet independent, fearful yet determined, with skin the color of rich dark chocolate, the kind that even doctors agreed was good for you. *Don't go there,* Nick cautioned himself, even as the thought to do so quickened his heartbeat. *Now is not the time.*

Nick's silence caused Tiffany to look away from the sensually dusky scene out the window and over to the picture of perfection standing less than five feet from her. She almost did gasp this time, the reality of her situation suddenly hitting her like a bolt of lightning. She was in the penthouse suite of a luxury hotel in Rome, Italy, with one of the finest men she'd ever seen up close and personal. She guessed he was around six feet tall, solidly built, his muscular frame perfectly proportioned. He had the type of body that in hugging, a woman could lose herself, Tiffany imagined. One that could communicate "Don't worry, I've got you" with one good squeeze. She followed Nick's tongue as he unconsciously licked a set of lips that were just the right size, casually nibbling on the lower one as he pondered some event to which Tiffany was not privy. His brow was furrowed slightly, and Tiffany took in the perfect arch of his thick, black eyebrows and the long, curly lashes that framed the bedroom eyes that had melted her in the airplane aisle. Before she could stop herself, her eyes traveled over his broad shoulders, down his strong back, stopping at his nicely rounded derriere before continuing to peruse a set of sprinter's legs and big feet that hinted at the promise of . . .

Promise of what? Tiffany mentally shook herself and hurried away from the window. The air had suddenly grown heavy and she found it hard to breathe. *Where is Tuffy?* In that moment she realized it wasn't her teddy bear, but the bear of a man on the other side of the room that she'd rather hug and squeeze right now. And just as quickly, she extinguished the thought. While she hadn't seen a ring on his finger, she was sure nonetheless that he belonged to somebody—maybe several somebodies. She thought of Joy, her best friend, and figured she was more the type of woman Nick would go after. Joy was a Tyra Banks type: tall, beautiful, long hair courtesy of European and Native grandparents instead of a weave, and confident beyond belief. And here she was, Tiffany, looking for an old-ass teddy bear! *Get your head out of the clouds, Tiffany!* Janice Matthews's voice rang in her head. Her mother was right, and Tiffany decided to obey her.

"Look, I'm going to—"

"Would you like to join me—"

Nick and Tiffany spoke at once, both silently aware that somehow, surreptitiously, the atmosphere between them had shifted.

"I—I was just going to thank you again for everything you've done, and then take a shower and lie down. It's been a long day."

"Surely it has, but aren't you hungry?" Nick knew that while there was food service in coach, it was nothing like first class.

"Not really."

Tiffany's stomach chose that exact moment to become vocal, and a loud, sustained growl emanated from its core. The sound of this base bodily function chased away the discomfort they both felt—brought about by unsolicited and unwelcome thoughts.

Tiffany's eyes went wide with embarrassment. How dared her body betray her, sounding common in front of this classy man and calling her a liar with pronounced vigor. "Ooh, excuse me!" she muttered, even as she pressed a hand against her flat stomach, mentally daring it to speak again.

Nick's laugh was deep and unfettered. "You may

not be hungry, but your stomach is. Join me for dinner. I'm going to one of my favorite restaurants and I detest dining alone." Actually, Nick was quite comfortable eating solo, and once through the doors of AnticaPesa, he was rarely alone for long. But he felt not one twinge of guilt playing the sympathy card to get Tiffany's agreement to be his dinner date. Something about her hesitation—and again, that flash of trepidation quickly replaced by resolve—made him want to be the one who relaxed her, who helped her feel comfortable in what was for her a strange, new place.

Thirty minutes later they were on their way to fine dining in the center of Rome. The slight discomfort returned, and was reflected in their silence as they waited on the chauffeur. Tiffany tried to still the nervousness combined with physical need that sprung up as soon as she walked from her bedroom to the living room. Nick was there, standing in front of the window, talking on the phone. It gave her a moment to behold him in all his glory: dressed casually in a black silk pullover and black pants. *Joy would probably know the designer,* Tiffany thought as she stopped and sipped the sight of him like one would a tumbler of fine brandy. Even with her lack of knowledge of all things fashion, Tiffany was sure the outfit had been tailor made. *There's no way that any piece of clothing could come off the rack and fit that perfectly.* She forced herself from the hall into the main living area and thanked her best friend for forcing her to pack the jersey dress she now wore.

* * *

"Joy Lynn Parsons! You *know* you shouldn't have gone shopping for me! How much did this cost you?"

"Don't worry about it. Just make sure it ends up in your suitcase."

"Look, my days will be spent in the kitchen and my nights will be spent in bed, alone. This is a crash course in upscale Italian cuisine, girl. I'm not going to have the time or place to wear something like this."

Joy had rolled her eyes. "Didn't your daddy ever tell you to always be like the Boy Scouts—prepared?"

"Sure. As long as I was preparing myself for something *he* wanted me to do."

"Well, these gifts to you are because of what *I* want, which is for you to stop being so serious and single-minded, and remember to have a good time." With that, Joy had reached into another bag and pulled out a pair of jewel-toned, strappy sandals.

"Girl, I don't wear stuff like this!" It was true. Tiffany was more likely to be found in cotton tops and jeans.

"You will in Rome. Who knows? You might star in your own Kiki series and become a rich man's wifey."

"Who's Kiki?"

"Kiki Swinson."

"Is that somebody at Randall's job?"

"Fool, this woman is far from working at UPS with my husband. She's a bestselling author!"

"Oh, please, you and your book addiction. Those fairy-tale endings only happen in fiction."

"And sometimes life imitates art," Joy fired back.

"Well, even if Kiki writes about a rich man who works in a kitchen, I'm sure my story's ending will differ from the one you read."

"No, you'll have to navigate the world of thugs and drugs to be in her story."

"Like I said, fiction isn't fact." Tiffany dangled the shoes in front of her, turning them this way and that, frowning as if what she held were foreign objects. "You need to take these shoes and stuff back to the store and get a refund," she said somberly.

"Tiffany, you're my best friend in the world, but as God is my witness, I'm going to beat your ass with those stilettos if you don't stop acting ungrateful!"

The women laughed and continued joking around as Tiffany tried on the outfit and modeled it for Joy. Her friend's taste was excellent and the choices spot on. The dress, which stopped a couple inches above the knee, spotlighted Tiffany's assets and hit her curves in all the right places. The sandals not only gave Tiffany height, but accented surprisingly long legs for someone so short. Tiffany looked gorgeous in the outfit.

Nick felt Tiffany's eyes on him and turned slowly, the words he was about to say to one of his partners dying on his lips. His eyes narrowed as he gazed upon the vision in front of him.

"Nick? Buddy, are you still there?"

"Let's touch base tomorrow," Nick said into the phone. He disconnected the call without waiting for a reply.

Tiffany's nerves increased under his intense perusal. Had she chosen the wrong outfit? Was this too dressy for where they were going? Was it too much, did it suggest something that she hadn't intended? *Why does he keep staring at me without saying anything?*

"I can change if this isn't appropriate," she blurted, suddenly feeling like the little girl who'd chagrined her father, which, with her choices, had often been the case.

"It's perfect," Nick breathed. He was trying to rein in feelings and emotions that had no place in this room, in this city, with this woman. It had been easier with the teddy-bear clutching girl in jeans; the task would be much harder with this sexy vixen with the hourglass figure he wanted to sculpt with his hands.

Once they were settled in the town car, Nick forced his thoughts away from how good Tiffany looked in the satiny dress she wore and turned them toward those good for casual conversation. After all, it would be another fifteen minutes before they reached their destination.

"I know this is your first trip to Europe, but have you ever been out of the States?"

Tiffany nodded. "If you count Mexico . . . Cabo San Lucas."

"I see."

Tiffany glanced over at Nick, who observed her thoughtfully while rubbing his mustache, something she deduced was an unconscious habit.

"Why Rome?" he asked.

Tiffany smiled, thankful for the familiar territory they were entering. "I'm studying to be a chef."

Nick's brows rose. "Really?"

"Yes. I just graduated from culinary school and am here to train under a master of Italian cuisine."

Nick's interest piqued, and he turned to face Tiffany. "Who?"

"You probably don't know him; he's famous in cooking circles, but not a name often heard in the outside world."

"It wouldn't happen to be Emilio Riatoli, would it?"

Tiffany's mouth opened in shock. "You've heard of him?"

Again, Nick blessed Tiffany with the deep, throaty laugh that made her love lair tingle. His eyes sparkled as he answered. "I've heard of him, yes."

Tiffany looked at Nick with new appreciation. Anyone who was enthusiastic for, let alone knowledgeable about anything or anyone in the culinary world gained credence in her eyes. "How do you know of Chef Riatoli?"

"This is one of my favorite cities, remember?" His smile deepened, but he said nothing further.

"He was on tour in the States and conducted a class at our school," Tiffany continued. "It was mainly on sauces, but he also demonstrated a couple dishes from another of his areas of expertise . . . seafood. He's a genius at what he does," she added, with more than a little admiration in her voice. "My dream is to open a restaurant in LA, one with cuisine similar to Chef Riatoli's specialties—but with my own interpretation, of course."

Nick's interest in and appreciation for Tiffany

grew. Here was a woman after his own heart, with dreams that complemented the future he visualized.

"What types of specialties would your restaurant serve?"

Tiffany sighed and sat back, at ease when talking about her ultimate life goal. It was the first time she'd felt totally comfortable with Nick since they met.

"I'd have several scallop-based appetizers," she began. "Served in various sauces, richly embodied yet never overpowering the fish's delicate taste. I love working with asparagus, especially white asparagus, and it's a perfect complement to this seafood. Chef Riatoli makes a dish that is amazing." Tiffany's mouth watered of its own accord as she remembered the dish Chef had prepared in their classroom kitchen.

I pettini al pomodoro e l'asparago, Nick thought. Emilio's simple yet succulent pairing of scallops with asparagus was his singularly favorite appetizer in all of Italy.

"What about salads," he prompted after Tiffany had reeled off several more variations on her scallop ideas.

"Simple, clean," she answered easily. "Too often, cooks make the mistake of putting too many ingredients into their salad creations. Chef Riatoli teaches that less is often more when it comes to marrying flavors. I've been playing around with an arugula salad that is nothing but greens, thin slices of fennel and tomato, with a basic vinaigrette that contains—" Tiffany stopped, realizing she was about to divulge a secret ingredient. "That contains a little something extra," she finished, her mouth pursing with the effort of not blurting out the very essences this man reminded her so much of—maple syrup with a hint of wasabi—sweet and hot.

The car turned the corner and entered a narrow street, typical of what one would imagine when thinking of Europe. The brick buildings on the left side of the street were adorned with flower-filled balconies and wooden shutters. The right side of the street was lined with cafés, all boasting outside seating enhanced with subdued lighting, candles, stark white linen, and canopies that bathed the setting in splashes of color. Belatedly, Tiffany realized she'd hardly noticed the city, so caught up had she been in sharing her dream menu. But now, as they approached the end of the block, she looked around and began reading the names of the restaurants and designer clothing and shoe shops on the other side of the street. Her heart beat faster as she read one sign that stated simply, Fia's.

"You'll love the area," Chef Riatoli's assistant had told her when he'd provided information to help Tiffany's transition. "And whatever you do, don't spend all your money at Fia's."

"Who's that?" Tiffany had asked.

"Only the newest and most sought-after designer in Rome," the assistant had explained. "Her shop is largely by appointment only, and her dresses are on probably half the actresses you see on the red carpet."

Tiffany had assured him that when it came to designer fashions, her money was safe in her purse. Now, had it been a culinary shop, with various pots, pans, and kitchen utensils? Tiffany would have been in trouble. It was designer knife sets, not designer knits, that warmed her blood. *But Fia's is right across the street from where I'll be working, he said. It's right across the street from—*

"Here we are, sir." The driver interrupted Tiffany's thoughts. "Safely delivered to your favorite place in Rome . . ."

"AnticaPesa," both he and Tiffany finished together. "You know him!" she gushed to Nick. "You know Chef Riatoli!"

"Guilty as charged," Nick said, his grin now full and unabashed.

The door on her side opened and the chauffeur waited to help her out of the car. Tiffany, however, remained glued to her seat.

"His delicacies await us, *mia bellezza*," Nick prodded. "Shall we?"

"I can't," Tiffany answered, feeling inadequate one minute, overwhelmed the next. "I'm here as Chef's cook, not his customer! I can't afford this place. I'm a student. I'm . . . What will he think of me walking into his establishment to eat?"

Nick stepped out of the car, walked around to Tiffany's side, and extended his hand. "Sweetheart, he'll think you're hungry. Come."

5

The maitre d' smiled broadly as Nick entered the warm and cozy foyer. *"Dominico, mio amico! Benvenuto di nuovo a AnticaPesa. Come lei è sono?"*

"Buono, grazie," Nick answered, before switching to English for Tiffany's benefit. "Very good, in fact. It's been far too long since I've been here, but I see you are managing well without me. The place is full, as usual."

"Too many customers," the maitre d' admitted, his English punctuated with a lyrical accent. "But that is a good problem to have, no?"

Nick placed a hand at the small of Tiffany's back and guided her forward. "My friend, Ms. Matthews," he said, his voice smoky and possessive. "Tiffany, this is Rolando."

The maitre d's eyes widened in appreciation. *"Bella donna,"* he gushed, bringing Tiffany's hand to his lips and kissing it gently. "It is my pleasure to feast upon such exquisite beauty."

Tiffany released a self-conscious giggle as Joy's voice swam into her consciousness. "Italian men love

Black women," she'd said as Tiffany modeled the
dress. "You might get ravished by a ravioli-eating—"

"*Grazie*," Tiffany answered softly, speaking the word
she'd heard Nick say earlier, that obviously meant
thank you. It was her first foray into Italian, and a
blatant attempt to turn her thoughts away from the
sexually oriented conversation that had preceded
Joy's comment.

"*Prego*," the maitre d' responded as they reached
Nick's reserved table. "Should we start with your usual
wine, sir?"

"No, I think we'll go for something a bit more celebratory. It's Tiffany's first visit to Rome."

"Ah, then let me send the sommelier to discuss an
appropriate choice for you and the *giovane donna*."
The maitre d' smiled at Tiffany, nodded at Nick, and
walked away.

Tiffany tried not to gawk. The last thing she wanted
to do was to come across like a country bumpkin
who'd been nowhere. But after a few seconds, her attempt at sophistication failed her. Because the truth
of the matter was that she was a bumpkin, albeit a city
one, who'd never been anywhere like this before. She
looked from the beautifully set tables to the beautiful
people occupying them, listened to the soft sounds
of classical music providing the subtlest of backdrops
for erudite conversations and, she imagined, more
than a few declarations of love. The place oozed ro-
manticism as well as wealth. Tiffany felt like Cin-
derella, her crystal-covered sandals as close to a glass
slipper as Tiffany needed. She only hoped her dress
wouldn't disintegrate at midnight, unless it was at
the hands of the prince sitting across from her.

Nick sat back and watched Tiffany. Her unsophisticated wonder captivated him, made him feel good. Her energy was so unlike Angelica's, who'd become bored with Rome and increasingly unappreciative of the city's cuisine. "I'm not crazy about it," she'd said of Riatoli's signature scallop dish, the one Tiffany had come to copy and conquer. But where Angelica had become jaded and taken life's luxuries for granted, Tiffany soaked them up with the appreciation due them. Nick was overcome with the desire to be the one who introduced her to the finer things in life, to his world. He was about to tell her so when Tiffany's eyes widened and dimples rippled with the smile that broke across her face.

One glance at her mentor walking in their direction and excitement replaced Tiffany's nervousness. This was the man who was going to fill her with the knowledge that would bring her closer to her dreams. "Chef Riatoli!" she whispered, when he stopped at her table.

Chef smiled at her but addressed Nick first. "Signore Rollins. It is my pleasure."

"As always, Emilio, the pleasure is mine." Nick looked at Tiffany and ignored the stab of jealousy that arose at the adoring way she stared at Emilio. "I believe you know my dining companion, Tiffany Matthews?"

"Indeed I do," Chef Riatoli said. "It is a thoughtful student who tests the dishes she'll attempt to master." He finally turned to Tiffany. "Welcome to Roma."

"Thank you, Chef. I hope you don't mind my coming to your dining room instead of the kitchen on this first visit."

"In the company of one of my best customers? Never!"

Chef Riatoli and Nick conversed a moment more before the sommelier joined them to discuss the wine list. "I'll leave you to this expert," Chef Riatoli finished. "But may I suggest the veal for your main course tonight? It's exquisite, grown especially for our kitchen."

"We'll take your suggestions for the entire meal," Nick countered easily. Before turning to the sommelier, Nick looked at Tiffany. "Do you prefer sweet or dry?"

"I'm not much of a drinker," she concluded honestly. "You decide."

Nick and the sommelier settled on a Dom Perignon Rosé, to start, as the waiter brought out a basket of focaccia, fresh from the oven. The flat bread was golden brown, topped with fresh tomatoes, basil, and olive oil, and a bowl of red caviar.

Over the next two and half hours, Tiffany learned about the man named Dominique "Nick" Rollins and ate the best food she'd ever tasted in her life. In between the perfectly cooked scallop appetizer, raw oysters on the half shell (which Tiffany loved, to her surprise), smoked mozzarella salad, and the palate-cleansing chilled celery soup, Tiffany learned about Nick's latest venture, a boutique hotel, and their shared dream of owning a five-star eatery with a three-star Michelin rating—the highest rating awarded by this industry bible, and a difficult score to achieve. During the fifth and sixth courses, braised monkfish followed by the medium-rare veal that tasted like ambrosia and melted in their mouths, Nick learned that Tiffany was an only child with an independent streak, a college graduate with a near four-point average, and a delicious mix of contradictions—a feisty woman with a childlike need for the security of a twenty-three-year-old teddy bear. While not spending much time talking about her parents, Tiffany showed open admiration for her grandmother, who'd encouraged her love of cooking. The food Nick and Tiffany ate was accompanied by a chilled Chardonnay, and later a mellow Cabernet Sauvignon. Though she'd only had one glass of each, Tiffany was feeling as warm and fuzzy as Tuffy by the time dessert arrived. The gelato-based treat was a Chef Riatoli original, and the alcohol Tiffany had consumed was the only logical explanation for how Nick's caramel-covered finger, which he'd dipped in the sweet masterpiece, ended up in her mouth.

6

"Um, it's delicious." Tiffany moaned as the mix of cool Italian ice cream danced with the warmth of the melted caramel sliding down Nick's long, thick index finger.

Nick had initiated the playful moment, almost daring Tiffany to loosen up by tasting Emilio's creation from this digit. But once again, Tiffany surprised him, this time with an unexpected show of boldness. The tables turned unexpectedly, and it now seemed as if Tiffany might beat him at his own game. He covered his growing ardor, and discomfort, with humor. "Yes, but how's the dessert?"

Tiffany finished licking the caramel off Nick's finger, laughing as she did so. "It's so good," she whispered, dipping her finger into the saucer in front of her and presenting it to Nick. "Here, taste it."

Nick's eyes turned almost black with desire as he fixed Tiffany with an unblinking gaze. Slowly, he leaned forward and with all due deliberation sucked her finger into his mouth. He took his tongue and swirled it around, even as he licked and then swallowed the gooey treat. "Um, you taste like brown sugar."

Tiffany sat mesmerized, like prey that belatedly discovered it had been captured. A warm heat started in her core, then spread in all directions—up her spine, down her throat, bursting into warmth like sun on her face; and down, lower, becoming wetness. Her breath caught and her nipples hardened. The caramel was long gone, but Nick continued to suck, as if her finger was a lifeline and he was a drowning man. Slowly he dipped each finger of her right hand into the dessert and methodically licked its dripping treasure. When he deigned to initiate her pinkie into this ritual, some of the caramel dripped from it to her chest and oozed down into her cleavage.

"Oops," Tiffany whispered, wishing Nick would do the obvious and come lick the sauce off her. And Nick would have probably obliged her, had not Chef Riatoli appeared at their table, breaking the magic and bringing both Nick and Tiffany out of their passion-induced fantasy and back to the private area of the restaurant where they sat.

"Oops," Tiffany said again, this time self-conscious of what had taken place. She hastily grabbed her napkin and wiped away what she could of the caramel down her cleavage. Her face burned with embarrassment, both at what she'd done and what Chef might have seen. *What has gotten into me?* For all intents and purposes, this was her place of employment, and here she was acting like a love-struck teenager out on her first date. Even as she tried to berate herself, her cootchie cooed at the very idea.

Nick and Tiffany would never know whether or not Chef Riatoli had observed their intimate playfulness. When he arrived at their table, he was his usual self—jovial and professional. "Was dessert to your liking, sir?"

"Perfection as always, Emilio. You've outdone yourself with this one." Nick sat back in his chair and wiped his mouth. "What is it called?"

"There's no name, sir. I created it just now, just for you, Dominique."

"Perhaps you should name it after your student," Nick said, nodding at Tiffany. "She found it . . . simply delicious."

Chef Riatoli simply smiled and bowed humbly. "Will there be coffee, an aperitif perhaps?"

Nick did have a particular chocolate liqueur in mind, one he'd like to drink from the valley of Tiffany's breasts. "Not tonight, Emilio. Just the check."

"Please, sir, consider this dinner my treat for your belated return. You always bring us luck when you come. A week after your last visit, our president dined here!"

Nick rose and walked around to help Tiffany from her chair. "You're a good man, Emilio Riatoli. The offer still stands for your relocation to Los Angeles. It would be an honor to have you head up the restaurant in Le Sol."

Moments later, Nick and Tiffany were on their way back to the hotel. The air between them was charged, full of unspoken desire and restrained expectation. The spell in the restaurant had been broken, or at the very least temporarily interrupted, and reality now accompanied the cool night breeze that caressed their faces. Nick tried to forget about the drops of caramel that even now he believed clung to Tiffany's skin. Tiffany tried to block the images of sucking and licking. They both had very good reasons, solid, practical reasons why the flirtation that began in the restaurant could go no further. Except for the barest of small talk, they traveled to the hotel in silence, a quiet that continued as they entered the elevator and rode to their floor. *I'll just say good night and go to my room,* Tiffany determined. *I'll suggest coffee for a nightcap and then go straight to bed,* Nick decided. These thoughts lasted until they walked into the penthouse and closed the door behind them. And then they were in each other's arms.

The first kiss was turbulent, mirroring their emotions, their tongues dueling, swirling, as hands explored and caressed. The heat was palpable, undeniable, pushing them both toward the inevitable conclusion. *Except it can't be,* the logical side of Tiffany's brain prodded. But something else was prodding her, something long, thick and hard—burning like a branding iron against her stomach. Tiffany moaned, deep and low, pressing herself deeper into Nick's arms.

"Are you all right?" Nick whispered against her ear, his breath hot and moist.

"No," Tiffany whispered back.

"What's the matter?" Nick said as he ground himself into her, sure he knew the answer and had the cure.

But once again, Tiffany surprised him. "My feet hurt."

7

Nick's deep, throaty laughter spilled into Tiffany's mouth. It was Tiffany's turn to use humor to try and defuse the intoxicating mood. The effect was at least partly as she'd expected. Nick stopped kissing her. But he didn't let her go. Instead, after a deep hug, he picked up Tiffany as if she were weightless.

"What are you doing?"

"Isn't it obvious? I'm sweeping you off your feet, brown sugar . . ."

"Really, Nick, I can walk—"

"Not on aching feet."

Tiffany was relieved when instead of the bedroom where she thought they were headed, Nick walked over and gently laid her down on the sofa. He knelt by her feet and gingerly removed first one heel, and then the next. "I love these sandals. You have great taste."

"Thanks," Tiffany said, after a hesitation in which she decided to leave out the fact that the choice he loved had been her best friend's, not hers. She was certain Joy would forgive her this omission.

Nick massaged each foot for a moment before standing abruptly. "Wait here. Don't move."

Tiffany allowed her head to sink into one of the velvet-covered sofa pillows, the alcohol still providing its own blanket of warmth. The liquor and the heat Nick generated provided an all-encompassing fire, so much so that the idea of getting buck naked and enjoying the balcony breeze held much appeal. Tiffany quickly banished the thought. She may have been tipsy, but shreds of common sense remained.

The soft sounds of smooth jazz seeped into the room, much like the caramel had earlier seeped down Tiffany's cleavage. Unlike many of her peers who ate and breathed hip-hop alone, Tiffany also loved jazz. She smiled and closed her eyes, settling deeper into the sofa, letting the velvet caress her. The saxophone bubbled, like the champagne had earlier, and the guitar licks melted into her eardrum, like the veal had in her mouth. Just as she began to enjoy this auditory feast, a hot, wet towel was wrapped around each of her feet.

"Don't move," Nick once again commanded.

Tiffany simply nodded, as something else besides her towel-wrapped feet became hot and wet.

Nick forced his mind still as he walked back to his bedroom, quickly undressed, pulled a couple of condoms from the box he always carried with him, and placed them within easy reach on the nightstand beside the bed. He pulled on a pair of black silk pajama bottoms, refusing to think about his previous declaration of "woman" and "complication" being synonymous. He was grown, and so was Tiffany. They both wanted the same thing, and for Nick, the four months since he'd broken up with Angelica and gone without sex had been entirely too long. For him, casual flings were not an option. The last one he'd had, with an independent contractor for one of his projects, had turned into a sexual harassment lawsuit when he'd said no to a more permanent arrangement. To avoid a long, drawn-out, and public court battle, he'd offered her a settlement, which she accepted. He'd learned from experience that sleeping with a female one barely knew could be costly. *But you barely know Tiffany.* Nick's lower head answered his upper one. *No, but I'm about to!* He reached for the avocado body butter he used instead of lotion and fled the bedroom and his cautioning thoughts.

The vision that greeted him as he turned the corner stopped Nick in his tracks. Tiffany had fallen asleep, and in doing so had turned on her side and pulled her knees to her chest. The jersey dress had ridden up, exposing an expanse of creamy skin and emphasizing the ample amount of buttocks the fabric caressed. Nick's member twitched its appreciation and moved Nick to action. He strolled over to the sofa, much like a panther ready to pounce. He gently lifted Tiffany's feet, sat down, and placed them in his lap. He quickly unwrapped the cooled towels and dropped them beside the sofa. Next, he picked up the jar of body butter, but before he unscrewed the top, he couldn't help but to satisfy a curiosity. He ran light, sure fingers across Tiffany's skin, and closed his eyes at the confirmation. *Soft . . . like this butter.* That question answered, Nick placed a small amount of the deliciously scented concoction into his palm, rubbed his palms together, and began slowly, gently massaging Tiffany's feet.

"Umm," Tiffany moaned. She turned onto her back

without waking up. The dress rode higher, barely covering her treasure. Something sparkly winked at him from between her legs. Nick forced his breathing to stay slow and even. After all, he reasoned, he had all night to savor this dish, which he was sure would be the tastiest of all the ones he'd eaten that day. He worked on Tiffany deliberately as she continued to doze. After massaging her toes, feet, and calves, Nick decided it was time for Tiffany to wake up and fully enjoy his ministrations. He smiled, remembering events from earlier in the evening, as he lifted her foot toward his mouth and placed a perfectly pedicured big toe between his lips. He began to suck it, his stiff tongue teasing the skin in between her toes. Tiffany squirmed and moaned again. And then her eyes flew open.

"What . . . Nick?" She tried to sit up.

"Shh, it's okay, sweetheart, just lie back, relax, and let me enjoy this second round of dessert."

Tiffany wanted to argue, but there was something about the way he was sucking her toes while running a firm hand up and down her legs that rendered her speechless. Of their own accord, her legs fell open, a fact Nick quickly noticed and upon which he capitalized.

Placing a knee on the couch while keeping his other leg planted firmly on the floor, Nick placed his hands around Tiffany's hips and slid the dress upward. The material was soft, as he'd imagined, but not as soft as Tiffany. Another mystery was solved as a gold thong—and not a pussy on fire—was the spark peeking out from Tiffany's dress. *I think it's about time for me to fan the flame,* Nick thought as he pushed Tiffany's knees farther apart and lowered his head to her paradise. Without preamble, and without warning, he dove in.

Tiffany's intake of breath was sharp and prolonged. Her entire body tensed at the unexpected yet delicious assault. She was fully awake now, and fully feeling. And she'd never felt anything like this before; a tongue so stiff and so skilled that her first orgasm was immediate, even though Nick licked her through her panties. The intensity of the feeling shocked her, but before she could contemplate what was happening, Nick moved aside the satiny fabric and slithered his tongue between her moist folds. Slowly, methodically, he lapped her nectar, alternately nipping and blowing to heighten the pleasure. The more Tiffany moaned, the deeper Nick traveled, placing his hands under her buttocks and forcing her closer. It felt as if he were reaching her very core, and try as she might to escape the pleasure that was so exquisite as to be almost painful, Nick held her in a firm, authoritative grasp. Just when she thought she'd topple over into an eternal ecstasy, Nick pulled back. But instead of stopping, his tongue became as light as a feather, subtly brushing her nub, over and over. Now Tiffany's body begged for what she'd tried to escape from just seconds before. She became the aggressor, blindly reaching for Nick's head, rubbing the soft texture of his hair even as she pressed his head between her legs. His laugh was intoxicating, tinged with knowing and victory. He knew what effect he had on her, and Tiffany didn't care. She just wanted him both to stop and to go on forever. Nick wanted to go on as well, to the next level of their lovemaking. He picked Tiffany up from the sofa and strode purposefully toward his bedroom.

The quick, deliberate action had a sobering effect on Tiffany. *What am I doing? I just met this man. He's the owner of a new, trendy hotel with plans for an award-winning restaurant. He could become my employer back in LA.* The playful conversation they'd had at the restaurant burst its way into the moment, warring with her tingling love nest and pulsating nub.

"I should put in an application for sous chef when your restaurant opens," Tiffany teased.

"Don't wait until it opens; send in your résumé as soon as you get back. Put it to my attention."

"Are you serious?"

"When it comes to business, Tiffany Matthews, I don't play around."

Working at a restaurant such as Nick envisioned could do wonders for her career. Nick had made her an offer. An offer that might be withdrawn, she decided, if she gave in to her desires for a one-night stand.

Tiffany jumped up as soon as Nick laid her on the bed. "I can't do this."

"Do what?" Nick asked dumbly, his lower head once again pushing out all common sense.

"This," Tiffany answered, backing slowly away from the bed. "With you."

"Why not?" Nick didn't want to sound like the whining, pimply-faced teenager he used to be, begging his schoolmates out of their panties. But that fifteen-year-old's voice was exactly what he heard in his ears. "Come on, Tiffany," he continued, trying to bring the Barry White bass back. "It'll be good, I promise."

That's what I'm afraid of, was what Tiffany thought. "I'm sorry," was what she said. And then she fled the room.

8

The sunlight awoke her. Tiffany yawned and stretched, belatedly realizing she hadn't closed her curtains last night. *Last night.* Fragments of the past evening flitted in by bits and pieces, as if pieces of a dream. The delicious cuisine and stimulating conversation about dreams and desires and . . .

Tiffany sat straight up in bed. Suddenly, it *all* came rushing back: memories of caramel, caresses, coital cultivation by a master. Her body began to tingle as the first mental pictures replayed on her mind's video. She reached for a pillow and hugged it to her chest. "Last night we almost . . ." She didn't finish the whispered acknowledgment, but rather turned on her side with a frown. In the light of a new morning, her decision to think rationally didn't seem so noble. Even without full intercourse and with her limited experience with three prior relationships, Tiffany knew Nick was an incredible lover, the best she'd ever had. It had been almost a year since she'd been intimate, since a failed, six-month affair with a former classmate ended when he relocated back to

New York. Their lovemaking had been satisfying, or at least Tiffany had thought so at the time. *How many orgasms did I have last night? Three? Four?* Tiffany couldn't remember, but she knew one thing for sure. It was the first time in her life she'd had more than one in the same night. *Why did I stop it? Why didn't I let Nick finish what he'd started?* Tiffany could almost see the look of compassion that would cover Joy's face upon hearing the story. "Tiffany," she'd say with a tinge of sadness. "You should have gone Zane." Zane, she'd been told after looking at Joy with a blank expression the first time her friend had used the quip, was the queen of erotic fiction.

Tiffany lay there a moment longer, remembering how good Nick had made her feel, both in his arms and with his tongue. His kiss had been powerful, all-consuming, as if he couldn't get enough of her. And that was just the beginning. When he'd parted her legs and touched her there . . .

Tiffany made a decision and threw back the covers at the same time. Joy was right. She needed to "go Zane." Life was too short to be so careful about everything. Who said that if they made love it would ruin her chances to work for Nick? Maybe it would increase her chances, Tiffany thought. *Yes, Ms. Matthews, what about that possibility?* Tiffany turned on the shower, determined to let Nick finish what he'd started the night before, for them to share the love they both wanted. Tiffany lathered her body all over, imagining that Nick's tongue would soon replace her hands. She laughed aloud at the prospect; she was so giddy she'd sing if she could. But she didn't want to wake Nick that way. She wanted to awaken him the way he'd awakened her . . . last night . . .

After finishing her shower, Tiffany brushed her teeth and finger-combed her short hair back away from her face. She was grateful she didn't feel the need to wear much makeup. That way the face men saw in the morning wasn't that different from the one they'd seen the previous night. She lotioned her body and sprayed her hair with perfume. She didn't want to spray the alcohol-laden product on her skin, didn't want the acidy taste to get in the way of the other tastes Nick so obviously and so thoroughly enjoyed. She eyed herself in the mirror, pinching her nipples until they stood at attention. After going back and forth between walking in naked and wearing the impulse buy she'd gotten just before she and her ex broke up but had never worn, she decided on the latter. Once again, she had Joy to thank that it was even in her luggage. She slipped the sheer thigh-length white nightie over her head, pulled on the matching white thong, and walked out of her room and toward Nick's master suite—before she could change her mind.

Just outside his door, she paused and took a breath. Every fiber of her body was on high alert. There had been no need for her to pinch her nipples; just the thought of what was about to happen had them standing at full attention. Tiffany ran her fingers through her hair, took one last calming breath, and slowly, quietly opened Nick's bedroom door. She took two steps toward the four-poster mahogany bed and stopped. It was empty. Tiffany's smile was devious as she looked at the closed bathroom door. She hurried over to the bed and climbed up onto it. Nick's masculine scent immediately enveloped her, a musky scent mixed with sandalwood. Tiffany pulled up the covers and waited, almost giggling with excitement. She imagined the look that would be on Nick's face when he saw her—surprise, glee, desire? Tiffany rubbed her body against the nine-hundred-thread-count sheets and breathed in Nick's scent. *Come on and get this, Nick Rollins. I'm all yours.*

Two minutes passed, and then five. Tiffany hated to ruin the surprise of his seeing her ready and waiting in his bed, but after another minute, concern overrode her desire to stimulate through shock. She arose from the bed, tiptoed to the bathroom, and knocked softly. "Nick?" She waited a few seconds and knocked harder, spoke louder. "Nick?" After another few seconds, Tiffany tried the door. It was unlocked and the bathroom was unoccupied. Then she remembered. Nick had mentioned he was an early riser, one of those rare individuals that needed only three or four hours' sleep a night. *He's probably having breakfast,* she decided.

Tiffany laughed out loud as she anticipated Nick's return. Figuring she'd hear him when he entered the suite, she enjoyed a stretch and walked around the room. Her gaze was casual as she ran a hand along the mahogany chest of drawers and the matching armoire. *He has great taste,* she thought, remembering the casual yet elegant way he'd been dressed on the plane and the stylish, chic man whom she accompanied last night. Feeling a bit like a voyeur, she walked to the closet and slowly opened it. The hangers were neatly aligned to the left of the closet—but not one stitch of clothing hung from them. Tiffany frowned, confused, but as she continued to look around the room and then walked into a bathroom devoid of personal toiletries, realization dawned. Nick wasn't simply out having breakfast. He was gone.

9

A million thoughts raced through Tiffany's mind as she walked over to the sitting area in the master suite. *Where is he? Why did he leave? Is it because I didn't have sex with him? Was I just a temporary diversion in his high-class life?* Tiffany remembered the way he had orally loved her, and refused to believe the sensations she felt were simply physical. The connection was deeper, stronger, than an orgasm. Or was it?

Even though she'd already looked, Tiffany walked around the room again. Aside from the hotel's room service menu, stationery items, and information catalogs, the tables were empty. So was the closet. Used, fluffy white towels were strewn across the marble bathroom floor. Tiffany imagined they were still where Nick had dropped them once he'd toweled off that gorgeous, hard body. She traced a finger along the marble countertop, which still contained the hotel's designer soaps, lotions, shampoos, and other toiletries. An unused bathrobe hung from a holder on the bathroom door. *What happened? Why did he leave?* A familiar feeling of abandonment began creeping into Tiffany's mind, memories from another tall, strong man whom she'd loved from birth, only to have him leave her, time and again. Tiffany fled the room then, trying to flee the unwanted thoughts of a certain absentee male in the process.

She didn't get far, only to the dining room table. There, in the center, was a single piece of the hotel's stationery. In her excitement to be with Nick, Tiffany hadn't even noticed it as she'd passed through the room earlier, on the way to his master suite. Her spirit began to lighten and she almost laughed with relief. Of course Nick wouldn't abandon her. He was too classy, too much a gentleman; he'd been her knight in shining armor and the only friend she had in Italy. The note would tell her where he was, and how soon he'd return. She bounced over to the table and picked up the piece of paper:

Tiffany: Business emergency, flying back to LA. Keep suite as long as needed. Take care. Nick.

Tiffany read the note once, twice, and a third time, trying to find a deeper, more personal message between the words of the brief, impersonal one she held in her hand. There was no term of endearment, not even a "*dear* Tiffany" at the beginning. "Brown sugar," as he'd called her much of last evening, was nowhere on the paper. There was no mention of the magical hours they'd shared, no reference to the intimacy that had rocked Tiffany's world off its axis. No thank you for the dinner company or the extra dessert provided by her body in the early morning hours. No, just a clinical explanation of his whereabouts, a charitable gift of a temporary roof over her head, and departing verbiage she might use with a customer, a stranger, or the cashier in the express checkout line: take care. *Take care?* It was impersonal and dismissive, like cold water poured unexpectedly on a warm dream.

Tiffany slowly crumpled the paper as she walked over to the window and looked out on a picture-perfect day. The sun was shining outside, but the warmth inside had gone. Once again she felt like the frightened young woman who'd slouched on her luggage in the airport, robbed of money and of spirit. She felt rejected, abandoned, easily tossed aside for something more important: business. The feelings of discomfort around Nick that had flittered in between the love and laughter came back full force. How she'd felt when he'd taken control of the situation without conferring with her at all, his domineering and know-it-all attitude with the airport officials and officers (even though he needed to dominate the situation and did seem to know it all), and this, the way he'd been able to leave her so easily without so much as a hug and good-bye. In an instant, clarity dawned, why these acts had made her so uncomfortable, and why they felt so familiar. It was because these actions reminded her of another man and another time, someone Tiffany detested and hadn't seen in almost five years . . . her father.

10

Thinking about her father, Keith Bronson, spurred Tiffany to action. Just as his actions had hardened her emotions—when he chose business over time with his daughter—Tiffany allowed the anger with Nick to build, quickly burning up the memory of their passion-filled night. She'd retrieved Tuffy from the bedroom after reading Nick's thoughtless note, but now threw the bear on the sofa and went to get her computer. Moments later, headset in place, Tiffany used Skype to phone Joy.

"Tiffany!" Joy answered. "It's about time you called! What time is it there, anyway? I've been waiting, impatiently I might add, to hear from you. Tell me everything!"

"I feel like crap," Tiffany began, and then proceeded to tell Joy what had happened since they'd hugged goodbye at LAX Airport. From first seeing Nick on the plane, getting her purse stolen, meeting Chef Riatoli, and her near one-night stand with Nick. "It's a good thing we didn't do it," she finished. "Then I'd really feel like a ho."

"I don't see why," Joy countered. "You're in Rome, darling. You're supposed to have one-night stands, didn't you know? You're much too hard on yourself. We're talking sex here, not surgery. I told you to loosen your butt up. And you went Zane, sistah! Now, aren't you glad you packed that dress? Looks like it did what it was supposed to!"

"What? Get wined, dined, and dumped? Thanks a lot."

"You are most welcome," Joy responded. "Anything for a friend. Look, you're approaching this situation from an entirely skewed perspective. Here's how I see it. You've met a fabulous man who owns a variety of businesses. So what that he had to leave you in a penthouse suite for as long as you need, while he takes care of business? He did say you could stay as long as you need it, right? Why are you trying to block your blessing, girl? You can save the money you were going to spend on an apartment and live in luxury's lap in the process, for a whole month!"

"Please, Joy. I won't be beholden to any man, especially for this kind of money. As it is, this one night is probably breaking my budget. And I'm determined to pay him back. Look, I've got to go. I need to find out if my checks or new debit card have arrived and get moved to the place where I'll be staying, the one I can *afford*. I'll call you back once I get settled."

"You'd better. And remember what I said, Tiffany. Don't crawl back into that shell where you feel so safe and comfortable. While you're over there in Italy? Go Zane."

II

Nick's brow furrowed as he disconnected the call to Italy and placed his iPhone on the table. He'd fully expected Tiffany to still be at the hotel, and he wasn't ready to admit how uncomfortable it made him that she'd rebuffed his generous suite offer and moved on. But given the quickness with which he'd had to leave the hotel in order to catch the first flight out, he'd figured offering her the use of his personal suite was the least he could do. Fortunately for him, the fire at Le Sol had been contained before it could spread to the restaurant, spa, gift shop, lounge areas, or any of the upper floors. The lobby would have to be gutted and redone, but things could have been much worse. Thanks to an all-inclusive insurance policy, the damage would be loss of time more than anything else. And most important, the worker who'd threatened to sue because of the gas leak that started the fire in the first place, had agreed to settle the matter out of court. All of this business had been handled the first day of Nick's arrival back in Los Angeles. He'd gone home, showered, and slept. His first thought after waking was of Tiffany, his first action to contact her. But to no avail; management informed him that Tiffany had checked out of the hotel the night before.

Nick walked into his kitchen and put on water for tea, still thinking of Tiffany. He'd been upset when she'd abruptly ended their lovemaking, leaving him hard and frustrated. But in the hours that followed, the frustration had turned into a fantastical, determined desire to finish what they'd started, to run his hands over the entire length of her smooth, supple body, to massage her heavy breasts and once again worship at her feminine shrine. He continued to tell himself that now was not the time for another serious relationship. He hadn't yet forgotten the hurt that Angelica had caused, and he knew the current hotel project would take his entire focus. Still, he couldn't get Tiffany out of his mind, the chivalrous streak of protectiveness once again blossoming where she was concerned. Where was she staying in Rome? Who was helping her navigate that sometimes unpredictable city? Then, remembering that Tiffany was there to work with his friend Emilio, it occurred to Nick how he'd reestablish connection with the woman who'd stirred his heart as well as his penis. He walked purposely to the living room and picked up his phone. The first call was to the AnticaPesa restaurant, the second, to his secretary.

"Christina, I need something done right away," he said as a greeting when his assistant answered the phone.

Even though it was Saturday, her off-day, Christina knew better than to point this out or act in any way other than ready to do her boss's bidding. "Yes, Nick?"

"I need a large bouquet of flowers sent to Antica-Pesa as soon as possible. Address them to Tiffany Matthews. Include this note . . ."

12

During the month she stayed in Rome, Tiffany rarely found the time to "go Zane" or anything else. For ten to twelve hours a day, she'd been at the elbow of Chef Riatoli, preparing sauces, making pasta, and mastering the intricacies of superior seafood preparation. At night, she was too tired to do much of anything but sleep. Her roommate at the apartment, a woman from England in Rome to perfect her Italian, tried to get her out and about to embrace the city; but aside from a couple days aboard an "on and off" tour bus, seeing such popular tourist sites as the Colosseum, Forum, Pantheon, and the now infamous Trevi Fountain, and a wonderfully enlightening afternoon at the Vatican, Tiffany could have just as well been in Rome, New York, as in the Eternal City. By the time her one-month internship was over, Tiffany was reeling with all that she'd learned, but more than a little ready to go home.

Instead of protesting Chef Riatoli's slave-driver schedule, however, Tiffany was grateful. The constant attention she was forced to pay in Chef's kitchen had made her all but forget about what's-his-name: Mr. First Class, Mr. Stiff Tongue, Mr. Disappearing Act. Tiffany had gotten her share of suggestive looks and a couple of date offers but had politely turned down all suitors. She'd conveniently left out these facts when talking to Joy. Her friend had already given her a "don't make me come over there" warning more than once when Tiffany, exhausted but happy, would phone her with the latest.

"Look, your learning how to make pasta from scratch is well and good," Joy said during one of their many trans-Atlantic chats. "But don't you think you should be working with something else long and edible while over there with all those fine Italian men?"

Tiffany smiled at the memory as she waited for the plane that would take her from Rome to Paris and on to Los Angeles to begin the boarding process. Tuffy was by her side, as usual, but this time he was sticking out of a tote bag instead of plastered to her chest. Tiffany studied her hands as she waited, noticed the nicks and scrapes from close encounters of the sharp knife kind, and the scar that still remained from when her wrist had stayed a little too long over a boiling pot of water. These were all wounds of war, she reasoned. All part of the price paid toward her dream of owning her own Italian bistro—or something similar.

The day after Tiffany landed in LA, the job-hunting began. Determined to pay Nick back for the twenty-five-hundred-dollar-a-night suite, plus replenish the savings she'd depleted to intern with Chef Riatoli, Tiffany scoured the papers for a job that not only paid higher than usual for a sous chef, but also would allow her to use the skills she'd learned.

After e-mailing several résumés to prospective employers and having a few unsuccessful interviews, Tiffany asked Joy to join her at a restaurant she hoped would hire her. That evening, they met in a chic Italian eatery in Beverly Hills, with Tiffany acting the part of a regular customer.

Tiffany's face fell after taking a bite of her seafood appetizer.

"What is it?" Joy asked, enjoying what she felt was a delicious minestrone soup.

"I can't work here."

"Why not?"

"Because if they can't turn out a simple cioppino, then how can they have perfected the scallop?"

"Let me taste it." Joy took a swallow of water to cleanse her palate and then tasted the fish stew. "Hum, it tastes good to me."

"You're saying that because you've never had Chef Riatoli's version." Tiffany tasted another spoonful and shook her head. "The shrimp is hard, the clams are rubbery, everything is overcooked. I don't think the herbs they used were fresh, and I'd bet my first paycheck that these tomatoes came from a jar or can."

"All of my tomatoes come from a can, what's wrong with that? The people coming into this restaurant probably haven't even heard of Chef Ravioli, let alone eaten his food. This is LA, not Rome, Tiffany. You're not going to find the same level of cuisine here that you do in Italy."

"Of course I can. I just need to keep doing my research until I find the place that has that kind of standard, that's all. And it's Chef Riatoli, not Ravioli."

"Look, whether the fool's name is rigatoni or macaroni isn't the point. The point is that you need to stop hiding from Nick Rollins and apply to work at the restaurant in his hotel, as he suggested. You know he has what you're looking for when it comes to Italian cooking, and you know you want to work there. I don't know why you're being so stubborn."

Tiffany knew Joy was right but, true to her obstinate nature, refused to agree. "Nick Rollins isn't the only one in LA who knows pasta," she countered. "There are plenty of places I can work besides at his hotel."

"Oh really? Is that why you're sitting here fussing over some nasty shrimp? Tiffany, what would be so bad about you calling and asking about the job he offered?"

"If he were really serious about my working for him, he would have contacted me by now."

"He did contact you, in a way."

"When?"

"When he sent the bouquet of flowers to where you worked in Italy. Didn't you tell me the note included a reminder to call the hotel when you got back to town?"

Tiffany shrugged. "Girl, those flowers were an 'I'm sorry' bouquet. He probably didn't think of me past the minute it took him to stop by his secretary's desk and give her my name."

"You're scared, that's what it is."

"Oh, please. Scared of what?"

"Scared that the next time Nick gets a hold of you, he'll put his pole in the hole and turn a sistah the rest of the way out. To hear you tell it, he had you singing soprano like Whitney on a good day. You're not used to being handled by a man like that."

"I think the note was a high C, I'll admit that. And I'll also admit that if I go to work for him, it will be strictly cooking, not coochie contact. I'm not one to mix business with pleasure."

"You're not one to mix much of anything with pleasure because you don't do pleasure much . . . but I digress. Let's put the c-word aside for a minute and look at this strictly from a professional point of view."

They paused while the waiter came to take away Joy's clean bowl and Tiffany's half-eaten stew. Soon, steaming plates of eggplant parmesan and three-cheese lasagna were placed before them.

Joy dug into her food with gusto, savored the bite, and then continued. "What is your ultimate goal where food is concerned? To own your own restaurant, right?'

Tiffany nodded, her mouth full of food.

"Then what better place than an upscale hotel to make the kinds of contacts you need and gain the experience that will help you in your own business later on? I mean, besides the restaurant itself, hotels cater parties and host private dinners. At least that's how it happens in the novels I read. You'll probably have a variety of different menus available depending on the size of the crowds you're serving. You'll be able to continue to work in the upscale environment to which you've obviously become accustomed and, if you're lucky, you'll get your man back. How's your eggplant?"

"Better than the shrimp," Tiffany admitted. "But I can tell that once again not all the herbs are fresh and this eggplant probably isn't organic. But it's okay."

The two women ate in silence while Tiffany pondered Joy's words. Everything she'd said had merit. The truth of the matter was, Nick's hotel would be the perfect place for Tiffany to work, and a real boost to her skimpy professional résumé. But it wasn't just about the job, it was about the fact that no matter how she tried, she couldn't get that night of ecstasy with Nick out of her mind. He'd awakened a part of her that she didn't even know existed, a part that begged for a culmination to what had begun in a foreign country's penthouse suite. The truth was, Tiffany was extremely attracted to Nick and at the same time afraid of what being attracted to him might cost her. He was a driven businessman, like her father, and she knew that often personal relationships suffered with men like him. She guessed he was at least thirty-five years old. That he was so driven in business was probably why he wasn't already married. Tiffany had another thought. Maybe he was married. Maybe that's why he hadn't tried contacting her anymore while she was in Rome. He knew she was working with Chef Riatoli, knew how to reach her if he'd really wanted to. She said as much to Joy.

"He's probably married, anyway, or at the very least has some lady living with him. A man like that isn't sitting at home twiddling his thumbs every night."

"You don't know what *a man like that* is doing. The only way you're going to find out is to get in touch with him. It's one simple phone call about a job offer. He has the restaurant and you're looking for work. What do you have to lose, Tiffany?"

Tiffany didn't answer, but rather continued eating. She knew that with a man like Nick . . . she could lose a lot.

13

Two weeks and ten restaurants later, Tiffany walked into the lobby of Le Sol. Instead of e-mailing her résumé to Nick, she'd decided to call the number on the ad she'd seen in the Sunday edition of the *LA Times*. She'd talked with human resources, e-mailed her résumé, and gotten a call back from the chef's assistant. If she got the job as sous chef, it would be on her own merit, not because of anything Nick did for her. She already owed him twenty-five hundred dollars for the hotel suite. She didn't want to owe him anything else.

By the time Tiffany finished the interview with Chef Wang, she was praying she'd get the job. What he had in mind for the menu was exactly the type of quality and variety of cuisine Tiffany wanted to work with. She was sure that Nick had had a say in the menu selections, which boasted pasta and Italian breads made on the premises and a healthy selection of seafood dishes, including scallops used both as appetizers and for a couple of main-course dishes. She'd toured the state-of-the-art kitchen furnished with professional kitchen supplier Citisco classics: dual-flame stoves, double-deck ovens, prep tables, warming units, food wells, and every other industry-strength appliance imaginable. The pasta machine was exactly like the one she'd trained on in Rome. The kitchen was stunning, a cook's dream.

"Do you think you could handle the pressure of a fast-paced environment?" Chef asked. "The owners plan for this to be an award-winning establishment, the draw of the property, besides the views of the rooms facing the ocean. We'll probably be full most nights, and in addition, be responsible for catering private parties and meetings that take place here in the hotel. You're short on experience but long on enthusiasm. Plus, you've worked with Emilio Riatoli which, frankly, is the reason we're thinking to hire you."

Tiffany turned to the chef and looked him straight in the eye. "I want this job more than anything I've ever wanted, and I'll work my heart out for you. I'll work long hours, weekends, and holidays. I'll help with the catering. I'll do it all! This job would be everything I could ever dream of, and I can tell just by talking with you that just like with Chef Riatoli, I would be working with a master." Tiffany didn't quite believe this last statement but was hoping that in this case, flattery would get her everywhere.

"If we do decide to hire you, when could you start?"

"The same day you call me."

Chef Wang laughed. "Well, in that case, stay by the phone."

Tiffany was beaming as she left the offices by the kitchen. She was almost positive she'd be getting a phone call and was already dreaming about perfecting a scallop creation to hopefully become her signature dish. Chef Riatoli's scallop and asparagus masterpiece was definitely the inspiration for her love of this particular seafood, and in time, after she'd proven herself, she hoped to add a piece of her imagination to the menu at Taste, the name Chef Wang said one of the owners had chosen for the restaurant inside Le Sol. *Probably Nick,* Tiffany thought, which was one of the reasons she tried not to like it. But she couldn't help it. The name was perfect for this eating establishment—from the décor to the menu. Nick was the last person Tiffany wanted to think about, so she pulled out her BlackBerry and began typing in the ingredients she'd need from the store, to experiment with various scallop recipes. Chef Wang had gotten her excited. She was ready to cook!

Tiffany hurried down the hallway, quickly crossed the lobby, and was almost to the revolving doors when she heard it. The voice she'd know anywhere. Firm and commanding, much like its owner. Tiffany stopped in her tracks, her thoughts quickly vacillating between running away and running into his arms. But since this was the owner of the establishment where she longed to work, there was only one choice.

Tiffany turned around. It took everything she could do to place a casual smile on her face. Nick was looking finer than she remembered, dressed in fitted black dress pants paired with a stark white shirt. He wore no tie, and the first couple buttons of the shirt were undone. She knew what that chest felt like, but Tiffany reined in her thoughts before they could continue. It wasn't time to think about that night, about how it felt with his arms around her. That incident was in her past and Tiffany was focused solely on her future. She waited patiently for Nick to cross the room with his sure, languid swagger. Inside, she was a bundle of nerves.

A smile lit up Nick's face when he finally reached her side. "Hello, Tiffany," he said softly, his voice belying the formalness of his businesslike handshake. "Were you going to come into my establishment and not say hello?"

14

Tiffany hid her disappointment at this formal greeting, even as the moment brought clarity to their polar-opposite positions. Nick was part owner of a luxury hotel and probably other establishments. She, on the other hand, was an out-of-work ex-intern seeking a job as a cook. *What did I expect? His tongue down my throat in the middle of the afternoon, in the middle of his lobby?*

Nick had acted business-like and professional, just the way Tiffany had told Joy she wanted their interactions to be. Yet even as she thought this, an image, one of Nick's head between her legs, popped into her mind. She willed the picture away, straightened her shoulders and held out her hand, hiding desire and nervousness behind dark sunglasses. "Hello, Mr. Rollins."

Nick's brows rose slightly at the use of his last name. "I would think my, um, late night dessert at the penthouse in Rome put us on a first-name basis, don't you think?"

Nick's reference to the mental image she'd just

erased almost caused her to shudder, but Tiffany remained as still as stone. Now was not the time for daydreams, fairy tales and lost control. *You're an out-of-work cook with bills and a mortgage,* she reminded herself. *This man is your potential employer. Keep your eye on the prize!*

"We're no longer in Rome," she said after a pause. "And as I am very much hoping that you will soon be my employer, I should probably follow the protocol of the others who are working for you."

"I see." Nick's eyes narrowed as he tried to figure out whether Tiffany's obvious discomfort was due to nerves, true dislike, or hidden desire. Sooner or later, he determined, he would definitely find out.

"Excuse me, Mr. Rollins." The hotel manager stopped several feet from where Tiffany and Nick were standing.

"Yes?" Nick answered him, but kept his eyes on Tiffany.

"You have a phone call. It's Mr. Price."

Nick turned to the manager. "I'll be right there." He turned back to Tiffany, his voice strictly business even as his eyes darkened when quickly scanning her body from head to toe. "We'll be in *touch.*"

Tiffany had barely steered her Prius out of the hotel parking lot when her phone rang. She figured it was Joy, calling for a play-by-play. She clipped on her headset and clicked the Talk button without checking the ID.

"Yes, he's still as fine as he was in Rome," she said by way of greeting.

"I thought you went to Italy to work. Who's still as fine as he was in Rome?"

Damn! "Oh . . . Mom."

"Well, don't sound so enthusiastic," her mother answered sarcastically. "Obviously you were expecting someone else. Now back to my question. Who's still as fine as he was in Rome?"

Tiffany barely suppressed a groan. The last person she wanted to be discussing either her past lust liaison or her future employment with was her mother. Her mind raced for a deft way to put the proverbial cat—that was almost out of the bag—back inside. "Oh, just somebody I had dinner with, a casual acquaintance. How's business? Did you get the airport contract?"

Normally any question about Janice Matthews's technology firm could send her into a nonstop spiel about the center of her world . . . her business. Now, however, was not one of those times.

"My business is fine. Now back to yours. Who's this *casual acquaintance* you met in Rome? Your comment didn't sound all that casual to me."

Tiffany had never found it easy to lie to her mother. She figured she would tell as little of the truth as possible and hoped it would satisfy her mother's curiosity. "Okay, Mom, you got me. Actually, he's not a casual acquaintance, he's the man who might be my boss."

"Tiffany, now, I know I raised you better than that. Office liaisons are the easiest way to throw a career off track, get you booted out of the workplace, and have you landing flat on your rump, pun intended. But then again, if this is another one of those kitchen jobs, that might not be such a bad idea."

"Look, Mom, I don't want to argue about my career choice today."

"Neither do I. I just wish you'd change it."

"I can't talk right now, all right?"

"Wait, Tiffany. There's a reason why I called. Your father is going to be in town this weekend. He asked about you. I gave him your new number. It's time you two talked."

Tiffany was stunned into silence. She hadn't talked to her father in over a year, hadn't seen him in almost five.

"I hope you're not angry at me for giving him your number. But no matter the differences you two have had in the past, he's still your father, Tiffany. Tiffany, are you there?"

"Yes, Mom. I'm here. What's the business that's bringing him to town?" Tiffany asked the question because she knew he wasn't coming just to see her.

"Some new partnership he's checking out. I don't know the details. Would you like his number? Just in case, you know, he gets busy? You know how single-minded he can be when he's working on a deal."

"Yes, Mom, I know all too well. But if he's too busy to call his only child, especially when we're in the same city? Then he's too busy."

Janice sighed at the sarcasm she heard in Tiffany's voice, even as she understood it. She couldn't blame her daughter for feeling resentful, and she couldn't deny that her daughter was right. Her father had always put business first—before his child and his marriage. She'd probably shared too much of the bitterness she felt toward him with her daughter, but at the time, she'd been too angry and hurt to care. That the divorce was acrimonious was an understatement, and for years after it was over, Janice tried to wipe every trace of Keith Bronson from their lives. That's why when she'd taken back her maiden name, she'd changed Tiffany's last name also—from Bronson to Matthews. She'd justified it at the time, saying it would be easier for her, her daughter, and the grandmother who was helping to raise her to have the same last name. Later she regretted it, and when Tiffany was sixteen, Janice asked if she wanted to have her father's last name again. But by that time, Janice's bitterness had become Tiffany's. She said no.

"Well," Janice concluded, "let me give you his number, honey, just in case."

"No, Mom, if Dad and I talk, it will be because he calls me."

An hour later, Tiffany pulled up to a familiar curb in the older, yet well kept neighborhood of Los Angeles known as View Park. The row of medium-sized, stucco-covered houses stood behind freshly mowed lawns and newly trimmed bushes. A profusion of color burst forth from bird of paradise plants that lined the walkway leading up to the bright red front door. As Tiffany approached the porch, a giddy lightness replaced the wisps of heaviness that still coiled around her heart following the conversation with her mother. The mood had lifted somewhat as she walked the aisles of her favorite market, gathering up items for the dinner she planned to cook. But it was only now, as she rang the doorbell shaped like a flower, that a smile flittered across her face.

"Tiffany!"

"Hey, Grand!"

Tiffany stepped into the cozy foyer and hugged Gladys Matthews, her favorite person in the world. It was at the elbow of Gladys, her maternal grandmother, that she had not only developed a love for great food, but a love for preparing it as well. While both her parents had adamantly opposed her decision to become a chef, one of the few things on which they agreed before, during, or since their ten-year marriage, Gladys had encouraged her to follow her dreams. Whenever Tiffany was at her grandmother's house, the world righted itself and everything was possible. If anybody could help her make sense of what was going on in her life, it would be the woman Tiffany simply called "Grand."

"Come on in the kitchen," Grand said, noticing the bags Tiffany carried. "What have you got here?"

"Dinner," Tiffany replied. "I hope you're hungry."

"Child, a little bird must have tweeted in your ear. I was just thinking about how I sure didn't feel like cooking tonight. And here you are."

Tiffany felt the tension begin to leave her body as soon as she stepped into Grand's kitchen. The familiar smells of the onions, peppers, and garlic that were hanging in a vegetable basket by the window, as usual, blended perfectly with the warm color of the kitchen walls and the copper pots that hung from a rack near the ceiling. Tiffany had helped Grand pick out the mellow yellow wall color almost ten years ago, and had chosen the bold, bright fabric depicting every kind of vegetable imaginable from which Grand had sewn curtains for the side and back windows. A well-worn teapot held its usual spot on the back burner. Grand was always ready to make peppermint tea. It was her favorite, which might explain why it was Tiffany's favorite as well.

"Well, it sure is good to see you," Grand said as she bustled around the kitchen to prepare the ladies' favorite brew. "I can't wait to hear all about your trip to Rome, and especially about the fella who has you wanting to cook up a storm."

"Grand! Who said anything about a 'fella'? I'm here because I wanted to cook for you, and so you can help me perfect my would-be scallop masterpiece."

"That may be so," Grand said as she walked to the other side of the island, which contained a massive cutting board. She picked out an appropriate knife from the butcher block and joined Tiffany in dicing vegetables. "But you've got a slew of food to cut on this here table, enough to supply a small soup kitchen. You got that habit honestly. I used to do the same thing when your grandfather was trying to court me and got on my last nerve in the process. I'd retreat to the kitchen and get to slicing and dicing. Better those vegetables than his neck! Now, tell me about the man who's got you practicing your cutting skills."

"His name is Nick," Tiffany said with a sigh. "But it's not how you think, Grand. We're friends, that's all."

"Uh-huh," Grand said knowingly. "And Mona Lisa was a man."

15

To say she had experienced first-day jitters at Taste was an understatement. Less than two hours into her new job, Tiffany had broken a nail, cut her finger, and shattered a glass mixing bowl. She wished she could have blamed her clumsiness on Chef's harshly barked orders. But Chef Riatoli had been a taskmaster as well, and possibly because she'd worked as a line cook in a super-busy restaurant while earning her culinary degree—and not buckled under that insane pressure—she'd blossomed under his heavy hand. Unfortunately it hadn't been the man barking orders in the kitchen who had Tiffany all discombobulated; it was the man who occupied the largest of the executive offices on the second floor.

While she tried to convince herself otherwise, Tiffany knew it was because of Nick that she'd gotten the job. Why else would she have gotten a call the day after her interview, before the chef would have had time to check her references and review her school transcript? She even wondered if it was her imagination that the chef seemed a bit cold and aloof toward her. Often, chefs were temperamental at best, but the last thing one would want was to be told who to hire in his or her kitchen. Because Tiffany felt this might be the case was all the more reason she determined to be the best sous chef in LA.

Fortunately for her, the fast pace in the kitchen had made her first week on the job fly by. She'd been too busy to think, for which she was grateful. Because if she'd given herself time to do so, then she'd have to give in to the hurt and disappointment she'd experienced yet again when her father had come and gone without calling her. Then she'd have to think about how angry she was at herself for being hurt and disappointed. She knew better. Keith Bronson was simply being true to form.

Another blessing: in the two weeks that had gone by since she'd started at Taste, she'd only seen Nick once. Considering how her kitty meowed at the very thought of him, this single sighting was a good thing. Having seen his picture on the Internet, Joy thought Tiffany was crazy not to date him. But Tiffany knew that if she saw him after dark, tackled him in the parking lot, and demanded he sex her real good in the backseat of his car—which was what she wanted to do—he'd think she was crazy, too.

Now, there were only two weeks until September, and the hotel's grand opening. Besides learning the way Chef liked his vegetables cut, pasta formed, and sauces prepared, Tiffany also had to familiarize herself with a new kitchen and cooking devices and get back into the groove of working in a fast-paced environment. The hotel had been accepting reservations via e-mail for over a month, and some of

Nick's well-placed connections, along with an A-list Hollywood premiere Chef Wang had catered, had created a buzz about the restaurant even before its doors opened. It was the anticipation of this onslaught, combined with Chef Wang's Type-A, perfectionist personality, that kept everyone frenzied, frazzled, and moving at a furious pace.

By the end of her third week, however, Tiffany began to feel her rhythm in the kitchen, and to develop the timing and anticipation necessary for a sous chef to meet his or her chef's demands. She'd also begun to interpret Chef's grunts and eye movements. One long grunt meant you hadn't done it right, rapid eye movements meant "are you kidding, throw it away and start over," and a brief head nod meant "good job." Today, Friday, Tiffany had gotten three head nods and only one grunt. She felt she was getting the hang of this job.

Feeling more comfortable in the kitchen meant that she could relax. But that wasn't the only reason, especially today. On her way into the building, Tiffany had overheard two secretaries talking. One, whom she assumed was Nick's assistant, seemed happy that Nick was going out of town. She was looking forward to not having to run some unexpected errand or set up a telephone conference in the middle of her Saturday afternoon. The other commented on how she'd set anything up at any time for their tall, dark, and handsome boss. The rest of the conversation faded as the ladies entered the building. But Tiffany had heard what she needed to. Nick Rollins was nowhere around. She could breathe easy for the next couple days before enjoying her first day off, two days from now. She reached for a large bowl of organic tomatoes, several bunches of fresh organic herbs, onions, peppers, and cloves of garlic. She was getting ready to make the basic tomato sauce that Chef had entrusted to her earlier in the week. She'd held her breath as he tasted it. He'd swirled the sauce, let it rest on his palate, swallowed, and tasted it again. Then he'd given one of his nonverbal signs, her first head nod.

Forty-five minutes later, Tiffany slowly stirred the sauce, thickened by a continual, low-burning flame. She knew from the smell alone that it was perfection, a fact that made her proud. Especially since tomorrow was such an important day. They would be feeding a select group of reporters and journalists from across the country. Everything had to be spot on. Tiffany reached for one of the smaller wooden spoons and dipped it into the sauce. After waiting a second for it to cool, she slowly placed the spoonful of sauce into her mouth. She tasted the concoction with a chef's palate, making sure that each herb held its own space, that the peppers, onions, and garlic didn't get lost in the tomato, and that there was just the right amount of raw sugar added to break up the balsamic vinegar that provided the right amount of acid to the pot. Closing her eyes, Tiffany rested back against the table and slowly ate the rest of the sauce off the spoon. *Umm, this is delicious.* "You've done it again, Tiffany Matthews."

"*I'd* like to do it again," a low voice murmured. "Can I have a taste?"

Tiffany froze in mid-lick. An involuntary shudder went down her spine and lodged itself just above her buttocks. Why now, in a rare moment when she was the only one in the kitchen, did Nick have to come around? She put what she hoped was a casual look on her face as she opened her eyes and turned around. "Hi, Mr. Rollins. What can I do for you?"

As soon as the words were out, Tiffany recognized the double entendre. But it was too late. Nick was advancing on her like a cat would a mouse. She retreated as he advanced, and stumbled over her words. "I-I mean . . . Chef's not here."

"I'm not looking for Chef." Nick kept advancing.

"Oh," Tiffany panted as her butt came in contact with the counter. She couldn't go any farther, but crossed her arms in an unconscious gesture of self-protection.

Nick stopped directly in front of her. "It looks as if you've been hiding out in the kitchen. So I thought I'd come say hello."

"Me? Hiding? Why would I need to hide from you?" Tiffany asked. Her voice was full of sistah-girl attitude, even as she scooted around him and virtually ran to the other side of the room. "We're just busy here, as I'm sure you're aware."

"Oh, I'm very aware." Nick began covering the distance between himself and Tiffany in long, sure strides.

But before he could reach her, Tiffany made a beeline for the stove and began vigorously stirring the sauce. "I'm really busy," she said, her voice coming out much higher than she intended, almost like a squeak. "Chef Wang is going to want to taste this sauce when he gets back."

"And I want a taste right now," Nick said, once again covering the space between them. "Of the sauce, that is."

Tiffany reached into a drawer for a spoon and

stayed at arm's length as she gave it to Nick. Nick's smile was predatory as he placed the spoon in the sauce, pulled it out, blew on its contents, and then savored the flavors. His eyes never left hers.

"How is it?" Tiffany tried not to react to the sight of Nick's tongue wiping the remainder of the sauce from his lips. She imagined her tongue doing it instead, and immediately stepped back to put more space between them. "Is it good?"

"It's delicious," Nick replied.

"Well, I'd better get back to work. Chef and the others will be back any minute."

"In that case, there's no time to waste. I'd better hurry up and get what I really came after." Nick took a step and closed the rest of the distance that existed between them.

Tiffany closed her eyes and braced herself for the kiss. Truth be told, it was what she wanted. She had been running from her own desires just as much as she'd been running from Nick. But he was right here, right now. And she didn't want to run anymore. Nick licked his luscious lips before lowering them toward Tiffany's already parted ones. She closed her eyes, barely breathing . . . and heard the sound of footsteps entering the kitchen.

"There you are!" Chef Wang sang in his choppy Asian accent. Seconds later he and the other crew members rounded the corner. "You're just the man I'm looking for, Mr. Rollins. The menu is ready for a taste test, as you requested, sir. I know you're anxious to try the food. Would you like it scheduled for later this evening?"

"No, I'll be busy this evening," Nick said casually, even as he adopted a business persona. "Have Christina

check my schedule for sometime tomorrow afternoon.
I'll make sure Bastion, the hotel manager, and other
appropriate personnel are there as well." He nodded
at the group and walked away.

Tiffany didn't let out the breath she'd been holding until Nick left the room.

16

When her workday was over, Tiffany had only one thing on her mind—avoiding Nick. That's why after putting her things into her work locker, she rushed toward the employee entrance, keys in hand. With any luck, she thought, she'd be in her car and on her way within minutes.

Ha! The coast is clear. Tiffany made a beeline for her car, popped the lock with the button on her keychain, and slid inside. She started the car and reached for her handsfree at the same time. It was time for a convo with backup. Smiling, she pulled out her Black-Berry and headed toward the parking lot entrance. But before she could punch in Joy's number, her phone rang.

"Meet me at Stanfords, I'll be there in five minutes."

"Nick? How did you get my number?"

Tiffany looked at the phone and knew she'd have to get the answer to this question in person. Nick had hung up, and the single line he'd issued before doing so hadn't sounded like a request, but an order. Tiffany copped an attitude immediately. She hadn't liked taking orders from her father and she had no intention of doing so with Nick. *But he's your boss.* Tiffany took a deep breath, and headed toward a new destination.

A few minutes later, she stepped inside Stanfords, waiting momentarily until her eyes adjusted to the dim interior. She also took this time to try and cool her ire, reminding herself yet again that Nick was her employer. *I don't care. He might have licked the kitty, but he isn't going to push me around!*

Tiffany followed the hostess into the restaurant. Nick was waiting for her in a corner booth, busy texting away on his iPhone. Tiffany approached the table slowly, taking in the rich décor of the restaurant/ lounge she'd heard about but never frequented. It was reportedly where celebrities and professional athletes hung out, and while Joy had often begged her to come, Tiffany had always declined. She had no desire to be with a man who was more high maintenance than her.

"Mr. Rollins," she said, sliding into the booth opposite Nick.

"Ms. Matthews," Nick drawled. "Let's shed the formalities. Yes, at work I'm Mr. Rollins. But you are the exceptional employee who may call me Nick."

Dang, why does he have to look and sound so sexy? Tiffany cleared her throat. "I guess you looked at the employee records to get my number."

"I did. Do you have a problem with that?"

"That depends. Is this a professional or personal meeting?"

Nick's smile lit up the dimly lit room. "Definitely personal. Do you have a problem with *that*?" When

Tiffany didn't immediately answer, Nick continued. "I've wanted to get you alone for a long time . . ."

Tiffany raised her eyebrows.

". . . to apologize for the abrupt way I had to leave you in Rome. It was business, couldn't be helped, but I'm sorry."

Tiffany shrugged. His excuse sounded much like the ones she'd heard from her father for years, sans the apology. "I heard about the fire."

"So you understand."

Tiffany's smile was bittersweet. "I understand. You don't owe me anything, Mr. Rollins." When Nick's eyes narrowed, Tiffany corrected herself. "I mean, Nick. Business comes first, right?"

Nick rubbed his chin as he listened to Tiffany. Her voice sounded strong and firm, but he detected hurt in her eyes. Had he caused that? He remembered the teddy bear. "How's Tuffy?"

The unexpected question made Tiffany laugh out loud. "He's fine."

"So what's up with a beautiful woman like you traveling with a raggedy teddy bear?"

Tiffany's smile disappeared. "What's it to you?" She hadn't intended the question to come out so rudely, but this man didn't know her well enough to talk about her friend like that! Since she was talking to the man who signed her paycheck, however, Tiffany tried to regroup. "We have a history," she said, glancing at Nick's handsome face to gauge his reaction. "It is a gift that has sentimental value."

"From one of your parents, I presume?"

"My dad."

Nick nodded, noticing the tightening around Tiffany's mouth. He also noticed how the pink lip gloss sparkled against lips he'd love to kiss again. "Are you close to your father?"

"Not really, but, Nick, I don't see how this is any of your concern. I don't mean to be rude, and I appreciate that you felt the need to apologize for how you left me in Rome, but now that you've done that, I probably should go."

"So it's you who's going to run away this time, huh?"

"Why would I have to run away from you?"

Nick grabbed Tiffany's hand and gently rubbed his thumb over the inside of her palm as he answered. "Because you're trying to deny this almost overwhelming attraction you're feeling for me, trying to hide the fact that even at this moment you're getting wet for me." His eyes darkened as he continued to stare at her lips, wetting his own.

"Don't flatter yourself," Tiffany retorted, even as she tried to ignore her throbbing nub and, yes, now damp thong. She gently but firmly removed her hand from Nick's, then grabbed her purse. "I'm leaving."

Tiffany was fast but Nick was faster. He grabbed her arm before she could run. "I want to go out with you."

"Why? You have your pick of any woman at the hotel."

"And I'm sure all of those women are special in their own way. But I want you." Nick released the grip he had on her arm, but did not remove his hand. Instead he stroked the inside of her forearm with his finger. "You're an incredible woman, Tiffany, and I'm attracted to you. I think we started something beautiful in Italy, and I'd like to see if what we felt there was real or just my imagination."

She couldn't think while he touched her. Tiffany

crossed her arms, staring into eyes she could drown in, and a man with whom she could easily fall in love. "I don't know, Nick. Mixing business with pleasure can be a risky proposition. And then there's your work. It will always come first. I understand that," she hurried on before he could interrupt. "But I'm not sure if I want to be with someone who's . . . you know . . ."

"Wealthy, successful? A man with varied national and international businesses, including a five-star hotel?"

"Don't sound so cocky."

"Don't sound so scared." Nick softened his tone. "I'm only speaking truth, love. What about me frightens you so?"

That you're just like my father! "I'm not frightened, I'm focused. I just started a new job and am determined to be a success there. I can learn a lot from Chef Wang. He's as skilled as Chef Riatoli, even more innovative in some areas. Besides, you don't really have time for a relationship."

"Maybe not." Nick looked at his watch. "But I do have time for dinner. Will you join me?"

Tiffany hesitated for a moment before relaxing her back against the booth's rich leather. "I guess so."

Nick's smile reached his eyes as he reached for Tiffany's hand, pulled it to his lips, and kissed it. He flagged down the waiter and ordered two glasses of Chardonnay. As they sipped the wine, he and Tiffany settled into an amicable conversation, learning more about each other. Tiffany learned that Nick was born Dominique LaSalle Rollins in Paris, France, where his Army father had been stationed. His family moved a lot before settling in Pasadena, California, where "Dominique" became "Nick," thanks to his high school b-ball playing buddies. He went back east for college and then, armed with a degree in business, set out to fulfill his dream of becoming a wealthy man. He bought his first property at twenty-one, Tiffany learned, an apartment building of ten units that he still owned. Along with various rental properties, both residential and commercial, Nick was a partner in various enterprises ranging from technology to agriculture. Hotel Le Sol was his latest venture, his first hotel, and the one of which he was most proud.

Tiffany found out a great deal about Mr. Rollins, but when the tables were turned, Nick learned that Tiffany didn't talk much about her private life.

"There's not much to tell," she answered, when asked to tell a little about herself.

"Uh-uh. I've sat here and told you everything that's happened to me since the age of five, and you're going to give me that? I don't think so." Nick eyed Tiffany thoughtfully as the waiter removed their dinner plates and set dessert menus in front of both of them. "I have a feeling there's a whole lot you can tell me about you, Tiffany Matthews. Now, I know you learned to cook from your grandmother. But what about your parents? Are they still alive? What do they do?"

"They're both in business, too," Tiffany responded, immersed in the menu. "Like you, it occupies a great deal of their time. Growing up, I hardly saw them. My mother was always at the office and my father was always away on business. They divorced when I was little. I guess you can say my grandmother raised me, mostly."

"But what about now that you're grown? Have you gotten closer to your mom and dad?"

"What is this, the *Dr. Phil* show?"

"No." Nick grinned. "It's the Nick-trying-to-learn-something-about-the-woman-in-front-of-him show. But if you're uncomfortable sharing who you are with me . . ."

"I shouldn't be, but your questions are making me realize that I don't talk much about my family. There is some pain in my past connected to my parents, especially my dad."

Nick sipped his wine slowly, drinking in the sight of this beautifully vulnerable woman sitting across from him. "Is that why you're scared of a relationship with me, scared I'll turn out to be just like your father?"

Tiffany was startled at the accuracy of his question, but chose to be honest nonetheless. "Yes."

"Will you give me a chance, at least?"

"I might give you a second date."

"Oh, is that what this was, a date?"

"No, this was dinner. Our first date was in Italy, or don't you remember?"

Nick allowed his eyes to travel slowly from Tiffany's eyes, down her face to her breasts and back up. "How can I forget?"

The waiter interrupted. "Would you two care for dessert?"

"No!"

"Yes!"

Nick and Tiffany spoke at once.

"Thanks, Nick, but I'm full, really, and I need to get home. We're preparing the personnel tasting for lunch and serving the journalists at dinner. It will be a long day."

"Just bring the check," Nick said to the waiter. "I'll get my dessert later," he said to Tiffany.

Nick walked Tiffany to her car and despite her mild protest, seared her with a kiss before opening her car door. "Keep Saturday night open," he said, as if she had no choice in the matter. "I'll call you."

"What if I already have a date?" Tiffany asked. She didn't like the way Nick assumed she'd be free.

Nick was already walking away from her car. "Cancel it," he said without looking back.

Demanding, just like Dad. "This will never work." Tiffany sighed as she started her car, but she couldn't help the smile that broke across her face as she watched Nick's lean, sure strides over to his Maserati. He must have known she was looking because before he got into his car, he turned around and waved. Tiffany waved back, turned on her engine, and steered in the other direction, out of the parking lot. Nick got into his car and sped off down the street, back to the hotel.

Somebody else turned on their car and headed down the street. Somebody who'd been sitting in the booth behind Tiffany and Nick, and had heard everything they said. Somebody who hadn't liked Tiffany from the beginning, and who hadn't been able to put her finger on the reason until now— because Tiffany was a threat to her own plans of climbing the corporate ladder.

The woman-turned-detective reached for her cell phone. "Angelica, this is Nick's assistant, Christina. I've got some news."

17

Angelica leaned back on the chaise lounge and twirled an errant sister-lock as she listened to the beans Christina spilled into her ear. As Christina rambled, Angelica remembered how Nick used to love burying his hands into her waist-length tresses, how he'd play with them while she orally played with him.

While rising from the chaise and walking to her kitchen, Angelica thought of how war made strange bedfellows. Angelica knew why Christina was calling. Her motive was about as invisible as Oprah shopping at Walmart. Angelica had always known about Christina's ambitions to use her position with Nick to snag someone of his stature, or to grab Nick's coattails and move up to manager or higher in one of his businesses. But what Christina didn't know was that Angelica didn't like having someone like Christina so close to her man. Christina was very attractive, with thick, brunette hair, sparkling blue eyes, and a nice, lean figure. Angelica figured it was just a matter of time before Christina's desire to have a man of Nick's stature turned into a desire to have Nick.

"So Nick has found another diversion," Angelica said with mock disinterest. No way would she let anyone, least of all Christina, know how she really felt. *Instead of you using me, little sister, I'm the one playing your naïve ass.* She poured a glass of cranberry juice and continued to listen.

"Yes. He sent her flowers after they met and suggested she apply for a job. But you know that employment isn't the only thing a woman like her wants from Nick."

"Yes, don't I know it." *This fool's too dumb to realize I'm talking about her!*

"Anyway, she's playing hard to get, but you know that's just a ploy. Oh, and she was acting all weak and helpless, telling Nick about issues she has with her father. Give me a break . . ."

Christina rambled on for another moment before Angelica had heard enough. "I appreciate your calling me, Christina," she lied. "But I'm really not interested in what goes on in Nick's life. We're no longer together and I've moved on. Perhaps your skills would be put to better use handling Nick's administrative tasks, rather than trying to handle his personal business."

"Oh, well, as a friend, I just thought you should know."

"I appreciate it, Christina." *Not.* "Good-bye."

Angelica ended the call, telling herself it really didn't matter who Nick was with. She was over him, wasn't she? He'd given her an ultimatum—either agree to have children, or end their engagement. She'd tried every argument she could think of to convince him that they would be much happier without kids; that there would be nothing to stop their jet-set lifestyle.

"But this is one of my dreams," he'd pleaded. "To have children, you and me. Don't you want to be a mother, baby? I thought every woman wanted children."

"Well, you thought wrong. I was born without the mommy gene."

They'd gone back and forth for over a year, the length of their engagement. This sticking point was why no wedding date was ever set. Then last year, during the holidays, Nick had applied the pressure by telling her that he wanted them to be married the following year, but only if it were clear that they'd be starting a family soon after. He'd argued that at almost forty, it was time for him to start a family before he got too old to run and play with his children. The discussion almost ruined their skiing vacation near Zurich, Switzerland, and had dimmed the brightness of the three-carat teardrop necklace he'd given her. Then finally, on the next to the last day of their vacation, she'd finally told him the truth. That not only did she not want to have children, but that she couldn't have them. A tubal ligation almost ten years before made that desire an impossible one. Not only had the doctor tied the tubes, he'd burned them. At the time, her body was reacting negatively to birth control pills and she found the diaphragm too painful. Knowing she didn't want kids, she'd been tied and sizzled. "But," she assured Nick with tears in her eyes, "nobody will ever love you like I do, baby. No one."

After that telling conversation, the relationship

was never the same. Belatedly, Angelica realized the extent of Nick's desire and the damage of her confession. More than once she wished she'd waited until after they were married to tell him the truth— that she'd told him whatever he wanted to hear long enough to become Mrs. Rollins. But it was too late for what should have happened. Nick was gone and someone else was in his place, someone with a smaller dick but a bigger bank account, someone who wouldn't pressure her to have kids or about anything else, for that matter. Someone who just wanted to have fun, give her money, and have sex. Angelica wasn't missing Nick for a minute. The new man in her life had made her all but forget about him.

As if summoned by her thoughts, Angelica smiled when she looked at the caller ID. "Bastion, my darling," she purred into the phone. "I was just thinking about you."

"Oh, well, that's nice."

Angelica's intuitive antennae immediately went on high alert. "Bastion, baby, what's wrong?"

Bastion cleared his throat. "It's, uh, it's not good news, I'm afraid, at least not for me."

"What's happened?" Angelica left the kitchen where she'd been sitting, and began pacing the dark mahogany living room floor in her deluxe two-bedroom Manhattan Beach condo, the one Bastion began paying for after Nick stopped.

"I hate to have to break this kind of news over the phone, Angelica . . ."

Uh-oh. This does not sound good.

"But . . . I can't see you anymore." Bastion said the words quickly, and all together, trying to get them out before he lost the will to do so. He was very fond of Angelica.

Angelica smiled. *Is that all?* Bastion wasn't the first married man she'd dated, nor the first to get a little skittish when the wife started asking questions or acting suspicious. She'd swam in these waters before, knew just how to navigate them.

"What, has the missus gotten suspicious? Or are you being paranoid? Either way, let's not be too hasty, darling, you know we're made for each other. If you want to cool it down for a few days or a week or two, I understand. But," Angelica dropped her voice to a sultry whisper, "me and my pussylicious will think about you every day."

Bastion stifled a groan. Sex with Angelica would be the hardest thing for him to give up. But he would give it up. Bastion wasn't the most moral man in the world, but he did have a conscience. His wife needed him now. And he'd be there for her, without distractions. "Jill has cancer," he blurted.

"Oh, I'm sorry," Angelica quickly replied, already wondering if the disease was terminal, how long it would take for Jill to die, and how soon afterward she and Bastion could marry. "You must be devastated." Angelica's voice held just the right mix of compassion and concern.

"I can't see you anymore," Bastion said, needing to end the call and the emotional attachment he felt toward this woman. "I'll put some money in your bank account. But this will be the last time I phone you, and please . . . don't call me again."

Angelica placed the phone down on the cradle and idly picked up a copy of *Black Enterprise* magazine. Bastion's wife's illness definitely added a wrinkle to her smooth plans. Since a ticking biological clock wasn't the issue, Angelica was totally prepared to wait two, three years for Bastion to wise up to the fact that he needed to leave his wife and marry her. That Bastion was Nick's business partner would make becoming Mrs. Price even sweeter—a constant reminder to Nick of what he could have had. But Bastion's wife getting ill was a glitch Angelica hadn't considered. How long could she afford to wait and see what happened?

Angelica looked at the magazine table of contents and turned to the reason she'd bought the magazine. "Influential Black Americans" was the article title. Before she could start reading the list, a familiar face caught her eye. It was Nick, looking fabulous in a tailored, charcoal gray suit with matching shirt and tie. "Feeding his bank account along with his clientele," the article stated. "A rising Black star in the worlds of hotel acquisitions and five-star cuisine."

After tearing out the page, Angelica placed the magazine on the table and headed to her bedroom. She opened the doors to her large, walk-in closet, stepped inside, and idly fingered her massive wardrobe. Deciding there was nothing in there Nick hadn't seen, she quickly stepped out of her lounger and into a pair of Anne Klein slacks and a classic Chanel blouse. It was time to go shopping. Because come Monday, she'd be paying a surprise visit to one Mr. Dominique Rollins at Hotel Le Sol, congratulating him on his making the list, and reminding him of what she could do from under his desk. She'd moved fast to forget Nick; now she planned to give him a lunch date he was sure to remember. Angelica was nothing if not adept at changing her plans quickly. Her smile was predatory as she grabbed her Prada purse and headed for the Mercedes in the underground parking lot, the car that Nick had gifted her with two years prior. *Oh yeah, baby, I'm getting ready to dress to impress.* Christina's call was timelier than Angelica had realized.

18

Nick had wasted no time on Saturday. He'd called Tiffany before eight A.M.

"Do you know what time it is?" she'd asked in a voice husky with sleep.

"Yeah, but . . . do you?" Nick had answered, his voice husky with lust. "What's your address? I'm picking you up tonight—seven o'clock."

It had been too early to argue; Tiffany had given him her address, hung up the phone, and gone back to sleep.

Now she stood in the middle of her bedroom with her fashion judge, Joy, lounging across her bed.

"So, how does it look?"

"The same way it looked when you tried it on last night. I wouldn't have let you buy the dress if it didn't look good on you."

"I don't know," Tiffany continued, turning this way and that in the mirror. "It's kind of tight. I don't want to give Nick the wrong impression."

"And what wrong impression would that be?"

"That I'm trying to come on to him!"

"Girl, please, the man is trying to come on to you. And from what you told me about y'all's little tryst in Italy, it's a little too late for you to act the prude."

"Whatever, Joy."

"Whatever, Tiffany," Joy mimicked. "I don't see why you're trying to turn down what's being offered to you on a silver platter: a fine, rich, Black man who's interested in you. If someone who looked like him came after me, I'd bring him home and eat his ass like steak on a plate!"

"Uh, wouldn't Randall have something to say about that?"

"Oh now, why did you have to go and bring up the husband?"

"Maybe because y'all have been together forever and have two kids?"

"Who's paying attention to pesky details like those?"

"Besides, I'm sure that Nick isn't short on women coming after him with . . . healthy appetites."

"All the more reason you need to work it while a brothah wants a taste of you. Men have short attention spans. If you don't give him what he wants, somebody else will. Remember Bernadine."

"Who's that?"

"The character in Terry's book *Waiting to Exhale*. Her husband ended up falling for the white woman at work who paid him the kind of attention he wanted. Angela played her part in the movie."

"Well, if somebody who looks like Angela can't keep her man . . ."

"That's not my point."

"Well, I wish you'd get to what it is."

"My point, Tiffany, is that you have also attracted somebody in the work environment who just happens to own said environment and wants you to put in a little overtime. Maybe his after-hours suggestion would take care of the reason you've been so bitchy lately. Don't think I haven't noticed."

"I'm bitchy because a certain friend keeps trying to run my business."

"Hmph. You're bitchy 'cause you keep running from Nicky's dicky."

"Ha! You're a mess, Joy."

"That's why you love me."

Tiffany plopped on the bed next to her BFF. "You're right. I am running. But that's because I don't want to get hurt, and that's exactly what will happen if I open my heart to Nick Rollins. Right now, I'm a goal, a little challenge for his ego. But what happens after dating a month or two? He'll move on to someone who's a better fit for his world. I'm sure there are plenty of women traveling in his circle who are wealthy, more beautiful . . ."

"Oh, stop being such a Libra and overanalyzing."

"Stop being such a Leo and bossing me around."

Joy ignored her and kept being bossy. "No, don't put on those sandals. Wear the Donna Karans. And did you spray on perfume, 'cause I don't smell any."

"Oh, shoot, I forgot." Tiffany walked over to her dresser. "Which one should I wear, Magnifique or Fabulosity?"

"Use the Baby Phat, because it has vanilla in it. Vanilla is supposed to be a natural aphrodisiac."

Tiffany rolled her eyes.

"Look, I'm just saying. Spray some on your titties and your coochie, too. But not where he's going to lick later on, only at the top."

"Joy!"

Joy laughed as she rolled off the bed. "Girl, your man will be here soon, I'm outta here."

"Are you and Randall going to take advantage of the kids being with their grandparents?"

"Maybe later. But right now he's hanging with some of his frat brothers and I've got a date with Mary B."

"I'm guessing she's an author and you have a date with a book?"

Joy nodded. "A sistah's learning how to be a man eater."

"Hmph, with two kids, I'd think you already know."

"It's about more than dickage, but come to think of it, you could probably use the book more than me. I'll finish it quick and bring it over."

"Yeah, *whatever*, Joy."

"Bye, chick."

Two hours later, Nick and Tiffany strolled down the Santa Monica Promenade. They'd enjoyed a seafood dinner and were headed to one of Nick's favorite jazz spots for a nightcap.

Nick slid an arm around Tiffany's waist and pulled her toward him. "Did I tell you that you look beautiful tonight?"

Tiffany smiled. "Once or twice."

"Um, and you smell good, too."

"Thank you." *Thanks, Joy.*

"Look, instead of checking out the band, why don't we go to my place? I've got a fully stocked bar, a nice jazz collection, and a magnificent view."

"Sounds like a place perfect for seduction."

"As fine as you're looking? I sure hope so."

"Look, Nick, I'm flattered that you're attracted to me and yes, the feeling is mutual. But . . ."

"But what?"

"I don't know how comfortable I feel with being intimate with you again. Things are different now. You're my boss. My career is important to me. I love where I work and I wouldn't want to jeopardize what could be a long-term career opportunity for something that might not last."

"You don't put much faith in yourself, huh?"

"I don't put much faith in you."

"Whoa!" Nick said, grabbing his heart. "You crush me!"

"It's not personal. I just don't trust men."

Because of your father? Nick thought the question, but wisely did not ask it.

"Baby, look, the only things guaranteed in life are death and taxes. Love is one of the most elusive, fickle emotions there is. I could tell you something that sounds good, but I don't want to give you any false promises. I only wish that you'd let us take this one step at a time, and see where those steps take us."

They reached the doors of the jazz lounge. Nick reached for his wallet but Tiffany stayed his hand. "What kind of jazz do you have at your house?"

Nick smiled and took her hand. Tiffany's palm tingled. By the time they'd pulled up to Nick's home in Malibu, something else was tingling—the spot at the apex of Tiffany's thighs. Nick twirled Tiffany around his massive living room to the sounds of Wayman Tisdale. The groove was seductive; the song, familiar.

"Who sang this first?" Tiffany asked, trying to get her mind off what Nick's deft hand movements were doing to her body. As achingly innocent as they were, stroking her shoulders, her lower back and neck, they had her strumming like Wayman's guitar.

"Barry White," Nick said, singing the lyrics to the song over Wayman's smooth guitar licks. He touched his lips to Tiffany's temple.

"You sing good!" Tiffany screeched, a little too loudly. She stopped dancing and stepped away from Nick in one movement. "I'm thirsty. Maybe I'll take that glass of wine now."

"There's no running away this time, woman. I've got something for you that's more intoxicating than wine."

Tiffany had backed up to the wall, and Nick must have figured that was as good a place as any. He rested his large palms on each side of Tiffany's head, lowered his mouth to hers, and nibbled her lips. "Hmm, my brown sugar . . ." He softly kissed the mole that sat just above the right side of her mouth before placing a hand on her chin and lifting it for better access. He licked her lips, gently prodding them apart with his tongue. He tweaked her nipple. Tiffany gasped and Nick plunged in, sucking her tongue into his mouth, pressing his hard, lean body against hers.

"Give me this," he ordered, even as he placed his hands under her buttocks and lifted her high on the wall. He held her there with his body while his fingers found their target. He pushed aside the wispy material of her thong and rubbed her already wet treasure. Still kissing her deeply, he expertly separated her nether lips and slid a finger inside her. Tiffany groaned her pleasure, wrapped her legs around Nick's hips and her arms around his neck. The move spurred Nick on. He withdrew his finger, placed his hands underneath Tiffany's butt once again, and walked them straight to the bedroom. Tiffany barely had time to take in the decidedly masculine black oak cabinets and platform bed. Nick wasted no time in placing her on the raw silk comforter, and following her down. He roughly pushed up her dress, his breathing slow and even. His gaze was so hot Tiffany felt he could see inside her very soul. His pupils darkened as he spread her legs and again began his fingered assault.

"Does this feel good to you?"

Tiffany nodded.

Nick withdrew his middle finger and plunged back in with two. "I can't hear you."

"It feels good," Tiffany stuttered. She could barely think, let alone speak. Nick had found her G-spot and was applying just the right amount of pressure to drive her insane. She tried to move away but Nick held her firm. Her climax was intense, just as she'd experienced in Italy.

Before she could catch her breath, Nick scooted her up to the head of the bed. He quickly took off her dress, drank in her smooth, chocolate body in the cream-colored Victoria's Secret bra and panty set. "I'm getting ready to eat you like a meal, baby," Nick whispered before ravishing her hardened nipples with his strong tongue. Once again, his fingers worked magic below as he nibbled her neck and licked her shoulders. When he reclaimed her mouth, he made love to it with his tongue, mimicking the sex act. His fingers followed suit, and soon Tiffany was spiraling over the edge again. This time, Nick withdrew his fingers, rolled over to his nightstand, and quickly donned protection. Without another word, he raised himself above Tiffany, and with one long thrust, plunged deep inside her.

"This is where I've wanted to be," Nick whispered. "This is what I want. You are what I want, Tiffany," he continued, branding her body with each push. "Give it all to me, baby, I want it all."

Both of their bodies became sweaty as Tiffany tried her best to give Nick what he asked for. She felt herself drowning in the ecstasy of having him inside her. He felt so good. *Maybe Joy's right. Maybe this can work.* Tiffany spread her legs wider, tried to take in more of him. She ran her hands across his taut butt, cupping his cheeks. He answered her unspoken request by pushing in deeper, filling her fully, even as he claimed her lips in a hot, wet kiss. The flutters of another orgasm began at her core. She whimpered, then cried out as her body shook with the force of her climax. Nick's rhythm increased, his thrusts deepened, and soon he moaned his own release.

That was perfect, Tiffany thought, as Nick's penis continued to pulsate inside her walls. She rubbed Nick's back and tenderly kissed his cheek. It was time to toss aside her rule of not mixing business with pleasure so that she could give her heart to this man who made her soul sing. "Nick," she began, but before she could continue—the phone rang.

"Hold that thought, baby," Nick said, as he rolled off her and looked at the ID. "I need to take this." He sat up and pulled the sheet over the lower part of his body. "Bastion. No it's okay. I knew it had to be important. Never mind that, just fill me in with what you know so far." Nick got out of bed, reached for his pajama bottoms and continued talking as he walked around the corner to the sitting area of the master suite.

Tiffany got up and stepped into her dress—not even bothering to shower. She refused to think about what had just happened, refused to break down. Knowing it would cost a fortune, Tiffany called a taxi as soon as she stepped outside Nick's house. Fifteen minutes later, she was on her way home. Five minutes after that, her phone rang. *Oh, now you remember that you had a guest.* Nick's call went to voicemail.

By the time she reached her condo, the wall around Tiffany's heart had been rebuilt. "Kiss my ass, Nick Rollins!" she hissed, as she unlocked her front door. *Hmph, his doing just that is how my problems started.* There was no humor in life's irony.

As she climbed the stairs, her mind threatened to return to the scene of the crime, and the moments before her and Nick's intimacy was so rudely interrupted. But Tiffany refused to go there. *That's it, I'm done.* She stripped and stepped into a steaming hot shower. The next time Nick saw her, she vowed, Tiffany would play by *his* rule book. "Business first." She quickly dried off, climbed into bed and hugged Tuffy close to her heart. Then, and only then, did she let the tears fall.

19

"Is he in?" Angelica's question was perfunctory, asked only as a courtesy to Nick's assistant. Angelica knew she was special to Nick, but she also knew protocol. She didn't want to barge in and interrupt something important.

"Angelica!" Christina said, genuinely surprised. "You look nice."

"I know." And she did. Angelica knew that the fire-red Ralph Lauren suit fit her 5'7", size-six body to a tee, that the short-cropped jacket emphasized her generous breasts and narrow waistline. She'd had the skirt tailored so that it fit her butt snugly and stopped a couple inches above the knee. She wore the teardrop diamond that Nick had bought her, along with his favorite perfume. She didn't wear underwear; didn't need them, for the visit she had in mind. "Is he with someone?"

"No, but it's Monday and you know how crazy it is after the weekend. He said not to disturb . . ."

Angelica was already halfway to Nick's closed door. She gave a brief knock, opened the door, and went inside. "Hey, handsome," she said, casually tossing her freshly twisted locks over her shoulder. "You are a sight for sore eyes." She slithered over to Nick's desk, sat in his lap, and tried to stick her tongue down his throat.

Nick was too stunned to move, but not for long. He reached behind his neck and unlocked her arms before pulling his face away from hers. Her blatant actions had instantly aroused him, but her presumptuousness had angered him as well. "What are you doing here, Angelica?"

"Isn't that obvious?" She attempted to kiss him again.

"What is this about, Angelica? This isn't us anymore, remember? You don't want what I want, so I don't know why you're here."

Angelica reached down and started rubbing Nick's penis through his slacks. "Can't a former lover remain a good friend? I'd think what we shared deserves that, at least."

"Fine, we can be friends. Platonic friends." Nick moved Angelica's hand off his dick and placed it in her own lap. "Get up, Angelica."

Angelica took Nick's hand and placed it under her skirt, onto her bare skin. "You sure you want me to?"

Nick took a deep, patience-inducing breath. "Positive."

"Fine," Angelica said. She got up abruptly and straightened her skirt. Deciding on another tactic, she walked toward Nick's office windows, which faced the ocean. "I always loved this view." When Nick remained quiet, Angelica turned around. "So how have you been, Nick? Besides busy."

"Fine. And you?" Nick felt pretty sure that Angelica

didn't know that he knew about her and Bastion. He decided to keep her ignorant of this fact, for now.

"Good . . . besides missing you."

"Spare me that line. A woman like you doesn't stay lonely for long."

"You always were smart. But there's only one Dominique Rollins, you know that."

"Is that what you came to tell me? That you've finally realized what I tried to get you to see for four years?"

"I came for a few things. To congratulate you, for starters. I saw your name in *Black Enterprise*. One of the most up-and-coming Black men in America."

"That list is overrated."

"Spoken like someone who's on it. But really, congratulations, Nick. I know how hard you work. And congratulations on this hotel. You and your partners did a bang-up job."

"Thank you, Angelica. So . . . now that you've congratulated me . . ."

". . . you can take me to lunch. I'm starved, and I hear there's a five-star restaurant not far from your office. I love the name, Taste, very clever. Your idea, I'm sure."

"Yes, I named the restaurant, which doesn't open for another week."

"But that doesn't matter when you're the owner, now does it? I'm sure your kitchen is up and operating. I heard about the taste testing for the staff and journalists last week."

"From whom?"

"Bastion," Angelica said, recovering quickly from her faux pas. "I ran into him and his wife at Stanfords."

Nick knew firsthand that Bastion and Jill hadn't

eaten out in weeks. Not since Jill's diagnosis. But there was no need to tell Angelica this. "Oh, really," he said instead.

"Yes, and he told me how impressed he was with the new chef, Wang, I believe he said his name was."

"You and Bastion had quite the conversation. What did you do? Join him and Jill for dinner?"

"Ha! Hardly. I simply commented on the dish he was having and he told me that it was nothing compared to a similar one made by Chef Wang." This conversation had actually happened, but it was Bastion and Angelica having dinner at Stanfords, in one of the private dining rooms, the ones that came with their own entrance. Jill had been nowhere around.

"I see." Nick hesitated in whether or not to take Angelica down to the restaurant. He didn't want Tiffany to see them together and get the wrong idea. Nick knew Tiffany hadn't returned his calls because she was angry, and he didn't want to chance further pissing her off. Her anger was justified. He'd been a jerk, staying on the phone so long. He hadn't intended to. *But the call was important!*

"Uh, hello?" Angelica interrupted Nick's reverie. "This isn't a complicated request, Nick. Just because we've broken up doesn't mean we can't eat together." She walked over, grabbed Nick's hands, and tried to pull him up from his chair. "Come on, darling, one hour. That's all I'm asking."

"I'm pretty busy here, Angelica."

"All the more reason to join me. A busy man has got to eat."

Nick knew how bullheaded Angelica could be, and how conniving. If she found out that a woman who worked there was why he didn't want to take her to Taste, she'd quite possibly become a permanent customer—just to annoy her. *I don't have anything to hide. Chances are, we won't even see Tiffany.* "All right, Angelica, one hour. And then I have to get back to work."

Tiffany wiped a bead of perspiration away from her face with the sleeve of her white uniform jacket. It wasn't that the kitchen wasn't well ventilated, but the steam from the boiling water that cooked the pasta she meticulously stirred was quite warm. The fact that she'd been told this dish was for her boss, who'd brought in someone to try the food—a client, Tiffany assumed—had her a bit hot under the collar as well. Were it not for the fact that she was a consummate professional, she would have laced Nick's ravioli with enough cayenne to burn off the tongue he used so well. Her inability to ruin perfectly prepared pasta, however, kept him safe.

"How much longer for pasta?" Wang barked to Tiffany.

"One minute, Chef!" She gingerly fished out a freshly made ravioli, placed it on a waiting saucer, speared it with a fork, and took a bite. *Thirty more seconds and they will be perfect.*

"Once you plate pasta, Tiff, chop basil."

"Yes, Chef."

"Roger, cheese freshly shaved?"

"Waiting for your go-ahead, Chef."

Wang gave a curt head nod.

Tiffany smiled, enjoying the easy way this team worked together, and how Wang bravely navigated his second language. He rarely saw use for articles such as "the" and "a," since there were none in the Chinese language.

Moments later, Nick and Angelica were served. The delicious aroma from Nick's crab-stuffed ravioli nestled in a lemon basil butter sauce wafted under his nostrils. Angelica's tarragon-infused salmon also smelled divine. For a couple moments, the tinkling of silverware on china was the only sound to be heard.

"The verdict?" Nick asked, after taking his napkin to wipe his mouth.

"Divine," Angelica answered honestly. "This place is going to be the talk of the town, Nick. Those other hot spots had better watch out."

"I don't know about all that," Nick replied, even as his chest swelled. He had to admit it, the food tasted excellent, especially his ravioli. He took another bite and then remembered why. Tiffany had been trained under Chef Riatoli, which meant that she probably prepared the pasta.

"Would you like to try a bite of pasta?"

"Sure." Angelica finished her bite and took a drink of lemon water to cleanse her palate.

Nick nodded at his plate. "Help yourself."

"My fork has bits of that wonderful salmon on it, Nick. I won't get a pure taste." Angelica batted her lashes seductively. "Feed me."

Nick speared a stuffed ravioli with his fork and held it out. Angelica slowly wiped the fork clean, and closed her eyes while she chewed.

"Melts in your mouth, doesn't it?"

"My gosh, where did you get this chef?"

"Stole him from a place in New York where I've eaten for years. I wanted someone else, but . . ."

"Let me guess. That chef in Italy."

"Exactly. But Emilio loves Rome."

"Well, Chef Wang is no slouch." From the corner of her eye, Angelica saw someone watching them from the hallway that led to the kitchen. Someone Black and female. "Here, try some of my salmon."

"Okay."

Angelica cut a piece of salmon, placed it on her fork, and lifted it up to Nick. Like her, he slowly eased the fish from her fork and savored the bite.

"Here, you have a little sauce on your mouth." Angelica leaned over, showing an ample amount of cleavage, and wiped the nonexistent dab from Nick's lip. She then took her finger and ran it over the same spot. "I miss these, you know," she said, her smile dazzling.

Nick looked at his watch. "Ten more minutes. I'd better eat up."

Angelica looked toward the hallway. The woman was gone. She leaned back in her chair, satisfied that she'd accomplished her goal. "I guess you're right. We wouldn't want our food to get cold."

20

Tiffany walked to her car and swore to herself that she wouldn't cry. Even if she had to peel a thousand onions when she returned to the kitchen tomorrow, not one more tear would she shed for Dominique Rollins. How was he going to sex her to within an inch of her life and not forty-eight hours later bring his ex to her kitchen? Okay, Chef Wang's kitchen in Nick's hotel, but still. *I know how he did it. The same way he sexed me then forgot I was there as soon as the phone rang. I'm just one of the many women he's screwed and scrapped.* Tiffany had seen the way Christina's eyes followed him everywhere, when the witch could barely speak to anyone else. And she'd heard other females whisper. They all thought Nick Rollins was the cat's meow. Yes, he'd made her cat meow, but that was beside the point. Tiffany didn't have time to have her heart speared like a fresh piece of asparagus. As much as it hurt, she was glad the night with Nick ended the way it did. His abrupt change of focus had brought her back to reality, shattered all illusions. It had been crazy to dream that she could have a relationship with a man like Nick and after seeing how quickly his taking care of business put her on the back burner, she realized she didn't want to.

As she pulled out of Le Sol's employee parking lot, Tiffany's thoughts were interrupted by her vibrating telephone. Her first thought was that it was Nick calling, this time to probably explain how lunching with Angelica was just *business*. "I could care less, Mr. Rollins," Tiffany said aloud. Her phone was buried at the bottom of her bag, so she simply clicked her headset. "Hello?"

"Tiffany, it's Dad."

Tiffany swerved, narrowly missing a white Beemer as she turned onto the boulevard. She hadn't heard his voice in a year. "Dad?" she asked incredulously.

The smile on Keith's face was heard in his voice. "I deserve that, pumpkin. I know I'm a rotten father who's neglected his only child her whole life. But believe it or not, the hard work's all for you."

"No, Dad, I don't believe it." Tiffany took a breath. "But I don't want to argue. Why'd you call, since you didn't feel the need to do so while you were in town last month." *Dangit.* The last part of that sentence had come out of its own volition.

Keith sighed heavily. "Look, your mother's already cussed me out for that. Can you not beat me up, even though I deserve it?"

Tiffany was silent a moment before answering. "I'll try."

"So . . . how are you, Tiffany?"

Angry. Exhausted. Hurting. "Fine."

"Your mom tells me you're working at a restaurant." Keith tried but failed to keep the disappointment out of his voice.

"Yes, Dad, I'm a sous chef for one of the leading

chefs in the country, Li Wang. His contemporaries are people like Emeril, Alton Brown, Mario Batali, Masaharu Morimoto, Bobby Flay. What am I doing? I'm sure you don't know who I'm talking about. But they're all famous chefs, *millionaire* chefs," she added, knowing that nothing got her father's attention like the mention of money.

"Wait, just hold on now. While I don't care much for the kitchen, you know I love food. I know the name of that Flay guy you mentioned. Sasha and I ate at one of his restaurants when we were in New York, a year or so ago."

"Wow, Dad, I'm impressed." And she was. Not only for the fact that her dad knew about Bobby Flay, but that she and her dad could possibly talk without arguing. "Which one was it? Mesa, Bar Americain . . ."

"Mesa."

"Cool. What did you have?"

"Baby girl, we eat out so much, I don't remember. Sasha has many talents, but cooking is not one of them."

Tiffany rolled her eyes and then remembered she was driving. She could just about imagine what talents the stepmother who was just a few years older than her possessed. Still, this was a civil conversation with her father, the first one in a year. She'd forgotten how cordial her father could be, and how much she missed him. "When are you coming back to LA?" The question was out before she could stop it. "I know you were just here, so I imagine it will probably be a while." She didn't want her father to know how much she needed to see him.

"That's one of the reasons I called, Tiffany. I've been thinking about how wrong I've treated you, how instead of waiting for you to make the first move in patching up our relationship, I should have been the one doing it. I'm the adult, you're the child, but I was the one acting immature."

Tiffany silently agreed with everything her father said. He had acted immature and selfish, like someone else she knew.

"Tiffany, you still there?"

"Yes, Dad."

The awkward silence continued, but Keith suppressed his discomfort. He was determined to make things right with Tiffany, especially after what he'd witnessed the past weekend when he'd attended the wedding of his partner's daughter. As he walked her down the aisle, it was obvious the two adored each other. His partner, Tim, looked so proud. It was a feeling Keith realized he might not ever get to experience if he didn't take action. "Baby girl, it's time for me to fix things. Make amends. How long has it been since I've seen you?"

Four years, ten months, thirteen days . . . "It's been a minute. About five years," she added.

"That long? No, couldn't be." Keith sighed audibly. "I'm so sorry, Tiffany. I feel like such a knucklehead. But the fact of the matter is, you're grown, with your own mind, goals, and dreams. I think that's been the problem in our relationship. I didn't want to accept that you're your own woman. There's some other things I need to say to you, but I want to do it face-to-face."

Tiffany navigated the streets of LA in stunned silence. Was it possible that she could finally have the father/daughter relationship she'd always wanted?

"I was wondering if you'd like to take a vacation,

just the two of us. We could go wherever you want, stay a few days. Get to know each other again and make up for the time we lost."

How do I get back a childhood, and all the times I needed you, but you weren't there? But for the first time, her father was trying to reach out to her. She decided to reach back. "Okay." The word was barely audible.

"Huh, pumpkin?"

Tiffany cleared her throat. "That would be . . . okay." Then she remembered her grueling schedule. With the hotel officially opening next week and the restaurant waiting list almost three months out, Chef Wang had warned them: no vacations for anyone in the foreseeable future. "Oh no, Dad, I can't."

"Why not?"

"It's work. See, the hotel opens next week and we're going to get slammed. There's no way I'll be able to get time off for months."

"Surely you can get a three-day weekend, Tiffany."

"Weekends are our busiest time, Dad."

"I don't like it, Tiffany. Sounds like they're working you like a slave, probably over a hot stove, griddle, or whatever you cook on. Baby, I could line up a nice management job for you—"

"Dad . . ."

"All right, all right, I'll let it go. But I can't help but to think what an excellent manager you'd make in my company. Probably triple what you're making now. At KJB, the sky would be the limit. I'd groom you to take over when I retire."

"Ha! Like that will ever happen. For you, work is like breathing."

"You're probably right. But for sure, you'd be my right-hand daughter."

Tears sprang to her eyes at his words. For a split second, she considered it. If nothing else, working side by side would definitely give her more time with her father. But the world of finance was his world, not hers. Keith loved to crunch numbers. She'd rather crunch a carrot. "Do you think you could maybe come to LA?" she asked, changing the subject.

"I don't know. We'll see. Tiff, I need to take this call. It's one of my managers."

And there it was; the moment of camaraderie was over. Now it was back to business as usual.

"Bye, Dad."

"Wait, Tiffany?"

"Yes?"

"I'll, uh, I'll try and get to LA soon."

"Yeah, okay." This time it was her headset that beeped. "I have to go, too, Dad. Hello?"

"How's my brown sugar? Can I come over and taste some of your sweetness?"

"I don't know, Nick," Tiffany replied. "Will you be using the same fork that Angelica used to feed you?"

Tiffany's unexpected comment, and the venom with which she spoke it, sat Nick straight up in his office chair. "You saw me in the restaurant?"

"I work there, remember?"

"Of course, Tiffany. I just didn't see you, that's all."

"Well, you were rather busy."

Nick leaned back and rubbed his eyes. "Having lunch, baby, that's all."

"And were your hands broke?"

"Tiffany. You're angry, and you should be. I'm sorry about the other night, neglecting you when my phone rang."

"No need to apologize, Nick. I've experienced a lifetime of neglect."

"Don't judge every man by your father's yardstick, Tiffany."

"Don't you dare tell me what to do!" Tiffany fired back, forgetting she was talking to the man who authorized her paycheck. "And don't presume to know about my life, or my father!"

"Well, let me tell you what I do know," Nick countered, his voice stern before turning soft, seductive. "I know that what we shared the other night was magical. I felt it, and I know you did too."

Tiffany's heart constricted. She had experienced the magic. But it was over. "This isn't going to work, Nick. I have a rule of not mixing business with pleasure and have learned from recent experience that it's one not to be broken. I love working at Taste, and plan to stay and learn as much from Chef Wang as I can. My earlier reaction was uncalled for. Who you dine with is none of my business."

She's more hurt than angry, although a lot of both. But anyone who knew Dominique Rollins knew he never backed down from a challenge. He simply changed tactics, and proceeded.

"Angelica came to the office because she'd seen my name in a magazine. She'd heard about Chef Wang from one of my partners, Bastion Price, and wanted to check out his skills. When I tried the pasta, I was sure you'd made it. I wanted her to taste the work of LA's finest sous chef. That's what you saw."

"Like I said, Nick, it's none of my business. You dated her a long time. She's beautiful. It's not hard to figure out why you're still in love with her."

"We were together a long time. And while I'll always love her, Tiffany, I'm not *in* love with her."

Tiffany snorted. "Same difference."

What on earth is wrong with this girl? I know I screwed up but . . . Nick's brow furrowed as his awareness heightened. *No, there's something more.*

"Tiffany, is seeing Angelica today the only thing that's bothering you? You nearly took my head off when you answered."

One thing Tiffany liked about Nick was that he was sensitive, and acted like he genuinely cared about her. "No, something else happened."

"Want to tell me about it?"

"I talked to my dad. For the first time in a year."

"I'll meet you wherever you want."

Tiffany knew just the thing that would make her feel better, and exactly where she wanted to meet Nick—his home, his master suite, his bed. But from now on, Tiffany intended to think with her head, not her heart. *Business first.*

"Thanks, Nick. I'm really okay. Just tired. I just want to go home."

"I can meet you there. Let me love you, Tiffany, help ease the pain, and make up for the hurt I caused you."

Every fiber of her body urged her to say yes, as memories of how she'd felt beneath him crashed into her wall of resolve. *It would feel so good! How can I say no to what I want so badly?*

And then Tiffany thought of the conversation she'd just had with her dad—the man who'd showed her what a workaholic looked like—and she knew how she would do it, how she would resist that which she craved so deeply. With three simple words. "No, Nick. Goodbye."

21

It was Labor Day weekend, the official opening for Hotel Le Sol. It had enjoyed a soft opening one week earlier, and select guests had enjoyed the hotel's ambience, spa, professionally equipped gym, and other facilities. But today was when Taste would open its doors. Nick was nervous, but could hardly wait.

Inside, the kitchen was a zoo. Chef Wang barked orders as the kitchen staff chopped, diced, sliced, seared, and stirred. From the moment the first order was taken until the last dessert was served, there was not a spare second. For ten hours straight, the cooks toiled over their assigned tasks, turning out perfection in dish after dish. At the end of the night, which was actually two in the morning, Chef Wang had given Tiffany a brief head nod as she stumbled out of the kitchen. She was too tired to smile, or to join the rest of the kitchen crew for a celebratory cocktail.

"You're gonna miss out," Roger said, after her initial refusal. "We're going to a fancy schmancy place—"

"I don't care if you're going to the moon," Tiffany interrupted. "All I want is my bed."

She reached her car and slumped inside. The only thing on her mind was a hot shower and a soft mattress. Tomorrow would demand a repeat performance. Tiffany wondered where she'd find the energy. Her phone vibrated. She ignored it. But just before she started the car, she changed her mind and read her text messages. There were three. The first was from Joy, wishing her good luck. The second one, from Nick:

> I know your feet hurt, and that you're tired. I've got something to make you feel better. Come over now.

Anger and irritation quickly replaced Tiffany's exhaustion. "Who does this asshole think he is?" She had absolutely no intention of dignifying his presumptive message with a response. Didn't he hear her when she said their little tryst was over? What part of professional relationship didn't he understand? When she saw that the third message was also from Nick, she almost ignored it. But curiosity won out. She opened the text message, and poised her thumb over the Delete button.

> In case you think coming over NOW is optional, or personal, it isn't. This is strictly business, and your appearance is mandatory. If you choose to ignore this message tonight, then don't bother showing up at Taste in the morning.

Just as her blood started to boil, Tiffany remembered Roger's comment. *So this is the fancy schmancy place he was talking about. Nick decided to throw a little get together for the kitchen crew.* "How nice." Even though this statement was said sarcastically, Tiffany actually admired Nick's kind gesture. He knew how hard they'd worked, and how common it was for crews to share a drink, even after pulling long, hard shifts. "So why didn't you just say that, Nick Rollins?" Tiffany asked aloud as she started the car and shifted into drive. *Probably just to piss me off,* she reasoned.

Less than ten minutes later, Tiffany pulled into Nick's spacious driveway. She yawned, the sleepiness that anger had pushed away now coming back full force. But only for a moment. As soon as Tiffany stepped out of her car, she was on full alert again. *What's wrong with this picture?* There was only one other car in the driveway. And it wasn't Nick's. *His is probably in the garage.* So who was the other guest?

There was only one way to find out. Tiffany steeled herself against the range of emotions she knew would come upon seeing Nick in his home setting, and marched toward the front door. She'd barely rung the doorbell when a strange man opened the door and greeted her.

"Ms. Matthews," the man said, bowing low. "It is my pleasure to meet you."

Tiffany frowned. "Where's Nick?"

The stranger, a slight, dark-skinned man with a wiry build, shock of black hair and angular face, offered a wisp of a smile. "Come." He bowed again, and opened the door wider as he stepped aside.

Tiffany cautiously stepped inside the door. She immediately detected an odor that wasn't food. "Where's Nick?" she asked again.

"He's not here. My name is Picchu, and I am a

masseur. He has employed my services for your pleasure and well-being. Please, right this way."

Tiffany's mind whirled as she followed the man down an unfamiliar hallway. They'd walked the opposite direction from Nick's master suite to a set of guest rooms. The scent she'd smelled in the foyer grew stronger as they came to the end of the hall. Her eyes widened when they entered the room.

The setting was like a fairyland, with dozens of white, pink, and green candles covering every inch of available space. New Age music mixed with the smoke that wafted from oil burners placed on a long table—the source of the floral, earthy aroma. Also on this table were a variety of smooth stones, several bottles of oil, and several large, fluffy white towels.

"What's all this?" she whispered.

"Please. I will give you a moment. Remove your clothes, and your jewelry. Lie on the table and cover yourself with a towel. When I return, I'll explain."

Moments later, Tiffany felt as if she'd died and gone to heaven. In between Picchu's firm kneading, gentle prodding, and light tapping, he informed her that he was from Peru, and had been a masseur and spiritual healer for twenty years. The blend of flowers and spices, he explained, served to relax, while stimulating the soul toward peace and positive expectation. The heated rocks he placed on various points of her back, stomach and legs were Basalt stones, designed to aid blood circulation while eliminating pain and stress. If Picchu said more, Tiffany didn't remember. She fell asleep on the massage table and woke up with a start—in Nick's bed.

A ringing phone is what had awakened her. Tiffany threw back the covers, puzzled yet thankful to see that she was wearing a long, cotton nightgown. "Nick?" she called out, even though his side of the bed was unruffled. She'd obviously slept alone. *Where is he?*

Her phone had stopped ringing but now rang again. This time Tiffany reached for the BlackBerry, which had been conveniently placed on the nightstand beside her. She eyed the clock also sitting on the stand and breathed a sigh of relief. It was only nine o'clock and she wasn't due at work until ten. Her sleep had been so deep and uninterrupted, however, she felt she'd slept ten hours instead of five.

Tiffany glanced at the Caller ID. "Hello, Nick."

"Good morning, brown sugar, how'd you sleep?"

"Like a baby. You shouldn't have gone to all this trouble, but I appreciate it."

"It was no trouble, but my pleasure. Picchu has been my masseur for years—"

"He's amazing."

"I knew you'd think so, which is why I had to pull the boss card in my texts earlier. Forgive me?"

"Where are you?" As soon as the question was out, Tiffany wished she could take it back. Where Nick spent the night was of no concern to her.

"At the hotel, where I spent the night. I wanted to experience what our guests enjoy. But I wish I were there. With you."

"Nick, listen—"

"Shh. I know. But what you think doesn't stop how a brothah feels about you." Nick paused. When he spoke again, his tone was professional. "You did great work last night, Tiffany. The guests raved and the *LA Times* gave us a good review. The kitchen should be proud."

"Thanks, Nick," Tiffany responded, already missing his flirtatious tone. But it was for the best.

"You're welcome, Tiffany. I'll see you later. At work."

"Right. At work. Goodbye."

Tiffany walked through the dressing room on the way to the master bath and was surprised yet again. Her uniform had been washed, and hung pressed and ready on an end hanger. Her shoes were beneath it, shiny and clean. *Who washed my clothes? Picchu? Is that who clothed me and put me to bed?* This thought brought only mild embarrassment. Something about the masseur's almost divine countenance separated him from the average man. She doubted he'd had an untoward thought at seeing her body, if he'd even looked at all.

Nick had thought of everything, had had her pampered like a princess. With all their similarities, Keith Bronson had never treated Tiffany like this. *What if Nick really is my prince?* Tiffany shrugged, knowing the answer to that question. Last night may have felt like a dream but today, in the real world, life was not a fairy tale.

22

By the time Monday after Labor Day rolled around, Tiffany was beyond tired. She hadn't had a day off in two weeks, and what little time she should have been sleeping was spent tossing and turning with thoughts of Nick. She'd only seen him twice since opening night and Picchu's massage. The first time he was talking to Chef. He'd looked up and smiled. The second time was after a bathroom break, when she encountered a group of important-looking men standing in the hallway that led to the kitchen. Nick was among them, listening to another man. He looked up as she muttered an "excuse me," before passing, but didn't acknowledge her. His focus zoomed right back in on the man who was speaking. All business, like she wanted.

I don't want to think about him. Tiffany reached for the stereo knob just as her phone rang. "Hey chick."

"Hey yourself. You'd better not tell me your butt is still at home."

"Okay, so I won't tell you."

"Tiffany Alana!"

"Joy Lynn! Ha! Chill out, girl, I'm on my way."

"You'd better be. You know what they say about all work and no play . . ."

"Yeah, well, my name ain't Jack."

"It ain't Jill either. And you might not be going up the hill with a pail, but you're still in the kitchen fetching water."

"Joy . . . you are ig-no-rant, you hear me?" Tiffany said, laughing.

"You know I've got a screw loose. Girl, Randall's been calling me for the past five minutes. Let me go in there and see what he wants."

"Later." Tiffany continued smiling as she hung up the phone, thankful that she had a friend like Joy. She thought about Joy and Randall's relationship, how it seemed to come so natural, how they'd gelled from the beginning. The opposite appeared to be true for Tiffany, where finding love was like finding a needle in the proverbial haystack.

There'd been her first love, Tony, whom she'd met her senior year of high school. He'd transferred to her school from Georgia, and she'd immediately been taken with his manners and gentle spirit. She gave him her virginity the night of graduation, the same night she'd had a terrible row with her father. She'd had only two serious relationships since then. The last one had ended when her culinary classmate decided to move to New York without her.

Within seconds of arriving at the Parsons residence, all thoughts of ex-boyfriends, and Nick, were forgotten—replaced by the noise and chaos that typified Joy's household. Tiffany had initially tried to get out of Joy's invite for dinner, but Joy wouldn't take no for an answer. Now, sitting in their living room, talking to the kids and munching on potato chips, she was glad Joy had "gone Leo" on her. For almost a month there had only been Nick and work. She'd rarely talked to her mother and hadn't been by Grand's house. Until now, Tiffany hadn't realized that she missed the rest of her life.

"Okay, it's not bourgie, but it's ready," Joy yelled from the kitchen. "Lecia, I thought I told you to set the table."

"She can do that?" Tiffany asked. "I'm impressed."

"Girl, don't be. Lecia's setting the table consists of putting forks and napkins somewhere in the vicinity of everybody's plate. But she wants to *help Mommy*," Joy continued, making air quotes. "So I let her."

Joy allowed it, but Lecia's brother, Randall, Jr., nicknamed Deuce, made sure he contributed as well. He promptly went behind his little sister and knocked the napkins to the floor as soon as she placed them on the table.

"Mama! Deuce is messing up my places!"

"I ain't neither," Deuce whispered, wanting to keep his taunting between the two of them. "Shut up, fool!"

"Mama, Deuce is pushing me. Tell him to stop!"

"Stop pushing her, Deuce," Joy said without feeling.

"She pushed me earlier," Deuce said.

"Don't push your brother," Joy responded in the same dull tone.

"Ooh, you lying!"

"Stop lying, Deuce." During this, their umpteenth fight of the day, Joy was answering by rote.

Deuce ran around the dining room table and shouted in Lecia's face. "I ain't lying. You lying!"

"Your breath stinks," Lecia said calmly.

"Your breath smells like your booty," Deuce yelled.

"All right, y'all, that's enough," Randall drawled from in front of the stove. He was from Alabama, and everything he did was slow and easy: cook (which he, too, had learned from his grandmother), talk, walk, and according to Joy, make love. In all the years Tiffany had known him, she'd never once seen him lose his temper. Joy assured her it was a sight she didn't want to see. Watching them interact, Tiffany saw yet again how perfectly Randall's laid-back personality complemented Joy's fiery style. He was the "steady Eddie" to Joy's flightiness, and the family's solid rock. He was loyal and dependable, had worked at UPS for fifteen years.

After a simple yet delicious dinner of round steak, gravy, mashed potatoes, and garlic toast, the kids watched a movie in their parents' room while Randall, Joy, and Tiffany chilled out in the living room.

"Heard you got a man," Randall said in his lazy verbal style. He flipped idly through the channels, but looked at Tiffany slyly with a twinkle in his eye.

"Yeah, well, your wife has a big mouth."

"That she does."

Joy jabbed him playfully. "You're not supposed to agree with her, fool."

Randall looked at her incredulously. "Woman, it's the truth!"

"In-tee-ways," Joy said, turning to her husband. "Things have changed. All is not perfect in paradise. If it were," she continued, looking at Tiffany, "girl-friend would be wearing that glow on her face."

"What glow?"

"The satisfied *pushy* glow."

Tiffany's response was an open mouth and wide

eyes. In the Parsons household, "pushy" referred to one's vagina, the word adopted after Lecia, then two years old, mispronounced what she'd heard her foul-mouthed father say.

"Girl, please, Randall knows all about the pushy glow. Don't you, baby?"

"You wearing it, ain't cha?"

"Damn skippy, baby." Joy's tone was sweet, but she turned to Tiffany and made a face.

"Well, all right then." Randall went back to flipping channels, and put his arm around Joy's shoulders in a possessive fashion. Joy snuggled closer, and rested her head on his shoulder.

"I guess I probably should leave you two lovebirds," Tiffany said, feeling a sudden pang of loneliness. "I only have this one day off. Tomorrow, it's back to the grind."

"I thought you were supposed to get perks when you sleep with the boss?" Randall's eyes never left the television, convincing Tiffany that he could talk and listen at the same time.

"Even if I was sleeping with him, the last thing I'd want is to be treated differently. I want to get to the top of the culinary world on the basis of what I do in the kitchen, not in the bedroom."

"Damn, girl, why you fucking him, then?"

"What a crass question, Mr. Parsons. You and Joy make the perfect couple," Tiffany said dryly. "I guess after a while the two really do become one."

Randall muted the television and gave Tiffany his undivided attention. "Look, he's getting more than being an employee out of you, you should get more than being a boss out of him. That just fair play right there."

"Okay, that's it, I'm outtie." Tiffany rose from the couch.

"Get a raise, an extra week's vacation or some shit."

"Bye, Joy. Bye, Randall."

"Don't be stuck on stupid, Tiff. Hit that rich mutha-fucka up for a car, a house, or somethin'!" Randall's rumbling laughter followed Tiffany and Joy down the hallway and out the door.

"Girl, don't pay him no mind. He's just jerking your chain."

"I know." Tiffany gave Joy a hug.

"I know y'all are having a little tiff, pun intended, but you do need that brothah to throw out some major ducketts . . . real talk."

"Joy . . ."

"Aren't you ready to move to Malibu?"

"On that note . . ."

"At least let him hook you up with a pedicure. I noticed your feet tonight, and those toenails are not cute."

"Forget you, heifah."

"Bye, girl."

23

"I'm sorry, Ms. King, but you can't go in there."

"Excuse me, Steven, are you talking to me?"

"Please, Angelica," the older man pleaded. Steven had worked for Nick at another of his companies before becoming head concierge at the hotel. He'd known Angelica for a couple years, and liked her. That's why he'd greeted her personally as she tried to step through the revolving doors. "I don't want to do this. But it's Nick's orders. Not telling you this can cost me my job! I'm going to have to ask you to leave the premises."

"This is a public establishment. No one—you, Nick, or anyone else—can keep me out."

Steven's voice dropped to a whisper. "We're to call security if you put up a fuss. I'd hate to do it, Angelica. But Nick's my boss."

"Your master, is more like it. I'm disappointed in you, Steven. I thought you had balls."

"Take care, Angelica."

"Fuck you, Steven." Angelica took a couple steps and then whipped back around. She walked up to him purposefully and put her manicured finger in his face. "This little fling Nick is having is temporary. I'm the one who will be around when the dust stops flying. I'll be back, Steven. And those who've crossed me are going to pay. You remember that."

"I'm sorry, Angelica."

"Yes, you are."

Angelica rang Nick's line for two straight hours. Finally, Christina had had enough. She knocked on Nick's door and, in an uncharacteristic move, didn't wait for his answer before walking into his office. Nick looked up, a frown on his face.

"I'm sorry, Mr. Rollins, please forgive me. But . . . it's Angelica. She's called repeatedly, for hours. The girls at the switchboard are going nuts and try as I might, I can't convince her that you're not here. I was just hoping you could take just one call so that she won't call back."

As if to underscore her point, the outer phone rang again. Christina walked over to Nick's phone, which showed the blinking light announcing a call but was silent. "May I?"

Nick nodded.

"Good afternoon, Mr. Rollins's office. This is Christina."

"Put him on, bitch."

"Angelica, it really isn't necessary for you to call me names—"

Nick hit the speakerphone button and motioned to close the office door.

"Look, I know that Nick is in there. I want you to put him on the phone, now! I've already been there once, and if I come back again, it's not going to be pretty. I don't care if you call the police. I want to talk to Nick and I intend to do just that."

"You're already doing it," Nick said. His voice conveyed the weariness he felt. "Thanks, Christina. You can go back to work now."

Nick waited until Christina had closed the door behind her. "All right, Angelica, you have my undivided attention. What do you want?"

"I want to know why you've barred me from the hotel, as if I'm a criminal. That is a public establishment. You can't do that, Nick."

"You and I are over, Angelica. Why would you want to come here?"

"For the food," Angelica spat, before her voice turned deceptively sugary. "There's no restaurant like Taste, the cooking is out of this world!"

She knows about Tiffany. In that moment, Nick was sure of it. He didn't know how she'd found out, but Angelica knew.

"Angelica, I'm seeing someone who works in the restaurant." Nick tried a direct approach. "The relationship is new, and tentative. I like this woman and want to pursue a relationship with her. You and I had something special, Angelica, but those times are over. We want different things out of life.

"You're a good woman, and there is someone out there for you." *Someone who isn't married, unlike Bastion Price.* "When you two find each other, you'll forget all about me."

"Don't flatter yourself, asshole. I already have."

24

Nick walked through Le Sol's elegantly appointed lobby. He stopped to chat with Steven, the concierge, and engaged in small conversation with a successful East Coast businessman who'd become a regular guest. Anyone observing him would have seen a calm and gracious man, his interactions more those of a host than a hotel owner. No one would have guessed the frustration that simmered beneath his placid demeanor.

When it came to women, Nick rarely let one get under his skin. But Angelica had done it today. He'd made the choice to date her, and could deal with her attitude. But the constant calls to the hotel had burdened his staff, and Christina had borne the brunt of Angelica's misplaced anger. His plate was much too full to have to deal with an egotistical female who refused to accept the fact that "they" were no longer "us." Her telephone call had riled him, and reminded him of what he didn't miss about his ex. But it had also reminded him of what he liked about someone else.

From the time Angelica hung up on him, Nick was preoccupied with the fact that Tiffany was just two floors below, no doubt working up a sweat as she worked in the kitchen. He'd thought back to another time when her body had glowed—from the sheen of their lovemaking. As he walked through the restaurant's dining room, he told himself that it was because of the private dinner Chef Wang was catering the coming weekend that he felt the need to visit the kitchen. But Nick knew it was because of one reason and one reason only—he missed his brown sugar.

Tiffany wiped an errant strand of hair away from her face, and beads of perspiration along with it. Her semi-regular visits to the hair salon were among the many aspects of her personal life that were being neglected. Her hair had grown out to her shoulders, and her highlights were dull. There was no place she'd rather be than this kitchen, but Tiffany's visit with the Parsons family yesterday reminded her of what was missing from her life. Seeing Randall and Joy together forced Tiffany to acknowledge the truth—she missed Nick. He'd been on her mind since she'd slept in his bed, and even though she'd thanked him again via a text message, they hadn't spoken since his call had awakened her the morning after the massage.

The holidays were over but the dining room remained full. Fortunately the lunch crowd was beginning to wane. Tiffany bantered with Roger as she helped him cook "the chow," the crew's name for the staff meal served before the morning shift, and again between the afternoon and evening shifts. Even though her back was to the door, she knew the moment Nick Rollins entered the kitchen.

Before Chef called out a greeting, something about the atmosphere changed, crackled, and she could have sworn the hairs rose on the back of her neck. From the corner of her eye, she watched him, noted how he was respectful of each person's job and their space as Chef took him to the hot prep area to taste the day's soup special—a hearty cioppino made with a zesty, herb-infused tomato base, and filled with a variety of straight-from-the-dock seafood. Tiffany hoped that Chef would tell Nick who made the mouthwatering sauce. *Maybe he'll remember.* In that moment, Tiffany did—remembered the day shortly after she'd began working, when Nick had tasted one of her first batches of tomato sauce and then a few days later, had tasted something else.

"Ow!" Tiffany snatched back her hand from the grill, having just gotten a quick lesson in not day-dreaming while testing the doneness of meat with one's fingers. She'd missed the halibut filet and touched the grill.

Nick was by her side in an instant. "Are you okay?"

"I'm fine," Tiffany mumbled, embarrassed that Nick had seen her make such a dumb mistake. Thankfully, he was the only one who reacted. In a chef's world, burns, cuts and bruises were par for the course.

"Let me see," Nick insisted, taking her hand before she could protest. His touch was gentle. Tiffany's heartbeat raced, and despite her efforts to the contrary, she could feel her body grow warm.

Nick held her wrist with one hand, and traced the

red burn mark with the other. "Shouldn't you run this under cold water? I believe that's how to treat a burn, correct?"

Tiffany jerked her hand away. She felt naked, exposed, even though the others in the kitchen seemed bent on their tasks. Even Chef had stepped away to speak with the pastry chef. Tiffany got the distinct feeling of being all alone with Nick, in a room full of people—a feeling that heightened her awareness of him, and shortened her breath. Especially with the way he looked at her, dark eyes boring into hers before dropping slightly and settling on her quivering mouth.

"Tiff!" Roger quickly stepped between Tiffany and the grill, bumping Nick in the process. "Excuse me, boss, but the sous here is about to burn our chow." Roger elbowed Tiffany playfully while turning the now overdone fish with his other hand.

Tiffany was mortified. Not only had she burned herself but even worse, she'd almost burned the food. In front of Nick! It wasn't like her to be a bumbling idiot, under any circumstances. She had to get away before she made a complete fool of herself.

"You know what? I think I will go and run water on this, just to make sure it doesn't blister. I owe you one, Roger!" she called over her shoulder, as she hurried toward the employee bathroom and away from the man who'd unnerved her.

Chef re-entered the kitchen as Tiffany exited. He and Nick finalized the menu for the weekend meeting, and Nick returned to the second floor. But his mind wasn't on meetings or menus. It was on Tiffany, and how he knew she'd felt the heat when he touched her, the same as him. She was a stubborn one, he'd give her that. But Nick was determined to work things out, to get them back on track. As he walked down the hallway of the executive offices, a slight smile played across his face. *You can run but you can't hide, Tiffany Matthews. I know where you work.*

25

"What's that smile about, Grand?" Tiffany's question broke the companionable silence that she and her grandmother were enjoying as they cooked shoulder to shoulder during this, Tiffany's first in-person visit in over three months.

"Oh, I'm just happy you got a new fella, and y'all are getting along." Grand took the pan of marinated fish and placed it in the oven.

"How are you so sure I have a new fella, much less how we're doing?"

"You think your grandmother was born yesterday? I know what it's like to be in love, and that pep in your step gives away the fact that someone has your nose wide open." Grand emphasized the word "wide" by spreading her arms. "I know you're getting along because you didn't bring that many things to chop for this visit. Even the potatoes are being baked. Yeah, child, there's some smooth sailing happening on the home front. And I for one am happy about that. You're not getting any younger, Tiffany Matthews. I want to see a great-grandchild in my lifetime."

"Well, don't hold your breath, Grand. I've got plenty of cooking to do before I think about taking time off to raise a family. I don't want to have kids just so someone else can take of them."

Both women became silent. Tiffany pondered Grand's erroneous assumption about her "fella," and wished it were true. She didn't have the heart to reveal that the man who'd put the pep in her step yesterday was not a suitor but Chef, who'd complimented her verbally—a rarity. He'd even told her that if she continued to learn and work hard, she could someday own her own restaurant. From anyone, but especially from Chef Wang, this was high praise.

As for kids, Tiffany meant what she'd said about them. If and when she gave birth, she didn't want a nanny raising her child. Tiffany loved her grandmother to death, but all of Gladys Matthews's love couldn't stop her from feeling like she'd been an afterthought in her parents' lives. Grand understood Tiffany's anger, but had told her that things could have been worse—that Tiffany could have been born and left to someone who didn't love her as much as Grand did.

"That fish should be about ready," Tiffany said with authority.

"Hmph, like I haven't cooked fish for the last fifty years. You just make sure those twice-baked potatoes don't taste like they've been cooked three times!"

"Ha! All right, Grand."

"All right now."

The uncomfortable energy of the past successfully defused, Tiffany and Grand enjoyed their dinner of pecan-crusted baked halibut, potatoes, asparagus tips, and Grand's homemade yeast rolls (which

Tiffany had yet to master). While eating this main course, the conversation centered on Grand's Monday-night bingo circle (where she'd recently won five hundred dollars); her neighbor's new, noisy Chihuahua (who didn't always get his poop scooped); and the Neelys, Grand's favorite cooks on the Food Network.

"If I was a little younger," Grand concluded, "I'd give Gina some competition for that tall sip of tea!"

As they topped off dinner with Grand's fresh-from-the-oven strawberry-rhubarb pie and Tiffany's homemade vanilla ice cream, the conversation returned once more to Tiffany's love interest.

"So Mr. Put-The-Pep-In-Your-Step. He good-lookin'?"

Tiffany thought of Chef Wang, and almost laughed. Chef wasn't unattractive, but neither would he win *People* magazine's Sexiest Man Alive. *Nick could.* "Honestly, I don't have time for a relationship. I'm focusing on my career right now."

Grand's fork clattered to the saucer as her head jerked up. "What do you mean, you don't have time? You're not getting any younger, child. You'd better make time. A career can't visit you on your deathbed. Family can."

"I don't plan on dying anytime soon, Grand. I'm not even thirty."

"The years can fly away before you know they're gone. While you're turning up the heat on the stove at your workplace, don't forget to light the home fires, that's all." Grand picked up her fork and chewed thoughtfully on a bite of pie. "What about that fella that had you slicing and dicing when you were here before? What happened to him?"

"Didn't work out."

"What happened?"

"Oh, Grand," Tiffany sighed. "It's a long story."

"Don't seem like y'all lasted a month—can't be too long."

Tiffany laughed. "Can't put one by you, huh, Grand?"

Grand winked. "You'd have to get up mighty early."

"First of all, there's no *new fella*," Tiffany said, deciding on the spot that Grand's counsel might not be a bad idea. "There's just this one guy I've been dating off and on. He owns the hotel where I work. I met him before I started working there and after getting hired, decided not to mix business with pleasure."

Tiffany continued eating her dessert, wondering whether her grandmother's reaction would mirror how her mother had felt—that interoffice dating was a bad idea.

"This here man, what's his name?"

"Nick. Nick Rollins."

"This here Nick Rollins, what kind of man is he?"

Tiffany thought for a moment. "A lot like Daddy . . ."

"How?"

"Focused, take-charge, all about business."

"Couldn't have been all about business else you two would not have met."

"True."

"Your father's not all bad, Tiffany. Keith has some good qualities. Nothing wrong with being focused and take-charge. You want a man to be able to handle his business."

"Right."

"And you say he *owns* the hotel?"

"Well, not only him. He's one of a group of partners who do."

"That sounds like a good quality right there. So
what other good qualities does your Nick possess?"

"He's not my Nick, Grand."

Grand simply grunted.

As they continued eating, Tiffany remembered
how Nick had come to her rescue in Rome, helped
her get hired at the hotel, loved her passionately, and
arranged the massage after the restaurant's opening
night. "He's kind," she said at last. "And thoughtful.
Made me feel protected when I was with him. But it
couldn't last. I could never come second to a man's
career."

"The way a man is coming second to yours right
now?"

It was Tiffany's turn to jerk her head in Grand's
direction.

"That's what you just told me, right? That you
didn't have time for a relationship because you were
focused on a career right now?

"Sometimes, Tiffany, living life is a lot like cooking.
You might have several burners going at the same
time, something in the oven and a slab on the grill.
But if you keep your wits about you, and pay attention to what you're doing, nothing has to overcook,
dry out or burn. A cook worth her salt can whip
up a three, four, five course dinner and never lose
her smile. Course, a meal always tastes better when
it's shared with somebody else." Grand nodded at
Tiffany's empty saucer. "You want another slice?"

Tiffany shook her head.

"And one more thing," Grand said, as she walked
over to place Tiffany's empty saucer on top of hers.

"Don't ever think nobody else's cooking is better than yours. Don't matter if their kitchen is bigger, or their pots are shinier. A man will eat beans mixed with love before he'll chew steak seasoned with spite."

Tiffany watched her grandmother sashay into the kitchen. Her heart swelled with love for the slight, feisty woman who even now was the wind beneath her wings. *She's right,* Tiffany admitted. The parts of Nick's personality that at times she detested weren't necessarily bad traits. They were undoubtedly the qualities that had made him a millionaire. As for his good qualities, Tiffany had purposely put those out of her mind. It made the thought of not being with him romantically hurt less, but did nothing to quench her desire.

She thought of Grand's beans and steak analogy, and concluded her grandmother had said a mouthful without even knowing it. The word *spite* definitely described Angelica's actions when she and Nick had dined at Taste. *She saw me watching them, read my reaction, and purposely rubbed the fact that they were dining together in my face.*

"But I cook with love," Tiffany whispered, repeating Grand's words. For the first time in weeks, Tiffany admitted that when it came to Nick Rollins . . . she wanted another taste.

Tiffany wasn't the only person remembering what they'd once tasted. So was Bastion Price. "You ever hear from Angelica?" he asked Nick, after they'd wrapped up discussion on their latest business venture—a megadeal involving a string of high-tech nightclubs in China.

Nick nodded. "Unfortunately. She's pretty much stopped calling, but the e-mails continue."

"You know, I don't know what I was thinking, taking up with Angelica when you two broke up. Granted, she's a gorgeous woman . . . smart . . . but Jill didn't deserve my infidelity. I just wish it hadn't taken her illness to get me to realize that."

Nick thoughtfully sipped a cup of decaf coffee. "Like you said, she's an attractive woman who made it obvious to you that she was interested. Stronger men than you have been felled by a woman's wiles."

"You still don't hold it against me that I went out with her? I mean, you guys were an item a long time."

"Believe me. You did me a favor." Nick put his cup down as a thought occurred to him. "When did you break things off with her?"

Bastion told him.

Right before her surprise visit that Monday. The pieces of the puzzle were falling in place.

"Why, if you don't mind me asking?"

"The timing suggests that Angelica began pursuing me again after getting the boot from you."

"She never stopped loving you, Nick. She told me that."

"Doesn't matter, I've moved on."

"Doesn't sound like she has."

"She will. Women like Angelica don't stay alone for long."

Angelica sat at home, wrapped in a bathrobe, calmly sipping a flute of sparkling champagne. She'd needed it after returning home from yet another unsuccessful date. There'd been nothing about Stan

Koespesky, whom her friend had raved about, that impressed her. Not his looks, dress, or conversation, especially his going on and on about how successful he was. She'd learned from experience that that was a telltale sign of someone who wanted to be a player but wasn't there yet. When men were at the top of their game, like Nick and Bastion, they didn't have to talk about it. Men like them just walked into a room and their success showed. Had it not been for the news Stan shared just before she ended their date, the evening would have been a total loss.

"Angelica, I sure hope we can go out again," Stan said as they sipped after-dinner drinks. "I'm going places, and you're the type of woman I need beside me."

"I don't know, Stan. I've been with some pretty powerful men in my life. You might say I'm a bit spoiled."

"I know about you and Nick Rollins," Stan replied calmly. "I also know that where he is right now is probably as far as he'll go."

He'd spoken this with authority. Angelica was intrigued. "Why on earth would you say that?"

"Because," Stan said, moving closer and lowering his voice. "I've just been hired by a very astute businessman who's working on a huge deal."

"How huge?"

"Millions."

"How many million?" In the circles Angelica traveled, *huge* was relative. Nick was worth about ten, twenty million, and she guessed Bastion, with the family's old money, was worth around thirty or more. So just hearing the word "million" didn't move Angelica. She said as much to Stan.

"What I'm sharing with you is in confidence, because I like you, Angelica. You're intelligent, beautiful, and you're not afraid to ask for what you want. This deal is with a group of business-men from China. It is an innovative concept in nightclubs—combining high-tech, top-of-the-line video games with great food, top-shelf drinks, and A-list entertainers. The kids in that country are going to go wild!"

Angelica asked more questions, and Stan patiently explained the venture to her. "I have to admit, it sounds fabulous," she said when he'd finished. "But I still don't understand what this has to do with Nick."

"The competition in getting this partnership with the men from China is now down to two groups. Nick is with the team of partners who are going to lose."

Angelica pulled on a silk nightgown and walked over to her laptop. *It's time to do a little homework,* she thought as she turned it on and waited for it to fire up. She'd agreed to give Stan a second date not be-cause she was interested in him, but because she wanted to meet the genius boss he'd bragged about. "Okay, Mr. Keith Bronson," she said aloud, while typing his name into a search engine, "let's see what your next love interest can find out about you."

26

Today was a big day for Tiffany. Her mother, the one and only Janice Matthews, had accepted an invitation from her daughter to eat lunch at Taste. Aside from having heard rave reviews about the city's newest restaurant, Janice had determined going there was the only way she'd get to see her always-working only child. She and a colleague were due to arrive at Hotel Le Sol around two—when the crush of the midweek lunch crowd would be slowing down. Tiffany wanted to make sure her mom and friend received superior, unhurried service. Chef Wang had agreed to let her prepare their lunches personally. While she now felt comfortable in the kitchen for the most part, today she was a nervous wreck.

"Need my help with anything?" Roger asked.

"Not right now, Roger, but if you can personally prep the vegetables later, that would be great."

Tiffany and Roger had become good friends as part of their trial-by-fire experiences. Roger prepped and was also a line cook whose work was fast yet methodical. He cared about the food he put on the customer's plate. Shortly after the restaurant opened, a catastrophe happened. Tiffany was cooking for an important group of clients on a tight schedule, an intricate lobster dish. She'd been so focused on getting the lobster to just the right consistency that the delicate cream sauce, made with a variety of freshly chopped herbs and shaved cheese, scorched. Roger had taken over a prep station, his blade moving so fast over a new group of herbs that one could hardly see it. He'd helped her prepare another batch of sauce in under fifteen minutes, which was still a record in the kitchen. They were friends from that day on.

When Janice and her associate, Barb, arrived, Tiffany made sure they were seated at Amber's station. Amber was an excellent waitress with a bubbly personality. On top of that she was very efficient, an important quality to a daughter who wanted the lunch to be perfect.

And it was. Tiffany sent out a complimentary scallop appetizer, followed by fragrant green salads. Janice's salmon and spinach fettuccini was just the right blend of textures and colors, complemented by a chilled Riesling. Barb ordered swordfish à la Siciliana, a hearty steak topped with an almost sinful tomato sauce mixture of raisins, onions, garlic, olives, pine nuts, and capers. Just before Amber was to offer them the dessert menu, Tiffany walked to their table.

"Hey, Mom," she said, leaning down to give her a hug.

"Hello, Tiffany."

After Janice introduced Tiffany to her friend and business associate, Tiffany continued. "I hope you've enjoyed your dining experience at Taste." She said this casually, playfully, but her heart was in her chest. Until now, she hadn't really realized how important her mother's approval was. Her parents had never validated her choice of career, but if her mother saw just how good she was at the job she loved—Tiffany reasoned—then maybe she and her dad would come to support her career choice.

"I was just telling your mother that this was the best piece of fish I've ever put in my mouth. And you'd better believe I've eaten a piece or two in my lifetime." Plus-size Barb put her hand on an ample stomach to underscore the point. "This was excellent, Tiffany. And you cooked it?"

"Yes, I prepared the entire meal for you ladies, including the pasta and the sauces, which were made fresh, from scratch."

"You made the fettuccini?" Janice asked.

Tiffany nodded.

"And that exquisite Alfredo sauce?"

Tiffany smiled broadly. "Yes, I did."

"Well, I must say, Tiffany, I'm impressed. That pasta was delicious, girl, and the smoked salmon nestled in that sauce . . ." Janice didn't finish the sentence, just put her hands to her mouth and shook her head.

"I'm sure your mother is very proud of you, Tiffany. She says you hope to own your own restaurant someday."

Tiffany's eyes widened in surprise. In an unguarded moment, she'd shared this dream with her mother. Her dream of cooking for others was the last thing she thought Janice would share with anyone, particularly someone in her world of technology.

That Janice shared this information in a positive way meant the world to Tiffany.

"Yes, I'd love to operate a small, five-star restaurant with an eclectic menu of healthy yet tasteful food choices. The experience I'm receiving here is invaluable."

The three ladies continued to share small talk as dessert was served. Fortunately, at three o'clock, Tiffany could afford to take the break. Her mother was in the middle of telling Tiffany that her father was planning another business trip to LA when she became distracted and her words died. . . .

Before Tiffany could turn to see what had so completely snatched her mother's attention, Nick was at her side, giving her shoulder a light squeeze. "Hey, chef," he said softly, his warm gaze belying the formal greeting. "Ladies," he said to Janice and Barb.

"Nick, uh, hi." Nick's unexpected presence had surprised her; the physical contact made her uncomfortable.

"Why, hello!" Barb flirted, not even trying to hide her attraction.

Janice's expression was a question mark as she looked from Tiffany to Nick.

"Mom, Barb, this is Nick Rollins. He, um . . ."

"I help run the place," Nick continued smoothly, shaking first Janice's hand and then Barb's. "And for you," he said to Janice, "a huge thank you is in order."

"What do you have to thank me for?"

"This is a very special woman that you brought into the world." Nick squeezed Tiffany's shoulder again. "And I'm sure you now know . . . a fabulous chef."

"Now I definitely know," Janice said, beaming with pride.

"I was on my way to speak with Chef Wang, but saw you ladies and had to stop. I immediately recognized the resemblance between you and Tiffany and now know where she got her good looks."

Janice's eyes raised in surprise as her skin warmed in appreciation. "She takes after both me and her dad."

"And that's a very good thing. It's been a pleasure. And please, accept the meal you've just experienced as my gift. But don't leave out dessert. The choices are sinful and not to be missed." Nick gave Tiffany's arm a final squeeze, winked at her mother, and was gone.

"Is that the man you met in Italy, Tiffany?"

Tiffany groaned inwardly. *Here comes the rebuke.* "Yes, Mom, but . . ."

"The boss you told me about on the phone, and are obviously still dating?"

"Mom, it's not what . . ."

"I think I know *exactly* what it is, and regarding those detrimental interoffice liaisons that I told you about? I take back everything that I have *ever* said. So, he's the general manager? And a handsome, courteous one to boot? Yes, darlin', you just handle your business and tell your mother to mind her own."

27

Angelica fixed Stan with a come-hither smile, flinging back her locks seductively. She took in his thinning blond hair, watery blue eyes, hawkish nose, and nonexistent lips. It was all she could do to flirt convincingly, but Angelica plowed forward because the end justified the means.

"I've always been interested in business." She placed her toffee-colored hand on top of Stan's freckle-blotched one that rested on the tabletop. The contrast in their skin color was nothing compared to that of their personalities. Stan was quiet, 5'9", a brainiac, who'd lost most of the family fortune in a day-trading scheme gone bad. It had happened almost a decade ago and he'd been trying to recoup the losses ever since. Angelica, on the other hand, considered herself a winner who only dated those who stayed on top.

Angelica got up, walked to Stan's side of the tucked-away restaurant booth, and slid in beside him. "I can tell you're good at what you do," she said, leaning toward him so that her breast touched his arm. "One of the best. I'm sure I could learn a thing or two from just, you know, being around you."

"Well," Stan stuttered, blushing at the praise. "I'm nowhere near where I want to be, or where I was, but like I told you the other night, that's all about to change."

"How is that deal going? Making any progress?"

"It's going beautifully. The Chinese partners are hoping to have the first ten clubs opened by 2012, expanding to one hundred clubs in ten years. It's an aggressive plan, but that country has the people and the money to make it a very doable goal."

"So, when is your next trip to China? Do men travel with their wives or . . . significant others? Because if so, I'd like to travel with you, make you look good." Angelica was dead serious, but defused her comment with a brilliant smile.

"Darling, you can come with me anywhere." Stan hadn't missed the envious looks cast his way when he and Angelica had walked into Stanfords. She looked darn good on his arm, he thought, improved his status and his stature. "Having you by my side would be terrific, Angelica."

She licked her lips seductively and kissed his cheek. Ever since she'd researched Stan's boss, Keith Bronson, Angelica's attitude toward the blue-eyed blondie had changed. Not her opinion: She still thought he was a trust-fund wimp, but he offered another kind of value. She'd never think of going to bed with him, but she acted in a way that made *him* think it was just a matter of time. By the time he found out otherwise, she would have used him and gone.

"So when's your next function?"

"There's a little gathering tonight, as a matter of fact. I hadn't thought to go to it but if you want to, I'm game."

"I absolutely want to," she gushed. "Now, what kind of gathering? Will there be food there? Because I'm starved."

An hour later, Stan and Angelica stepped into the foyer of a Holmby Hills mansion. A large chandelier glistened overhead and the sound of ivories being tinkled wafted from somewhere beyond. As the doorman was taking their coats, the hostess came forward, arms outstretched.

"Stan, darling," she said, offering air kisses to his cheeks. "It's about time you accepted an invite. And I can see why," the effervescent, heavily yet attractively made-up brunette continued. "You've got someone to show off." She winked at Angelica and offered a warm handshake.

After assuaging their appetites at the lavishly furnished buffet, Stan and Angelica worked the room. Stan introduced her to a variety of professionals: a bank president, CEOs, real estate moguls, a politician. Halfway through the soiree, they stopped in front of a distinguished-looking man, handsome in a stately kind of way. He and Stan exchanged cordial greetings before Stan turned to introduce his date.

"Angelica, I'd like you to meet one of the finest businessmen I know, Keith Bronson. Keith, this is Angelica King."

"It's a pleasure," Angelica said softly, accepting Keith's handshake.

Their eyes met and held as Keith covered the hand he held with his other one and squeezed. "The pleasure is mine."

28

"I can't believe it's been five years since I've seen him." Tiffany eyed herself critically in the mirror above her fireplace before joining Joy on the couch. She reached over for Tuffy and smashed him to her chest. Joy eyed her friend with concern. "Calm down, Tiff. You don't want to work yourself up into a panic attack."

"You're right, I don't." Both women knew it was circumstances like these, when Tiffany felt claustrophobic, or in this case extremely nervous, that could bring one on. Tiffany took a deep breath, loosened her hold on the bear, and continued. "Here I am at twenty-eight years old, acting like I'm five. Some father/daughter relationship, huh?"

"Better some than none at all," Joy countered as she munched on a chicken finger Tiffany had made. "My daddy could walk right by me and I wouldn't even know it."

Both ladies became quiet as they pondered this unfortunate commonality. Not having fathers in their lives was one of the things Joy and Tiffany had found they had in common when they met at a suburban school during seventh grade. They'd both been part of just a handful of African Americans in that environment, bussed in as part of the nation's continued attempt at integration and cross-cultural relationships. Along with the absentee father status, they also shared a love for In-N-Out Burger, Michael Jackson, Kris Kross, and fellow seventh-grader heartthrob Mario Vasquez. Their anthem was Hammer's "2 Legit 2 Quit," outfit of choice: baggy pants, bright-colored T-shirts and suspenders like their girl-group idols TLC. Tiffany had grown up in a protective environment, not allowed to play in the South Central streets her mother deemed unsafe. Few children lived in Grand's View Park neighborhood, where she could ride her bike up and down the street. So much alone time in those early years gave Tiffany a shy, almost withdrawn personality, the exact opposite of the boisterous, mischievous Joy, who waylaid Tiffany in the hallway the second week of school.

"Ooh, girl, your braids are the bomb. Are those beads heavy, though, 'cause I can't have my hair falling out."

Before Tiffany could form a response, Joy had plowed on, rolling her eyes at a beautiful, curvy redhead walking in the opposite direction, with an equally handsome, high-top-fade wearing football jock.

"Honey, these 'itches around here better back the bump up 'cause ain't too many brothahs even go to this school. Ooh, but I like him, though." She slowed down as they passed the locker of an earring-wearing Latino. *"Yo hablo español, papi,"* she flirted. The boy, who they later learned was named Mario and whom Joy would date from eighth to eleventh grade, showed a set of even, pearly white teeth as he smiled at her.

"Shoot, I can't stand Mr. Calvin's evil ass," Joy had continued as they kept walking. "Those math equations are stupid hard. Good thing I'm sitting by the smartest boy in class, 'cause I'm sure going to copy off his test, you watch. Hey, what time is your lunch period? You should meet me by the gym 'cause me and some seniors are going to ditch that crap they call food in the cafeteria and head to In-N-Out. Wanna come?"

"Yeah, I guess so." And with those four words, the only ones in what was an otherwise one-way conversation, Joy and Tiffany became best friends.

Tiffany's ringing telephone shook both women from their ruminations. "It's Dad," Tiffany said after she'd peeped at the ID. "Probably calling to cancel as per usual. Hey, Dad."

"Hello, Tiffany. I'm just calling to make sure we're on for lunch. I'm in Beverly Hills. We can either meet here or I can come toward Culver City. Which do you prefer?"

"Why don't we meet in the middle, maybe Jerry's Deli?"

"Why don't we choose something a bit more up-scale, honey? I haven't seen you in five years, let's make it a celebration of sorts."

"Okay."

"Tell you what. I need to take this call, make another one, and then I'll phone you back with the place. Work for you?"

"Works for me, Dad."

"Tiffany, honey, I'm looking forward to it."

"Me, too."

An hour later, Tiffany sat across from her dad at Chart House, a medium-priced restaurant with marina views. He devoured his crab-stuffed mushrooms while she nibbled on seared, peppered ahi tuna, served with mustard, ginger, and wasabi. It was prepared very well, but Tiffany didn't have much of an appetite.

"You look good, Tiffany," Keith said, for the second or third time. "You're twenty-eight years old, but I still can't get over the fact that you're a grown woman!"

"Time flies, I guess," Tiffany said softly.

Keith put down his fork. "I feel horrible about it being so long since we've seen each other, Tiffany, about so many things, really. Too late, I'm realizing how neglectful I was to you, and to your mother while she and I were married."

"Can't change the past." Tiffany shrugged. "I came out all right."

"Better than all right, according to Janice. She told me about her trip to your restaurant, and how excellent you are at what you do. I'd like to experience your cooking sometime."

Tiffany snorted. "What's with the change in attitude? Sasha leaving you for a younger man has you seeing the error of your ways?" When Janice had told Tiffany about her dad's latest separation, she'd immediately assumed that that was the reason for his sudden change of heart where she was concerned—his loneliness brought on a case of the guilts. She hadn't intended to speak so harshly, but since it was an honest question to which she wanted to hear the answer, she let it hang in the air instead of apologizing.

Keith paused while the waiter delivered his lobster bisque and Tiffany's chopped spinach salad. "I know I was pretty hard on you about your career choice. It's only because I wanted what I thought was best for you at the time. You'd graduated with honors, a degree in business. I wanted you to work with me, follow in my footsteps.

"Now I realize that was my dream, not yours, that maybe you knew a little more about what you wanted to do than your old man. And yes, Sasha walking out on me has me taking stock of my life, and what's important." Keith then told her about the wedding he attended, and how seeing Tim with his daughter made Keith miss Tiffany. "You've always mattered to me, Tiffany, even though I wasn't around to show it. Yes, I worked for me, for the success and prestige, but I also worked to secure your future. My heart was in the right place even if my actions weren't. I can't undo what happened in the past, but I'd really like to try and establish a relationship with you. Do you think you can forgive me, and let us work on that?"

"I can try, Dad. But you've said some pretty mean things to me over the years. Those words don't just wash off. Nor does the fact that you weren't there when I was growing up and really needed you."

"I'm trying to be here now." Keith reached into his suit pocket for a handkerchief and gave it to his daughter, whose cheeks were stained with tears. He took a deep breath and continued. "Honey, I apologize for those hurtful, unkind things I said in anger. They were immature and stupid, spoken by a man who's been self-centered for far too long. If I could take them back I would, but I can't. I can only try my best to do right by you now. Will you help me do that?"

Tiffany nodded and finished off her salad. With every word of Keith's apologies, her appetite grew.

Through courses of parmesan-and-cracker-encrusted snapper, topped with lump crab and shallot butter on a bed of rice pilaf, tenderloin medallions and sweet potato rings, Dungeness crab clusters and pan-seared sea scallops, Tiffany and Keith began the tedious process of rebuilding their relationship. Keith shared parts of himself that Tiffany was hearing for the first time: how he grew up poor and lacking in Detroit's mean streets, his own father an absent figure from his life. He came of age in the turbulent sixties to a soundtrack dominated by Motown. When it became clear that he wasn't going to follow in the footsteps of crooners Marvin Gaye, Smokey Robinson, or the Four Tops' lead singer, Levi Stubbs, his attention turned toward world events. He threw his share of Molotov cocktails in the '65 riots, the same year Malcolm X was assassinated, and was an Afro-wearing, dashiki-dressing thirteen-year-old when Martin Luther King was killed in 1968. By the time he was seventeen, many of his classmates were on drugs or in prison, and if it hadn't been for a certain high school teacher who saw Keith's potential, he might have ended up there, too.

"He helped me to focus, work hard to keep my GPA up. That's how I earned a scholarship, and what brought me to California, and your mother."

"Dad, I just can't picture you wearing a dashiki with your fist in the air."

"Baby girl, your old man was the stuff back then.

You should have seen me in my Superfly suits and platform shoes! I'm telling you, your pops was outta sight!"

Tiffany laughed at the thought and soon Keith joined her.

"Your aunt has tons of pictures from that era. Come to think of it, your mom does, too. Ask her about them the next time you're home."

"Oh, I will most definitely do that. I don't think I'll believe it until I see it!"

Their conversation had started out tentatively, but by the time they split a decadent slice of hot chocolate lava cake, its chocolate liqueur molten center covered with vanilla ice cream, warm chocolate sauce, and Heath bar crunch, Tiffany and Keith had discovered they were more alike than different, and that after all was said and done, they might be able to not only love each other, but to like each other as well.

It was nine P.M. Keith sat in his hotel suite quietly sipping a snifter of premium Courvoisier. He felt good, better than he had in a long time. Thinking back to his time with Tiffany that afternoon, he laughed at her dry sense of humor. *I can't believe how much of me I see in her. How could I have missed that before?* As Keith walked to the minibar to replenish his drink, he heard a light knock on his door. He walked toward the sound, pulling down his V-neck cashmere sweater and straightening out his gabardine slacks as he did so. He didn't have to look through the peephole to know who it was, but he did so anyway. His smile was bright as he opened the door.

"Hello, Angelica."

"Keith." Angelica held a model's pose, showing off her coral, stretch silk Nicole Miller dress, tailored to fit her body like a glove.

Keith reached for Angelica's hand and led her inside. "You look beautiful. But then again, I'm sure you know that."

"I've been told a time or two," Angelica replied playfully.

"Something to drink?"

"Grand Marnier, if you have it, on the rocks." Angelica continued into the suite and stopped at the floor-to-ceiling windows with a view of Westside Los Angeles all the way to downtown.

Keith joined her at the window and gave her the drink. "What shall we toast to?"

"Hmm . . . to new friendships, perhaps," Angelica said as she took a step toward him.

"What about Stan? I thought you two were friends."

"We are, but that's strictly platonic."

"Is that what you want this to be, another platonic relationship?"

"Hardly," Angelica said. She boldly stepped up to Keith, who immediately embraced her with his free hand. He ran a casual hand down her back and cupped her backside. Angelica licked his lips, reached down, and stroked his manhood. "When it comes to this relationship, Keith Bronson," she breathed huskily, "I think we both want *exactly* the same thing."

29

Tiffany reclined on the lounger by Nick's pool and tried to relax. It wasn't easy. Not when she'd vowed that this visit would be strictly platonic, yet felt her insides quiver as she watched Nick swim. The muscles in his arms, legs and back rippled as he sliced through the water. *Damn.* Fluctuating feelings aside, Tiffany was glad to be here with Nick, glad she'd accepted his invite to join him for a casual dinner. Especially when he said he'd cook. Tiffany smiled, remembering the conversation.

"When is your next day off?" Nick asked, after Tiffany had answered her phone and they'd exchanged opening pleasantries.

"Tomorrow, why?"

"Because I want you to come over."

"Look, Nick—"

"No, Tiffany, you look. I want to see you, and at the risk of sounding incredibly arrogant, I believe you want to see me too. I miss our time together, and it's obvious you could use a break. I had one of my managers bring up the crew schedule. You're working too hard."

"It's what I love, Nick."

"Well, you know what they say about all work and no play . . ."

"Geez, what is it with that line? You sound like Joy."

"Who's Joy?"

"My best friend. I've mentioned her before. She used that same tired cliché."

"Joy sounds like a smart woman, and a good friend. Come over for dinner tomorrow, Tiffany. You won't have to do anything but relax, and unwind."

"Oh, really? So our meal is being catered? Or do you have a chef?"

"I'll be the chef tomorrow."

"You?" Tiffany laughed. "Seeing you in an apron is worth the price of admission."

"So you'll come?"

"For dinner and conversation, nothing more. And it needs to be early. I only have one day off and want to get a good night's sleep."

When I'm finished with you, you'll sleep like a baby. "Okay, then, what about five o'clock? Better yet, make it four. You'll miss rush hour traffic and can take a dip in the pool."

"Four sounds good, but I'll pass on the swim. I have a hair appointment in the morning."

"That's fine. But bring your suit. I want to see some brown sugar."

"Nick . . ."

"Baby, you know you're fine. I can look, can't I?"

"Look, but don't touch."

"If that's what you want."

"It's what I want."

"Fine, see you then."

So here she was, and so far, Nick had been a man of his word. Tiffany had not lifted a finger. On the contrary, she'd felt like a princess as Nick insisted she rest on the lounger while he plied her with wine, cheese, and fruit. And aside from a brief hug and chaste kiss, there'd been no physical contact either. But as she watched Nick walk up the steps on the other side of the pool and then turn to come toward her, she knew that him keeping his hands off her was the last thing she wanted.

"Ready to eat?" Nick asked, as he reached for the towel on the lounger next to Tiffany and began drying off.

"I don't know," Tiffany said, still not convinced Nick's food would be edible. "What are we having?"

"Ha! Still don't believe I can cook, huh. Girl, I can throw down! I know you don't want to swim, but why don't you at least enjoy the Jacuzzi while I finish our meal."

"It'll sweat out my hair, Nick."

"Okay, baby, then just relax. Dinner will be served shortly." He bowed formally, and winked at Tiffany before walking back into the house.

Just under an hour later, Nick and Tiffany dined on swordfish burgers, organic root chips, an awesome salad, and chilled Chardonnay.

"This burger is amazing. Did you buy these at Whole Foods?"

"I had the fish filets delivered, and then assembled the burgers so they could marinate overnight."

"You made this swordfish burger from scratch? But it's seasoned so well, the spices and . . ."

"I told you I could cook."

"What kind of salad is this?" Tiffany asked, around a mouthful.

"A 'whatever' salad."

"I've never heard of such."

"You haven't? It's easy to make. You just open up your refrigerator and whatever is in there goes into the mix."

After poking through the salad and discovering romaine lettuce, cooked spinach, corn, black beans, tomatoes, onions, rice, raisins, sprouts, pine nuts and items she couldn't identify, Tiffany found the name to be appropriate. "It's good . . . what kind of dressing is this?"

"A secret kind."

"Oh, please."

"You're the cook, figure it out."

Tiffany took a sip of lemon water and cleansed her palate. She took her finger, wiped it around the rim of the bowl where drops of dressing clung, and tasted slowly. "Olive oil, balsamic vinegar, some type of mustard for emulsion, spices . . ."

"What kind of spices?"

Tiffany wiped the bowl again. "Cinnamon for sure . . . that's different, but nice. A little ginger maybe, and some coriander."

"You're good."

". . . poppy seeds, and what's making it sweet . . . agave?"

"Your finger."

"C'mon, Nick, I'm serious."

"So am I." He laughed as Tiffany pouted. "Yeah, it's agave."

"What about the other ingredients, was I right?"

"Just about."

"What did I miss?"

"Woman, are you trying to make my mama turn over in her grave? Because that's what would happen if I told you the whole recipe!"

"I didn't know your mother cooked."

"Not just her, but all the neighborhood mothers. That's how they often passed time on the base, hanging out in the kitchen and cooking up all kinds of dishes. My mother got pretty good at dressings, sauces, even jellies and jams. I totally ignored them, or so I thought. But I obviously picked up the love by osmosis."

Conversation flowed easily as Nick and Tiffany finished their early dinner. "That was delicious, Nick. Thank you." Tiffany stood, and reached for his empty plate.

"Sit down, woman. Guadalupe will clean up."

"Oh, right," Tiffany said as she sat down. "You have a housekeeper."

"Yes, and you're not doing any work today, remember?"

Tiffany smiled. "As much as I enjoy cooking, it felt good to be served."

"Service isn't over, *bella*," Nick said, rising. "I hope you left room for dessert." He held out his hand. "Come."

Tiffany slipped into the jean skirt she'd worn over her swimsuit and soon joined Nick in the great room. This room, with its bold colors, abstract art and cushiony, oversized furniture, stood in refreshing contrast to the formality of the other rooms. She sank into a tan, suede-covered sectional, placed her bare feet beneath her and picked up her dessert bowl.

"Yum, you can never go wrong with chocolate," she said, before taking a bite of chocolate chip cheese-cake. It melted in her mouth. Tiffany looked point-edly at Nick. "You didn't make this."

Nick laughed. "No, this is Donny's handiwork." Donny was Taste's prized pastry chef.

"I should have known. It's delicious."

They continued chatting while eating dessert. Tiffany plied Nick with humorous stories about the war zone otherwise known as the Taste kitchen, while Nick briefed Tiffany on a new, huge business venture.

"You sound really excited about it, Nick," Tiffany said sincerely, but with a tinge of sadness.

"I am, but it doesn't sound like you're too happy for me."

"No, really, it sounds great. Your enthusiasm just then reminded me of my dad, that's all. I can re-member being a little girl and hearing him talking on the phone about this or that business deal. He'd sound so excited! I'd run into the room, wanting to be a part of it all, a part of his world. He'd shoo me out of course, and later, when I'd ask him about it, he'd say, 'just work, baby girl.' And then, he'd be out the door again."

Nick poured them both a cup of decaf coffee from the urn on the tray he'd brought in earlier. "How is your dad?" he asked, knowing he was stepping into sensitive waters. "I know you guys talked recently. Have you spoken to him again?"

"I saw him just the other day, for the first time in almost five years." Tiffany's voice was barely above a whisper. Unconsciously, she withdrew into herself, wrapping her arms around her body and nestling against the sectional arm.

Nick reached over and eased Tiffany's leg out from under her. He began softly massaging her foot. "That must have been hard."

"It was, at first." Tiffany recounted parts of the conversation she'd had with her father, including the new things she'd learned about him. "We're a lot alike," she concluded. "I'd never really realized that before."

Nick let that statement hang in the air as he motioned for Tiffany to place her other foot in his lap, and he quietly continued to massage her feet. His hands itched to move higher, but he knew that such a move—caressing calves, thighs, and beyond—would likely send an already skittish Tiffany running for home. Nick knew that touching her at all was pushing it, so he let well enough alone. If there was a move to a more intimate encounter, she would have to make it.

Tiffany leaned back against the couch, relaxing as Nick massaged her feet. "That feels good, Nick," she whispered. *Wait, did I say that out loud?* She'd been thinking it from the moment he touched her, and once he started massaging her feet, the rest of her body had cried out for attention.

"I can do your calves too, if you'd like. You're on your feet for hours every day, and that affects your calves, knees, everything. That has to take a toll after a while."

Tiffany remembered how good her legs had felt

after Picchu's massage. "I guess that will be okay," she said, closing her eyes.

Nick finished massaging her heels, and then slowly slid his hands to the meaty part of her calves. His strokes were slow and deliberate. He kneaded her muscles, adding just the right amount of pressure to release the kinks. Tiffany's moan was barely audible, but Nick heard it. He dared move his hands over her knees, to her thighs, and continued the massage.

Stop him, Tiffany. Stop him now! But she couldn't. His hands felt so good, and her pussy longed to be massaged as well. She squirmed, remembering how his mouth felt on her, how his dick felt inside her. She moaned again, louder this time, and shifted her body slightly.

You want it, brown sugar, and I want to give it to you, baby. But you'll have to tell me. Nick eased his hands back down to her calves, and rubbed slowly to her feet. Then he stopped, and gently lifted her feet off of his lap. "Does that feel better?"

"Much better," Tiffany said, forcing herself to a sitting position. Her stubborn logic warred with her sizzling body. *Don't stop touching me, Nick. I want to feel you* . . . Tiffany reached for her coffee cup. "Is the coffee still warm?"

Nick nodded. He leaned toward her, poured the coffee, and placed the carafe back on the tray. Tiffany stared at his large hands, at the strong fingers that gripped the pot handle, as if mesmerized. She wanted something hot, but it wasn't coffee. Logic snapped, and senses took over. She put down the cup, leaned into Nick, and seared him with a kiss.

Nick returned the kiss, but kept his hands by his side.

Tiffany wanted more. She straddled him, and kissed him again. Nick devoured her mouth, and hardened beneath her. Tiffany ground herself against his shaft, then reached for his arms and put them around her. "Nick," she breathed into his mouth.

"Yes, love?"

"Ooh, please . . ." She placed her hand on his manhood.

"What do you want?" Nick slowly rotated his hips, pushing his hardness against the bikini bottoms under Tiffany's skirt.

In an uncharacteristic act of boldness, Tiffany reached behind her and unfastened her top. Her heavy breasts sprang from their confines, her hardened nipples ready for sucking.

"Tell me what you want, brown sugar," Nick said huskily. "I will only do what you tell me to."

"I want you to touch me," she whispered.

"Where?" Nick placed his hands on her waist, but didn't move them.

Tiffany shifted her body and pushed her nipple between his lips. Nick hungrily twirled the areola with his tongue before taking as much of her as he could into his mouth. *His tongue feels so good! Oh my God* . . . Tiffany's nana tingled as she remembered just how good his tongue felt in other places.

"Nick, I want us to, I want you to . . ."

"What, baby?"

"Lick me . . . there . . ."

Nick smiled against Tiffany's skin. "Where?"

"Here," Tiffany cried softly, taking his hand and placing it under her skirt.

"But you said you didn't want me to touch you like that . . ."

Tiffany jumped off Nick's lap abruptly.

Oh, hell, Nick thought. *Time to run away.*

But running was the last thing on Tiffany's mind. She knew what Nick was doing, and understood why he was doing it. She had rebuffed his advances and insisted on a platonic relationship. But now she was getting ready to show this man that it was a woman's prerogative to change her mind. She hurriedly shed her skirt and bikini bottoms, lay on the couch and spread her legs. "Here, okay?" she said, pointing toward the area she'd decided to have waxed after getting a manicure/pedicure. I want *your* tongue *here!*"

Nick chuckled, pleasantly surprised by Tiffany's brazenness. He wasted no time in fulfilling her request, stripping off his shorts and then burying his head between her legs. Before long, Tiffany's moans turned to loud whimpers as Nick orally plucked her feminine flower. He placed his hands under her butt and lifted her for better access, teasing her crevice with a long, strong finger as he tongued her folds, tickled her nub, and then pushed his tongue as deep as he could inside her. Tiffany's body began to shake with the oncoming orgasm. As she reached the peak and cried out, Nick spread her wide, plunged inside, and took them both on a raw, erotic journey.

Later, Tiffany cuddled next to Nick. A fire burned in the bedroom fireplace, and Sade's sultry alto filled the companionable silence.

"We didn't use a condom," Tiffany said.

Nick turned to face her. "I know. You have nothing to worry about. I was tested before, during and after my break-up with Angelica, and have only been with you since then."

This fact surprised Tiffany, but she remained silent.

"What about you?" Nick asked.

"I've been tested too."

"Have you been with anybody else since . . ." Nick wasn't sure he wanted to know the answer. The longer she hesitated, the more convinced he became that he absolutely did *not* want to know.

"I haven't been with anybody else, Nick. And, truthfully? I don't want to be with anyone else."

Nick's smile was broad as he pulled Tiffany into his arms. With that simple statement, Tiffany took up a little more space in his heart. "I want to spend Christmas with you," he said, as the pulsating Brazilian tempos of Gil Gilberto replaced the Sade soundtrack. "I want us to fly to Italy for New Year's, and visit our favorite chef. Rome is magical during the holidays. You'll love it."

"Sounds beautiful, Nick, but I'll be working. Chef has already told us no vacations for kitchen staff under after January tenth."

Nick pulled Tiffany closer. "That statement doesn't apply to you. You have connections. If Li doesn't want to give you the time off, I'll fire him."

Tiffany laughed. "You wouldn't."

"Messing with my brown sugar? I'd drop his ass like a hot potato."

"I like Chef Wang, and am learning a lot from him."

"More than Emilio?"

"Chef Riatoli is still my favorite. I'd love to return to Italy someday," Tiffany continued, after a pause. "I was working so hard that I barely saw the city. Can I take a Rome rain check, perhaps?"

"Absolutely."

Tiffany nestled into Nick's chest. It felt good to be

back in his arms. She refused to think past the moment, to examine potential implications or complications, and instead focused on how happy she was right now.

"I want you to spend the night," Nick said. "I haven't had enough of you."

"You're insatiable," Tiffany responded. "Sex-crazed. In fact, do you know that every time I've been alone with you, I've ended up in your bed?"

"Well, maybe," Nick drawled, slowly twirling her nipple into a hardened peak, "that's because," he slowly slid his middle finger into her heat, "in my bed is exactly where you belong."

30

Nick twiddled the straw in his freshly squeezed orange juice, wondering for the umpteenth time why he'd agreed to come here. It was bad enough that he was in LA during the holiday season, the first time in years that he hadn't been overseas or on an island. But he'd wanted to bring the new year in with Tiffany. So here he sat, in the Beverly Hills Four Seasons, wondering what he'd been thinking when he drove down.

This is a mistake. He pulled a twenty from his wallet and was just getting up when Angelica rounded the corner.

"Am I late?" She stopped and looked at her watch.

"No, I just . . ."

". . . concluded that you didn't want to meet me and was just about to leave."

Nick laughed. "Guilty as charged."

"I won't keep you long, Nick, and I'm really happy you agreed to meet me." Angelica sat in the plush brown chair facing Nick and made eye contact with the waiter. He approached at once. "An olive martini, please."

"Right away, ma'am." The waiter left and returned moments later with her drink and a crystal bowl of gourmet mixed nuts.

"You look well, Nick."

"Thanks, Angelica." He looked at his watch.

"I wanted to end this year on a good note, by apologizing for my unscrupulous behavior at your hotel. I guess I went a little crazy when I saw you moving on without me. Quite an adjustment, you know?"

Nick remained silent, remembering Angelica's lip-wiping performance in the restaurant, the one he'd later learned was for Tiffany's benefit.

"You'll be happy to know that I've finally gotten it together and have truly moved on. I've met a wonderful gentleman, and we're enjoying each other. It's new . . . don't know where it's headed, but . . . it's nice having someone in my life again."

"I'm happy to hear that, Angelica, and I accept your apology. I only want the best for you."

"Yeah, me, too."

They sat silent a moment, and then Nick spoke. "So who is the lucky guy?"

"A businessman from Chicago, but he has business here as well."

"I see."

"In some ways, he reminds me of you. Has the same sort of drive, tenacity . . . not that I was trying to . . . I mean . . . I met him at a dinner party." Angelica wasn't usually nervous around any man, but Nick's penetrating stare gave her the shivers. It was important that she play her hand just right. She had to, if her plan was to succeed. "What about you? Still with . . . *the help* . . . the woman who works for you?"

"I am."

"Is it . . . are you guys serious?"

"I don't think you really want to hear the details about Tiffany and me."

"No, I guess not."

Nick looked at his watch again.

Angelica finished her drink. "Well, I've said what I came to say. I'm sure you've got things to do, so I'll be leaving. I hope that I've cleared the air between us. The LA business circle can be a small one. If we run into each other, I hope we can be cordial."

"I don't waste time holding on to hard feelings, Angelica, you know that."

"Yes, I know. It's one of the many things I admire about you."

Nick stood. So did Angelica. "Oh, there's one more thing. If you talk it over with Tiffany, and she has no problem with it, I would love to patronize your restaurant again. My guy has heard about it, and I'd rather not have to explain that I've been barred for stalking the owner." Angelica laughed. "I'll be on my best behavior, promise."

"I'll ask. If it's okay with her, then it's fine with me."

"Thanks, Nick. I really appreciate it. I'm happy for you, really, I mean that. Can I get a hug for the holidays?"

Nick hugged Angelica briefly, as a father would a daughter. "Good-bye, Angelica."

"Good-bye, Nick." She sat back down in her chair and watched the man she used to love walk out of the bar area. He'd loved her, too, once, she remembered, so very thoroughly. *But now he's with another woman. And I don't like it.* Angelica ordered another martini, requested the bar menu, and plotted her next move in using Keith Bronson to help ruin Nick Rollins. Nobody broke Angelica King's heart and got away with it. Angelica's eye twitched as she sipped her second martini. *Nobody.*

31

Tiffany worked at a furious pace. She thought things would let up after the holidays, but the restaurant remained full with a month-long waiting list. Tiffany readjusted the scarf tied around her lengthening tresses and concentrated on an original scallop dish. She'd expanded the menu selection from Chef Riatoli's asparagus delight and created several of her own. Today she was fixing a bacon-wrapped concoction cooked in a coconut oil/tamari/agave blend and seasoned with fresh ginger, lemongrass, white pepper, and a hint of saffron. A dozen at a time were then placed on large square platters sporting an oriental-inspired symbol drawn with some of the pan drippings and offered free by handsome, white-coated waiters to waiting diners in the bar area as an *amuse-bouche*. The idea of offering this bite-sized hors d'oeuvre to reservation holders having drinks in the bar had been Tiffany's idea, and was a huge success. Patrons had written letters praising the classy move, and Nick was impressed and pleased. After showing one such correspondence to Tiffany, Chef Wang had given her a curt head nod and uttered a single word—"good." Tiffany had almost fallen over at the rare verbal praise.

"How's that steak working?" Tiffany asked Roger.

"Coming up, Chef!" Roger responded. Chef Wang was taking his first days off in the form of a three-day vacation, leaving Tiffany in charge of the kitchen for the first time. Any anxiety she'd felt about this responsibility had been quickly relieved as the workers treated her with the same respect and deference they would have given Chef Wang. He'd picked a dedicated, top-notch team. In a world that often had a high rate of turnover, not one kitchen or wait-staff employee had left. This restaurant was a plum place to work, and everyone knew it.

"Farah, we need to finish that risotto."

"It's ready, Chef."

Tiffany finished the last of the scallops and moved over to lift a lobster claw from its boiling confines. She placed it on a plate, removed the meat, and filled the bottom of the shell with the creamy risotto. After replacing the meat, she drizzled it with a citrus-infused butter, another of her creations. She decorated the plate with fried sage leaves and placed it steaming on the counter. "Order up! Serve it quickly!"

"Yes, Chef!"

Tiffany went right to work on the next dish, dreaming about the trip to Italy that she and Nick were going to take at the end of January—two weeks away.

"Chef." Amber walked into the kitchen, careful of the handles, knives, and other potentially dangerous utensils scattered about. She knew how quickly the team worked in back; one had to keep their wits about them.

"Your father's here."

Dad? What's he doing here? Then Tiffany remembered the phone call she'd gotten right before her shift started. She recognized his number and had made a mental note to call him back first chance she got. She was still waiting on that chance. Unfortunately, her father had come at the height of the dinner hour. Talking to him would have to wait.

"Tell him it's pretty busy right now," Tiffany panted, checking on a delicate white sauce with one hand while she fished buckwheat penne rigate from a pot with her other one. She threw a handful of large prawns and fresh herbs into the pot and gave the mix another stir. She then plated the pasta, covered it with the sauce, and sprinkled the entire dish with freshly shaved parmesan reggiano, pearl onions, and capers. "Order up!"

Amber checked on other tables as she made her way back to Tiffany's father. After delivering his daughter's message, she asked if they were ready to order.

"What will you have, Angelica?"

Angelica looked at Amber. "What do you recommend?"

"Well, everything Tiffany cooks is amazing, but the salmon, scallop, and lobster dishes are the most popular. Oh, and her filet mignon dish is to die for—that gets ordered a lot as well."

After placing their orders, Keith and Angelica settled back and awaited the first course. He'd never admit it, but after vowing to not get serious ever again, he was falling hard and fast for this woman. Finally, he'd found someone who was everything he wanted: beautiful, independent, driven, and smart. And in bed . . . he'd never been with someone whose sexual appetite was so voracious. She could run rings around Sasha, even though she was five years older than his soon to be ex. He'd had to stock his shelves with Viagra just so he could keep up!

Angelica smiled at Keith. She slid off her sandal and discreetly ran her foot up his leg. In the two months since they'd been dating, things had progressed brilliantly, just the way she wanted. She'd had no such notion when she first put the plan in motion, but now she wouldn't be surprised if summer came with a marriage proposal. She'd already spent considerable time in his posh condominium on Lake Michigan Avenue, in the same building as the one Oprah owned. And he'd started saying "we" when referencing his future—a very good sign. Keith was brilliant, as smart as Nick, in her opinion. She had no doubt he'd give Nick a run for his money, and if she had anything to say about it, beat him to China. Angelica could hardly wait for Nick's reaction when he saw her on his primary competition's arm. But in the meantime, she'd have to settle for Tiffany's reaction when she found out her man's ex was now screwing her father.

Angelica's eyes shined at the deliciousness of fate. *What were the chances that the man who will help me bring Nick down is also the father of the bitch who replaced me in Nick's bed and heart? The gods could not have been kinder,* Angelica had thought, when during a recent conversation Keith had mentioned why he so wanted to visit Taste—because his daughter, Tiffany, worked there. Angelica had phoned Nick immediately, told him of her lover's impending visit, and asked if she'd be welcome at Taste. Nick had phoned her back that evening with the go ahead, and had again wished her well with the new relationship. *Ha! Thanks for the well wishes, Nicky baby. Although after you find out I'm screwing the competition who just happens to be your woman's daddy, you might take back your blessings and I might get barred again!*

Angelica slid down a bit in her seat and placed her foot squarely on Keith's inner thigh.

Keith reached down and captured Angelica's bare foot. "All right, baby girl. Don't start nothing, won't be nothing."

Angelica moved her leg higher, placed it near his crotch. "I think I've already got something started." She began to massage him with her toes.

Keith shifted himself away from her. "Behave, Angelica." But his smile belied the gruffness in his tone. This girl turned him on something fierce!

Forty-five minutes later, they had finished their third course and were waiting on the main course when Keith's phone rang. His eyes widened and a big grin broke out on his face as he listened to the caller on the other end. After a few brief comments, he hung up the phone.

"Baby, we have to leave, now."

"Why, Keith, what's wrong?"

"Nothing's wrong," Keith said, signaling for Amber. "Everything is getting ready to be more than right. That was the president of J.P. Morgan. We've just been invited to his house, for an impromptu dinner. He has some people he wants us to meet."

Angelica's initial disappointment was replaced with excitement. She loved to move among society's movers and shakers, and even more, this invite could have something to do with the China project. "Whatever you say, darling," Angelica purred, taking her compact from her purse and refreshing her lipstick. There would be another day to surprise Miss Tiffany. Angelica knew that moment would be well worth the wait.

After waiting another minute for Amber, who was busy at another table, Keith took out four crisp one-hundred-dollar bills and placed them on the table. "That should cover the cost of the meal and leave a generous tip." His daughter, and the main course she was preparing for him, never crossed his mind. "She'll see it when she comes back here," he said, referring to Amber. "Ryan's in Pacific Palisades. Let's go."

Tiffany carefully cut the tenderloin her father had ordered. It was a juicy medium rare, the mustard, avocado, and panko crumb coating perfectly done. She smiled as she plated the cut, topping it with cold organic avocados and slices of purple, yellow, and red heirloom tomatoes. This would be served with a potato, turnip, and parsnip medley, paired with sautéed green beans.

At the same time, Roger was plating for the person dining with her father, a glamour gal, was how Amber had described her. Tiffany had thought it interesting that her father had brought a date. Tiffany had met only a handful of her dad's many women. Most of those meetings had been memorable—and not in a good way. But her father was changing the way he lived his life. Maybe he was changing the type of woman he dated, which meant maybe this woman was closer to his own age. Tiffany smiled, actually looking forward to meeting this woman and visiting with her father. They talked almost weekly now. How their relationship had grown in this short time was nothing short of miraculous.

"You ready, Roger?"

"Yes, Chef."

Tiffany picked up her father's dishes and headed to the door. She'd told Amber she'd deliver their order personally. She wanted to see her father's reaction when he tasted her food. She'd just started down the short hallway into the dining room when Amber came around the corner. She was not smiling.

"I don't know what happened, Tiffany, but your father's gone."

32

Tiffany slowly took off her soiled apron and placed it in the laundry bin. She was thankful that the dinner crowd had kept her busy—the steady stream of customers hadn't abated until well after ten o'clock. But now, as she walked to her car, the thoughts that she'd held at bay came back full force.

She pulled out her cell phone, put on her headset, and navigated out of the parking lot. Before listening to messages she called Nick and got voicemail.

"Hey, baby, it's me. I just got off, was going to stop by. My dad came to the restaurant but left before I could see him. I wish you were there, Nick. I need you."

She ended the call and punched the Message button. She had four new messages. The first was the earlier call she'd seen from her father.

"Hey, Tiffany, it's your dad. I'm in town, but not for long, maybe only a day. Would love to see you, maybe even stop by your restaurant. Give me a call when you get this message. Good-bye."

The second call was from Joy, the third from Grand. The last call was another message from her dad:

"Hey, Tiffany. I was at the restaurant, but you know that. I hate that I had to leave without seeing you, but I got an urgent call from a business partner. A very big deal, baby, and a crucial meeting. We're headed over to his house for dinner right now. If my calendar will allow it, I'll stay an extra day to see you. If not, I should be back in a couple weeks. Oh, I had one of your taster scallops. Something about being amused?" Tiffany could hear a woman's laughter in the background. "Anyway, it was delicious, baby. All the food I ate tonight was outta sight. If you cooked that food, baby girl, you're a first-rate chef. I love you."

Tiffany played the message again, and a third time. On the one hand, the message disappointed her. It was her dad being his old self, putting business first. This had been the way they'd rolled from the time she was born. She thought that with their reestablished connection, his actions would be different. But she'd thought wrong. With her dad, business would always come first.

Which brought her thoughts to Nick, who also gave business first priority. Yes, he was loving, kind, and attentive, but he was also a driven man who thrived when doing what he loved—making deals and making money. Lately, his schedule had been busier than ever, some new project he and the partner she'd met, Bastion Price, were working on. He'd been out of town most of the new year and when he wasn't, was closeted away in one meeting or the other. She'd only seen him once since they'd brought in the new year together. Tiffany had been too busy to notice she missed him, until now.

Tiffany pushed the Message button, going through the messages until she reached the last one, from her father. She smiled when his message neared the end. If she could, she'd put that last part on a loop and play it over and over again. Because she couldn't be certain, but she thought she was in high school when she'd last heard her father say those three magic words.

"Dad," she said softly to the wind around her, "I love you, too."

33

It was another rare day off. Tiffany had been working so much that she barely knew what to do with all the free time. There were errands to run and bills to pay, but after an hour online, she'd decided there were better things to do. Which was why she was ringing Joy's doorbell and sipping a vanilla latte from Starbucks.

"Hi, Tiffany," Deuce said when he opened the door.

"Hey, Deuce. Where's your mother?"

"Where she always is . . . on the couch."

"I heard that," Joy yelled out.

"Reading," Deuce whispered, with a frown.

Tiffany laughed. "You don't like to read?"

Deuce shook his head vigorously.

"You've got to read to get good grades, right?"

Deuce shrugged.

"Of course you do. What's your favorite subject?"

"Recess!" Deuce quickly shouted, and then dodged past Tiffany and ran outside.

"Your son's a mess," Tiffany said, laughing as she

walked into the living room. "But he's right about one thing. You've always got your head in a book."

"You know this is my guilty pleasure. But I guess it is pretty bad when you have to get your excitement from a book."

"What are you reading now?"

"I'm re-reading all of E. Lynn Harris's books. Man, he was one of my favorite authors. Even after all this time, it's hard to believe that he's gone. A part of me is still waiting for his next novel to come out." Joy reached for the crumpled lottery ticket that doubled as a bookmark, marked her place and closed the book. "Okay, girl, tell me what's up."

"It's nothing really, same old, same old." Tiffany crossed over to the well-worn couch, stepping over toys and clothes and gossip magazines. Joy would never win the award for housekeeping, but she might nab one for most read books.

"Well, tell me about same old, same old. You want some chips and dip?"

Tiffany followed Joy into the kitchen and told her about Nick's ramped-up meetings and business travel, her own crazy schedule, and her dad's visit to the restaurant, ending with his untimely departure.

"Damn, that's jacked up."

"Tell me about it."

"But at least he called you and told you what happened."

"But I had cooked this amazing dish for him and he just up and left without a second thought."

"His phone call is proof he thought about you, Tiff. Don't beat yourself up over it, girl. What's done is done."

"Yeah, I know you're right."

"Have y'all talked since then?"

"Yeah, he wants me to visit him in Chicago. Can you imagine? I haven't been to a home my father's owned since college."

"I haven't been to my daddy's house in my life, never even *seen* my sperm donor. For all I know, he could be Dr. Huxtable. So don't think you've got the market cornered on colored-girl stories, okay?"

After spending an hour at Joy's house, Tiffany left and headed for Grand's. She started to call her, and then decided to just drop by—like her Grand said they used to do back in the day. Nick was out of town once again, and she didn't feel like going home, with only Tuffy for company. She pulled up just in time to see her grandmother closing and locking her front door. She was wearing some cute capri jeans, an oversize top, and sandals. She was carrying a large tote bag in one hand and a bottle of water in the other.

"Hey, Grand."

"Hi, Tiffany. Girl, what are you doing over this way?"

"I thought I was coming to see you." The two ladies met and hugged in the middle of the sidewalk.

"Come on, you can go with me."

"Where are we going?"

"You said you came to see me, so does it matter?"

"I guess not."

She got into her grandmother's Mercury and fastened her seat belt. "I know how wild you drive," she teased as Grand slowly backed out of the driveway. They rode down Crenshaw, sharing small talk. Her grandmother passed the Baldwin Hills Crenshaw Shopping Plaza, turned left onto MLK Boulevard,

and turned into a parking lot just before reaching
La Brea.

Tiffany put a hand to her head as realization
dawned. "Oh, Grand, *please* tell me that this is not your
bingo spot."

Grand chuckled. "Okay, so I won't tell you."

"Grand, this isn't funny. I'm not trying to spend
my night around a bunch of old folk. Nothing personal, Grand, but . . . c'mon now!"

"No, *you* come on. Mess around with you and all
the good seats will be gone!"

Tiffany had never played bingo in her life, but
by the time the second half of the evening came
around, she was acting like an old pro. She'd increased the two cards she'd started with initially to
six, and—like her grandmother—was a dobbing
fool. But when it came to cards, Tiffany couldn't believe how her Grand held it down. Not only did she
mark her own ten cards, but she leaned over and
caught numbers Tiffany had missed as well.

"Girl, you better keep up!" Grand warned. "Don't
watch out, you're going to sleep on a bingo."

Tiffany hunkered down and tried to focus. Her
eyes flew from her cards to the big, lit board up front
that showed the called numbers. *Ooh, I missed one.*
Tiffany scooted to the edge of her chair. Checking
her card again, she got excited. She only needed one
more number, I-19.

The elderly man calling out the numbers reached
into the popper for another white ball. "I . . ." *Oh my
gosh, this is it, he's going to call my number!* ". . . eigh-
teen, I-eighteen."

"Bingo!" Grand held up her card and waved it in
the air.

"Grand! That's not fair, he was supposed to call I-*nineteen*."

Grand laughed and placed her winning card in front of Tiffany. "Read it and weep, baby, read it and weep!"

"So how much was that prize for, Grand?"

"It was the big one, baby. One *thousand* dollars!"

By the time the night ended, Tiffany had eaten bad junk food, dobbed cards until her hands were stained with blue and red ink, laughed harder and had more fun than she'd had in a while. They topped off the night with a pass through Taco Bell's drive-thru and got hot, sugary churros, just like they used to do when Tiffany was young. When she hugged Grand good night and got into her car, Tiffany was smiling. An entire evening had passed, and for the first time since she'd met him, and especially since their time apart had increased, she hadn't thought about Dominique LaSalle Rollins . . . not even once.

34

The air was so thick, it could be cut with a knife. Tiffany and Nick were in the sitting area of their master suite, and Tiffany was not happy. She'd been looking forward to the Italy vacation with Nick for weeks. And here he was canceling at the last minute? No, Tiffany was not amused.

"Baby, I feel horrible about this, worse than you do. You know how much I've wanted to go back to Italy with you, shoot, just to get some quality time with you. We've both been so busy since the holidays. If there was any way I could get out of going to New York, I would. But what's happening now threatens to unravel months and months of negotiations. If my partners and I don't move, right now, this venture might be snatched right out of our hands. It's the biggest deal I've tried to seal in my life." Nick's countenance turned stormy. "I'm not about to let that happen."

Nick's words were heartfelt, but they didn't remove the pout from Tiffany's face. "So what am I supposed to do with this time off, and you in New York?"

"Baby, you're welcome to come with me, you know that."

"And sit in a hotel suite by myself all day? No, thank you."

"Granted, these meetings will be long and intense. I probably won't have much down time. But who knows? The talks may go smoother than I anticipate and if that happens, we'll still have time to enjoy the city . . . and each other." Nick walked over and sat on the love seat next to Tiffany. He took her in his arms, but she did not return his embrace. "Baby, it's business. It can't be helped."

"Don't say that!" Tiffany shouted. "Don't give me that crap about business first and everything else second. You sound just like my father!" With that, Tiffany ran out of the room. The muffled sound of a closing door soon followed. Nick had no doubt that if his doors weren't equipped with special springs that prevented them from being slammed, his ears would now be ringing.

Nick sighed, still looking in the direction Tiffany had run. She'd shared a little bit about her and her father's previously strained relationship. But they were doing so much better now, weren't they? That's what Tiffany had led Nick to believe. So why was the business aspect of his life still such a sore spot for her?

Nick walked over to the sliding doors, opened one, and stepped out onto his patio. He inhaled a deep breath of salty ocean air. As he continued to ponder the situation, anger replaced compassion. Hell, it wasn't like Tiffany didn't know what he did for a living. She knew she was getting involved with a businessman. He'd never hidden his ambition. In fact, he'd shared his goals and dreams with her, had been open with his desires. *I've supported her career, encouraged her every step of the way.* So why should he stand here feeling guilty about simply being who he was?

"This is bullshit," he muttered. Walking back into the house, he strode purposefully toward the master suite. He turned the knob on the door: locked. "Open this door, Tiffany! Dammit, girl, you will not lock me out of a room in my own home. Tiffany!"

Two minutes passed, then five. Nick prowled the halls like a angry bull. Another five minutes went by. By the time he remembered the master key he kept in a kitchen cabinet, Nick was furious. He couldn't get to that drawer fast enough, and once he'd retrieved the key, he stormed back down the hall to the bedroom suite as if Usain Bolt, the world-record holder for the one-hundred-meter sprint, was behind him. Just as he was about to put the key into the lock, the door swung open. Tiffany walked past him without speaking, her carry-on bag trailing behind her.

Nick's heartbeat quickened, and after being momentarily stunned into immobility, he followed Tiffany down the hall, catching up with her just as she reached the front door.

"What is this, Tiffany?"

"What does it look like, Nick?" Tiffany popped her car trunk and placed the carry-on inside. She walked back to the house.

Nick followed. "Ah, the runaway tactic. Of course. Tiffany doesn't get her way about something, so she's just going to take her ball and bat and play in somebody else's yard?"

Tiffany remained silent as she went into the master suite, retrieved a large tote from under the bathroom counter, and began methodically clearing off the toiletries that had accumulated at Nick's house during her many stays.

"Tiffany, look. You're being unreasonable. This is one trip, baby, out of a lifetime of opportunities to be together. You know the only reason I canceled our vacation is because I had no other choice!"

Tiffany eyed Nick a moment before slamming down the lid to the case, snatching it off the counter, and brushing past him. She didn't get far. Nick grabbed Tiffany's arm and swung her around. "Oh, you think you're just going to up and walk out of my house?"

"No, Nick. I'm going to walk right out of your life. Now, let me go."

They were both breathing heavily, staring at each other without speaking. Finally, Nick released his hold on Tiffany. He put his hands on his hips and watched as she turned and walked back down the hall.

This time he didn't follow her. Nick wasn't going to apologize for who he was or what he did. Scarred childhood or no, Tiffany was being unreasonable. If she couldn't understand why he had to cancel, how important this trip was to his life and future, Nick reasoned, then she wasn't the woman for him.

"I don't have time for this," Nick said angrily. He walked to his patio doors, put his hands on his hips and took a deep breath. A phrase that he'd heard a motivational speaker spout years ago came to mind, and he decided to heed it. *If a friend can walk away from you . . . let 'em leave.*

35

Tiffany and Joy were quiet as they strolled barefoot in the sand. It was a stunningly beautiful day in California, the late January weather a mild seventy degrees. Deuce built who knew what in the sand several yards away. Lecia created havoc in the pigeon community, offering them no peace as she relentlessly chased them. Every now and then, Joy would look over at her downtrodden friend. Tiffany was often not a woman of many words, but this was the quietest Joy had ever seen her. She'd barely mumbled a coherent sentence while on the phone a few nights earlier, and had said almost nothing on the ride to the beach. Joy broke the silence with an uncharacteristically subdued approach.

"Ready to talk about what happened?" She and Tiffany continued walking, the quiet broken up only by the crashing waves, a screeching bird call, or occasional shouts from the volleyball players on the nets nearby. It wasn't her style, but Joy waited. She could tell that now was not the time to be her direct, rambunctious self.

"It never would have worked. He's just like Dad."

Joy waited a moment before responding, watched a pair of bikers zooming down the path. "It worked for a while," she said quietly.

Tiffany shrugged. They remained silent and walked. Finally, Tiffany stopped, pulled out the towel that was in her tote bag, spread it on the ground, and sat down. She picked up handfuls of sand and watched the tiny grains spill from her fingers back to the earth.

"Deuce, don't go so far out in the water! Lecia, come here and let me put some more sunblock on you." After spreading lotion on Lecia's face, arms, and legs, Joy handed Lecia the juice box she'd asked for and then turned her attention back to Tiffany. "What changed, Tiffany? Between the time you met him and last Thursday night, what happened?"

Another long moment passed before Tiffany answered. "I remember when I first saw him," she said with a sad smile. "Sitting in first class, looking like a million-dollar bill. My first thought was . . . could anybody really look that good?" Tiffany laughed, but the sound held no trace of happiness. "My second thought was that he was out of my league. Then I lost my purse . . . and he helped me. I don't know what I would have done without him. My third thought, though, was that he reminded me of my father. That's the thought I should have focused on. If I had, I wouldn't feel like I do right now . . . like there's a stake in my heart."

"Mama, can I have one of those juice boxes, and some potato chips?"

"Boy, stop dripping that cold water on me!"

Deuce responded by shaking his hair and spraying

the remainder of water in it over the ladies. Joy laughed. Tiffany didn't react at all.

"Here, boy."

"No, Mama, I want grape."

"No, you want to drive me crazy, that's what you want. Here!"

"Thanks, Mama."

Joy had barely packed the food back in its container when Lecia ran up. "Mama, Deuce won't share his food!"

Joy mumbled under her breath while pulling out a couple of individual bags of chips, some cookies, and some Now and Laters. "Here. Now, I want you and your brother to leave me alone. Take this towel and you guys sit over there. Tiffany and I are talking."

While Joy took care of her children, Tiffany's eyes fastened on a couple strolling hand in hand down the beach. The woman said something to the man; he laughed and began chasing her. When he caught her, they tumbled in the sand and began kissing. Tiffany's eyes watered, but she quickly dried the tears and turned away.

"I can see how Nick might remind you of your father in some ways," Joy said. "They're both in business, and from what you've told me of Nick and what I know of your dad, very motivated. But that didn't seem to stop you guys from hanging out, and to hear you tell it, having a very good time. So what happened, Tiffany, to have you cut and run all of a sudden?"

Tiffany reminded Joy that she was sitting next to her in Venice, California, instead of hanging out in Rome with Nick, as she was supposed to have been. She told her about Nick's meeting in New York.

She omitted the fact that he'd invited her to join him. "He put business first, before me, before our vacation. It didn't matter that it had been planned since before the holidays. I grew up without a father around; I sure as hell don't plan to be in a relationship where my man is MIA."

"Let me ask you something. Say there was a cooking opportunity, one that if handled successfully would give you the opportunity of a lifetime . . . to open your own restaurant. You'd have the building, the money, everything . . . but you had to go to this meeting for it to happen. Here you are, just a trip away from your dreams, but lo and behold, the meeting is the same time you and Nick are taking a vacation. Are you saying that you would pass up that chance and go on vacation? Or would you explain how important the meeting was to you, and ask Nick if y'all could postpone your rendezvous until later?"

Several long moments went by before Tiffany responded. "You know what, Joy?"

"What?"

"You get on my damn nerves."

Joy hid her smile. "You're welcome."

36

She should have felt rejuvenated and refreshed. Isn't that how one was supposed to feel after a vacation? Especially since she and Janice had enjoyed a girls' day at Burke Williams, where they'd been patted and pampered from head to toe. Instead, Tiffany felt more tired than ever and her nerves were on edge. She hadn't had a good night's sleep since leaving Nick, and especially since after calming down, it had occurred to her that she might not have a job. That day, she'd almost called him. But it felt hypocritical. She'd ended their relationship because of Nick's focus on his career, so now to call him about her job instead of their relationship seemed . . . well . . . as if she was putting business first

So here she sat, in Hotel Le Sol's employee parking lot, looking at the back door and dreading going in. If she had been fired, would Nick have called her? For sure, Chef Wang would have. It was the million-dollar question: did she or didn't she still have a job? *There's only one way to find out.*

Amber was the first person Tiffany encountered.

"Hey you!" she said, giving Tiffany a hug. "Welcome back! How was your vacation?"

"Long." Tiffany hadn't intended to respond so honestly, but it was the truth, anyhow.

"Whoa, that's not an answer I expected. But then again, it is hard to live without people like me."

Tiffany laughed, and Amber continued, filling her in on what had been happening in her absence. Amber's sunny personality was catching, even through the thunderstorm otherwise known as Tiffany's mood. Her steps were a bit lighter as she continued to her locker, donned her chef coat, and proceeded to the kitchen.

"Chef!" Roger walked over and cupped Tiffany's chin with his flour-laden hand.

"Roger, you jerk!"

"Ha! Missed you, too. And hey, you'd look good as a white chick!"

"Shut up! You're disgusting." His "disgusting" ways had widened the smile initiated by Amber's chatter.

Chef Wang barely looked up from the dish he was plating. "Hi, Tiffany. Feel good?" Without waiting for an answer, he continued, "Need one hundred scallops prepared for bar. Different kinds. Chop, chop!"

Now the feeling on the inside matched the smile on the outside. Tiffany was back in her element, and she still had a job.

Five hours later, Tiffany was still turning out plates, with only a ten-minute break. She wasn't complaining. The work felt good. It gave her something else to focus on besides Nick. But now, as the lull after lunch and before dinner began, so did the ramping up of her thoughts. Was Nick here, at the hotel? Was he still thinking about her? Did he meet someone else while in New York? *Maybe he used Angelica's shoulder to cry on.* That last thought really put a frown on Tiffany's face, especially with the news Amber had shared while Tiffany rested her feet in the break room. Angelica had dined at Taste just after Tiffany had gone on vacation. According to Amber, she came in with three other ladies, all acting as if they'd put the "d" in divas. Unfortunately for Amber, they sat in her station. According to her they were rude, demanding, and after sitting in their booth for almost three hours, left a puny tip! Tiffany was only partly glad that she'd not been here to cook for them. Had she been present, she might have been tempted to spit in Angelica's food! Not that Tiffany would actually follow through on this desire, she was too much of a professional. At least that's what she'd thought while listening to Amber. But now, thinking about it again, she wasn't so sure.

Nick was out of her life, so what Angelica or any of his other exes did was none of her business. Still, she couldn't help but be curious as to the turn of events that had Angelica hanging out at the hotel. *To get back with one of the owners, perhaps?* That would explain why Angelica had told Nick about some new male friend who wanted to check out the restaurant, and then conveniently showed up with her girlfriends. Tiffany would have been happy to never again see Angelica in the Taste dining room but when asked, it had seemed petty to tell Nick it wasn't okay for her to visit. It was a public place and a free country. Angelica could do whatever she wanted. So could Nick. Nick . . . Angelica . . . none of her business. If she kept telling herself that, she deduced, maybe she'd eventually believe it.

The "none of my business" mantra wasn't working. As Tiffany walked back into the kitchen, she wondered if Nick was back at work. Had he had time to chill out after his meetings? They were so important to him; how did they go? Was Nick able to carve out some time to chill, and if he was able to relax, did he stay in New York, or worse, did he end up flying to Rome without her?

And then there was the probing question Joy had posed. How would Tiffany have felt if Nick got pissed and broke things off because of an action she felt was important, even pivotal, to her career? *How would I be feeling about that right about now?* While a part of her felt justified in the actions she'd taken, another part of her felt unreasonable. Tiffany realized she'd been selfish and shortsighted when Nick canceled their vacation. She'd been so angry when he told her. It was only much later that she remembered how he'd encouraged her to go and enjoy Italy without him. *Whatever I remember about him doesn't matter now. What's done is done. Nick is probably happy to be rid of me.*

Nick sat in his office idly twirling a paperweight. He'd wrapped up early in New York but instead of hanging out in one of his favorite cities, he'd flown back to LA and returned to work early. He wasn't one for a lot of idle downtime, and without Tiffany, that's exactly how the week would have felt. So after a two-day DC side trip to see his sister, brother-in-law, and their children, Nick was back in his office, trying to hang on to the deal.

Nick set the weight on his desk, leaned back, and clasped his hands behind his head. What had happened? Who was this other group that had seemingly gotten the upper hand in negotiations with the businessmen from China? Nick and Bastion had thought their becoming partners with them was as good as done—at least that's how they'd felt after their week-long trip to China in December. Nick was almost sure J.P. Morgan was backing them financially; his contacts at Citicorp hadn't come up with anything. Nick knew from experience that someone moving a billion dollars couldn't hide too easily from those with access. Still, the New York trip had been successful. Nick and his boys were still negotiating, but the partners in China had made it clear that they were weighing both proposals. One wrong move and Nick, Bastion, and the other associates could topple to second place in the negotiations. Unfortunately, in this particular game, first place was the only one that mattered.

Nick rocked forward and picked up the paperweight. He knew Tiffany was down in the kitchen but he'd be damned if he sought her out. In the forty years he'd been on the planet, he'd never chased a woman. He didn't intend to start now. Nick smirked as he imagined Tiffany's focused intention as she was indirectly working for a man she despised. For the first time Nick had an employee who dared defy him, one he couldn't control, though firing her had crossed his mind. But Nick would never play the game that way. Personal was personal and business was business. Tiffany was an excellent sous chef. Wang had mentioned during their last meeting how well they worked together in the kitchen. The sous chef was an important component in how the service to his dining room ran. Tiffany's *amuse-bouche* idea had been copied by a competitor restaurant, one that would probably like nothing more than to have her in their kitchen. No, he wouldn't jeopardize the positive buzz his restaurant was receiving over a personal issue.

"Mr. Rollins?" Christina's voice interrupted Nick's thoughts.

"What?"

"Angelica is on line two, sir."

Nick's pause was brief before he picked up the phone.

"Angelica."

"Happy New Year, Nick!"

"Oh, I guess we haven't talked since then. Happy New Year."

"Except . . . yours doesn't sound too happy. And that is absolutely no way for a man as magnificent as you are to sound. Tell me who did what so I can kick their ass!"

Nick laughed. "I think I can take care of myself." Nick couldn't deny the fact that Angelica was good for stroking a man's ego. Tiffany liked to show her love more than express it, but Angelica had always made Nick feel as if he was the most important thing in her world. He missed feeling that way. "So, besides the well wishes, to what do I owe this phone call?"

"Not much, just thinking about you. I just arrived back in town from Chicago, where I've been for the past three weeks."

"Oh, yeah? You and dude pretty hot and heavy, huh?"

"He's a good man, this guy. I think I'll try and hang on to him. Not let him get away the way another one-of-a-kind man slipped through my fingers. He'll remain nameless," she hurried on. "No need to get all caught up in the details."

Nick and Angelica kept talking and, for the first time since breaking up over a year prior, fell into the easy banter they used to regularly enjoy. Angelica was full of witty quips, and had the latest lowdown on all the LA insiders. She told him about a married-with-children, A-list, African American actor who was carrying on with his male agent, and floored him with the news of a forty-year-old singer carrying a twenty-three-year-old basketball star's baby.

"Uh-oh, another Usher and what's her name?"

"Tameka . . . but no. There was only ten years between those two; this woman could have *birthed* Jamal. Hey, Nick. I was on my way to Stanfords to grab a bite. Have you eaten?"

"Not since a late breakfast."

"Cool. Meet you there in, say . . . half an hour?"

"More like forty-five minutes, but yeah, I'll see you there."

Angelica dressed to impress and literally danced out of her front door.

37

"You look good, Angelica." Nick and Angelica sat in one of Stanfords's cozy booths, sipping a vintage, over-priced champagne that she had insisted on buying.

"Thank you."

"This new relationship obviously agrees with you."

"It does."

"What's his name?"

"Careful, Nick," Angelica teased. "You're coming precariously close to prying into my affairs."

"Oh, is that what this is?"

"I don't mind." Actually, Angelica thought it might work to her advantage to discuss Keith now. That way, later, it wouldn't seem suspicious, as if she'd been hiding information all along. If she found out Tiffany had talked to Nick about her father, this too would be information she could use. "His name is Keith Bronson."

Nick rubbed his chin thoughtfully. "Don't know him."

"Didn't think so. I don't think he's quite in your altitude, darlin'. You're in a class all by yourself."

"You always were prone to flattery."

Angelica reached over and squeezed Nick's hand. "Only when it's deserved."

Nick looked at Angelica's hand covering his, and smiled. "You're too much, Angelica King."

Angelica winked. "I thought you knew."

"C'mon," Joy pleaded. "We don't have to stay long."

"How do you even know he's there?"

"Girl, I've got it on good authority that Jamal Sproles is holding court there. You know I had to have solid proof to get torn from Brenda Jackson and those Westmoreland men!"

"The men in your books are harmless, Joy. They're a fantasy. But actually hanging out trying to hook up with somebody . . ."

"I'm not trying to hook up. I'm just trying to shake things up a little bit, add a little spice to my life."

"Does Randall know about this spice?"

"No, his shaker is empty, and that's the problem. I love Randall. We're coming up on our ninth anniversary. There's no harm in looking, as long as we don't try out the merchandise, right? At least, where I'm concerned this is true. But where you're concerned, you need to put it on, take it home, and sleep with it. One hour, that's it. I'm already in Beverly Hills. You can meet me at Stanfords in fifteen minutes."

Twenty minutes later, Tiffany pulled into Stanfords's parking lot. She'd only been there the one time before, when a summons from Nick had turned into a delightful dinner. She knew Joy had been there once as well, about a year ago. Joy had seen Derek Luke and a couple other faces that she recognized from television, and after finding out this was

a popular spot for athletes as well, had bugged
Tiffany about hanging out there more often. But
when you worked in a restaurant, you didn't really
feel like *hanging out* in one. That logic had quieted
Joy's pleas—until now.

"I don't know how I let that girl talk me into
things," Tiffany scolded herself. *Oh, well, it's just an
hour.* The outing would probably be good for her. It
would definitely help to lift her dismal mood after
learning that Nick had been at the hotel all day. It
was just as well he didn't seek her out. Even though
she'd finally agreed that her abrupt departure from
Nick's house was probably extreme, she was resolved
to keep it a clean break. She loved Nick immensely,
which was why she hurt so much. And which was also
why she'd admitted the obvious: it was over—for
good this time.

She'd probably have to leave the restaurant. Even
though it was for the best that she and Nick separate,
and as much as she loved Chef Wang and the rest of
the crew, it just might prove too painful to try and
stay there. Who knew? Maybe she'd end up with
Chef Riatoli in Rome.

These were Tiffany's thoughts as she entered Stanfords. Joy was the first person she saw. She was sitting
at the bar in a bright yellow sundress, four-inch
heels, and sunglasses. Inside. Tiffany smiled and admitted her girl looked fabulous.

"Hey, chick."

"Damn, girl, you could have put on some lip gloss
or something."

"Hello to you, too, Joy. And for the record, I just
finished working nine hours. You'd better be glad I
came here at all. But if all I'm going to get from you

is insults, then . . ." Tiffany turned and took a step toward the door.

"Chill out, girl. And stop taking out your haven't-had-it-hit-in-a-month frustration on me."

Tiffany plopped on the bar stool next to Joy. "I can see right now I'm going to need a glass of wine to get through this hour." After placing her order, Tiffany looked around. "So, where is he?"

"In one of the private rooms," Joy replied, flirting with the bartender while he fixed drinks for another couple.

"Girl, you need to quit. So how do you plan to hook up with him, or meet him, or whatever, if he's in a private room? And why do you want to meet him anyway? Isn't he just a few years older than Deuce?"

Joy turned to Tiffany and began to speak as if she were addressing a two-year-old. "First off, I'm not trying to get with Jamal. It's those around him I want to get to know. I hear his agent is thirtysomething, and hot! I hear he throws some of the best parties, knows some of everybody and, well, I want a change of scenery. I want to rub shoulders with the beautiful people."

Tiffany looked at her friend with concern. "Joy, what aren't you telling me? What's going on with you and Randall?"

"I told you, Randall is losing his sex drive."

"Uh-uh."

"Well, something like that. He's always been able to get down, to satisfy. But since he's gained weight, gotten a little older . . . I think it's affected his libido."

"Old? Randall is thirty-three."

Joy shrugged. "Maybe it affects different men in

different ways. But between you and me? Randall has become the two-minute man."

"So you're thinking about sleeping with someone else?"

"No . . . not yet. Look, I'm going to stay faithful to Randall. I just want to put a little spice in my life." Joy scooted a bit closer to Tiffany and lowered her voice. "See, Daaimah Poole wrote this book about some ladies that chased ball players and got paid!"

"Oh—my—God."

"No, wait, hear me out."

Tiffany leaned back against the bar stool, crossed her arms, and stared at Joy.

"I *said* I'm not going to cheat on Randall. But what I might do is . . . have a brothah thinking I'm going to play on my hubby, and get a few trinkets—a diamond, some designer clothes, hell, just the feel of what it's like to roll on that level. And," Joy paused while she sipped her drink, "I might let him do a little licky licky."

"What you're thinking about doing sounds dangerous. Men don't like to be played. As for 'that level,'" Tiffany said, making quotes with her fingers, "it's overrated."

"That's easy for you to say. You were practically living in Malibu until you started trippin' and messed up that good thing." Joy put up a hand to stop Tiffany's protest. "You were tripping, Tiffany, but we'll get to that in a minute. Right now I'm talking about me.

"I know I probably keep my head buried in too much fiction, but lately, some of the stories have got me thinking . . . about my life. I've basically been with the same man for over ten years, married for eight of those. I've got two kids, a decent house in Inglewood, but no life of my own! Besides wife and mother, how do I define me?"

"And you're thinking the term 'gold-digger' might work?"

"In this other book, this woman lived a double life. By day, she was the perfect suburban housewife, but at night? She became 'Candy,' an exotic dancer that drove men wild!"

"Joy, you're starting to worry me. How much have you had to drink?"

"I'm clean and sober, trust. These are virgin daiquiris I'm drinking. I'm not drunk, Tiffany, I'm bored!" Joy's eyes widened as she looked across the room. "Don't turn now," she said out of a mouth that didn't appear to be moving. "But somebody's coming in this direction."

"Who, Jamal?"

"No, your boy Nick. And he's not alone."

38

Tiffany froze. *Maybe he won't see me. Maybe he'll just walk straight past and . . .*

"Hey, Nick!"

Dammit, Joy!

Nick groaned inwardly. What were the chances that Tiffany would visit Stanfords tonight—a million to one, maybe? She'd told him on more than one occasion that she didn't like the pretentiousness of the place. Yet here she was with . . .

"Joy, we met a couple months ago, remember?"

"Of course." Nick said, shaking Joy's outstretched hand. But his eyes were on Tiffany, who'd not turned around. "Hello, Tiffany."

I don't care who he's with. Tiffany turned around. "Hi, Nick." Her heart clenched. She did care.

"How are you?" Nick's eyes devoured Tiffany; he spoke as if they were the only two in the room. Angelica placed a hand on his arm. He shook it off and stepped to Tiffany. "How was your time off work?"

Tiffany looked at Angelica as she answered. "I see how yours was . . . *uneventful.*"

"Baby, this is *nothing*," Nick whispered.

Angelica flung back her locks as she moved closer to Tiffany, almost hitting Joy in the face. "Um, excuse me, Nick, but I don't think I've met your friend."

Joy jumped off her bar stool. "Well, bitch, if you don't back up, you're getting ready to meet the *fist* of his friend's friend!"

"Joy, don't go there." Tiffany slid off her bar stool and stepped in front of Joy.

"Oh my goodness, how utterly *ghetto*," Angelica exclaimed.

"Yeah, I got your ghetto, and if you say one more word to me it's about to go down!"

The once-flirty bartender hurried over, his expression serious. "This is a respectable establishment," he said, sounding like Carson Kressley on *Queer Eye for the Straight Guy*. "You'll have to keep your voices down."

Angelica turned to Nick. "Honey, I think we should call the police."

Nick's eyes never left Tiffany's. "Angelica, you need to leave."

"*Me?* Baby, what did I do?"

"You're trying to act like this is more than the meeting for drinks that it is, with your 'honey' and 'baby' nonsense. Just leave, Angelica."

Angelica looked from Nick to Tiffany and back. *So all's not perky in paradise, huh? Very interesting.* She upped the ante on her innocent act. "Nick, I'm sorry. I didn't know your relationship was in such shambles. I never would have asked you to come out and celebrate with me if I knew your new woman was insecure."

Tiffany had heard enough. "Joy, I'm leaving." She brushed past Nick and headed for the exit.

Angelica prepared to follow, but Joy blocked her path. "I don't think so."

The drama on the inside of Stanfords didn't match the one on the outside. Nick was right on Tiffany's heels.

"Baby, wait . . ."

"Don't *baby* me!" Tiffany picked up her pace. So did Nick.

"Tiffany, you're blowing this way out of proportion. If anybody should be pissed off, it's me!"

Tiffany spun around. "What?"

"You heard me. From the time I canceled our vacation, you've acted like the only person who had a say in our relationship was you! Did you try and understand my point of view? Did we discuss it rationally? No. You just packed your bags and closed the door. Forget the fact that you broke my heart in the process. Now, just because I'm here with Angelica you get pissed and storm out? I've known her for almost fifteen years so yes, we still talk. But I told you that wasn't nothing going on beyond that. You're acting like someone did you wrong when I'm the one who should be angry."

Had Nick screamed this at her, Tiffany could have stomped off to her car, slammed the door, and peeled off. But he'd delivered this tirade quietly, pointedly, his deep brown eyes boring into hers. How could she get him to understand that it had taken her a lifetime to erect the wall that was around her heart, to shield herself from being hurt and disappointed as she'd been in the past? *His* heart was broken? *Well, join the club. Mine was broken, many times, by an expert.* But how did she tell him? How could you convey what it was like to have your heart ripped out without even realizing that could happen, and to have it be your father who did it?

"Tiffany Alana, your father's on the phone!"

Unlike the sulkiness that usually accompanied her preteenaged movements, Tiffany bounded to the phone. "Hi, Dad!"

"Hey, how's my baby girl?"

"Good! Are you still taking me to Disneyland for my birthday tomorrow?"

"You bet. I'm going to wrap up my business and fly out tonight. Did you invite some of your friends along, as I suggested?"

"Uh, just my best friend, Joy."

"You sure, honey? The limo can hold six to eight girls comfortably."

Tiffany whooped. "You're renting us a limo, Dad?"

"Oops, that slipped out."

"Mom, Dad is taking us to Disneyland in a limo!"

"That's nice, honey." It was said pleasantly enough, but Tiffany hadn't missed Janice rolling her eyes.

As soon as Tiffany ended the call with her father, she rang Joy and spent the next two hours discussing what they'd wear and what cassettes they'd bring to listen to on the ride to Anaheim. Before they ended the call, Joy's mother asked to speak to Janice, and they coordinated dropping Joy off the next morning.

Tiffany was so excited she could barely sleep. She walked to the mirror and looked at herself for the umpteenth time. Tomorrow, she would be thirteen! Would she look any different, feel any different? Would she finally get her period? Joy had gotten hers six months ago and was constantly reminding Tiffany that she wasn't a woman yet. She leaned in to the mirror and fingered a small pimple on her chin. She didn't dare mess with it, otherwise it would grow to the size of a horn and totally ruin her fly look for tomorrow. Running a hand over her freshly done braids, adorned with pink, blue, and yellow beads to match her outfit, Tiffany began dancing to Naughty By Nature's latest hit. She continued while Whitney talked about being somebody's baby, and a brush became her microphone as she sang about what love would do with Janet.

The morning of her birthday, Joy's mother called with a change of plans. Instead of dropping Joy off immediately, they would pick Tiffany up for a birthday breakfast at McDonald's. After filling up on Egg McMuffins, pancakes, orange juice, and milk, the girls were dropped off at Tiffany's house. Joy helped Tiffany put the final touches on the makeup her mother was letting her wear for the first time.

"What do you want to ride first?" Joy asked.

"It's been so long since I've been there that I don't remember all the rides," Tiffany responded. "I know I want to get on a roller coaster."

"Yeah, me, too. And go in 'It's a Small World.'"

"How are you going to turn thirteen and go on that kiddie ride?"

"What's wrong with the Small World ride? It's fun! I like it."

"The only reason I'll ride it is because it's your birthday. But you better hope nobody from school sees us. We'll never live it down!"

As it got closer to eleven o'clock, the time Keith told the girls to be ready to leave, Tiffany and Joy set up watch by the big picture window in the living room. Joy tried to get Tiffany to watch *The Young and the Restless,* but Tiffany was too excited. She kept going outside and looking down the street, waiting to see this big white limousine her father had promised. When twelve o'clock rolled around, Joy suggested Tiffany call her father. She left messages on both his office and home voicemails. By the time one o'clock arrived, Janice offered to make lunch. The girls declined; they wanted to save their appetites for hot pretzels and funnel cake. By two o'clock, Janice placed another call—this time to Keith's assistant—and made the girls grilled cheese sandwiches . . . just to tide them over. Shortly afterward, Janice had to leave for work. "I'm sure he'll be here any minute," she'd reassured an increasingly sad Tiffany. "His plane was probably delayed is all."

By three o'clock, reality set in. Her father was a no-show. On this, her most important birthday that she'd asked him about six months ago and that he'd promised to witness, something else was more important than his daughter. When a sobbing Tiffany called her mother, a very pissed-off Janice tried to make it up to Tiffany. She called Grand, who saved what remained of the day. Grand drove the teenagers to Universal Studios, where they rode rides while she watched a movie and enjoyed a rare restaurant meal. Grand helped Tiffany put the fun back into turning thirteen.

But the damage had been done. Tiffany stopped trusting men on her thirteenth birthday. Tiffany started building the wall around her heart, the one that would prevent it from hurting again, on the night of her entry into her teenaged years. Because when her father finally called, he didn't want to hear about her disappointment. Instead he went on and on about an unexpected and unavoidable business meeting, and how she might have just turned thirteen, but she wasn't old enough to understand the pressures he was under to "build a future for her." Tiffany had listened as he railed, tears rolling down her cheeks. They continued once the call was over, because on top of everything else? He forgot to do what no father should ever forget, especially one who'd just acted the biggest ass without even apologizing. He forgot to wish Tiffany "Happy Birthday."

Tiffany looked up and realized Nick was still staring at her, waiting for an answer. And even though she knew it was irrational and that perhaps she should feel otherwise, she chose to ignore her feelings and protect her heart.

"You're right, Nick. I have no right to be angry.

Someone like Angelica is probably a better fit for you anyway."

"I know exactly the type of woman I want in my life. And it isn't someone like Angelica."

Tiffany stared at Nick, stubbornly refusing to say that she was wrong. Defiance from years past rose up within her. "Well . . . it isn't someone like me, either."

39

Tiffany was numb. She stopped at red lights and turned corners on autopilot. The radio was on, but Tiffany couldn't hear it for the conversation looping over and over inside her head.

. . . you've acted like the only person who had a say in our relationship was you!

Tiffany felt horrible about what Nick had said, how she'd hurt him. She'd never felt about anyone else the way she did Nick, which meant he had the power to hurt her like her father had. All these years later, the memory brought tears to her eyes. It was one of the reasons she didn't date until her senior year in high school, and didn't have another boyfriend until her junior year in college. It was why she chose to focus on her culinary career—because that choice felt safe, predictable, and one she could control.

Did you try and understand my point of view? Did we discuss it rationally? No. You just packed your bags and closed the door. Forget the fact that you broke my heart in the process.

Tiffany raised a shaky hand to her mouth as realization dawned. Nick was right. She hadn't listened to his side of the story, the same way her father hadn't listened to how she felt fifteen years ago.

But what if she and Nick had talked? Would anything she said have mattered? By the time he came to her, Nick's decision to cancel their vacation was made. He'd canceled his flight and booked another one to New York *before* he talked to her. Was that what she'd have to look forward to if her future included Nick? A man who made important decisions without her. Tiffany's phone vibrated, but that fact barely registered. She looked down at the ID. *Joy.* She ignored the call, but she couldn't ignore Joy's words from that day at the beach. It was as if her friend was sitting right there in the car:

Say there was a cooking opportunity, one that if handled successfully would give you the opportunity to open your own restaurant. Are you saying that you would pass up that chance and go on vacation? Or would you explain how important the meeting was to you, and ask Nick if y'all could postpone your rendezvous until later?

Joy had asked a very good question. And the answer was that Tiffany would have done the same thing Nick did—she would have taken the business trip. And would she have loved him any less because of that? Would that decision mean that she loved cooking more than Nick? Tiffany turned down her street and lowered her visor to hit the garage opener. Tears flowed down her cheeks. Her doubts about men, which began with her father, had caused her to act irrationally with a man who deserved far better. And for what? Her heart still hurt. And not only had she ruined a fairy-tale romance, but she'd pushed away the most amazing man she'd ever met. *What have I done?*

Tiffany heard Joy's voice as soon as she opened her door.

". . . and I mean it, Tiffany. You'd better call me back in the next thirty minutes or I'm coming to Culver City, and it won't be pretty. It's about, let me see . . . what time is it? Look, I don't know what time it is except to say it's time your ass called—"

Tiffany picked up the phone. "Joy, chill, I'm not in the mood."

Tiffany's subdued response quieted Joy even as it worried her. "Girl, I've been calling and calling you. Where's your cell?"

"I was going to call you when I got here."

"What happened?"

"Nothing."

"What do you mean nothing, you and Nick didn't talk?"

"Not really."

Joy's loud sigh was her response. "He didn't want to talk?"

"I didn't want to listen. I've messed up, and it's too late to do anything about it. What happened with you and Angelica?"

"Ha! That wench knew she didn't want Joy to bring pain."

"That's not like you, Joy, to get in somebody's face like that. I appreciate your having my back, but was that really necessary?"

"Probably not, and you're right. I think I've been reading too much Wahida and Kiki. I better go back to ReShonda or Mary Monroe, maybe throw in a little Gwynne Forster so I can chill the bump out."

Tiffany's mind was too mixed up to follow Joy's ramblings, though the mention of the name "Mary" suggested that these were authors of books Joy had read.

"But it felt good stepping to chick, though. As soon as Nick left, you should have seen her hightailing it out of there. And guess what? Just as I was making my grand exit, who stops me but Basketball Jamal, *and* his agent. Your girl still has a little game going on. I focused on the agent, Myron Wilkes. He gave me his card, and now I don't know what the hell I'm going to do with it, to be honest with you." Joy's laughter met silence on the other end. "Tiffany, you all right, girl? Do I need to come over?"

"No, just tired. I'll be fine."

"Okay. But I've got dibs on girl time your next day off, no excuses."

Tiffany hung up the phone, undressed, and stepped into the shower. There, she let the tears fall in earnest. Tears for a lot of things: her father's absence, her mother's indifference, her introverted personality honed through years of solitude, rejecting Nick. Here was the man of every woman's dreams pleading with her to listen. And she'd walked away. She told Joy she'd be fine, but right now, Tiffany didn't even believe that lie herself.

40

Tension was palpable in the executive office. The usually unflappable Chef Wang was, well, flapping. "I don't know what happen. She come in, hand me this. Reservation still months out. I need Tiffany."

Didn't you know, Li? Tiffany runs away from people who need her. Nick's outward demeanor remained calm, but his blood boiled. For Tiffany to leave him was one thing, but for her to quit working at Taste, and throw a wrench into restaurant operations, was something else. She knew how Li ran his kitchen, and how meticulously he'd chosen his help. The restaurant could handle the high customer volume because the kitchen staff ran like a well-oiled machine—a machine that had been running with the same parts, translated people, since it opened.

Nick leaned back in his chair. "Did she give a reason for this two-week notice?"

Chef Wang shook his head, his brow furrowed. "Not really. She no say she have other job. She no moving other state. I don't get it. She love this job. Do you think you can talk to her?"

I'll talk to her all right, right before I hand over her severance check, and escort her out the door! Again, Nick thought how easy it would be to simply fire Tiffany . . . get her out of his life. *An easy fix, but not the most prudent.* Not only was Tiffany a damn good chef, but this job was her livelihood. That she would up and quit had never crossed his mind. "I'm not sure that that would help the situation. She probably has her reasons for leaving, even if she is not sharing them with you."

"I don't care! Kitchen run perfect now! Excellent team. You the boss. Talk to her. Make her stay." Chef Wang realized he was being a bit forceful with not only Tiffany's boss but his as well. "Please," he added. He stood up and bowed slightly in Nick's direction.

"I'll think about it. In the meantime, start going through the other résumés we have on file. We need to be prepared for whatever happens."

Nick made a couple of phone calls, trying to get back into the flow of the business day. But it wasn't working. His mind was where it had been all weekend—on Tiffany. *What in the hell happened?* One minute they were laughing, joking, and cooking together, the next minute she was throwing her belongings into a carry-on and hauling ass. The change had happened so abruptly it didn't even make sense.

The reality of the matter was that for as much time as Tiffany and Nick had spent together, he hardly knew her at all. Most of their conversations centered around him, his business, world affairs, music, and food. She hardly ever talked about her family, and even when coaxed, kept the topic to a two or three sentence maximum.

It doesn't matter. The last thing I need in my life is a

temperamental female. Nick decided to keep his mind focused, stay busy. *That's all.* With resolve, Nick picked up the phone. "Bastion, Nick."

"Hey, Nick."

"Wondered if you wanted to do a dinner meeting tonight? Go over plans for the meeting with the delegation from China in Vegas."

"Well, I'd love to, Nick, but Jill finishes her last round of chemo today. It's been a tough road. We just want to spend a quiet evening together, appreciating life."

"That's beautiful, man."

"Any other time, I'd . . ."

"No worries, Bastion. You're doing exactly what you should be doing tonight. Give Jill my best."

"Will do. Hey, maybe one day soon we can invite you and Tiffany over for dinner."

So much for using business to keep her off my mind. "Enjoy yourselves tonight, friend."

"Bye, Nick."

Nick ended the call and immediately placed another one to the financial component of the Project China team.

"Pat McKennan."

"Patrick! Nick."

"Hey, buddy, how are ya?"

"I think we'll all feel a little better next week, and we'll be floating a month from now if everything works out."

"For sure. What can I do for you?"

"I was wondering if you had those latest numbers crunched, and if you could bring them to a dinner meeting."

"Tonight?"

"Yes, well, I know it's late notice, but I'd like to have those numbers for a report I'm preparing."

"Got daddy duties tonight, pal. It's my son's birthday. Tell you what. I can have Katie print out what we have and messenger them to you. Will that work?"

No, because I'll still be home alone. "Sure, Pat, have them sent over."

"You got it."

"Enjoy the party."

"My wife has convinced me to dress up as a clown. Don't know how much I'll enjoy it."

Nick laughed as he hung up the phone. He thought for a moment, and then once again hit the speaker button. "Jonathan, Nick!"

"Nick Rollins, my man!"

"Everybody knows it's your world . . . the big JV!"

"What can I do for you, man?"

"I was wondering if you wanted to hang out tonight, shoot some hoops or something."

"Aw, man, that sounds like the ticket right there. But you know my daughter imagines herself to be the next Lisa Leslie. I promised I'd watch her play tonight. You're welcome to join me."

As much as Nick wanted to keep busy, he didn't see a high school gymnasium anywhere in his immediate future. And hearing his friends talk about their children made him keenly aware of his single, childless state. "Thanks for asking, but I think I'll pass."

"Wasn't for the fact that my daughter is playing, you wouldn't be the only one. You know once I left high school, I swore I'd never go back."

"Ha! That makes two of us. Take it easy, brothah."

Nick shuffled through papers for several moments but soon gave up the pretense. He pushed away from his desk and stood. Looking around him, he surveyed the trappings of his empire: a vast office the size of a living room, complete with full mini-kitchen, living room area, and shower. The deep French walnut of the executive desk and bookcase was carried over into the living room area by way of a heavy, square coffee table. Similar matching end tables anchored a Henredon leather sofa. Its rich tan color softened the look of the masculine room, which was further warmed up by a silk rug that Nick had personally selected on his first and so far only trip to India. The kitchenette was all stainless steel and granite, outfitted with Kosta Boda crystal and Lenox china. The floor was a mosaic of cappuccino onyx; the curtains, a mix of silk and fine linen. After surveying his office kingdom, Nick walked over to the bar, discreetly positioned between the kitchen and small dining area, and in a move that was totally unlike him, poured himself a finger of Courvoisier. He was looking out at the ocean waves, sipping his drink, when the intercom buzzed.

"Excuse me, Mr. Rollins?"

"Yes, Christina?"

"There's someone on the phone who's demanding to speak with you. Her name is Joy and she said it's personal, in a very rude way, I might add. I tried to get more information from her but—"

"Put her through."

"Oh, okay. Right away, Mr. Rollins."

This should be interesting. . . .

"Nick, I'm sorry to bother you, but this is Joy, Tiffany's best friend."

"The one who was ready to start a brawl at Stanfords? Is this Joy, or Floyd Mayweather?"

"Anyways," Joy said with a smile in her voice, "I'm calling about Tiffany."

"I'd rather Tiffany talk to me, not through you."

"She doesn't know I'm calling, and I hope to keep it that way. Look, Tiffany is trying to act as if it's over between you two, and I want to know if you feel that way. You might not think this is my place, or my business, but she's been my best friend since junior high, and I care what happens to her. I never saw Tiffany so happy as when she was with you. So if you still have feelings for her, I think you should act on them. And I think there are some things about her that she won't tell you but that you need to know."

Nick put down his drink and reared back in his chair. "I'm listening."

41

"You've been summoned." Roger whispered the cryptic message into Tiffany's ear.

"Quit playin'," Tiffany said with a smile. She was trying not to think about how much she'd miss this place in two weeks but focused on enjoying the atmosphere and the people to the fullest during the time that remained. It was the best job she'd ever had. She would never forget them, or Chef Wang.

"Serious." Roger twirled a dish towel and popped it near Tiffany's behind. "I just left Chef Wang. He told me to deliver the message."

"Oh." Tiffany wiped her hands and removed her apron. She'd delivered her resignation when she came on at one. There had been no time for discussion during the rush hour. But now that it was the lull before dinner, he probably wanted to discuss her leaving. It would be hard, especially if Chef Wang tried to convince her to stay, but Tiffany had made up her mind. She was leaving Taste.

Tiffany decided on a light approach. She pasted a smile on her face and walked purposefully and jauntily toward Chef's office. She even tried to hum a line or two. Anything to counter the fast beating of her heart. "Chef Wang! I know this is about my—Nick!"

"Sit down, Ms. Matthews." Nick, who'd been lounging by a set of shelves bulging with books, walked over and sat behind Chef Wang's crowded, messy desk. On the surface, he was all business, but inside, his heart was melting. Tiffany didn't know how good she looked with her sweated-out hair pulled back in a simple ponytail and a streak of flour on her cheek. Nick noted the defiant tilt of her chin and defensive crossing of her arms. *The stubborn, unbreakable woman with a heart of stone.* But Joy had known better and now, so did Nick.

Tiffany sat opposite Nick, without a word. She did notice, however, what Nick was holding in his hand— her resignation letter.

Nick looked at her for several seconds without speaking. "Ending our relationship was one thing, Ms. Matthews, but running out on a chef who's invested considerable time in your development, and with a measly two-week notice, no less, is quite another."

"I think two weeks is—"

"Frankly, I've heard enough about what you think, Ms. Matthews."

Nick's forceful attitude rendered Tiffany speechless. She opened her mouth but no words came out.

"Chef Wang came to my office today. I've never seen him so upset. Out of a dozen qualified sous chefs, yes, some with more qualifications than your résumé showed, he picked you. Not for your experience, but for your attributes overall—education, training with Emilio, determination, passion—strengths he felt would be a good addition to his team. The team he built with an eye toward the long term. It is no accident that not one person has left his team, not one! Because he picked every person based not only on their cooking skills, but on their character."

"Now, wait just a minute, Nick."

"This isn't personal, this is business. Which is why from here on out you will address me as Mr. Rollins."

"Fine, Mr. Rollins," Tiffany spat. "There is nothing wrong with my char—"

"What is wrong, Ms. Matthews, is that you are letting personal feelings get in the way of professional integrity. When Chef Wang hired you, he thought he was getting someone who'd matured beyond childish pouting and selfish actions. And so did I."

Tiffany was so mad she couldn't see straight. *The nerve of this sanctimonious asshole! Sitting over there looking so smug and judgmental . . . and fine, and sophisticated, and smelling so good . . . damn!* She wanted to stomp her foot in anger. But that would have looked . . . childish.

"Chef Wang was perplexed as to the reason you gave for leaving." Nick looked down and read from Tiffany's letter. "'. . .to pursue various cooking styles within different institutions.' He thought that reasoning strange, to say the least. You and I both know it's bullshit."

If I didn't need the check from these last two weeks, I'd tell you where you could put your bullshit! Though she felt like a volcano about to erupt, and that a panic attack was imminent, Tiffany forced herself to calm down.

"Now, Chef thought a raise might convince you to stay. But I told him I wasn't sure. Because, Ms. Matthews, I'm not sure you've got what it takes for a long-term career in such a highly pressurized industry, and we both know the food industry is one of the hardest, most competitive of all. The five-star culinary world takes a particular talent, much more skilled and tougher than an average restaurant, or even a three- or four-star. He wonders if the pressure is too much and whether you'd fare better in a place with lower standards and uncomplicated menu choices. I personally think you may want to consider getting out of the kitchen altogether and becoming a food buyer, or perhaps the manager in a high-end market. There you could still assuage your love for cooking, but without having to deal with the stress that the restaurant business demands."

Tiffany was about to choke on the litany she wanted to spew at him. But she was determined not to say a word, if it killed her.

Nick looked at Tiffany and noticed the marks she was making in her arms by holding herself so tightly. *Yeah, she's pissed, all right. Just like Joy said would happen. There's no way she's leaving now.*

Satisfied that he'd done what he set out to do, Nick stood. "I'll simply tell Chef that there's nothing that will keep you in a kitchen of this magnitude, not even a ten percent increase. I will alert him that he needs to hire your replacement immediately, this week if possible." He walked quickly to the door.

"That won't be necessary."

"Excuse me?" Nick asked, without turning around.

Tiffany would be damned if Nick Rollins would be proved right by her leaving. "I-I'll talk to Chef Wang, and if *he* feels the restaurant would be better served by my staying here, then I'll withdraw my resignation or at least . . . wait until Chef finds a suitable replacement."

Nick spun around. "I'll consider your change of

mind, but only because of the precarious position Chef would be in because of your hasty, unplanned departure. But know that if you pull a stunt like this again, not even Chef Wang will be able to save you from the unemployment line. I will not stand for this type of temperamental behavior in any establishment that I own. And once I put the word out about your volatile attitude, no reputable five-star in this town will touch you with a ten-foot pole. Is that understood, Ms. Matthews?"

Tiffany was fairly shaking with rage.

"I don't think I heard an answer."

Her eyes narrowed and her lips barely moved. "Yes," she hissed.

Nick ignored her insubordination, turned, and walked out of the office. It was a good thing she couldn't see the smirk that was on his face, or else she'd have really kicked his ass.

42

It had been one month since Nick canceled their vacation and Tiffany broke things off with him. One month, six days, and about seven hours, not that Tiffany was keeping track. It had also been four days since she'd given and then taken back her notice, and had the encounter with *Mr. Rollins*. It wasn't until she got home that she admitted how much his words had hurt her. One thing she loved about the Nick she used to know was how much he supported her career choices, how much he'd encouraged her in her culinary endeavors. *And how much did you encourage him in his work?* "What difference does it make?" she mumbled under her breath. *I've destroyed the feelings he had for me.* Even though a stack of vegetables had already been prepped, Tiffany grabbed an onion and minced it to within an inch of its life—anything to stop herself from thinking. She placed the onions on a grill and caramelized them to top the steak of a regular customer who liked it when she went off menu a bit. Next, she focused on a pot of fettuccine.

"Damn, this order is crazy! And right in the middle of lunchtime!" Roger shook his head as he walked by the computer. He printed out the order and placed it on Tiffany's station. It was for a table of eight, and it was as if they'd fixated on the menu's most labor-intensive dishes and then placed their order.

"This is a pretty crazy order," Tiffany agreed, even though she and not Chef Wang would be handling the order. He'd left the kitchen for two hours, for a doctor's appointment. Tiffany was secretly thankful for the challenge. With an order like this, she'd have no time to think about anything, or more importantly, anyone else.

She shouted out various directives to the other sous chef and line cooks for oysters, lump crab, whole crabs, shrimp, salmon, mahi mahi, flounder, swordfish, abalone, lobsters, and tenderloins. There'd also been a special request for a fresh batch of her bacon-wrapped scallops. *And Nick doesn't think I belong here. Ha! Evidently the customers don't agree with him!* Tiffany and crew sped up their already furious pace, each member concentrating on their piece of the culinary masterpiece puzzle. For the next hour they barely stopped to breathe. Tiffany wiped away sweat with the arm of her chef coat as she meticulously butterflied a tenderloin, cutting the prime piece of beef in half to within a quarter of an inch, and after lightly seasoning, fanned the two sides out on the hot grill. While she kept an eye on the rapidly cooking meat, she placed a handful of onions in a stainless steel skillet, along with garlic, peppers, celery, fresh basil, and mint. The herbs released a pungent fragrance into the room.

"Order up!" Roger shouted, hurriedly taking two plates to the counter.

"Tenderloin ready," Tiffany told him, slipping into Chef Wang's abbreviated English pattern that she had unconsciously adopted. "How's clam chowder?"

"Ready, Chef!"

"Focaccia?"

"Just placed five more in the oven, Chef."

Tiffany released a deep breath. Everything was running smoothly, perfectly. Ever since Nick had questioned her abilities to man a five-star kitchen, she'd been in mental competition with his doubts, trying with every dish to prove him wrong and reassure herself. But delivering this complicated order in a timely fashion was the ultimate test of her abilities. She leaned back on the counter as the last plate for that table was taken from the kitchen.

A few minutes later, Amber walked into the kitchen. "Chef, your presence is being requested. Looks like a table of influential people were quite impressed with their meal."

Tiffany nodded, mentally thumbing her nose at Nick's words. *Wish you could talk to some of your clients, Mr. Rollins. The ones who want to see me!* "I'll be right out. Thanks, Amber." Rarely one to fret over her looks, Tiffany stopped at the mirror in the hallway. She wiped her face with the white cotton scarf she wore to keep her hair back, then tied it back around her head. To add a touch of femininity, she pulled a few of her curly locks out to dangle around her face and down her back. *There, that's better.* Satisfied that she looked more like a sexy mama than Aunt Jemima, Tiffany bounced out of the kitchen and into the dining room.

Amber passed Tiffany as she walked out. "Table one," Amber said.

"Got it." Tiffany turned the corner into the more isolated part of the dining room where corporate bigwigs or entertainers were often seated. The nook allowed for more privacy, while a small, shimmering wall waterfall provided a soothing ambience. The only thing that was brighter than the lights in that area was her smile.

Then she saw him, and the smile ran away from her face. It threatened to leave the room but she caught it, pasted it back on, and after a stutter step, proceeded to the table. Nerves had replaced confidence and her once dry hands became clammy. She cursed her body for its reaction to Nick Rollins.

He was looking fine, as usual, wearing a crisp beige suit with an open-collar starched white shirt. His face was clean-shaven and smooth as butter. Her fingers itched to caress it. His hair looked freshly cut, close to the scalp, creating a pattern of mini-circles and a natural sheen. She didn't have to get close to smell his fragrance, a woodsy sandalwood with an undertone of citrus. This refreshing odor cut through all the others in the restaurant. It was an odor she'd memorized from their beginning, when his body covered hers, pounding . . .

"Here she is!" Nick said to the group. "One of LA's finest up-and-coming chefs, Tiffany Matthews." He stood, with hand outstretched, his smile at once deadly and benign. "The lunch was excellent."

"Thank you." Tiffany didn't want to take his hand, afraid that one touch would melt her resolve to be done with him, to focus on her career, to keep her heart safe. She tried not to look at the broad shoulders, tried to steer her eyes clear of the long, curly lashes and the succulent mouth opened just enough to reveal gleaming white, even teeth. *Get it together, Tiffany! If he can act detached and professional, so can you.*

Tiffany swallowed discreetly and shook Nick's hand. Her body shivered in spite of her resolve. The sexual libido that Nick had awakened with his touch, and which she had tried to tamp down over the past several weeks, came roaring back again. How could a man affect her so with a simple touch?

When Tiffany would have pulled away, Nick held on firmly but gently. *Baby, you feel so good . . . so soft.* "Tiffany, meet some of my colleagues. They will become regular guests at Taste. These are names you'll want to remember." Nick finally released her hand, but as she reached out to shake the hands of the other men around the table, Nick kept a slight yet unmistakable hand lightly rested on her lower back. Unobtrusive, yet very effective. Tiffany didn't know how the man did whatever he was doing, but . . . he was doing it.

"It's a pleasure," she said even as she shook the last hand. "Please come back to see us soon. I really must get back to the kitchen. Thanks again for coming." With that, Tiffany hurried away from the table, and from Nick.

Nick watched her hurry away, his thoughts bittersweet. He was so proud of her, yet so aggravated at her stubbornness he could shake her, *no, sex her,* silly. He knew that for them to be intimate again, Tiffany would have to make the first move, she'd have to be sure that he was who she wanted. Nick wanted to believe that that move was inevitable, because Tiffany was the most succulent morsel he'd ever tasted. How long was a brothah supposed to wait?

Once inside the kitchen corridor, she rested her body against the wall, tilted her head back, and took long, deep breaths. More than ever she wondered what drug she had been on to ever let this man out of her grasp. And now that he was doing exactly what she thought she wanted, keeping things strictly professional, she realized professionalism was not what she wanted from Nick Rollins at all. Now that she'd satisfied his food hunger, she wanted to assuage another of his appetites—the healthiest appetite of all.

It's too late for that, sistah. You blew it. With resolve, Tiffany went into the kitchen and began the next order. It was for a seared sirloin carpaccio with white truffle aioli. Unfortunately, she thought, this was the only type of meat she would handle tonight.

43

From that day on, Tiffany began to see Nick regularly. He'd eaten at the restaurant several times in the past two weeks. Most of the time, he was with clients, but occasionally he'd request a specific dish be brought up to his office, and he'd request that Tiffany bring it. This was for strictly professional reasons, of course, so that Chef Wang would not be pulled from the kitchen, but Nick could still ask specific questions about ingredients and preparation. He'd discuss either the dish's possible inclusion in or deletion from the menu, or how it could be mass-produced for the ever-increasing number of A-list events catered by Taste.

For Tiffany, these meetings were excruciating. She wanted to hate Nick, but she couldn't. In his professional role, he was courteous, respectful, intelligent, and *fine*. He asked good, solid questions and had a hard, solid body. He tasted and tempted with his mouth. Little by little, Tiffany let her guard down and tried to relax around him. But as easy as it seemed for Nick to go from lovers to friends, the same wasn't so for Tiffany. She was still in love with her boss.

"I can't take it." As soon as her workday was over, Tiffany punched in Joy's number on the speed dial.

"Girl, I was just getting ready to call you! You're not going to believe what happened!"

"Yeah, well, neither are you."

"Okay, you first," Joy said excitedly.

"I saw Nick today."

"You work for him, Tiffany," Joy said dryly. "Don't you see him every day?"

"In his office."

"Okay." Joy drew out the word.

"Alone."

"And . . ."

"Joy, I can't take it! The man is about to drive me insane!"

Good work, Nick. "Why, what's he doing?" Joy's voice was as innocent as a newborn babe.

"Nothing! And that's the problem."

"Okay, sistah, start at the beginning."

Tiffany did, telling Joy about her renewed attraction to Nick, his increased presence in and around the kitchen, and the newly begun requests for private dinners in his suite, due both to the catering boom and to Nick and the partners toying around with another, stand-alone Taste restaurant.

"That sounds great, Tiffany. It sounds like exactly the career path you say you wanted."

"It is, but . . ."

"But what?"

"It's just that . . . never mind. What's happening with you?"

"Baby, your friend is about to be all up in the

pro-ball business. You're talking to a woman who is now employed."

"Joy, you haven't worked a day in your life."

"I beg your pardon. What do you call raising two children and taking care of a husband?"

"I mean a *real* job."

"Trade places with me for twenty-four hours and I guarantee you'll agree that it's a job for real!"

"All right, I don't want to argue. What on earth made you trade in your book reading for a nine-to-five?"

"More like eleven to three, and it's an assistant position with Myron Wilkes, Jamal's agent!"

"You're kidding."

"Not at all. I called him last week, and went on and on about how much I admired him. Of course, I'd Googled his ass and found out everything he'd ever done since he graduated from Duke. I also told him about an idea I had about athletes, especially newbies, getting exposure outside of the sports world. Girl, basically, I talked myself into a job. I think he said yes just so I'd shut up!"

Tiffany laughed. "Only you, Joy Parsons. And what does Randall have to say about all this?"

"He doesn't know yet. I figure I'll spring the news once I get us a four-pack to a UCLA–USC game."

"Are you sure there isn't more to this than your needing excitement?"

"Like what?"

"Like you and Randall. Is everything okay?"

"Why do you keep asking me that?"

"Because I don't trust the answer you've given so far."

"Look, if I decide to step out on hubby, you'll be

the first to know. Instead of worrying who I'm with, why don't you focus on Nick."

"Joy, he looked so fine today, I could barely stand it."

"Standing isn't the position you should be thinking about."

"It's too late. He's seeing Angelica again."

"No, he is not."

"How do you know?"

Shoot, Joy, you and your big mouth. The day Joy called him, Nick had told her exactly how he and Angelica had ended up at Stanfords, and how much he loved Tiffany. "Did he stay with Angelica in the restaurant that night, or follow your fleeing behind out to the parking lot?"

"Oh, shut up, who asked you?"

"I rest my case."

"You need to, because it's a tired one."

There was a moment of silence, and then Joy and Tiffany cracked up laughing.

44

"Angelica! You look great!"

"I know it." Angelica really meant this statement but she offered the obligatory giggle behind it as if she were joking. "You look good, too, Christina." *In a Catherine Zeta-Jones on a bad hair day sort of way.* "You're working that cut. Didn't Victoria Beckham wear that look last year?"

"No, hers was shorter. This is more like Kelly Clarkson from a couple years ago."

And that's a good thing?

"I just got up the nerve to cut my hair."

"You want a coffee, macchiato, Frapp? I'm buying."

After Angelica and Christina received their orders, they settled at an outside table of the Starbucks on Little Santa Monica Boulevard. Normally such a place was a bit too common for Angelica, but she didn't want to chance Nick seeing her and she was fairly certain that wouldn't happen here.

After about ten minutes of general chitchat, Angelica got down to why she'd asked Christina to meet. "So, how's your handsome boss?"

"Still as gorgeous as ever."

"Still working too hard, probably."

"Yes, especially since he's working on plans to open a second Taste location."

Angelica's ears perked up, as did her body. "Really?"

"Oh, no, you don't know about that? I'm sorry, I probably shouldn't have said anything. I know you guys are still friends and thought that you talked."

"We do," Angelica said quickly to quell Christina's doubts. "And of course I knew about the second location. I just didn't know he'd actually put the plans in motion. When he discussed it with me, it was just an idea. You know I spend much of my time in Chicago these days."

"Right, with the the finance guy. Sounds like things are heating up."

"Are they ever." Angelica dropped a few tidbits about her life with Keith in Chicago—eating at Table Fifty-Two, owned by Oprah's ex-chef, shopping on Michigan Avenue, and attending Bulls games with Michael Jordan—then she steered the conversation back to Nick. "So, tell me. What's going with Nick and Tiffany? You know he never did like to talk much about his private life, and I didn't want to pry. But he works so hard. I worry about him."

"I don't know." Christina shrugged. "I guess they're okay. She's in his office all the time, fixing private lunches and stuff. He eats at the restaurant regularly. Guess he likes her cooking, among other things."

This was not the news that Angelica wanted to hear. Even though she'd already vowed to destroy him, it bothered her that Tiffany was getting the good loving that she'd given up. "Nick has really lowered his standards to sleep with the help," she said dismissively, hiding her anger.

"I think she's a little more than that."

"Why would you say that?"

"Um, I don't know if I should say anything. It's something I accidentally saw on Nick's desk, in a file marked confidential. I think he's planning it as a surprise."

"I'd never betray a friend's confidence, Christina. You can tell me."

Christina looked around and leaned forward. "The new restaurant he's planning is called Taste Too, and it's for Tiffany."

45

Nick stood still under the pulsating showerhead. Even after a two-hour workout, he still felt wound up. *Hell, brothah, you are wound up.* And the one person with whom he wanted to unwind was still stuck on stubborn. Sponging his hard body with a natural soap of palm oil, shea butter, and aloe vera extract, Nick smiled as he recalled Tiffany in his office earlier that day. She'd tried to stay nonchalant, but he knew he'd worked a nerve or two. It was no accident that when she came in, he'd taken off his suit jacket, unbuttoned a couple buttons, and rolled up his sleeves. He didn't consider himself a vain man, but he knew he had a little "sumpin, sumpin" to offer the ladies. He kept an extra bottle of her favorite cologne in his desk drawer, and had purposely stepped in and leaned over as she described the ingredients of the seafood paella, a Spanish dish, he'd asked her to prepare. Like everything else she cooked, it was amazing, and gave him confidence when it came to the plans for his second restaurant, Taste Too. It would have the same ambience, décor, and standard dishes as Taste, but instead of Italian, it would boast a cosmopolitan theme—taste-sized offerings from all over the world. The input she provided and dishes she created were for her own restaurant. Nick laughed out loud at the reaction he imagined would happen when he told her about that! *She'll be a perfect partner,* he thought, not only because of her passion for cooking but also because of her culinary creativity and eye for eating trends. Because of her observations, this restaurant would also offer a diverse array of vegetarian and vegan dishes. He, too, had been following the meatless industry, and with its increasing popularity, especially in California, and Americans becoming more diet and health conscious, he knew that now was the time to put his foot more deeply into those waters.

Nick stepped out of the shower and toweled himself dry. He lazily dried his dick and thought about Tiffany. While a lover of all things intimate, Nick had always been a discriminating man. And now, if the woman wasn't Tiffany, he was an uninterested one as well.

After putting on his favorite pajama bottoms, made from fifteen-hundred-thread-count Egyptian cotton, Nick walked into his den, a room he rarely visited. He brushed a hand over the seven-foot-tall plants that framed the doorway as he took in the warm surroundings. In the corner was a baby grand, not because Nick played piano but because he hoped his children would. He walked over to the glistening instrument, lifted the lid, and randomly fingered keys. *Tiffany will make a great mother.* These thoughts were all the more reason why Nick was determined to succeed with the venture in China.

This single deal would make him and his lineage financially independent.

Nick heard his phone ring and walked over to answer it. When he saw it was Bastion, he almost didn't pick up. Seconds later, he wished he hadn't.

"Someone is definitely trying to elbow us out of China. If they convince the local partners that their money and short-term plan is a more secure investment, we're screwed."

Nick resisted the urge to pound his fist on the marble sofa table he was standing by. "What do you know?" His voice was deadly calm.

"Not what, but who. Keith Bronson. Do you know him?"

Nick's mind raced to place the name. It sounded familiar, but how? From whom? He relayed this to Bastion.

"Well, here's what I know. He's a broker with a medium-size firm but major connections."

"Where's he from?"

"Chicago."

Chicago. Angelica! "You said Chicago?"

"Right, ring a bell?"

"Unfortunately, it rings two. Let me make a phone call. I'll call you back."

"Call my cell if it's late. I don't want to wake Jill."

Nick ended the call to Bastion but didn't immediately make another one. *So this is the man Angelica is dating. How much does she know?* Angelica was nobody's fool; chances were slim she knew nothing of his business interests. And if that was the case, how was she involved in this Bronson guy trying to cut Nick and his partners out of the deal?

Nick reached for the phone but, on second thought,

put it back on the cradle and walked toward his bedroom. Once there, he quickly exchanged his pj's for a pair of jeans and a simple black pullover. This business with Angelica, he decided, was much better done in person. He didn't want to give her a heads up with a phone call, so he hoped she was home.

46

Angelica started from a deep sleep. *Was that my doorbell?* She sat up, disheveled, disoriented. There it was again. Someone was definitely ringing her bell at—she looked at the clock—*midnight!* Angelica passed a hand over her eyes and looked again. Surely she was still asleep, because none of the men she messed with would dare come to her house without calling, especially at this time of night. Nobody, that is, except . . .

In one fell swoop, Angelica tossed back the covers and hopped out of bed. There was only one man who would have the audacity to ring her bell at this hour. She sauntered to the living room door, not bothering to cover her nudity. Anybody bold enough to come calling at midnight would have to be able to handle what was on the other side of the door. She looked through the peephole and smiled. It was just as she'd figured.

"Nick?" she said in a raspy voice. She peeked from behind the door, allowing her hair to partially cover her face.

"I need to talk to you, Angelica."

"Right now?"

"Uh, that would be the reason I'm standing here, yes."

"Nick, it's late. How do you know I don't have company?"

"Tell whoever it is that this won't take long."

"You're pretty bold," Angelica said, stepping away from the door. "Come in."

Nick took a step inside and stopped. He didn't expect Angelica to be naked, but on second thought, that was *exactly* what he should have planned for. "I'll wait until you put something on."

"Well, you'll be waiting till morning. You know I sleep nude." Angelica continued into her living room and called out, "I'm only giving you five minutes, so I suggest you start talking."

Nick took a deep, calming breath. Now was not the time to go off. If he was going to get any information on Keith Bronson from Angelica, he needed to keep things cordial. He stayed in the hallway and began talking without looking at Angelica. "I heard some interesting news today."

Angelica turned the dimmer on low and reclined on the couch. "You hear interesting news every day, so I hope you didn't come over for that. Are you really going to stand in the hallway, Nick? Isn't that a bit childish for someone who knows me as well as you do?"

"I'm respecting your relationship with Keith Bronson."

"What Keith doesn't know won't hurt him."

"Did you think it would hurt me, Angelica? Is that

why you hooked up with him, because you knew he was vying for the China conglomerate?"

Ah, so that's why you're here. "My world used to revolve around you, Nick. But not anymore."

Nick didn't buy that line for a minute, but he let it pass. "Who's he working with? Are all his partners located in Chicago?"

"Keith is old school. He doesn't believe his woman's place is to involve herself in his business affairs."

Nick walked even farther away from Angelica as he continued, crossing the living room and standing in front of the fireplace, with his back to her. But he continued to use the information he'd received during another call from Bastion on his drive to her home, offering yet another name. "Not involved? So you've never been to a dinner party with him, or any of his associates?"

"Yes, but Stan didn't add titles when he made introductions. He just wanted to show me off."

Nick's jaw clenched as he closed his eyes. If Angelica was lying, and he was sure she was, then she was probably knee-deep in whatever waters were swirling around the Chicago elite and the players of the company trying to usurp them. His thoughts were interrupted by a hand on his back. Angelica had walked up on him soundlessly and, after his eyes flew open, she leaned her body into him. "I'm sorry I don't have information for you. Is there anything I can do to make up for that fact?"

Nick turned and quickly walked around Angelica. Granted, she was a beautiful woman, but how had he stayed with her four years and not seen the extent of this manipulative side of her?

"Sorry to disturb you, Angelica. Good-bye." Nick

covered the distance from where he was to the door in long strides. It was clear that he was not going to get anything from Angelica tonight . . . not anything that he wanted.

Angelica eyed the door that Nick exited. She looked at the clock on the wall—*twelve-thirty . . . two-thirty in Chicago. Probably not a good idea to call at this hour.* With purpose, Angelica walked to her bedroom, retrieved her iPhone, and sent a text:

Hey, baby. Please call me as soon as you get this. Someone here in LA is asking questions about you and the venture you're doing in China. I might have some useful information.

47

It almost felt like old times. Tiffany and Nick sat eating lunch at the table in his office. As usual, Tiffany had outdone herself. It was a dish she called "Seafood Symphony," a combination of shrimp, scallops, clams, and lobster claws, cooked in a spiced wine reduction and plated atop a mound of angel hair pasta.

"This is delicious, baby, I'm sorry, Ms. Matthews." There was a twinkle in Nick's eye as he chewed his food.

"Okay, *Nick*," she said pointedly. "Maybe we've gotten past the point where we have to use last names as additional barriers. Personally, I'm glad we can be civil again. We both share this love for food and quality restaurants and, well, I'd really like to continue working with Chef Wang and improving the diversity and ingenuity of food at Taste."

"What would you think about a place of your own?" The question came out before Nick could stop it, but since it had, he anxiously awaited her answer. Her reaction delighted him even as it made his heart skip a beat.

"Are you kidding?" Tiffany's eyes shone wide with excitement. "That is my ultimate dream. To have a cute little spot with amazing, somewhat exotic food, a funky bar menu . . ." Tiffany looked away and into the future. She wasn't aware of the sexy smile simmering on her face.

"I probably should wait to tell you this, but . . ."

Tiffany's head whipped around to look at Nick. "But what?"

"I've been kicking an idea around for a while, a different kind of establishment for the LA crowd. The success of this location bears out the fact that with the right marketing to the right people, this part restaurant, part see-and-be-seen spot could be successful from day one. And with the right chef, of course, one who's willing to think outside the box, come up with fresh ideas." Nick's eyes bored into Tiffany's.

"Me?" Tiffany breathed.

Nick simply smiled.

"Oh, Nick!" In her excitement, Tiffany forgot her new "never touch Nick" rule, leaned over, and threw her arms around him.

Nick returned the favor, closing his eyes as he hugged the body he'd been missing for two months. Within seconds, his hands were roaming over her back, and lower. . . . With a mind of its own, his mouth sought and found Tiffany's, and a kiss prevailed, a kiss that neither of them could stop. The passion that both had tried to restrain when around each other was unleashed. Nick pulled Tiffany from her chair into his lap, devouring her mouth as he had devoured her "symphony" seconds before.

"Oh, baby . . ." he moaned, placing a hand under

her top, finding and tweaking a nipple. "Baby, I've missed this so much. I want you so much." He deepened the kiss, slid his tongue along her neck and ears before reclaiming her mouth—heated, desperate.

Nick's words wound through the cloud of passion pulsating through every fiber of Tiffany's being. *Missed this . . . want you . . .* She willed her body to follow her brain's directive and pull away from this man. He'd just offered her a restaurant. She couldn't let physical need get in the way of mental clarity. She and Nick could be great together, as long as their relationship didn't venture beyond business.

Tiffany's mind thought that, but her body refused to listen. It was as if she were a desert, and Nick water, filling up her dry places, tamping down her heat. He pulled up her top and she welcomed it. He tongued her nipple into hardness even as his hand sought a lower paradise. Her legs opened involuntarily and she reached for the zipper of his pants, feeling wanton and wild and ready for Nick to take what had always been his.

"Excuse me, Mr. Rollins?" Christina's voice chirped through the intercom.

Nick didn't slow his pace or remove the tongue reaching for Tiffany's tonsils.

"An urgent call from Mr. Price. . . . Mr. Rollins?"

Damn. "Um, baby, I have to take this," he whispered softly. And then a bit louder, to Christina, "Tell him I'll be right with him."

Tiffany attempted to move from Nick's lap even as she struggled to slow her breathing. *Good. A reality check. A phone call to remind me of Nick's priorities.* She tried again to remove herself from Nick's grip.

"No," he said softly, "I won't let you leave me." He

lifted her away from him, but keeping her hand, walked them both over to Nick's desk . . . as easily as he could with his engorged manhood standing both at attention and in protest. When he reached his desk, he sat down and pulled Tiffany down with him. He hit the speaker button. "Bastion."

"Nick, I've just gotten off the phone with the other partners. We need to go to Vegas, buddy. Some things are going down and we need to be there."

"When?"

"Tonight."

Tiffany tried to rise again. Nick stilled her with his hand, and then began stroking her stomach and kissing her neck.

"How long?"

"Just a couple days, I hope. But basically, until we know for sure that our position is locked in. I have some information about the players in Chicago, as well as an inside to J.P. Morgan that might be able to shake things up a bit. You on board?"

"Of course."

Nick hung up the phone. Reluctantly, Tiffany removed Nick's hand from under her shirt. "I really need to get back to work, Nick." She tried to keep her voice light and casual, but Nick knew better.

"Actually, I'll walk down there with you. I need to talk to Li and let him know that you'll be gone for a couple days. You're coming with me to Vegas."

48

"Ooh, I know I didn't just hear you say you were going to Vegas with Nick." Joy spoke into the phone while shuffling a stack of papers at her new office space.

"Yes, you did."

"I knew you wouldn't be able to stay away from that lovin'. You held out for a minute, girl, but I'm glad you've finally started acting like a woman with sense."

"This is business," Tiffany responded, remembering what Nick had told Chef. "I'm just calling so you'd know where I am. Speaking of, you at work?"

"Yep."

"How's that going?" Tiffany placed the cordless phone under her chin, pulling items off their hangers and packing while she listened.

"Better than I could have imagined."

"Randall know yet?"

"Told him last week, just before I gave him the four tickets Myron gave us to last night's game. We were in the fifth row. Randall and Deuce went to the locker room afterward. He came out talking about a gym membership. Five minutes around those buffed-ass athletes did more than two years of my nagging him to lose the beer gut."

"Only you, Joy, could have a twisted scheme work out in your favor."

"Honey, that's only the beginning. Randall laid the pipe last night like he's on a city contract. Guess he noticed the cute little outfits I've worn to work. Now it's as if he is in competition with Myron, Jamal, and the rest of the team. He's trying to win the prize!"

"And y'all just might get a prize while you're at it . . . another little Parsons."

"Tiff, don't even joke like that. I'm having fun and not even trying to hear any baby talk right now."

"Well, I'm happy for you, sistah."

"I'm happy for you, too. And listen, I want you to let Nick hit it until your coochie hurts, okay? Your face needs that pushy glow."

"I do miss sleeping with Nick, Joy, but that's not us anymore."

"What about the other day? In his office?"

"A momentary lapse in judgment."

"When it comes to Nick, you're always having those lapses. And you need to have another one when y'all hit the strip."

"Goodbye, Joy Parsons."

"Bye, girl."

Tiffany continued to smile as she hung up the phone. *Admit it, Tiffany. You're happy because of Nick.* While designated as a business trip, with Tiffany assuming she'd be cooking private meals for the six men who were renting out a nine-bedroom, gated villa just outside of Las Vegas, Tiffany couldn't help but admit that she wished more could happen between her and Nick. But it couldn't. Not now. Not when having her own restaurant was on the line. She and Nick were cordial again, getting along. Tiffany decided it best to leave it at that.

Three hours later, Tiffany was aboard her first chartered plane. A company car had picked her up at her apartment and whisked her to the private plane strip at LAX. When she arrived she didn't see Nick, and she felt a bit uncomfortable. Two men, she assumed Nick's partners, were quietly conversing next to the plane's stairs. A woman and another man had looked up when she exited the car, but had gotten on the plane. Was she supposed to get on the plane? She didn't have a ticket. Did someone have her name? If there was one thing Tiffany didn't like, it was feeling out of control. She reached into her purse and was just about to call Joy when she saw a stretch limo coming toward them. Was it Nick?

With all the stress he was under regarding the stakes in China, Nick felt he probably shouldn't be so happy about or preoccupied with Tiffany. Fact was, he was delighted she was coming with him. Something about her presence inspired Nick. He simply felt better having her around. He smiled as he noticed her countenance, a slightly raised chin, eyes shaded with large glasses, offering a confidence Nick was sure she didn't feel. His Tiffany. Strong, yet supple. . . .

Nick exited the car. The two men immediately waved and began walking toward him. He stayed them with his hand and walked over to Tiffany. Her heart swelled. *Who was I trying to kid about not wanting this man in my life?* In that moment, Tiffany absolutely knew she wanted Nick in her life and hoped, in time, she could share these feelings with him.

"Ms. Matthews," Nick said. His voice was business-like even as his eyes drank her in like water.

"Mr. Rollins."

After exchanging brief cordialities, Nick glanced at his watch. "Please board the plane. We'll be leaving in about ten minutes. I'll be sitting up front with my partners, but if there is anything—anything at all that you need—just let me know."

Tiffany hoped her face didn't reveal just how much she needed what she needed! Figuring that distance was the best way to calm her nerves and her desire, she simply nodded, turned, and boarded the plane.

The trip was mercifully short. It was apparent from the beginning that the two other ladies sitting in the back of the charter were friends, and that they didn't like Tiffany. To drown out what Tiffany felt was mindless chatter, about designer dresses and luxury cars, Tiffany pulled out several cookbooks and her ever present three-ring notebook. She still wasn't sure which meals would be her responsibility, or if all of them would, so she wanted to be prepared for any scenario. By the time the plane touched down forty-five minutes after boarding, she had designed several food combinations that would satisfy any meal request.

When Tiffany stepped onto the stairs leading from the plane, she was surprised to see Nick at the bottom, obviously waiting for her. "How was your trip?" he asked as she reached the last step.

"Fine," she answered, taking the hand he offered. "Definitely better service than I get on a regular airline."

Nick smiled. "With the money we spend to have them at our disposal, I sure hope so. Come this way."

Tiffany frowned slightly as Nick directed her toward a waiting limo. She'd assumed the execs would ride together and the ladies would ride in their own car, the same way they'd been separated on the plane. *Of course, the menus,* Tiffany concluded. *He wants to go over what I've planned for dinner tonight.* As soon as the driver closed their door, Tiffany began asking the needed questions: how many would be dining, what time was dinner expected, and if there were any dietary restraints or concerns. After Nick had answered these questions, she outlined her proposed menu. "It's late, and you gentlemen will probably be working into the night. So how about something light yet nourishing? I'll have to check how the house is stocked, of course, and, wait, will I have an assistant? If not, we may need to push back the time. Not trying to arrange your schedule, you understand, but—"

"Tiffany."

"I know you're trying to impress these men, and it sounds like this meeting is important, so—"

"Tiffany," Nick said, a little louder.

"I just want things to be perfect, Nick. I'll need scallops, of course, the freshest. That's my signature appetizer, you know. Well, of course you know! I—"

Nick's sigh was barely audible before he leaned over and extinguished Tiffany's nervous chatter with a searing kiss. His probing tongue left her breathless, but as soon as she recovered, Tiffany spoke again. "What did you do that for?"

"To shut you up," Nick said, with a laugh that softened the harshness of his words. "Do I need to do it again?" When he saw the scowl that formed on Tiffany's face, he quickly continued. "I didn't bring you with me to cook, baby. I intend for things to get hot, don't doubt that. But not in the kitchen, not for you and me."

As Tiffany digested Nick's words, her frown deepened. So this wasn't all about work? *It's about you being presumptive, and thinking that just because you might help me open my own restaurant that I'll open my legs?* Tiffany crossed her legs, because for Nick, right now, her legs would fall open on command. But she couldn't let Nick know this. Now that she'd cooled down from their afternoon tryst, it was time to set Nick straight again. And she didn't care if her job as the sous chef at one of LA's most sought-after restaurants was on the line.

"Look, Nick . . ."

"No, Tiffany. I know what you're thinking, and you're mistaken. I didn't fly you out here just for physical release. I can get that anywhere, anytime."

Tiffany's eyes searched Nick's. *Can I believe you?*

"I miss you, Tiffany," Nick went on, showing a rare face of vulnerability. "I miss us."

Tiffany remained quiet, but instead of looking at Nick, she gazed out the window at the passing scenery. Abstractly, she thought of how dull the rest of Las Vegas appeared compared to the strip.

"I've been thinking a lot about what you said the day you walked out of my house. The day you compared me to your father, said I sounded just like him putting business first. In a way you were right, Tiffany. No matter how I rationalized the trip to New York, and even though I felt it had to be done, I did put business first. Before pleasure, before you."

Tiffany turned her attention to Nick, but remained silent.

"I lost my dad when I was thirteen," Nick continued, his voice lower, softer. "It was a very hard time. He'd been the leader of the family, the breadwinner. His passing threw our house in turmoil, because his was a lingering illness that chewed up their retirement. By the time he died, their savings were gone. My mother, a homemaker, realized how lost we all felt without my dad's physical, emotional, and financial support, and how quickly all you had could be taken. With the help of our grandparents, we made it through this tough time. My mother took a secretarial course, got a job at the local bank, and was one of the vice presidents when she retired. But almost from the time they laid my father's body in the ground, she drummed the importance of education, hard work, and financial security into us. Even after the promotions, when our family was once again solid financially, my mother still maintained that money was the means to all-around security. She told us over and again that we could never rest on our laurels, that something could happen at any moment to snatch away all that we'd built. Her words are what has driven me for the last twenty years. And it wasn't until you said what you did that day that I actually took a step back and dissected just where this blind ambition, this tremendous drive I have to succeed that makes me a workaholic comes from. It comes from losing my dad, and my secure world, at thirteen."

Tiffany lowered her eyes, awash in a sea of emotions. Her thirteenth birthday again flashed before her. She knew how vulnerable one felt at that age. Nick's story also reminded her of the one her father had told, how the lack of a father figure had played a part in his drive to succeed. This thought gave her perspective, yet frightened her at the same time. Keith Bronson had never been able to outrun the demons of his childhood, and was working on his fourth marriage as a result. Was this to be Nick's fate—jumping from woman to woman, and relationship to relationship? Sure, he'd had a relatively long-term affair with Angelica, but her parents were married for ten years. Tiffany's on-again, off-again relationship with her father let her know that if she ever found love, she wanted it to be the once-in-a-lifetime kind. Before she could articulate these thoughts, Nick spoke again.

"One of my favorite movie lines comes from *Mahogany*. Have you seen it?"

"I've heard about it," Tiffany replied. "With Diana Ross, right?"

"Uh-huh, and Billy Dee Williams. It's a great movie. The role Diana Ross plays reminds me a lot of myself—driven, ambitious, wanting to escape surroundings and circumstances. I won't spoil the storyline for you, but at one point Billy Dee Williams, who plays Diana's love interest, delivers this line: 'Success is nothing, without someone you love to share it with.' It's true, Tiffany. I can go anywhere, buy anything. I'm content, but not truly happy. Because I want it all—financial and career success, yes, but also marriage and family. I want to share all that I've achieved with someone else . . . with you."

The limo door opened. Nick's frown was apparent as he turned to the intruder. "We're here, sir," the driver offered quickly, realizing he'd interrupted. Nick gave a curt nod and turned back to Tiffany. Neither of the two backseat riders had realized the car had stopped, and the driver closed the car door so softly that they barely heard it.

But Nick obviously had. He began speaking as soon as the large door clicked into place. "I'm sorry for that interruption." He took a deep breath and reached for Tiffany's hand. "This deal is very important to me, and not just for the significant return on investment that it represents. This is going to be my last deal for a while, Tiffany. I'm going to speak with my partners about it shortly after this meeting, but I've already made up my mind. Once this deal closes, which should be in the next few weeks, I'm going to bring on an assistant who can manage the day-to-day of my business affairs and cut my workload in half. And in about ninety days or so, after the transition, I'll be able to focus on creating the future I want. I don't want to be that man for whom business is his life. I want my life to be about my wife . . ."

At the word "wife," Tiffany's eyes widened.

". . . and children." Nick became quiet then, even as his eyes bored into Tiffany's, probing, questioning.

Five seconds passed, fifteen, thirty. A full minute went by and no one spoke. Tiffany's mind whirled with too many thoughts to process, much less speak out loud. When she'd left work, the last thing she'd been prepared for was a conversation like this one. She'd been ready to slice and dice vegetables, not hear Nick's recipe for a happy life. Deep down, the life Nick described was the one Tiffany wanted, but it was also the one she felt she could never have. People got hurt when they fell in love, people who married didn't stay together. That's what life had taught her. Being with Nick had taught her something else—it was hard to stay in control around him. Tiffany liked being in control.

"Nick," she whispered, "I don't know what to say. I came here to cook. I had no idea . . ."

"I know," Nick answered. Again, he was interrupted, this time by a slight tap on the window before the door opened.

"Sorry to disturb you, buddy, but the other players are here." Bastion peered into the limousine and smiled slightly at Tiffany before turning back to Nick. "The meeting should begin in about twenty minutes."

"Thanks, Bastion. I'm coming." After the limo door closed, Nick reached into his pocket. "The limo is at your disposal, to take you anywhere you want to go. Here's a little something for you to get something to eat, maybe do a little shopping, a little gambling if you'd like. I'm not sure how long the meeting will last, but I hope we can finish this conversation later tonight."

Tiffany's eyes widened once again as Nick handed her a large stack of cash. "Nick! I can't take this money from you. It's too much."

Nick opened the car door and placed a foot on the pavement. "Woman, that's just today's allowance. There's more where that came from. So stop tripping, being stubborn and independent, and have a good time." He quickly leaned over and kissed her temple. "I love you."

Before she could counter his argument or react to his declaration, Nick was gone. *I love you?* "He loves me?" Tiffany whispered. She sat in the backseat of the compact limo, bewildered. *What do I do now?* Tiffany had no idea. But she knew who would. "How do I put your window up?" she asked the driver, with less knowledge than she needed and more bravado than she felt.

"It's the top button on the console next to you. But first, where to, miss?" the driver replied.

"I don't know. Where is a good place for shopping?"

"There are several designer shops in hotels on the strip."

"Then take me there." The driver pushed the button to close the partition as Tiffany pushed the speed dial on her phone.

49

"He did what?" Tiffany's news made Joy throw down Deidre Berry's latest release, jump from the couch, and begin pacing the room.

Tiffany recounted the unexpected chain of events that began shortly after she'd landed in Vegas. "I don't know what to do," Tiffany finished. "Nick's in a meeting, and I'm sitting in this big car with money that I can't spend!"

"Can't sp—girl, what are you talking about? Are all the shops closed? Did somebody break your legs so that you can't walk? Are you locked inside the limo? Because unless your answer to one of these questions is yes, I don't understand why you're on this phone instead of at a blackjack table or in a store's dressing room! How much did he give you?"

"I don't know."

"Oh my God," Joy whispered. *This child wants me to leave my children home alone and board a plane just to smack some sense into her!* Joy stopped pacing and spoke as if she were speaking to Randall Junior when he was two. "Count the money, Tiffany."

"Why? I'm not going to—"

"Count the damn money before I lose my mind up in here!" Joy's words came out in a rush, with no room for breath in between.

Tiffany unwrapped the stack of bills, all bearing the face of Benjamin Franklin. She counted them quickly. "Ten thousand dollars," she said when done.

Ten thousand . . . Joy took a breath to calm down, and continued. "Where are you now?"

"Hold on a second." Tiffany found the button that controlled the window between her and the driver and pressed it. Once the glass slid down she asked where they were. "Aria," she repeated to Joy.

"Isn't that next to Crystal, the luxury shopping center?"

Tiffany asked and found out that it was.

"Perfect. Tell the driver to wait for you."

"Why? So I can feel like a kept woman, like somebody is buying my love, again? This is the same shit Daddy pulled when he couldn't be there in person. He'd throw money at me, or a car or a trip, and think that replaced the feel of his arms around me. It doesn't, Joy, not even close. Money can't keep you warm at night—"

"Then buy a cashmere blanket, fool!"

Tiffany was waffling between anger and self-pity, and anger was winning. The last thing she wanted to do was say something to her best friend that she didn't mean and would have to take back later. "Look, Joy—"

"No, you look, Tiffany! God keeps sending you blessings and you are determined to block them. So you had an absentee father, so what. You wish your childhood had been different. Well, join the club, sistah. Keith gave you money instead of love. Well, at least he gave you something! At least he's in your life now. For all the time that I've known you, which is most of your life, you've invited me to your deadbeat daddy pity party and I've accepted the invitation, drank the champagne, and ate your appetizers. Well, no more. You keep living the present based on stuff in your past, and it's fucking up your future. You can't see the forest for the trees, so your friend is getting ready to remove a big branch for you. It's a major news flash, so listen up. Nick is not your father! Nick is the man trying to give you the love that your daddy didn't provide!"

Joy paused, took a breath, and lowered her voice to a calmer level. "You're living the life that most women could only dream about, and you're sitting on stubborn and stuck on stupid, letting a chance at happiness pass you by!"

The air fairly crackled as these words settled like an electric blanket around Tiffany's shoulders. A part of her wanted to slam her phone shut and throw it *and* her decade plus relationship with one Mrs. Joy Parsons out the window. But the other part had heard her best friend's words, and was starting to let them sink in. Nick was a good man, and he said he loved her. Tiffany hadn't even allowed herself to examine how those three words made her feel, nor did she acknowledge that she loved him too. She was too scared to go there, too afraid that to acknowledge those feelings would be to act on them. "I have no idea what to do with this money," she said at last, wiping away an errant tear that had escaped from her eyelid. "What should I buy?"

"Whew, thank you, Jesus!" Joy collapsed onto

her sofa. "Now you're talking like a woman who's learned a thing or two from hanging around me, proving that all this novel reading I've been doing is not in vain. What are you going to buy? You're going to buy the kind of stuff that will make that brothah turn over his paycheck with a smile!"

Two and a half hours later, Tiffany entered the palatial mansion the company had rented. Joy had stayed on the phone with her almost the entire time, until she had spent all but fifteen dollars of the money Nick had given her. She was greeted by a housekeeper who showed her to the room she'd be occupying. Nick's clothes weren't in there, which meant he hadn't been presumptive in knowing she'd sleep with him. *He did that because he knows how I am,* Tiffany thought. He knew, and he'd been considerate of it.

After making sure the door was closed and locked, Tiffany pulled items from her many shopping bags and laid them out on the four-poster mahogany bed. Even long distance, Joy had been the perfect shopping companion in helping her pick out just the right garments. In addition to a casual outfit from Carolina Herrera and a Versace dress, Tiffany had purchased a handbag, matching shoes, and underwear from Roberto Cavalli; two pairs of sunglasses from Ilori (one pair as a surprise gift to Joy); and her first strand of pearls—rather, a three-pearl drop pendant—from Mikimoto. "To show those bitches you have class," Joy had so "classily" explained. Lastly, she'd gone into Tiffany and purchased Nick a set of silver cufflinks. "Never forget your man when you're spending his money," Joy had advised. "And make sure you're wearing some of that money the next time he sees you."

It was almost nine o'clock when the same house-keeper who'd brought an excellently prepared seafood salad to Tiffany's room for dinner returned with a summons from Nick. "He's in the library," the housekeeper said before turning to lead the way. Tiffany appreciated the elegance of the mansion as they walked down carpeted corridors lined with gilded glass and rich marble. They descended a flight of stairs and walked to a set of double doors. The housekeeper turned to Tiffany, nodded, and left.

Tiffany put a hand on the crystal doorknob. Her heart was racing. *Will he like the outfit I'm wearing? Was it presumptuous of me to buy him a gift? What does Joy know about these kinds of men? And to think . . . I spent all of his money! Ten thousand dollars!* Tiffany opened the door abruptly, before fear forced her to flee back to her room.

"Hey, Nick." Tiffany tried to find calm as she walked into the well-appointed library. To the left was a sitting area—a cozy love seat, two wing-backed chairs, and antique end tables. Tiffany, further un-nerved by the way Nick stared at her, walked to the first chair and sat down. "How did your meeting go?"

Nick could barely remember there'd been a meet-ing, or his name, for that matter. He knew the woman in front of him had no idea what she did to him, or that she was a sight so lovely it could cause a blind man to see. He continued to drink her in as he joined her in the sitting area. Hers was a look of casual elegance—a pair of dark gray slim-legged pants and a light gray shell that hugged her breasts and waist, with a V-neck that showed off a black pearl pendant to perfection. He rarely saw Tiffany's hair down and liked how the big, loose curls framed her face and teased her shoulders. She wore little makeup, and needed none. She was naturally stunning. He wanted to ravish her then and there. But the look in her eyes warned him to proceed with caution.

"You look lovely," he said at last. "The black pearls are a nice touch. Where'd you get them?"

Tiffany told him. She almost blurted out that everything she wore, and everything she'd purchased, had been Joy's idea.

But then Nick spoke again. "So I take it you enjoyed shopping on the strip?"

Tiffany nodded, too nervous to speak. She imagined the yelling match that would happen once Nick asked for the rest of his money back and she gave him a ten and a five. "Would you like to see what all I bought?" she asked, hoping to delay the ugly moment.

"I think I prefer to see it on you, the way I'm seeing your outfit right now. You've got great taste, baby. But I don't want you to feel limited in the amount you spend. I'll call ahead to your favorite shops and set up an account so you can buy what you want, *everything* that you want."

"Nick, that's very generous of you, but—"

"No buts—"

"I really don't need . . ."

Nick narrowed his eyes and looked at Tiffany thoughtfully. "Did you spend all of what I gave you?"

Tiffany swallowed, hard.

"Well, did you?"

"Yes." Her eyes were downcast as she waited for the fallout.

"Good girl."

Good girl? Did he just compliment me for spending ten thousand dollars in less than three hours? Tiffany raised her eyes to see that Nick had got up from the couch and was over by a minibar. "Red or white?" he asked.

"Whatever you're having," Tiffany replied, still digesting how casually Nick took the news of her spending what was almost a third of her annual salary in a single shopping spree, and that he was pleased that she'd done it. "I bought you something," she continued when Nick rejoined her in the sitting area. She placed the Tiffany bag on the table between them.

Nick looked genuinely surprised. "For me? Why? What is it?"

Tiffany relaxed for the first time since walking into the room. "Open it and find out," she said, chuckling.

Nick took out the box and opened it. He stared at the cuff links for a long moment.

"If you don't like them we can have them exchanged," Tiffany offered.

"I love them," he said finally. When he looked up, Tiffany could have sworn that his eyes were misty. "I've sent many women on shopping sprees," Nick continued. "No one has ever brought me back a gift. I think that because I've got money, they figure it's not necessary. But everyone likes presents, and even more, to know that you were thinking of me while you were out."

Tiffany made a mental note to kiss Joy the next time she saw her. Maybe reading all those romance novels was beneficial after all! Especially now, as the way Nick was looking at her almost made her melt.

"May I have a kiss?" he asked.

Tiffany nodded.

Nick walked over to her, leaned down, and lightly touched his lips to Tiffany's. Then he kissed her nose and forehead. "Thank you," he said again. He walked back to his chair and reached for the wine that had gone untouched. "To a beautiful woman who is the light of my life," he said softly. "I want you back with me, Tiffany. I want us back together. Is that what you want?"

50

Moments later, Tiffany entered Nick's room—one of the mansion's master suites, located in the same wing as her room. Little had been said after Nick's pivotal question and Tiffany's tentative yet affirmative nod. After they'd quickly finished their glasses of wine, Nick had simply stood and extended his hand. Together they'd walked back up the stairs. Tiffany had no idea where the two assistants who'd ridden with her in the back of the plane or the other partners were. It was as if she and Nick were the only ones in the house.

Nick whispered terms of endearment in Tiffany's ear as he helped her undress. When she reached behind her head to unclasp the necklace, Nick stayed her hand. "No, I like the pearls, leave them on. I want to see you in them . . . and nothing else."

Tiffany shivered. Not from cold, but from wanting. In this moment, all her fears, all her logical reasons for not dating Nick, all the similarities between him and her father flew out the window. The only thing that mattered was the feel of Nick's arms around her, his lips touching her skin.

Nick gently lifted Tiffany and placed her on the bed. When she reached for the cover, he again stayed her hand. "Just lie there. Let me look at you."

Tiffany obeyed, yet felt vulnerable, exposed. She told this to Nick. "You're making me vulnerable," he replied. "And you're turning me on, more than I've ever been turned on in my life."

He stared at her as he stripped off his beige silk shirt and unfastened the tailored chocolate brown slacks that fit to perfection. His desire was evident as he pulled his undershirt over his head before sitting on the bed to remove his shoes and socks. Tiffany shivered again, remembering what the desire she saw outlined in his briefs felt like—and knowing that she'd soon feel it again.

Nick joined Tiffany in the middle of the bed. He lay on his side, resting his head in his palm as he looked at her. Tiffany stared back for a moment, and then closed her eyes.

"Uh-uh. Look at me," Nick whispered, placing a tendril of errant hair behind her ear.

Tiffany opened her eyes and looked into Nick's. She could have drowned in the love she saw there. "I'm scared." This truth came out in a rushed whisper before she could stop it.

"I know. So am I."

"You are?" Tiffany asked, her brow raised. She couldn't fathom this strong, confident man next to her being afraid of anything.

"Love is a risk, Tiffany, for all of us. Men are not excluded from the fear factor. When I . . ." Nick stopped, not wanting to bring Angelica's name into the moment. "There have been times when I swore I'd never love again. That I would live my life in the moment, with whoever was convenient at the time. Many men do it, but that's an empty life for me. I want a life that is filled to the brim. If we get married, how many kids should we have?"

Nick's abrupt change of subject surprised Tiffany. First, the "I love you." Now, marriage? Kids?

"This is a very important question for me, love."

"I've never thought about kids," she said honestly, after a pause. "Marriage either, for that matter." When Nick continued to be silent, Tiffany went on. "I'd say to start with one, see how we do, and then decide."

Nick laughed. "Spoken like a true planner. My sweet sous chef. Brown sugar . . ." Nick leaned down and placed feather kisses on Tiffany's mouth, nose, cheeks, ears . . . "So . . . sweet." He moved back to her mouth and plundered it, thrusting his tongue deep inside. They both moaned as the kiss deepened even more, even as Nick languidly rolled Tiffany's nipple between his thumb and forefinger, bringing it to a hardened peak. His assault continued as he left one breast for the other, and then abandoned both to trail his fingers across her stomach and over her hips. "Open up for me," he quietly demanded after brushing his hand across the patch of rectangle-shaped pubic hair.

Tiffany spread her legs slightly, and Nick wasted no time in searching for her treasure. He touched her nub, and Tiffany's legs spread further of their own volition. He touched and teased, fingering Tiffany's body like the keys of a piano. All the while, he kissed her senseless, murmuring his undying devotion and his thanks for her belief in their love. When his tongue followed the trail his fingers had blazed earlier, and he buried his head at the juncture of her thighs, Tiffany became overwhelmed with emotion. Tears sprang to her eyes as he lavished her, ravished her, caused her to reach one orgasm, and then another. Soon, his moans replaced hers as she worshipped at his engorged shrine, taking in as much as she could, trying to pour the depth of her feelings into the skill of her tongue. They were both on fire when Nick placed Tiffany on top of him. "Ride me, baby. I want to watch you take your pleasure."

Tiffany balanced herself, and then closed her eyes as she slowly sank down onto Nick's long, thick rod. Her breasts swayed with the slow, deliberate rhythm. Wanting to feel every inch as he entered her, she raised up again, tightened her muscles, and slid down, even slower than before.

Nick watched Tiffany from half-closed eyes. He moaned his appreciation, even as he grabbed her hips and quickened the pace. "This is mine, Tiffany," he whispered, repositioning them so that he could enter her from behind. "No more running, this is mine."

They made love and talked until the morning. Nick had an early meeting, but encouraged Tiffany to sleep in, and then go shopping. Tiffany smiled as she snuggled back under the covers after kissing Nick goodbye, thinking of how he had claimed her again and again. He'd said he didn't want her to leave, that she was his. He was right. Nick had unlocked treasures she hadn't known existed, had helped to open a part of her soul. She wasn't going anywhere.

51

"Baby, that sounds like a chapter out of Zane Presents," Joy whooped, after hearing Tiffany's description of her and Nick's last night in Vegas. "Rooftop Jacuzzi, melted white chocolate, sex toys. Tiffany Matthews went Zane!" Joy shook her head and laughed. "Who knew?"

Tiffany placed her feet on Joy's couch and hugged her knees to her chest. "I was embarrassed when he pulled out those . . . balls . . . but I liked them." Tiffany felt herself grow warm, remembering the way Nick had used those balls, demanding that she let herself go and enjoy all the pleasure he had planned for her.

Joy had read about Ben Wa balls but had never held them, much less tried them. But from the pushy glow on Tiffany's face, they worked quite well. "And the next day, how much money did he give you?"

"What?" Tiffany immediately got an attitude at what Joy's question implied.

"Not for the sex, fool. The day after you bought him the cuff links, spent all his money, and made sure you were wearing some the next time he saw you—like I told you. How much?"

"Oh, that." Tiffany giggled. "He, uh, set up accounts at various stores . . . so I could buy as much as I wanted."

"And did you?"

"Matter of fact, I did. I'll be right back." Tiffany went to her car and retrieved a large bag from the trunk. "For you," she said once she'd returned to Joy's living room.

"Girl, you didn't!"

"I most certainly did."

Joy whooped again when she reached into the bag and pulled out a Roberto Cavalli bag. "I said spend the money on you, not have Christmas in March for your friends. What else is in here?" Joy asked, without a breath between sentences. "Oh, girl, you know I've got to sport these shades *today*!" Joy leaped from the couch and preened in front of the mirror.

Tiffany basked in Joy's delight. "Looks like somebody doesn't mind Christmas in March."

"You know it," Joy agreed. "Baby girl getting ready to work it!"

"Work what?" Between their squeals and the music playing, neither had noticed Randall come in.

"Oh, uh, baby, I'm just getting ready to work those pots and pans and fix you dinner. Yeah, that's it!"

"I thought so," Randall said, a mock scowl on his face as he came over and hugged Joy. "Nuckas down at the office think they can steal my *pushy*. They'd bettah recognize. Joy belongs to Randall with the handle." He rubbed himself against Joy's backside. She responded by turning and placing her tongue down his throat.

"Oh, please," Tiffany moaned. "Get a room. On second thought, let me leave."

The couple broke their kiss and laughed. "All right, we'll tone it down for company," Randall said.

"Naw, go on and handle your business. And I must say," Tiffany continued, "you're looking rather *toned*, Randall."

"His seeing the b-ball vultures circling his favorite pushy made him step up his game."

"Aw, I wasn't worried," Randall drawled as he kissed Joy again and then headed out of the room. "Between my skills in the bedroom and the kitchen . . . you ain't going nowhere!"

"I sure ain't!" Joy agreed.

"Wow, ten years together and y'all acting like new-lyweds."

"Yeah, especially since I brought home those edible panties—"

"Damn!" Randall exclaimed from the kitchen. "You tell that girl everything!"

We'll talk later, Joy mouthed. "Tell Nick I said hello," she said in a regular conversational tone.

"I will. Be sure and call me later."

Joy hugged Tiffany. "Be sure you stop screwing long enough to pick up the phone."

52

A week later, Joy entered Tiffany's condo, ready to help with the big move. "I can't believe it," she said, shortly after Tiffany had opened the door for her to enter. "Miss Independent is going to actually move in with a man."

"I know, me either," Tiffany replied.

"But that big dick wore you down, huh?"

Tiffany playfully pushed Joy. "Shut up! This move makes sense economically, since I'm in Malibu most nights anyway. Moving in with Nick and renting this place out is practical. The rent price I've set will be enough to cover the mortgage and see a little profit as well. So that's why I'm moving, Miss Thing, just so you know!"

"Yep," Joy replied, unconvinced. "Whenever you get through with that economical advantage bullshit, we can talk truth—he's got you whipped."

Tiffany picked Tuffy up and placed him in a box headed for Malibu.

"I know you are not going to take that scruffy-ass bear into that beachside paradise."

"Why not?"

"Tiffany, you're getting ready to move in with a multimillionaire. You are a college graduate and the sous chef at a five-star restaurant. I know it was a gift from your father and assuages a part of you that still longs for what you never had. But don't you think it's time to cut the Tuffy cord?"

"Maybe," Tiffany replied as she placed the bear in the box and reached for the tape. "But Tuffy is moving with me to Malibu. Speaking of teddy bears," Tiffany continued after a pause, "I still can't get over Randall's transformation. How much weight has he lost?"

Joy knew Tiffany had purposely steered the conversation away from her father, but she went along. "Only about ten pounds, I think. But it's the crunches and losing that gut, that's what makes people think he's lost more."

"I was so against your going to work for Myron, was so sure you were getting ready to have an affair. But now I see what you were doing, just making Randall pay attention."

"You give me too much credit, sistah, because an affair was definitely on my mind. Randall shocked you and me both with this transformation. But at the end of the day, I'm happy things turned out the way they did. I love my husband, my kids, my family. And from seeing up close and personal how many women these ball players are juggling, and the backstabbing shenanigans of the wannabes trying to come up, I now know that the grass is definitely not greener on the other side of the fence. I could write a book about the month I spent in that camp."

Tiffany stopped in mid-pack. "You should do it, Joy!"

"Do what?"

"Write a book! You love to read, you were excellent in English class back in the day, always made As. God knows your imagination is always working overtime. You should do it. You should write a behind-the-scenes book about women chasing ball players!"

"I don't know. Daaimah's already covered that territory with *A Rich Man's Baby*."

"Da-who?"

"Daa-i-mah Poole. She wrote a book about these stupid hoes trying to date ballers, get pregnant and get paid. I told you about her."

"Was it good?"

"I loved it!"

"Well, then. That's all the more reason why you should write one from your perspective. You're a voracious reader, and if you loved her story line, I'm sure that other zealous readers will love reading the story from your point of view."

Joy pulled a box from the closet. "What about these clothes?"

"Put those to the side, that's for Goodwill."

Joy immediately opened the box and began going through it. "First, let me make sure I don't want to be your charity case."

"Girl! Make sure you put what you don't want back in the box, tape it back up, and label it. I don't want to give the wrong stuff away! So . . . are you going to take on this project I've suggested?"

"Writing a book?"

"No, cooking a soufflé. Of course, writing the book!"

"I might."

"You should. It would give you something to do,

a way to focus your mind so you don't dream up another wild scheme and get into trouble."

Tiffany's phone rang. "Speaking of trouble," she said to Joy before answering the phone. "Hi, Dad."

"Hey, Tiffany. How are you?"

"Fine."

"Good to hear it. Listen, I'm calling because I'm in town and wondered if you were free for lunch or dinner tomorrow."

"I work tomorrow." Tiffany started to invite him to Taste, but she didn't want to be disappointed by another no-show.

Fortunately or unfortunately, her dad had the same idea. "I could come by your restaurant . . . if that's okay. Make up for the other time when I had to run out on you."

"Sure, if you'd like."

"What time is your break? Maybe you could sit with me while I try out the food your mother raved about."

"Mama told you about my food?"

"*Raved,* I said. What time would you like me to stop by, honey?"

Tiffany and her father made plans to meet the next evening. When she hung up the phone, her mood was subdued.

"He'll love your cooking," Joy said.

"It doesn't matter," Tiffany lied, shrugging away the nervous flutters that filled her stomach. She automatically reached for Tuffy, forgetting that she'd already taped up the box that instead of containing a security blanket held a security bear. Tiffany sighed as she reached for the last items on her bed, placed them in an empty box, and sealed it. *If only it were this easy to seal up the need for Daddy's approval,* she thought. Granted, he'd had the chance to try a couple of her dishes, before he'd abruptly left the restaurant, and said they were good. *Out of sight,* were his exact words. But had he accepted her career choice? What Keith Bronson thought about her chosen profession mattered. Even though Tiffany was reluctant to admit it, her father's approval meant everything.

53

"I know you didn't cook this," Keith murmured as he placed another mouthful of succulent Kobe beef into his mouth.

"I cannot tell a lie," Angelica admitted. "A chef prepared this dinner, and then left before you arrived."

"We could have gone out to eat."

"I know, but I wanted us to share an intimate evening . . . just the two of us."

Angelica smiled as Keith continued to enjoy the scrumptious meal she'd had catered. So far, the night was working out just the way she'd planned. If things continued to move as smoothly, the chef would more than earn the hefty price tag that came with three hours of personal service—his last hour cut short because Angelica wanted to serve the meal herself. She watched as Keith speared the last asparagus on his plate, placed it into his mouth, and chewed with his eyes closed. "More?" she asked, already reaching for the tongs.

"No," Keith replied, patting his stomach. "I'm trying to watch my weight. But that was delicious."

"I hope you saved room for dessert," Angelica purred. She rose from her seat, walked over to where Keith sat, and kissed his cheek. "Your sweet treat will be served in the bedroom. Follow me."

An hour later, Keith and Angelica emerged from the shower, where they'd washed away the remaining traces of edible chocolate and the proof of their love-making. Angelica dried off and donned a flowing silk kimono. Keith put on the bottoms of Angelica's gift to him—a pair of black silk pajamas.

"Mind if I smoke?" he asked when Angelica reentered the bedroom. He rolled a large Cuban cigar between his short, stout fingers before snipping off the end with a pair of gold scissors.

"Let's go out to the patio," Angelica responded. She hid her chagrin at the habit that so annoyed her. Once the deal was done and Nick's plans had been ruined, Angelica would demand that Keith quit smoking. But she decided to not make waves . . . for now.

"Will you be moving to Los Angeles?" she asked, making sure she sat on the other side of the cigar smoke's circuitous journey into the night air.

"Why would I do that?"

Angelica shrugged. "Your partners are here. I'm here . . ."

Keith took another thoughtful puff from his cigar. "I like Chicago."

"This nightclub chain is going to be the most lucrative business deal of your life. Good food, great live music, and high-tech games—a perfect marriage for the innovative Chinese culture. Baby, do you have any idea how much money this is going to bring? Your share alone should be ten, twenty million dollars a year, easy. I think you'd love Pacific Palisades, or even Palm Springs. You could get a mansion there for three, four million dollars."

Keith's eyes narrowed as he pondered Angelica's words. Granted she was a gorgeous woman, and intelligent to boot. But Keith was old school. The last place he wanted the woman in his life to be was all up in his business. "You know, babe . . . you'd be better served to use that gorgeous mind of yours to keep yourself groomed, in shape, and up on the latest fashion. You're by my side to make me look good, not to stick your nose in my finances or try and tell me where to live."

"Of course, Keith." Angelica's submissive response masked her anger. *Don't patronize me, you son of a bitch. I'm the reason Stan shared information on Bastion and Nick, and why you're poised to seal the biggest deal of your life.* Angelica decided to send Keith a subtle reminder in a passive/aggressive manner. "Stan called earlier."

Keith's brow furrowed, as Angelica had hoped. "What's he calling you about?"

Angelica stood and walked over to a view that sparkled with lights from a thousand homes and businesses. "Probably just wants my opinion about something. He often uses me as a sounding board regarding business ventures."

"Are y'all still fucking?" Keith asked brusquely.

"Why, Mr. Bronson. Do I detect a note of jealousy?"

"What you detect, Ms. King, is the sound of a man who won't be messed with. You're just a little too interested in matters that don't concern you. When it comes to my personal and business relationships, it's like oil and water . . . they don't mix."

Angelica could feel Keith's hard stare, but didn't turn to face him. Instead, she slowly sipped her snifter of Grand Marnier, tossed her thick, coiffed sister-locks, and again purposely shifted the mood. She felt she'd made her point for now, that she wasn't one to be messed with either. "Stan is not only someone I dated, but a very good friend. Even so, Keith, you must know that he doesn't hold a candle to you. You are more educated, intelligent, and street savvy. Not to mention the best lover I've ever had."

Angelica cleared her throat, afraid the lie she just spoke might get lodged there and cause her to choke. No one had better lovemaking skills than Dominique Rollins. But Angelica wisely decided this was a fact best kept to herself. "I only mentioned it because hearing his message reminded me of something else I heard through the LA business grapevine. Nick Rollins and his partners rushed to Las Vegas last week for a closed-door meeting with some . . . men from China. I know you don't want me in your business affairs, Keith, and I'm not trying to elbow my way in. I'm really not."

Angelica rose from her chaise and eased herself down onto Keith's prone body. She kissed his chest, nose, and lips. "I just want to see you get what you deserve," she whispered, even as she reached beyond the elastic on his pj bottoms. "I want to see you get everything."

54

Tiffany wiped away a bead of sweat from her brow as she gently shook the small stainless steel skillet. She sautéed scallops in garlic-infused butter even as she stirred the spinach wilting in another pan. Once finished, she plated the scallops atop the greens and drizzled the remaining butter over the dish. "Order up!" she said, pleased with the presentation. She immediately called out for two live lobsters before searing a prime cut of beef.

"Do you want me to drop them, Chef?" Roger asked as he brought the snarly crustaceans over to the stove. Tiffany nodded. A hiss soon followed as he submerged the lobsters in a pot of boiling water. He nudged Tiffany playfully, happy to act as sous chef as Tiffany was once again allowed to cook for her dad. "So, do you think your old man's gonna stick around this time?"

Tiffany cut a mean look in Roger's direction. He'd hit a nerve, especially since she'd just been thinking about the last time she took dishes out to an empty table. Her father had apologized, and offered an explanation for his hasty departure. He didn't have to. She knew—business.

"Whoa, sorry!" Roger said. "Didn't mean to push a sore spot with you, Chef."

"Don't worry about it," Tiffany replied. "It's hard to avoid sore spots where my dad is concerned."

Roger walked close to her and dropped his voice. "Look at it this way, Tiff. At least you still have a dad to get angry at. Me and my pops were at each other's throats all the time, up until he died two years ago. I'd give anything just to hear him yell at me just one more time." He said nothing more, just walked over to the food processor, dropped in some ingredients, and turned it on.

Tiffany pondered Roger's words as she cooked, having never given thought to her father being permanently removed from her life, dying. *How would I feel with Daddy gone for good?* She removed the steak from the fire and set it on a board to rest, then reached long tongs into the large pot and pulled out the cooked lobsters. *I know we have our differences and I know he hasn't been the best father, but I still love him.* She placed the lobsters on a cutting board, chopped off the claws, and split open the tails. After plating the herbed spinach pasta she'd made from scratch, she took seasoned melted butter and placed it in a ceramic creamer to be used tableside. She began slicing the steak for plating, noting that the meat was cooked to perfection. Even though the restaurant was near capacity and there were orders to fill, Tiffany reached for the plates holding the food she'd prepared. Roger's words had hit their mark. Tiffany decided that she, and nobody else, would be the one to serve her father.

* * *

Keith admired the restaurant's décor as he sipped his Chardonnay. The perky waitress had been right—it was the perfect complement to the succulent scallops he'd enjoyed before the palate-cleansing celery soup. It was hard for Keith to believe that his daughter had actually prepared these dishes. Over the years, he'd eaten in his share of five-star restaurants, and couldn't remember any dish that had surpassed what he'd experienced so far at Taste. The service, the understated elegance of his surroundings . . . Keith had to admit that he was impressed. And he didn't impress easily.

As he watched the people around him obviously enjoying their meals, Keith sat back and searched for memories of Tiffany, the little girl turned woman whom he hardly knew. Smiling, he remembered her as a baby. She was a small newborn, yet feisty and full of life. Her eyes used to light up when she looked at him, and when she grabbed his forefinger, she held on for dear life. The toddler years were a blur. He'd traveled so much during that time—as a salesman, then a project manager, and later as sales director for a commodities firm. He'd been so focused during those early years, determined to shut up the naysayers: racist jerks, jealous coworkers, and the voice of a father who said he'd never amount to anything. He did remember one birthday, though, when Tiffany was five years old. Her birthday landed on a Saturday that year, and Keith was home. Janice had a party and invited the neighborhood children. Keith went to the mall himself, a rare occurrence, and picked out a big, brown teddy bear for his little girl. When

Tiffany unwrapped it, Keith remembered her eyes widening in amazement. "I wuv it!" she'd shouted. The stuffed animal was almost as big as Tiffany, but she refused to part with it, even for a minute. She dragged it around as she played the games. Keith chuckled aloud as he remembered that after Janice served the cake, the bear had as much cake frosting on his face as Tiffany did.

Keith rubbed his brow as another scene came to mind. This one happened much later, when Tiffany was twenty-three years old. She'd just gotten her master's degree from UCLA, and since Keith didn't see a husband or children anywhere in her future, he'd laid aside his chauvinistic views and made big plans for his only child to follow his footsteps into the business world. He'd taken her out to a fancy restaurant, much like the one he sat in now, and along with introducing her to his latest wife, laid out his plans for her future.

"I'm so proud of you, Tiffany."

"Thanks, Daddy."

"I am, too," Keith's wife had echoed.

Tiffany had suppressed the desire to roll her eyes and simply smiled.

After a bit of small talk, Keith had made an announcement. "I have a surprise for you, baby girl!"

Tiffany's smile widened—her graduation present! For high school, her dad had bought her a shiny red Nissan. The down payment on her condo had been her undergrad gift. Tiffany couldn't imagine what she would get this time.

Keith reached into his inner breast pocket and pulled out an envelope. Tiffany's heartbeat quickened as he held it out to her. "What's this?" she asked.

"Only one way to find out." Keith winked at his wife and placed his arm around her. He beamed at Tiffany, who was staring at the envelope. "Well . . . open it up!"

Tiffany did, and quickly unfolded the letter inside, written on Keith's company's stationery:

Dear Miss Matthews:
   Your father has taken the liberty of forwarding your college transcripts to this office and we are quite impressed with your scholastic achievements. We are pleased to make an offer to you for a junior management position. Your starting salary will be $75,000, with additional company benefits including full medical and dental insurance, profit sharing, two weeks' vacation . . .

When Tiffany had looked up at her father, hers wasn't the happy face he'd been expecting. Instead, tears threatened as she quietly refolded the paper, stuck it back in the envelope, and placed the envelope near her father's plate.

Keith frowned. "What's the matter, baby?"

"I can't accept that," Tiffany whispered.

Keith nodded his understanding. Of course. She wanted to prove herself and not think that she got the job simply because her father owned the company. "Baby girl, I can assure you that nepotism doesn't play a part here. You were not the only candidate considered for this position. There were four other applicants that we—"

"I'm going to be a chef!"

Tiffany's sentence seemed to push air out of the room, and took sound with it. It was as if time stopped. Keith immediately thought about the tens of thousands of dollars he'd spent to provide his daughter with a top-notch education. *And she wants to trade in her diploma for an apron? To sweat over a stove in somebody's kitchen?*

"You want to do what?" Keith asked slowly, enunciating every word.

"Daddy, I love to cook. And I'm good at—"

"You want to do *what?*" Keith bellowed the question this time, and every patron in the restaurant turned to hear Tiffany's answer. "Do you think I just spent almost a hundred thousand dollars preparing you to work in my company so that you can throw it all away for a hot stove?"

"It's not like that, Daddy. I don't just want to cook. I want to be a chef, own my own restaurant. Nothing I've learned will be wasted; it will all be put toward eventually opening my own five-star restaurant."

Keith looked at Tiffany as if she'd grown an extra head. "You listen to me, Tiffany. No daughter of mine is going to spend her life as a glorified cook. Now, I don't know where you got this cockamamie idea, but you'd better forget about it, and quick. Do you know how many graduates would kill to get the offer that's been handed to you on a silver platter? People with five, ten years' experience don't have jobs like the one that's just landed in your lap!"

Keith realized he was still talking loudly even as his wife placed a calming hand on his forearm. He took a deep breath, lowered his voice. "You have a month to take a break from all your hard work of the past six years. You name the place and I'll pay for the vacation, for you and a friend, wherever you want to go. Then in July, just after the holidays, I expect you to move into your new office at KJB. If you don't, then . . . you're on your own. I'll cut off all financial support, so that you can see how a *cook* lives. I'll let you keep the condo, and other gifts . . . but no more. Join the KJB family and, well, the sky's the limit for what you can achieve."

"No!" Tiffany heard herself say. She took a breath and looked her father in the eye. "I spent the last six years of my life getting the degree that you wanted me to have. Now it's time for me to get what I want. This fall, I will be enrolling in culinary school, to get a degree in the culinary arts."

Keith never said another word. He simply folded his napkin, placed it on top of the half-eaten dinner, rose from the table, and left the room. His wife cast a sympathetic look at Tiffany before hurrying behind him. After Tiffany paid the almost two-hundred-dollar bill for a dinner no one ate, she too left the restaurant. Keith and his daughter didn't see each other for the next five years.

Keith looked down at his cleaned plate, and

for the first time was ashamed at how he'd treated his daughter. *She was right and I was wrong.*

"Dad?" Tiffany asked cautiously, aware that her father was deep in thought. When he looked up, his eyes were misty. Tiffany placed his dinner in front of him. "Dad, are you all right?"

"You were right and I was wrong, Tiffany," he muttered, anguish evident in his voice. "I was wrong to squash your dreams of being a chef, of trying to force my idea of success on you."

It was the first time Keith Bronson had come anywhere close to an admission of wrongdoing, much less an apology. Tiffany's heart swelled at the sound of his words, but she knew if the conversation continued on its present course, she'd break into an ugly cry. And as the sous chef of a five-star restaurant in one of Los Angeles's premier hotels, that would not be cute.

"Let's talk about that later," she said, forcing a cheerful sound to her voice. "We don't want your food to get cold." Tiffany donned her professional hat, explaining the food she'd prepared for her father. "The butter has been infused with ginger, smoked paprika, and lemon zest," she concluded, "and can be either poured over the lobster or used for dipping. Bon appétit."

Keith looked at his daughter another long moment before spearing a chunk of the lobster, dipping it in the butter, and placing it in his mouth. The spices immediately tickled his palate, even as the lobster almost melted in his mouth. He closed his eyes, chewed slowly, and savored the taste. "It's absolutely incredible, Tiffany," he said when he'd finished. "The best food I've ever tasted."

Tiffany tried to swallow the lump that leaped into her throat. "Well, enjoy, Daddy," she said hurriedly. "I have a few more orders to get out, but I will come back and join you for dessert." Without waiting for an answer, she rushed out of the restaurant, bypassed the kitchen, ran into the bathroom, and burst into tears.

Forty-five minutes later, Tiffany watched her dad scoop up the last of his apple dumpling, which had been served warm atop Tiffany's caramel ice cream. When she'd returned to the table and her father had tried again to apologize, Tiffany had cut him off. "Let's have this talk later, Dad. You'll make me cry, and that's not professional." Her father's smile was bittersweet as he'd simply nodded and changed the subject. The time they spent talking during Tiffany's fifteen-minute break centered on family and politics, specifically the presidency of Barack Obama, which next to business was Keith's favorite subject.

"When it comes to worldwide diplomacy, Obama's been walking a tightrope for the last two years. No matter which country we're talking about, he's damned if he does and damned if he doesn't."

"I think he's doing a fabulous job," Tiffany countered. "And Michelle is the perfect complement, tackling issues important to women everywhere. Wow, what I wouldn't give to fix them dinner . . . just one time. And speaking of, I'd better get back to work."

Keith wiped his mouth and placed the napkin on his cleaned plate. He leaned back, crossed his arms, and stared at his daughter. "The food was simply amazing, Chef," he said sincerely. "I love you, Tiffany."

Tiffany stood, once again tamping down her emotions. "Me, too, Dad. Catch you later." She leaned over, kissed him on the cheek, and left.

Keith eyed his watch. Dinner had taken longer than he'd intended, but he'd enjoyed every moment. So much so that he thought about taking the evening off. Maybe he'd pick up Angelica and do something casual—maybe take in a movie or go to the beach. He'd just reached for his BlackBerry to dial her, when it rang. "Bronson."

"Hey, Keith. It's Stan. We've got a situation, and we need to act fast. How far are you from Bel Air?"

"I'm in Malibu."

"Shit. Well, your source was right. While we were watching out for a meeting here in Los Angeles, those bastards were having it in Vegas. We need to act fast."

"I'm on my way." Keith quickly threw down two one-hundred-dollar bills and exited the restaurant. He was in such a hurry that he almost ran over the tall, lean man who rounded the corner. "Oh, excuse me, brothah," Keith said as he looked up. Recognition came immediately as he took in the immaculately dressed Black man. "Nick Rollins," he said to himself.

"Yes," Nick replied. "And you are?"

"In a hurry," Keith replied before quickly exiting the hotel.

Nick's eyes narrowed as he watched the man scurry from his establishment. *Who is he?* Nick thought. *And why is he in such a hurry?*

55

Tiffany yawned as she unlocked the door to her new home. She was exhausted, her shoulders and feet ached, and she needed a shower. At the same time, she'd never felt better. For the first time in a long time, in fact, since she could remember, her father had complimented her for doing what she loved. His praise lay like a blanket around her, causing all the physical aches and pains to recede into the background of her mind.

"Nick?" Tiffany walked into the master suite and immediately began pulling off her clothes. *He's probably in his office.* Tiffany smiled as she stepped into her favorite part of this bedroom—the custom shower. It was made of pure marble and was as large as her old walk-in closet. Six pulsating showerheads enveloped her in a liquid massage, with dual seating for at-home pedicures—or as was more often the case with Tiffany and Nick, lovemaking. Tiffany twirled around, luxuriating in the feel of the soft water flowing from all angles against her skin. She could have stayed in the shower indefinitely, but remembering the good news she wanted to share with Nick, she quickly washed her hair. After toweling off and rubbing on her favorite vanilla-and-jasmine-scented lotion, Tiffany donned a skimpy, silk pajama short set and went in search of her man.

"Hey, you," she said when she found him, looking out the window in his home office. She snuggled behind him before walking around and searing him with a long kiss. "I'm so glad to be home."

"I'm glad, too," he drawled, dipping his head to kiss her again. "Especially now."

"And I'm so happy! You'll never guess what happened to me today!" Tiffany almost bounced around the room as she told Nick about her father's visit to the restaurant. She gave him a rundown of all the dishes she served and a recap of their conversation. "He loved my food!" Tiffany finished. "He said I was a top-notch chef, and that I made him proud! The one and only Keith Bronson—proud that his daughter's a cook! I can't believe it."

Nick's head jerked up at this last comment. "What did you say?"

"I said that I can't believe that my dad is proud—"

"No, his name."

"Keith Bronson."

Nick's brow furrowed. "But your last name is Matthews."

"My mother's maiden name. It's a long story, but she changed both of ours after their divorce. But that's not the point! The point is that for the first time in my life, my dad gets it. He finally gets why I love to do what I do!"

"That's great, baby, that's real good." Nick hugged her tenderly.

Tiffany stepped back and looked into Nick's eyes. She'd been so wrapped up in her own happiness that she hadn't noticed his subdued mood until now. "What is it, Nick? What's wrong?"

What was wrong? That was the fifty-million-dollar question—literally. It was the question Nick had wrangled with since leaving his office around six o'clock, after spending hours on the phone. When he'd finished making calls and having them returned, he knew all he needed to know about Keith Bronson, the financial whiz behind the other contenders for the chain of nightclubs in China. Everything but the fact that he had a daughter named Tiffany.

Competition aside, Nick admitted to having a grudging respect for Keith Bronson. He was a man who, like Nick, had pulled himself up by his own bootstraps. Keith was brilliant with numbers, and tenacious when it came to getting the deal. He'd been labeled "silent but deadly" in business circles, the one who would verbally cut you with such finesse that it was only days later you realized you were bleeding. While being persistent, Nick learned that Keith stopped short of being ruthless. And he had a soft side, as his informant had found out. Keith had almost single-handedly funded the children's ward of a low-income hospital in Detroit, where he grew up. Nick was in turmoil with what to do about what he knew, and how much to tell the woman who stood nestled in his arms.

Nick reached for Tiffany's hand and walked over to the large office chair. He sat down and pulled her into his lap. *How can I tell her?* He ran his hand through her still damp hair and kissed her neck, but remained silent. *How can I tell her that my competition for this business venture, the one that will set me up to give Tiffany the life and relationship she wants . . . is her father?*

56

Nick paced his office. Various conversations from the past few days vied for attention in his head—especially Bastion's pleas and the other partners' appeal for caution where this monumental decision to bow out of the China venture was concerned. As loud as those voices were, however, they paled in comparison to the conversation he'd had that morning, when a trustworthy informant had confirmed his suspicions about Stan. Their finance guy was definitely playing both sides against the middle, and Nick believed he knew why. Angelica. Obviously, Stan had become more enamored with her than Nick had realized, enough to where he would betray one set of partners for another. But why?

"Mr. Rollins?"

Nick frowned at the fact his musings had been interrupted. "Yes, Kim?" Kim was the woman sent from the temporary agency to replace a hastily fired Christina—whom he'd let go after questioning her about Angelica. Christina denied sharing any confidential information with Angelica, but admitted she had talked to her since the breakup, and had initiated some of those conversations. That was enough information for Nick to lose faith in her, even though he felt she was lying as well. Nick liked to run a tight ship and a drama-free life. He had to trust everyone who worked for him, and he no longer trusted Christina. So she had to go.

"Tiffany is on line one."

Nick smiled. Tiffany was the one who could make him happy that his attention had been diverted. He walked behind his desk and sat down. "Hey, baby."

"Hey, you. Sorry to bother you, but I'm on break and was thinking about this Sunday. I have the day off, and thought about inviting Joy and her crew over. Do you have plans?"

Nick glanced at his planner. "Nothing urgent. I'll fix my world-famous grilled steaks."

"You and Randall can fight over the grill. Joy and I will handle the side dishes. Say . . . three o'clock?"

"Or earlier, if you'd like. And make sure the kids bring their swimsuits."

"Thanks, Nick."

"You're welcome."

"Okay, bye."

"Uh, hold on a minute. Aren't you forgetting something?"

There was a pause on the other end before Tiffany answered. When she did, there was a smile in her voice. "Oh, that. I love you, Nick."

Nick's chest swelled with pride and his manhood with longing as he hung up. They still hadn't taken their relationship public but he knew from Steven, the head of the concierge and all-around ears in the lobby, that people were starting to whisper about the amount of time Tiffany spent in his office. Nick had not one ounce of shame that a few of the meals Tiffany had brought him to taste had turned into another type of tasting altogether. *Just another couple months.* Once Nick and his partners sealed the restaurant/ nightclub deals in China, Nick was going to surprise Tiffany with what she'd always wanted—even though she'd have to promise to work part-time. Nick had no intentions of cutting down his heavy schedule while his wife became a workaholic. *Wife? Where did that come from?* Nick knew from where. That thought had come from his heart. Tiffany's exuberance for cooking and passion in lovemaking, combined with the naïve, vulnerable side that she tried so hard to keep hidden, was an attractive combination that Nick couldn't resist. Nor did he want to. He thought they were perfect together, and thought that Tiffany would make a wonderful mother. He only hoped he could be a good dad.

Thinking of fatherhood brought Nick's thoughts back to Keith Bronson. His frown returned. To navigate the situation between Tiffany and her father was tricky at best. If he got the deal, would Tiffany be angry that he'd won against her dad? If Keith got it, and Nick had to put the life he wanted for them on hold for several years, would Tiffany's trust in him fade? Would she be able to tamp back her fears that he was like her father? Nick felt guilty withholding this information from the woman he loved, but if he could just find a way to either pay Keith off or get him to somehow back out of the deal . . .

"What am I thinking? That will never happen," Nick said to the empty room. He ran a weary hand across his face, got up from his desk, and walked over to the magnificent ocean view that always calmed him. *If it comes down to a choice between this deal or Tiffany . . .* Nick didn't doubt his love for Tiffany. *But is it enough for me to walk away from fifty million dollars?*

"How can I do this?" Nick murmured to himself. "How can I get rid of Stan, make a case with Keith to back out of the deal, and expose Angelica for the snake that she is?"

"Mr. Rollins?"

"Yes, Kim?"

"Steven is here and would like a moment with you."

Steven? What could he want? "Uh, sure, Kim. Send him in."

Seconds later, his head concierge and longtime employee walked into the room. "Sorry to bother you, Mr. Rollins, but Angelica and an older man are in the restaurant. Keith, I believe she called him. I know you lifted the ban on her being here, but thought you'd like to know."

Interesting. "I appreciate it, Steven. Thanks." Without thinking twice about it, Nick walked toward the door. Most of the time, when it came to business, Nick was meticulous in his planning, dotting every *i* and crossing every *t.* Now was not one of those times. Now he was going on instinct alone, following his intuition. Two of the three people he'd just thought about wanting to deal with had just walked into his restaurant. *Angelica's idea,* he figured, as he crossed the lobby. And then another thought hit him. *Tiffany can't possibly know that Angelica is dating her father!* Nick's steps increased. He couldn't get to the restaurant fast enough.

57

"Hey, Tiff, your dad's out there." Amber said this as she reached for two plates on the counter and then balanced two more in her right hand.

"He is?" Tiffany was surprised her dad was still in town. She was even more surprised that he was back at the restaurant.

"And he's got company," Amber added before pushing open the door with her backside and scurrying out.

"You fix meal?" Chef Wang asked.

"Uh, oh, sure." *Who did Dad bring with him? One of his business partners?* Tiffany smiled. If her dad brought someone he did business with to the restaurant, then he was absolutely proud of what she'd served. *But maybe it's his latest love interest.* Tiffany tried not to have this thought bring a downer to her afternoon. After all, her dad had a right to happiness, even though she didn't believe he always made the best choices. "Maybe this one will be different."

"What?" Roger walked over to her station with a batch of sliced tomatoes, ready for sauce making.

"My dad brought someone to the restaurant," Tiffany replied. "I know that doesn't sound like much, but considering the fights we've had about my career choice, believe me, it's major!"

Nick entered the restaurant and walked directly up to the table where Keith and Angelica dined. "Angelica! This is a surprise." He leaned down and kissed her lightly on the cheek, before turning to Keith. "Nick Rollins," he said, with hand outstretched.

Nick's abrupt appearance caught both diners off guard. Angelica had intended to make sure Nick was aware of her presence, but later, after she'd shocked Tiffany with the news that they might become family, and to let the cat out of the bag about her father's great deal happening in China. Now she'd have to play her cards a little differently. Both she and Keith recovered at the same time.

"Keith Bronson," Keith said, standing slightly to shake Nick's hand. "I see you know Angelica."

Nick smiled as he motioned for Angelica to make room for him in their booth. "Oh, yes. Me and Angelica go way back, don't we, Angie?"

Angie? Who is this fool talking to? I've never been called Angie in my entire life! Angelica was flustered. She knew Nick was playing a game and hated having to learn the rules on the fly. "It's Angelica, and you know it," she said finally, with just the right touch of huffiness. "And if you don't mind, Nick, this is a private lunch."

"Keith Bronson," Nick said, ignoring Angelica. "So the rumors I've heard are true."

"What rumors are those?"

Conversation stopped for a moment while Amber took their appetizer orders. "The scallop dishes are superb," Nick commented while they decided. "They are my favorite appetizers, and our sous chef makes some of the best dishes I've tasted in the world."

Keith looked at Nick a long moment before deciding on the scallop medley—a plating featuring the scallops cooked five different ways—and Angelica decided on a crab salad.

"Amber, have one of the 1995 Rieslings brought out . . . the ones I have reserved for special guests." Nick smiled and winked at Angelica, further flustering her.

What are you up to, Nick Rollins?

The wine was brought out in seconds and their small talk was once again interrupted while the sommelier opened the bottle and made sure it was to Nick's liking. Nick waited until both Keith and Angelica had held up their glasses and knew that later, they would both wonder where the toast he offered came from: "To strange bedfellows."

Keith put down his glass without taking a drink. He looked at Nick. "What's going on here?"

"I'm sorry, man, please drink up."

Keith hesitated again before taking a sip of the wine. "You've heard rumors? What kinds of rumors?"

"Angelica tells me that you're vying for a certain new venture being developed for the . . . Asian market."

This time, Angelica could not hide her shock, nor could she mistake the anger that flashed across Keith's face. "I did no such thing, Nick, and you know it!"

"Man, don't sweat it," Nick continued, his voice

low, conspiratorial. "I'm sure you know Angelica and I used to date and are still close."

Keith's eyes narrowed as he glared at Angelica.

"Oh, no, not in that way, man," Nick said, with a laugh. "No, there's only one woman who has my heart now, Keith. Most likely it is her expertise that you're tasting today. She's a fine sous chef and even finer human being. I'd love for you to meet her. Her name is Tiffany."

"You're dating my daughter?"

Tiffany stopped in her tracks, sheer will keeping her from dropping the appetizer plates she held in her hands. What was Nick doing having lunch with her father?

There were a million thoughts running through Keith Bronson's head, and right now he was trying to keep most of them from showing on his face. The man he was determined to take down by any means necessary for the Asian market was dating his daughter? And used to date Angelica? *What kind of game is this woman trying to get over on me?* Keith would have to wait for the answers.

For now, he tried to erase the frown from his face as he motioned to his daughter. "Tiffany."

Tiffany! Nick's face remained blank while his heart plummeted. *Did she hear what I just said? And wait until she sees . . .*

"Angelica?" Tiffany asked, not trying to mask her surprise. Her hand slipped and the plate of scallops crashed to the table. Unfortunately, it clipped one of the water goblets on the way down. The glass fell directly into Angelica's lap.

"Ow!" Angelica tried to leap up from her seat but

was wedged between the middle of the booth and the table.

"I'm sorry," Tiffany mumbled, still in shock from seeing not only her father and Nick sitting down together, but Angelica as well. Tiffany had no love for Angelica, and while dropping the plate was an accident, she would just as soon have thrown the glass of water in her face. What was she doing at Taste with Nick and her dad?

"She ruined my outfit. Do you hear me, it's absolutely ruined. This is Dolce and Gabbana, brand new. It cost over seven hundred dollars. Nick, I want you to do something about your employee, now!"

"Calm down, Angelica," Nick said sternly.

"That's my daughter you're talking about," Keith warned.

Meanwhile, Amber had heard the commotion and came up next to Tiffany with towels to wipe up the water, and to soothe Angelica's nerves. "We are so sorry, ma'am," Amber said, moving the plates and wiping the liquid. Any other time, she would have made the offer on behalf of the hotel to handle any cleaning bill or other expense that resulted from the accident, but since one of the owners of said hotel was sitting at the table, she wisely thought to leave such gestures to Nick.

"I'm sorry," Tiffany said again, once Amber had cleared the table. "I'm just surprised to see you here . . . with my dad." Tiffany looked at Nick but didn't comment on his presence.

"So, Tiffany, I take it you know Angelica?"

Unfortunately, yes. "We've met." Tiffany hoped her voice sounded neutral, though she was hardly trying to act as if she and Angelica were friends.

Keith looked from Angelica to Nick to Tiffany. The tension was thicker than the black bean paste. For the first time since Steven had delivered the news and he'd left his office, Nick questioned his hasty decision to confront Keith and Angelica in the restaurant. How was he going to explain this to Tiffany, and how angry would she be once she was aware that he knew about her father's connection to Angelica and the China venture?

Before Nick could take control of the situation, Angelica spoke. "Keith, I want to leave, immediately. I'm soaked, and upset and . . . I just want to get out of here."

Keith started to object, and then decided that leaving was the best thing. He needed answers, and he needed to sort out just what was going on between Nick and Angelica, and what that had to do with Angelica's fast track into his life. Granted, he'd welcomed her with open arms once she entered, but now he had to ask—why was she there?

He stood abruptly from the table and reached for his wallet.

"Please," Nick said, staying his hand. "The wine and your next meal are on me. Angelica, send the cleaning bill for your pantsuit to the hotel. We'll gladly cover it. Keith, I think we need to talk. If you have any free time while in LA, please give me a call." Nick reached into his jacket pocket and pulled out a business card.

Keith took the card. "I'm not sure there's anything *you* and I need to discuss." He gave Tiffany a long, hard look, and then followed a huffing, puffing, and dripping Angelica out of the restaurant.

58

Nick breathed a sigh of relief. Tiffany's car was in their driveway. She'd gone back into the kitchen as soon as her father left, without a word to him, and when he called down to the kitchen, she was adamant about not discussing what had happened while at work. As angry as she'd seemed when she left the table, he'd not been at all sure that he would find her here. Within minutes, he was walking through his dark, quiet mansion. He walked straight to the master suite and called out softly. "Tiffany?"

He stepped inside and allowed his eyes to adjust to the darkness. *Is she sleeping? Should I turn the light on and wake her up?* For a man often said to have nerves of steel while making multimillion-dollar decisions, Nick felt more than a little uneasy. He'd second-guessed his earlier decision during his entire drive home. Especially after he'd called her cell and she hadn't answered. *Should I have told her what I knew about her father being my stiffest competition on a deal that mattered most?* Nick had wanted to spare her from what could have become a confrontational situation.

He'd hoped to have some type of resolution to the matter and *then* tell her everything. But Tiffany was a grown woman. Belatedly, Nick realized he maybe should have allowed Tiffany to make that decision for herself.

"Nick." Tiffany called to him from the hallway.

Nick spun around and walked out of the bedroom. "Baby," he said, his arms outstretched.

"Uh-uh. I don't feel like hugging right now. I feel like listening—to the reason why you were with my dad and Angelica, of all people, today at the restaurant. And why you didn't think the fact that you know my father is something you should tell me!"

"That's exactly what I want to do, and why I was looking for you. Can we sit down?" Nick asked, pointing toward the master suite.

"In the great room," Tiffany countered. She didn't want to discuss this in the same room where they'd made passionate love the night before.

Tiffany sat at the end of the long couch. She crossed her arms. And waited.

"I was trying to protect you," Nick began. "I ran into Keith yesterday, at the hotel. Or rather, he ran into me."

"You saw my dad yesterday, too?"

"I didn't know he was your father, not then." Nick explained the brief, mysterious encounter when Keith had bumped into him. "He knew who I was. But when I asked who he was, he hurried out the lobby. I went to the restaurant and asked Amber if she knew who the gentleman was who'd just eaten there. She told me it was your dad."

"And you didn't come to me then because . . ."

Nick sighed. "Because she told me his name." Nick

understood Tiffany's confused expression and hurried on. "Tiffany, Keith's firm is vying for the China nightclub project. His is the group I've been competing with to get this deal. I'd never met him, so didn't know what he looked like. I'd seen file photos of him, had an idea. But he brushed by me so quickly that it didn't register . . . until I talked to Amber." He was quiet a moment, allowing the enormity of what he'd just said to sink into Tiffany's understanding. "I went back to the office, made some calls. And the more I learned, the more certain incidents of the past few months made sense. Especially where Angelica was concerned."

"That was going to be my next question. Why was she there?"

Nick's stare met Tiffany's. "She and Keith are dating."

"What?" Tiffany lost her calm demeanor and jumped off the couch. "You have *got* to be kidding me! Tell me you're lying."

"I wish I were."

Tiffany began pacing the large expanse of the room. "What in the hell is she doing with my father? And why didn't I know about it?"

"Angelica didn't want you to know, Tiffany. She didn't tell your father that she knew you. You can trust me on that. Angelica knew about this project. I first heard wind of it when she and I were dating, engaged, actually. I knew then that this venture could be a career-defining moment for me, and I shared this excitement with her. So, my guess is that following our breakup, she found out who the opposing players were. This wouldn't necessarily be hard. Angelica and I dated for four years. She met several of the high-powered men I do business with. She then got to Keith—I'm not sure whether at this point she knew he was your father—but she latched on to him as her next *sponsor*. Angelica only dates men who are wealthy and can keep her in the lifestyle to which she's grown accustomed. She's also vindictive. So it probably didn't hurt that your father was trying to get a deal that meant so much to me."

Tiffany stopped pacing and walked to a table where several expensive pieces of crystal were displayed. She idly fingered the intricately carved pieces, thinking how something so valuable, so beautiful, could be shattered in an instant. *Is this what will happen to what Nick and I share?* Tiffany tried to keep out negative emotions and focus on what Nick had said. But there were still so many things she didn't know, didn't understand.

She walked back over to the couch and sat down. "I still don't get why you didn't come to me after you found out Keith was my dad."

Now it was Nick's turn to get up and pace. "Maybe I should have. But I was so shocked, and this all happened so fast. I know how you feel about your father, and how he's always put business before you. There were nagging questions that I needed answered before I said anything to you."

"Like what?"

"Like whether or not Keith knew about us, whether he was somehow using you to get closer to my businesses, to get information."

"Wait. You thought I might be working in cahoots with my father?"

"No, baby, no," Nick said as he walked over to the couch and sat next to Tiffany. She stiffened, but he persisted in taking her hand and looking her straight in the eye. "I trust you more than anyone else in the world, Tiffany. Don't ever doubt that. But—and don't take this personally, baby—but I don't trust your father. Some people will do crazy things when the stakes get this high, and I couldn't discount the fact that Angelica may have told your father about us, in some distorted way, to push Keith's desire to win this project over me even higher. What if she'd told him I was using you, or that if he won this deal it would get you away from me? Women like Angelica are more conniving than you can believe.

"I didn't want to come to you until I had the facts straight, and until I had the chance to talk with Keith face-to-face, and man to man. I wanted him to understand this deal was not just about me . . . but about us."

Tiffany jerked away from Nick and stood. "Now who's using me to get the deal? You think your dating me is going to mean a thing to Dad? Ha! I bet I'll have the last laugh on that one. Because if you think my father is going to bypass big money just because I'm his daughter, then you've still got some homework to do. Keith Bronson is about one thing and one thing only—m-o-n-e-y. So if you thought I was going to be your ace in the hole, you'd better keep digging." Tiffany wanted to run out of the room, but instead simply turned her back on the man she loved and stared out at the starry night. She didn't want to believe that Nick would use her as a pawn in business, but all of the old voices—the ones from the years when she came in second with her father— were speaking to her now. She'd been so close to living the life of her dreams—having a cozy, funky restaurant and running it with the man she loved.

But now she had to question whether she even knew the man she'd been sleeping with off and on for the past eight months. Maybe who she thought he was, was too good to be true.

"I didn't tell him about us to affect the outcome of the business deal," Nick said softly. "I told him because you're his daughter, and I thought he should know." He waited for a response, and when he didn't get one, walked over to Tiffany and took her hand. "Come here."

"No!"

"Please, Tiffany. Let's talk this through."

After a long moment, Tiffany walked around Nick and sat on the couch. She sat on the edge of the cushion, her back ramrod straight, as if to take flight at any second.

Nick joined Tiffany on the couch, and took her hand.

Again, she snatched it back. "Look, can't you just say what you have to say without touching me?"

"No, I can't." He calmly took both of her hands in his. "Look at me, Tiffany."

Slowly, reluctantly, she complied.

"Perhaps I should have handled this whole situation with your father differently. I can see how my actions could be interpreted as suspect from your perspective. I was trying to protect you, keep you out of the middle of what was going on, at least until I was sure exactly what that was.

"When I first heard the name Keith Bronson, I had no idea he was your father. I only knew of his involvement with Angelica which, given our history, already had me quite concerned. Then last night, when you mentioned his name and 'father' in the same sentence, baby, that just took an already crazy situation to another level. I could only imagine what hearing about Keith and Angelica would do to you, so I decided to try and get more information, find out the exact nature of their relationship, learn Angelica's angle in dating him relative to our mutual business interests, and, yes, to speak with your father about the China project. I'd hoped to tell you what was going on once things were resolved, one way or the other."

Tiffany stood and whipped around. "What kind of resolution can there be to this mess? My dad is screwing a woman who can't stand me *and* who just happens to be your ex, while also vying for the same 'once in a lifetime' deal that my man wants. Neither of you are going to back out, Angelica is going to continue being a bitch, and me? Don't ask me to choose, Nick. Ours isn't the best relationship, but he's still my father. I guess I'll just have to wait and see what happens."

"You won't have to wait long," Nick said, as he too stood. "And you won't have to take sides."

"How do you figure that?"

"I've thought this entire situation through, and I've stacked up the deal against what you mean to me. Baby, the scales tip overwhelmingly in your favor. If you want me to, Tiffany, I'll walk away from this deal. Right now, today. I mean it."

59

Tiffany sighed as she placed the last bite in her mouth and swallowed. Since the incident involving her dad and Nick the week before, and since canceling the barbeque with the Parsons family, she hadn't had much of an appetite. Leave it to Grand to bring it back. As had happened during her childhood, Grand's beef stew made her feel better. It was chock full of succulent beef, loads of vegetables, and round pasta. But mostly, the dish was filled with her grandmother's love.

"That was delicious, Grand," Tiffany said. "I need to come over here and watch you make it because my stew doesn't come out like this."

Grand chuckled even as she warmed at the praise. "Come over anytime, baby. But there's some kinds of cooking that has to be lived through, rather than taught. Tastes that come from repeating the process, and refining it, and pouring years' worth of 'know that you know' into the pot. You can already cook rings around me in some things. But beef stew, and these feel-good dishes? They come

from years of stirring them together, after you and
the recipe have had a chance to dance together for
a while, get to know each other. And from having
someone around you where you want to pour not
only food, but love into the bowls."

The two ladies cleared the table and walked into
the kitchen. Tiffany ran the dish water and began
cleaning the plates. Grand hummed while she put
on a pot of coffee and then began storing the remainder of their meal. "Well, do you want to talk
about it while we're washing dishes, or afterward,
when we have dessert?"

"What makes you think I have something to talk
about?"

Grand said nothing, just started humming again.

Several moments passed before Tiffany spoke. "It's
about Nick, the man I'm dating."

"Uh-huh."

"No, actually it's about Daddy."

Grand stopped and looked at Tiffany. "Well, which
one is it about, your fella or your father?"

"Actually, Grand, it's about them both."

"I tell you what," Grand said. "These dishes can
wait. Cut us a slice of that pound cake and take it in
the living room. I'll get the coffee." When Tiffany hesitated, Grand continued, "Conversations like these
are always easier with a little sugar around." She
winked and nudged Tiffany toward the cake pan.

Soon afterward, Tiffany was sitting in one of
Grand's well-worn recliners, eating cake and telling
her story. She told Grand everything—about how she
and Nick met (well, she did leave out some parts of
that story), deciding not to date him when she got
hired at Le Sol, and then changing her mind and

dating him anyway. She talked about Angelica and the run-ins they'd had. And finally, she told Grand about Nick and her father vying for the same lucrative venture in China, and how she found out about it.

"What's your daddy got to say for himself?" Grand asked, when Tiffany finished.

"I don't know." Tiffany shrugged. "We haven't talked."

"He didn't call after running into you that night?"

"He called once and left a message asking if I was okay."

"And why haven't you called him back?"

"Because . . . a part of me isn't sure I want to hear what he has to say."

"And he hasn't called again."

Tiffany shook her head.

Grand took a sip of coffee. "And what about your fella? What is he saying?"

Tiffany told her about Nick's offer to bow out of the deal if that was what she wanted.

"Do you think he meant it?"

"I don't know. I've never had anybody put me ahead of their work, but deep down, I really do think he meant what he said. Oh, Grand, this love stuff is so complicated. I don't know what to do!"

"If that young man meant what he said, that he'd turn down millions to make you happy, then I'll tell you my opinion."

Tiffany welcomed another opinion. Lord knew she'd talked Joy's ears off and still didn't know how to feel. "Please, Grand, what do you think?"

"I think you done found the man who can help you perfect your beef stew!"

* * *

Tiffany had been gone for more than an hour before Grand made the call. She'd just gotten off the phone with Janice, who hadn't been home when Grand had left a message earlier. Janice had been curious, even hesitant, about giving Grand Keith's number, pointing out that they hadn't spoken in two or three years. But Grand reminded Janice that she was mama in this conversation, and assured her that she had a very good reason for wanting to speak to Keith Bronson.

"What do you want to talk to him about?" Janice had asked her.

"That's between me and him" had been Grand's reply.

Grand dialed the number carefully. She waited, and frowned when the call went to voicemail. Figuring this was not something to be left "after the beep," she hung up and immediately dialed the number again.

This time, Keith answered. "Hello?"

"Keith, this is Gladys."

A beat of silence and then, "My mother-in-law?"

Gladys chuckled. "You know more than one Gladys?"

"Uh, no," Keith sputtered. "But I'm just rather surprised to be hearing from you, that's all."

"I know it's been a while. Janice gave me this new number."

They shared a few pleasantries, inquired after each other's health. "So, what can I do for you, Mama Goodness?" Keith asked, using the endearment he used to call her.

"It ain't about what you can do for me," Gladys replied. "It's about what you can do for your daughter. You need to call her. And you need to have a conversation that is long overdue."

"Tiffany? I don't mean to be rude, Gladys," Keith countered, suddenly feeling his ex in-law was not so dear, "but I don't see where my relationship with my daughter is any of your business."

"She ain't been much of your business, either."

"Wait a minute. You listen here—"

"No, you listen. I'm not judging you. I'm just calling it like I see it. That child needs you, and you ain't always been there. But, son, if I have anything to say about it . . . that's all about to change."

60

"You can't be serious."

"I am."

Bastion shook his head, got up, and walked to the elaborate bar in his Santa Monica home. "Care for a drink?" When Nick shook his head, Bastion placed two ice cubes in a tumbler and poured himself a generous amount of bourbon. "Nick, I know you love Tiffany, but backing out of the deal if she feels uncomfortable. . . . Man, I've known you for almost twenty years, have been your partner for a decade. This just isn't like you."

"I know. But there's more to life than business, Bastion."

Bastion rejoined Nick in the sitting area. "Look, I know you're getting older, you want to marry, have a family. You've still got time to do all that, Nick, plenty of time! Don't throw away the deal of a lifetime because some woman can't understand how important it is! Tiffany's great, but if she would ask you to choose between her and your livelihood, is she really the woman you want to spend the rest of your life with?"

"Tiffany hasn't asked me to do anything. It is my decision to show her that she means more to me than money."

"We're not just talking money, Nick," Bastion said, in a raised voice. "We're talking over a hundred million dollars in the next few years!"

"You don't have to remind me, Bastion. I know how much the deal is worth! Okay?"

"Okay, buddy, calm down."

"You calm down!"

Bastion's blue eyes pierced Nick's, but he remained silent. Nick stared right back before dropping his gaze. He could count on one hand the times he and Bastion had argued. Ninety-nine percent of the time they were on the same page. Nick hoped they could get back there on this issue, but even if they didn't, Nick's mind was made up.

Nick took a deep breath. "I'm sorry for hollering at you, B. This situation is crazy, and it's got me on edge. And believe me, it's not just Tiffany that has me rethinking my alignment with this group. It's Stan."

"I agree. It wasn't right for him to share confidences with Angelica. We're prepared to mete out a consequence for that breach. But we need him with us. He's crunching the numbers, Nick. And we're too close to nailing this thing to change personnel. You know how long it took for our Chinese partners to develop their confidence in us. They like to take things slow, get to know all the players. If we changed up now it just might . . . Stan's an asshole. Maybe we'll buy him out after the deal is over, but right now . . ."

"I know, it's tricky."

"Which is why you cannot bow out of this deal.

Tiffany's a smart girl. She'll support you, Nick, I know it."

After discussing a few matters regarding other businesses, Nick left Bastion's house. He appreciated Bastion's belief in Tiffany, that she'd never make him choose between his work and her love. Nick believed in her, too. But he also knew her vulnerabilities in this area, because of her father. Putting his business first could cost him Tiffany. He didn't want to take that chance.

61

Keith pulled his carry-on into the foyer and closed the door. He stopped and looked around. He'd been spending so much time in Los Angeles that his Chicago home seemed almost foreign to him. He stopped at the hallway table, where the housekeeper had neatly stacked the mail in a copper holder. There was nothing urgent in the contents, he knew, but he thumbed through the pile anyway. As he figured, it was mostly junk mail: sale papers, donation requests, and offers for another dozen credit cards.

After showering off the tiredness from a grueling week and a three-plus-hour flight, Keith headed to the kitchen. The housekeeper had stocked the refrigerator in anticipation of his arrival. He eyed a container of salad and another marked "tuna." He pulled these from the refrigerator, placed the tuna steak in the microwave, and cut a large chunk from a loaf of French bread on the counter. As he placed the salad on a plate, he remembered another meal— one prepared and served by his daughter.

Keith took the plate and walked to his large dining

room table that seated ten people. He'd lived in this house for almost ten years and had never used all the chairs at one time. Aside from the various wives and girlfriends who'd inhabited his life, and his business associates, Keith's life after Janice had been rather lonely. He hadn't really thought about these things before. But his conversation with Gladys had caused him to think about a lot of things, especially the time he'd missed with Tiffany, and how little he knew about the woman who—because of her mother's anger and hurt following their divorce—did not bear his last name.

"Nobody ever got a visit from a dollar bill on their deathbed," Gladys had said near the end of their conversation. "When people are preparing to meet their Maker, it's family they think about and who they want to have around."

He no longer had an appetite, so Keith left his untouched plate at the table and began walking aimlessly through his three-bathroom, four-bedroom, twenty-five-hundred-square-foot condo. Tiffany had never been there; in fact, Tiffany had never visited him in Chicago. It was the first time he'd pondered this truth, and it didn't feel good. He walked through the living room that had been decorated by a renowned designer, Candice Olson. She was a star on the HGTV Network, and in heavy demand. He'd had to pull some strings to get her, and the living room design alone cost more than fifty thousand dollars. Every piece was tailored, matched, and had its place in the subdued elegance of gray and black. He took in the artwork on the wall, all originals, as he left the living room and walked up the spiral staircase to the great room. There, the subtlety of the living room was left behind for a bolder mood. Bold colors enhanced the theme of black and gray that had been carried from the living room, and the original Salvador Dalí that Keith had personally escorted from Spain anchored the room. *I have it all,* he thought as he continued the spontaneous tour through his Lake Shore Drive abode, including the master suite, home office, and library in a separate wing. *So why am I feeling empty?*

Keith eventually returned to the dining room, where he threw away the tuna but ate some of the French bread and salad. He then opened a bottle of Pinot Noir, and took that and a wineglass back to his bedroom. He drank and thought into the night, almost until dawn. He analyzed his whole life—from the mean, lean streets of Detroit to conference-room meetings with some of the most powerful men in America. He thought about his ex-wives, and about Angelica. He tried to see his life five years from now, and to imagine how he wanted it to look. *In five years, I'll be sixty years old. It's time to think about what I'll do for the last third of my life, and who will be here with me.* Which was why, Keith concluded, the Chinese venture was so important. It would set him up for life.

Keith slept until noon, a rarity. When he awoke, he called his assistant and told her to cancel the meetings for which he'd flown back to Chicago, and book him on the next flight out to LA. He'd left some unfinished business back on the West Coast, and he refused to let another day go by without taking care of it.

62

When Nick returned to his office from the restaurant, where he'd spoken to Chef Wang, someone else was waiting for him.

Keith stood as soon as Nick entered the executive suites lobby.

"I told him he needed to make an appointment," Kim said, before Nick spoke.

"It's okay, Kim," Nick replied. He walked over to where Keith stood with a hand outstretched. "Keith."

"Nick, I need to speak with you. I asked for Tiffany downstairs and they said she was ill. Is she okay?"

"A little exhausted, stressed, but she'll be fine."

Keith didn't miss the unspoken message, that he was part of the reason for Tiffany's anxiety. "I know I don't have an appointment, but what I have to say can't wait."

Nick eyed Keith for a moment, and then shook his hand. "Come into my office. Kim, hold my calls."

The two men were silent until they'd entered Nick's spacious office and he'd closed the door. Nick bypassed his desk and walked over to the sitting area with a magnificent view of the ocean. He gestured for Keith to sit in one wing chair, while he sat in the one facing him.

"Nice view," Keith began.

"It is, but I don't think that's why you came to my office. I'm not sure Tiffany is why you're here, either."

"Let's get this straight off the bat. I love my daughter."

"Does she know?"

Two powerful, determined Black men eyed each other for a long moment.

Keith wrestled with his emotions. On one hand he despised the man in front of him, the one aligned with the competition that could take his dream. On the other, there was a begrudging admiration for the success Nick Rollins had built through hard work, tenacity, and intelligence. And then there was the fact that he was involved with Keith's daughter, and from what he could see, loved her. He knew he'd have to tread lightly to keep this meeting civil.

"Not that it's any of your business," Keith began, just to show he wasn't a pushover. "But I'll admit that I haven't always been the best father where Tiffany is concerned. I had my reasons, and I don't expect you to understand. But I'm not here to rehash the past. I'm here with a clear view toward my future." Keith took a deep breath and uttered the sentence he knew could change his life. "My company is backing out of the negotiations. I don't know about the other players, but as far as I'm concerned . . . the China deal is yours."

Nick looked at Keith, his chin resting on steepled fingers. He wasn't sure what to say. *Is this an underhanded ploy to get us to drop our defenses, slow down the negotiation process? Or is this really about Tiffany?*

There was only one way to find out. "Because of my relationship with your daughter?"

Keith stared out the floor-to-ceiling window, then rose and walked over to it. He watched as the waves lazily kissed the shore and in that moment realized that while he should have been tense, uptight, on edge—he felt just like the scene before him, calm. What he was about to do may have looked crazy, but it felt right.

"I was twenty-six when Janice got pregnant," he began, with his back to Nick. "I wasn't ready. See, I wanted to have a nice nest egg in the bank, a house that was paid for or close to, and be well established in my career before bringing kids into the equation. Janice disagreed . . . one of the many things Tiffany's mother and I didn't see eye to eye on. Janice said she hadn't meant to get pregnant, but I didn't believe her. I thought she did it to tie me down. Back then, I was traveling four to five days a week, home mostly on weekends. That didn't stop just because I had a child.

"My father wasn't able to provide for me, so I was determined that Tiffany would want for nothing. And no," Keith said, finally turning to face Nick, "it wasn't just for her. It was for me. To prove that I had what it took to be the best at what I did. I know what it's like on the other side of the tracks, and I never want to go back there. I wanted to have it all, at all costs. And I've come close to fulfilling my dreams. But it seems I may have lost something in the process.

"Tiffany's a beautiful woman, and I feel I hardly know her." Keith sighed, turned back to the ocean view. His eyes became misty, and Keith never cried. *So much time has been lost . . . years I can never get back.*

"She's a lot like you," Nick finally said.

"Hmph. That's been part of the problem—we're both stubborn and want to live life on our own terms. So," Keith clasped his hands together, his voice changing from one of nostalgia to being all business, "that's why I'm here. I've already talked to my team and told them that I'm pulling out to focus on other ventures. And, because I know your success involves Tiffany, I'll pass on any information that might help you close this deal."

Nick stood then, and walked toward Keith. Nick was taller, but Keith had bulk. Both were studies in strength and resolution. "You're a good man, Keith Bronson," Nick said when he reached him. He reached out his hand and the two performed a soul brothers' handshake. "Tiffany will be ecstatic when I share this news."

"Yeah, eyes on the money, just like her daddy."

"No, Keith, her eyes are on you. She'll be happy because you put her first."

63

Tiffany didn't know she'd dozed off to sleep until the phone rang. "Hey, Joy."

"Hey, girl. How are you feeling?"

Tiffany struggled to a sitting position and yawned. "A little better, I think."

"I can still come over there if you want me to."

"Thanks, sistah, but I'm okay."

"Have you tried eating anything yet?"

"No. I'll try and drink some juice after I wash my face and brush my teeth. Nick said he'd come home early to take care of me."

"And to think you almost quit working for that man. You'd better be glad I—" Joy clamped a hand over her mouth.

Tiffany rolled out of bed. "I'd better be glad you what?"

Dangit! She'd never told Tiffany about the phone call she'd made to Nick and the advice she'd given that led to Tiffany rescinding her resignation. "Oh, uh, never mind."

"Never mind, my behind. What did you do, Joy?"

Tiffany walked into the master bath, put the phone on speaker, and began washing her face.

"I, uh, look. Don't get mad at what I'm about to say. It's because of me you're living a fairy tale."

Tiffany put toothpaste on her brush. "I'm listening."

"I called Nick that week you resigned, after he canceled your vacation plans and flew to New York. I knew that you were just being your usually stubborn self, and since you wouldn't listen to me, I called to see if Nick would."

Tiffany stopped brushing her teeth. "And?" she asked around a mouthful of toothpaste.

"And I told him how you didn't like to be told what you couldn't do and if he actually agreed that you weren't cut out for a five-star restaurant, they'd probably have to pry your fingernails away from the stove."

"You heifah! Wait a minute." Tiffany quickly rinsed her mouth, wiped off the excess water with a towel, and picked up the phone. She knew exactly the conversation Joy was talking about, when Nick had questioned her abilities to be a top-shelf chef. She'd been livid, and at that moment became more determined than ever to succeed. Tiffany forgot all about being sick. She stomped into the kitchen and snatched open the refrigerator. "Nick didn't mean those things he said? He spouted that B.S. because you told him to?"

"Worked, didn't it?"

"What is it with everybody interfering in my life? First Grand," Tiffany said, remembering Grand's message that she'd spoken to Tiffany's father. "And now you!" Tiffany poured a glass of Perrier, hoping the carbonation would help her stomach's queasiness.

"People butt into your business because they

love you, Tiffany. Your grandmother does, and so do I. We want to see you happy, and I'd never seen you happier than when Nick Rollins walked into your life. So," Joy continued when Tiffany remained silent, "you can thank me now, or later."

Tiffany finished drinking her water. "Thank you," she said, then belched.

"Ooh, that's foul. I'm getting off this phone."

"Yeah, but it made me feel better." She belched again.

"Bye, Tiffany."

"Hey, Joy. What about the book? You said you were getting ready to send me what you wrote. That was a week ago."

"Yeah, but I read it again and thought it was whack. Writing is hard, girl. Makes me have mega-respect for all my favorite authors."

"So what are you going to do, give up?"

"Have you forgotten you're talking to Joy Parsons? I found an online writing course. My first class is next week."

Tiffany whooped. "Now that's what I'm talking about!"

The two best friends made plans to hang out on Tiffany's next day off. After ending the call, Tiffany wasn't sure which had made her feel better—the spirited conversation or the sparkling water. Her stomach had settled enough that she felt like taking a shower. She had just pulled on a pair of cashmere sweats when the tinkling chimes announced the front door opening.

Minutes later, Nick walked into the room. "Hey, baby."

"Hey."

"You feeling better?" he asked, his voice full of concern. Nick held his hand to Tiffany's forehead.

"A little bit. Still don't know if I can eat anything, though."

"I thought that that might be the case. Which is why I had Chef whip up some delicious vegetable soup for you. Are you up to joining me in the living room? I have someone I'd like you to meet."

Tiffany frowned. "Nick, I'm sick. I'm really not up for company."

"Please, baby. This won't take long."

"Who is it?"

"A businessman. He's only in town until tomorrow, so . . ." Nick didn't finish because there was no legitimate end to the sentence.

"I'm going out just like this," Tiffany said finally.

"You look beautiful, baby," Nick said, kissing her forehead.

Tiffany rolled her eyes as she slipped her feet into flat sandals and followed Nick out of the room and down the hall. She stopped short when they turned into the living room.

"Dad?" Tiffany shot a look at Nick, and then looked back at her father.

"Hello, Tiffany. I went to the restaurant to speak with you. They said you were ill. So I spoke with Nick, and . . . here I am."

Tiffany stared at her father, speechless. Nick quietly left the room.

"You've always been first in my heart, Tiffany," Keith began, speaking softly. "But you've never known this because I've never shown it. I think it's about time I did."

With those two sentences, twenty-eight years' worth

of hurt and misunderstanding began receding from
Tiffany's heart. And by the time Keith Bronson left
Nick and Tiffany's home two hours later, the healing
balm of a father's love was working its magic.

Shortly after they'd said good-bye to her father,
Nick and Tiffany cuddled in bed.

"I can't believe it," she whispered. "I can't believe
he turned his back on all that money . . . for me."

"That's what happened."

"How did you talk him into it, Nick?"

Nick turned his body so that he could look into
Tiffany's eyes. "It wasn't me, baby. Your father came
to my office and delivered the news. Said he'd been
doing some soul searching, and wanted to make
some changes."

"It had to be something that Grand said. It's probably too late to call her tonight, but—"

"Baby."

"Yes?"

"Stop it."

"Stop what?"

"Stop trying to come up with a different reason for
why your father did what he did. Accept it for what it
is, baby. He did it for you. He walked away from the
deal because he wanted you, the daughter that he
loves, in his life."

Tiffany began crying.

"Feels good, huh? To know your father loves you
so much."

"Yes, but it's not just that. Now, I feel kinda bad that
he backed out, that I was so insecure in how he felt
about me that it took something of this magnitude to
believe him." The more Tiffany thought about it, the

worse she felt. "It's not right, Nick! What if later on he resents me for what he could have had?"

Nick took Tiffany in his arms and began rubbing her back. "I told Keith the deal was his, Tiffany. That *I* would back down. But your father said no. It was his decision to walk away. You have nothing to feel bad about. Besides, Keith Bronson is one helluva businessman. He'll be all right."

Keith took his seat in first class, his two reasons for coming back to LA completed. He'd given Angelica a face-to-face verbal thrashing along with her walking papers, and he'd made things right with Tiffany.

The flight attendant came over immediately. After ordering a gin and tonic, Keith pulled out his Black-Berry and began checking messages. A few minutes later, it rang.

"Bronson."

"Keith, it's Nick."

"Nick. How's Tiffany, is she okay?"

"Tiffany's great, man. You'll never know what you did, bowing out of the deal like that."

"Well, I'll have to retire a few years later than I would have with this venture, but it's worth it. The look on my daughter's face last night showed me more than anything could that I did the right thing. I'm not in on this deal, but there'll be others."

"That's why I'm calling, Keith."

Keith perked up, took a sip of the drink he'd been given. "Yeah? You've heard about something coming down the pike?"

"Actually, this had to do with the China situation.

We've had an abrupt change in personnel, and I'm wondering if you know anybody good with numbers."

Keith froze, sure he'd heard incorrectly. "Good with . . ."

"Stan Koespesky is no longer on the project. We're down to the wire, so whoever takes his place will have to get up to speed on what's going on immediately. You know anybody who, say, has a working knowledge of this situation—and has the experience, expertise, and confidence to come on board a project like this?"

A slow smile began to creep across Keith's face. "I might know somebody," he said. "If the price is right."

"I'm thinking of him getting an equal percentage as all the others on the team. He will take the share meant for Stan. After all, the real work is going to start after this deal is signed."

Keith chuckled. "You're a good man, Nick Rollins."

"I figured since one day you'll be my father-in-law, this move might help me get in your good graces. And it will make your daughter a very happy woman."

"I think you've already done that, man."

"No happier than she's made me, Keith. That girl's my heart."

64

Tiffany wanted everything to be perfect—just how her life felt right now. She spread another light layer of the Hawaiian barbeque sauce she'd created on the baby back ribs, and placed them back in the oven. She checked the coconut rice. It was flaky and moist. Looking around the kitchen, she felt confident in taking off her apron. She only had to sear the scallops, which had been crusted with a secret ingredient. That bit of cooking wouldn't be messy, and besides, she wanted to look sexy for her man. The dinner was easy, relatively speaking—a simple salad and her soon-to-be-unveiled scallop appetizer the only other courses . . . besides dessert. Tiffany smiled as she imagined the things that would happen with the caramel and cream swirl she'd made. She actually shivered as she heard the sounds of jazz wafting from the living room. Nick had told her not to come out of the kitchen until she heard music.

She smoothed down her simple silk mini and walked barefoot down the hall. As she did, she thought about the whirlwind of the past two weeks, all that had happened, and how her life had changed. Never in a million years had she believed she could feel a true sense of family, as had happened at her grandmother's house last week. It had been years since she'd seen her parents in the same room, laughing, talking, and seeming to truly enjoy each other. And it was the first time that she'd introduced a man to the three most important people in her life. Her mother had met the few boyfriends she'd had previously, but her father had only met the guy she dated in college. She'd never felt a man worthy to take to Grand's house, until now. When Grand had called earlier, the first thing out of her mouth after hello was "Where is that fine hunk of prime rib?"

Tiffany turned the corner and saw her "prime rib" standing by the entertainment center, flipping through CDs. He looked up as soon as she entered, as if he sensed her presence. His dark brown eyes bored into hers, as if drinking her in. Her stomach clenched and fluttered, and there suddenly seemed to be less air to breathe.

Nick sauntered over to where Tiffany stood. "If dinner tastes as good as you look," he said, "then I'm going to be a very happy man."

"It's almost ready," Tiffany whispered. Nick enveloped her in a tender hug, and then began swaying to the sounds of Wayman Tisdale. She clasped her hands behind his neck as they danced; the sound of Wayman's guitar stirred their strings of passion. "Everything is so beautiful," Tiffany continued, when she finally reopened her eyes as they moved together in a slow circle. Nick had filled the living room with white flowers: orchids, roses, and lilies. White candles in various sizes and shapes were the room's only lighting, save a dimmed overhead chandelier. Nick rubbed his hands across the fabric covering Tiffany's body. The white halter-style fit her to perfection, just like he knew it would when he saw it in a Bloomingdale's catalog. Nick wore white as well, a pair of linen Calvin Klein slacks paired with one of his trademark stark white shirts, unbuttoned to mid-chest.

"I think I've heard this song before," Tiffany said, partly because it was true, and partly to divert her attention from the tiny kisses Nick was placing near her temple. His touch drove her wild, but she wanted to keep her wits about her until after dinner was served. She'd been working on what was to be her signature scallop dish for a couple weeks, and no one besides her had tasted it. There was no doubt that Nick was stirring up another appetite, but she was determined to assuage the one of the stomach before satisfying that which stemmed from . . . other areas.

"You don't remember?" Nick lazily replied. When Tiffany didn't answer, Nick continued, "That's Wayman Tisdale covering Barry White. It's what we danced to the first night I met you, when I brought you back to my room in Italy . . . to seduce you."

Tiffany stopped dancing and raised her head off Nick's shoulder. "I knew it!" she said with a gleam in her eye. "You probably had the whole thing planned, paid the staff to say the hotel was sold out just so you could get some nookie!"

Nick burst out laughing. "Nookie? Girl, I haven't heard that word in a minute!"

Tiffany smiled, too. "That's what Mom calls it. Or I could have said 'pushy,' like Randall and Joy."

"Or you could have said 'pu'—"

"Anyway," Tiffany interrupted. "You set me up. You probably mapped it out during that long flight over."

"I will admit I thought about you. Wanted to come back in coach so you could squeeze me like you were squeezing that teddy bear!"

Tiffany gave Nick a playful swat. "I needed Tuffy. I'm prone to panic attacks when I get really scared, or sometimes feel claustrophobic in planes. But you'll be happy to know that since I now have you to hug, I've packed away my furry friend."

Nick chuckled again as he pulled Tiffany back into his embrace and they resumed dancing. "I've got a lot of pull in a lot of places, but fate was on my side that day. Everything had to work out perfectly for us to be together—taking the same flight, your purse getting stolen, my stopping to talk to an airport administrator, which is why I was still there. And the crème de la crème, my favorite hotel being sold out of rooms. I need to find out which association was having that conference so I can send them a thank-you card."

"Nick?"

"Yes, love?"

"There's something that I really, really want to do right now."

Nick stifled a moan. It was what he'd been thinking about for most of the afternoon. He placed a hand under Tiffany's chin and aligned her face with his. After kissing her in a way that left Tiffany shivering, Nick lifted his head and stared into her eyes. "I'm never going to give you up," he whispered. "So tell me, what do you want to do?"

"Eat," Tiffany said. "Food," she hastily added when she watched Nick's pupils darken. "I'm starved."

"Woman, I'm going to get you for that!" He spoke gruffly, but was smiling as Tiffany led him to the dining room table.

"Sit," she ordered.

"But I love watching you cook!"

"I know, but what I'm about to serve is prepared with secrets I can't reveal. What you can do," she added after starting toward the kitchen, "is open up one of those delicious white wines."

"How about Riesling? I think its lightness will pair nicely with the scallops."

"You're the expert. Be right back."

Tiffany took a couple deep breaths to calm her ardor and refocus. Because of Nick, cooking was the last thing on her mind right now. After drinking a glass of water, she walked to the refrigerator and pulled out the container of scallops that had been marinating in some of her secret ingredients: the zest and juice from blood oranges, rosemary, and fresh mint. She then reached for the cast-iron skillet she'd used to caramelize onions earlier. Those onions were now piled atop the baby back ribs, but Tiffany added a small amount of coconut oil (another of her secret scallop ingredients) to the pan drippings, and when the oil was heated, she dusted the scallops with her final undisclosed weapon—pistachio nuts ground to a fine powder—and gingerly placed the scallops into the skillet. This time, she heard Nick come up behind her. "I thought I told you to stay away from my kitchen," she said, not turning around.

"And I thought I told you that I couldn't stay away," he responded. "Besides, I wanted the chef to taste

the wine and confirm its appropriateness with her
dish before I poured our glasses."

Tiffany turned and smiled. "You're a piece of work,
you know that?"

Nick smiled, nodded, and poured a small amount
of the chilled wine he held into a stemmed glass.
Tiffany took it, swirled the liquid around, sniffed
it, and then took a sip. She held the liquid in her
mouth for a second before swallowing slowly so that
she could taste the "textures" inside the drink. She
detected fruit, especially apple, and smiled when the
citrusy flavor fought for recognition. It would bring
out the blood orange essence in the scallops and
provide the kind of bite her grandmother would call
"heaven on a plate." She finished the small amount
he'd given her. "It's perfect," she said. "Now get out.
I'm ready to serve our first course."

Tiffany kept the plating simple. First, a light driz-
zle of aged balsamic vinegar creating an Asian-
inspired design topped with a wispy sprinkle of
pistachio crumbs. These items simply served as the
backdrop for the showstopper—two perfectly seared
scallops, one sitting slightly atop the other, in the
center of the dish. A sprig of mint and a celery flower
finished the presentation. She picked up the plate
and walked to the dining room.

With a great flourish, she set the plated scallops in
front of Nick. "Dinner is served." Tiffany sat down
next to the head table seat Nick occupied.

"Where's yours?"

"I wanted to serve you first." She placed her chin
in her hand and watched him with the same anticipation as a child who was watching someone open a
Christmas present.

Nick leaned over, placing his nose near the plate, and inhaled. "Wow . . . baby, this smells delicious." He sniffed again. "So there's mint . . ."

"Good job, Sherlock, since there's a sprig of it directly under your nose . . ."

"And some citrus, lemon, I'm guessing."

"Keep on guessing," Tiffany said with a smile.

Nick gently pricked the scallop with his fork. "Did you coat this with something or is this crust from the cooking process?"

"Will you eat it already? Before it gets cold?"

Nick laughed. He picked up his knife and cut the scallop in half. Tiffany's heart beat a little faster as she watched him lift the morsel up to his mouth. Nick closed his eyes as he chewed the food, slowly, thoughtfully. He swallowed, nodded, and brought the other half of the scallop to his mouth. "Unh," he said as again he chewed slowly, licking his lips after he'd finished.

When he started on the second scallop without having said a word, Tiffany could stand it no longer. "Well?" she asked, with barely veiled exasperation in her voice.

"Well, what?" Nick answered. His eyes danced with glee. He knew Tiffany was waiting for a verdict, knew that he'd been given the honor of being the first one besides her to taste the dish she planned as the signature dish for the establishment he'd given her.

"Dominique Rollins," Tiffany said as she narrowed her eyes and picked up her knife. "Don't make me . . ."

"All right, all right," he said, laughing. "Let me have one more bite." He halved the remaining scallop on his plate. "Baby, this dish is exceptional." He ate the remaining scallop half, groaned his satisfaction, and placed a light kiss on Tiffany's mouth. "Baby this is what love tastes like."

Tiffany's eyes sparkled with happiness. "So you like it?"

"I *love* it."

"You think it's good enough to be my signature dish?"

"It's good enough to be your *only* dish."

"Even better than Chef Riatoli's?"

"Chef who?"

Tiffany laughed even as she got up to hug Nick. "I'm so happy you like it," she said. "You've eaten at some of the best places in the world, so your opinion means a lot to me."

"It's amazing, baby. I think Taste Too is going to have a long waiting list."

Tiffany started for the kitchen to get her plate, but Nick grabbed her wrist and pulled her into his lap. "Nick, come on, I want to taste my signature dish . . . my Scallops Tiffany!"

"And I want my brown sugar."

They kissed. And after a candlelit dinner of scallops, a kale and blood orange salad, fall-off-the-bone baby back ribs served over gold Yukon rosemary mashed potatoes, and a caramel cake dessert, Tiffany Matthews and Dominique "Nick" LaSalle Rollins assuaged another appetite by enjoying the dishes they loved best—each other.

Want more?
Turn the page for Zuri Day's

Lessons from a Younger Lover

Available now wherever books are sold

Turn the page for an excerpt from
Lessons from a Younger Lover . . .

I

There were two things Gwen Smith never thought she'd do. She never thought she'd move back to her rinky-dink hometown of Sienna, California, and she never thought she'd come back as a forty-year-old divorcée. Yet here she sat in the middle seat of a crowded plane, at the age where some said life began, trying to figure out how the boring and predictable one she'd known sixty short days ago had changed so quickly.

The first hitch in the giddyup wasn't a total surprise. Her mother's dementia had become increasingly worse following the death of Gwen's father, Harold, two years ago. Her parents had been married forty-four years. It was a tough adjustment. At the funeral, Gwen told her husband that she knew the time would come when her mother's welfare would become her responsibility. That she thought Joe would be by her side at this crucial time, and wasn't, was the fact she hadn't seen coming.

But it was true nonetheless. Joe had announced his desire to divorce and packed his bags the same evening. Two months later she was still reeling from that okeydoke. But she couldn't think about that now. Gwen had to focus on one crisis at a time, and at the moment, her mother was the priority.

"Ladies and gentlemen, the captain has turned on the seat belt sign indicating our final descent into Los Angeles. Please make sure your seat belts are securely fastened and your seats and tray tables are in their upright and locked . . ."

Gwen stretched as well as she could between two stout men and tried to remove the crook from her neck. Still, she was grateful she'd fallen asleep. Shut-eye had been all too elusive these past few weeks, when ongoing worries and raging thoughts had kept true rest at bay. Fragments of a dream flitted across her wakened mind as they landed and she reached into the overhead bin for her carry-on luggage. Gwen didn't know if she wanted to remember it or not. Lately, her dreams had been replaced by night-mares that happened when her eyes were wide open.

"Gwen! Over here, girl! Gwen!"

Gwen smiled as a familiar voice pierced the crowd roaming the LAX Airport baggage claim area. She turned and waved so that the short, buxom woman, wearing fuchsia cutoffs and a yellow halter top strain-ing for control, would know that she, God, and every-one within a five-mile radius had heard her.

"Gwendolyn!" Chantay exclaimed, enunciating each syllable for full effect as she reached up and hugged her childhood friend. "Girl, let me look at you!"

"You just saw me last year, Tay."

"That visit went by in a fog. You know the deal."

Gwen did, and wished she didn't. Her last time home was not a fond memory.

Chantay stepped back, put her hands on her hips, and began shaking her head so hard her waist-length braids sprayed the waiting passengers surrounding them. "What are we going to do with your rail thin behind? You couldn't find enough deep-dish pizzas to eat in Chicago? No barbeque or chicken and waffle joints to put some meat on your bones?"

Gwen took the jab good-naturedly. Her five-foot-seven, size-six body had caused her heftier friend chagrin for years. No matter that Gwen had never mastered how to show off her physique, put on makeup, or fix her hair. The fact that she could eat everything, including the kitchen sink, and still not gain a pound was a stick in Chantay's craw.

Chantay enveloped her friend in a big bear hug. "You look good, girl. A day late and a dollar short on style with that curlicue hair straight out of *A Different World,* but overall . . . you look good!"

Gwen's laugh was genuine for the first time in weeks. "You don't look half bad yourself. And opinionated as always, I see."

"Honey, if you want a feel-good moment, watch *Oprah.* I'm going to tell you the truth even if it's ugly. And speaking of the *u* word, those *Leave It To Beaver* pedal pushers—"

"Forget you, Tay! C'mon, that's my luggage coming around."

A half hour later, Gwen settled back in Chantay's Ford Explorer as they merged into highway traffic for the two-hour drive to Sienna. The air conditioner was a welcome change to the ninety-degree July heat.

"I still can't believe you're here."

"Me either."

"You know you've got to give me the full scoop.

First, I never thought you'd ever get married, and if you did, you'd never, *ever* get divorced!"

"Obviously life wasn't following your script," Gwen muttered sarcastically.

"Oh, don't get your panties in a bunch, sistah, you know what I'm saying. And I'm not the only one. Who did everyone vote the least likely to, uh, get married?"

"I believe the exact description in the high school yearbook read 'would die an old maid.'"

"Well, I was trying to save you the embarrassment of quoting it verbatim but . . . who was it?"

They both knew the answer was Gwen. But rather than help make the point, Gwen answered the question with one of her own. "Who did they say would probably have ten kids?"

"Hmph. That's because those nuckas didn't know that fornicate does not equal procreate. After being stuck with raising one *accident* and another *oops* by myself, I had my tubes tied. I told the doctor who did the procedure that if a 'baby I pulled out' number three showed up in my pee sample, his would be the name in the father line. So believe me, if there's a sperm bad enough to get past the Boy Scout knot he tied, then that's a baby who deserves to be born."

Gwen looked out the window, thought about Chantay's two daughters, and watched the world whirl by while Chantay pushed past seventy and flew down the surprisingly light 405 Freeway. While Chantay had often said she didn't want kids, Gwen had always looked forward to motherhood. She was still looking, but couldn't see any bassinet or baby bed because a divorce petition was blocking the view.

Chantay scanned for various stations on the radio

before turning it off altogether. "Why are you making me drag the details out of you?" she whined, exasperation evident in her voice. "What happened between you and Joe?"

The name of Gwen's soon-to-be former husband elicited a frown. "You mean *Joey*?"

"Who the hell is that?"

"That's what he calls himself now."

"I call him 'bastard,' but I digress. What happened?"

Gwen sighed, sat up, and spoke truth straight out. "He met somebody else."

"You have got to be kidding. Corny-ass Joe Smith, the computer nerd who could barely pull the garter off at y'alls' wedding?"

"That would be him."

"What fool did he find to listen to his tired lines?"

"You mean besides me?"

"Girl, I didn't mean that personally. Joe has some good points. He seems to know his way around a computer better than anybody."

"That's one."

"We've got ninety minutes of driving left. I'll think of something else."

Gwen laughed, appreciative of the levity Chantay brought to a sad situation.

"So . . . who is she?"

"Her name is Mitzi, she's twenty-two and works in his office. They both like motorcycles, Miller Lite, and poker. He tattooed her name on his arm and moved into her studio apartment last month. But I don't want to talk about him right now."

"Whoa, chick! You're sure going to have to talk about him later . . . *and* her. That was way too much information to leave me hanging. But I can wait a minute, and in the meantime change the subject to somebody you can talk about . . . Adam 'oh, oh, oh, oh' Johnson!"

"Chantay, you are too silly! I haven't thought about that line since we left high school." Gwen, Chantay, and a couple other misfits used to substitute his first name in Ready for the World's hit, "Oh Sheila." Chantay would hum it as he passed in the halls and the other girls would break into hysterical laughter, making them all look like fools.

"That is the single welcome surprise I've had these past few weeks—that Adam is the principal at Sienna. Can you believe it?" Gwen said.

"No, because I never thought a brothah with that much weight in his lower head would have any brains in his upper one."

"Well, there's that, but even more the fact that he's back living in our hometown. After being such a standout at Texas A&M and going on to play for the Cowboys? I guess a lot happened to him since he was sidelined with an injury and forced to retire early."

"I can't believe his wife would agree to move back to such a podunk town. She looks too hoity-toity for Smallville, but I only saw her one time on TV," Chantay said.

"They're divorced."

"What? Girl, stop!"

"Yep, he told me that when we talked. He was nice actually, not the cocky, arrogant Adam I remember. He wouldn't admit it, but I know he's the reason why my getting this post is, to use his words, 'in the bag.'"

"Don't give him too much credit, Gwen. You're a first-rate teacher, and it's not like our town has to beat off qualified educators with sticks."

"Maybe, but the way everything happened . . . I'm just happy to know I have a job secured, or at least I will after my interview next week. Mama has some money saved up but that's all going into her assisted living expenses. I still need to support myself, and pay half the mortgage on the condo until it's sold."

"How's Miss Lorraine doing?"

Gwen shrugged. "Mama's about the same, I guess."

"Isn't she a bit young for what the doctors say is happening to her?"

"From what I've learned, not really. The disease usually comes with aging, but can actually occur at any time, from a variety of causes. It's usually given a different name when it occurs in someone, say, under fifty-five. But whatever the title, the results are the same—a long-term decline in cognitive function."

"Just be glad she's still here," Chantay replied. "You can always hug her, whether she knows you or not."

"Oh, she recognizes everybody, and remembers more than she lets on, I'm thinking. But I hear what you're saying, Chantay, and I'm grateful."

They were silent a moment before Chantay changed the subject. "Joe's a lowlife. He could have stayed in the condo and split the rent with the fool he's sleeping with until somebody bought it. He's just an asshole."

"That would have been too much like right. But it is what it is. Don't get me re-pissed about it."

Chantay started humming "Oh Sheila." "Wouldn't it be ironic if you moved back to town and snagged its star player after all these years? Now, we'll have to give your dated butt a makeover, but by the time I'm done with you . . . you'll move over all those other silicone-stuffed heifas in town."

"I wonder who else from our class still lives there."

"Girl, it don't even matter. Keep your eye on the prize." Chantay shot another sideways look at her friend. "Um-hmm. If it's Adam Johnson you want—trust, I can help you get him."

Gwen had thought about Adam, and what a nice balm he might be for the hurt Joe had caused her. Not that she'd get into anything serious right away. It would be months before the divorce came up on the backlogged Illinois court docket and was finalized. But since speaking to Adam, she'd fantasized a time or two about the heartthrob she remembered: tall, lanky, chocolate, strong, with bedroom eyes and a Jheri curl that brushed his shoulders. She never dreamed she'd get another chance with someone like Adam. But as she'd learned all too painfully in the past few months—life was full of surprises.

Look For These Other
Dafina Novels

If I Could
0-7582-0131-1

by Donna Hill
$6.99US/**$9.99**CAN

Thunderland
0-7582-0247-4

by Brandon Massey
$6.99US/**$9.99**CAN

June In Winter
0-7582-0375-6

by Pat Phillips
$6.99US/**$9.99**CAN

Yo Yo Love
0-7582-0239-3

by Daaimah S. Poole
$6.99US/**$9.99**CAN

When Twilight Comes
0-7582-0033-1

by Gwynne Forster
$6.99US/**$9.99**CAN

It's A Thin Line
0-7582-0354-3

by Kimberla Lawson Roby
$6.99US/**$9.99**CAN

Perfect Timing
0-7582-0029-3

by Brenda Jackson
$6.99US/**$9.99**CAN

Never Again Once More
0-7582-0021-8

by Mary B. Morrison
$6.99US/**$8.99**CAN

Available Wherever Books Are Sold!

Check out our website at www.kensingtonbooks.com.